BEST
WESTERN STORIES

BEST
WESTERN
STORIES

Selected and introduced by
SCOTT MEREDITH

SPRING BOOKS · LONDON

PUBLISHED 1964 BY SPRING BOOKS
WESTBOOK HOUSE · FULHAM BROADWAY · LONDON
© THIS EDITION COPYRIGHT 1964 PAUL HAMLYN LTD
PRINTED IN CZECHOSLOVAKIA
T 1225

CONTENTS

page

Introduction by SCOTT MEREDITH   7

POSSE *by C. Hall Thompson*   11

WELL OF ANGER *by Morgan Lewis*   25

TWO-FACED PROMISE *by Bill Gulick*   40

THE FRAUDULENT SKUNK *by A. B. Guthrie, Jr.*   48

LONESOME RIDE *by Ernest Haycox*   56

PRIDE IN HIS HOLSTERS *by Robert W. Lowndes*   75

A MAN CALLED HORSE *by D. M. Johnson*   81

THE GHOST LODE *by William Brandon*   96

THE TRAP *by Roe Richmond*   111

THE MAN AT GANTT'S PLACE *by Steve Frazee*   120

CAMPAIGNING COWPOKE *by Clark Gray*   148

FEAR IN THE SADDLE *by H. A. De Rosso*   164

THE SOUND OF GUNFIRE *by John O'Reilly*   174

SERGEANT HOUCK *by Jack Schaefer*   183

THE LAST SHOT *by Frank O'Rourke*   204

THE OUTLAWS ARE IN TOWN *by Bennett Foster*   217

THE FIRE KILLER *by Steve Frazee*   231

HANGING FIRE *by Richard Deming*   266

THE UNBELIEVER *by D. M. Johnson*   275

MAN-TAMING WOMAN *by Michael Fessier* 290

DUEL IN CAPTIVE VALLEY *by Will C. Brown* 304

SHADOW OF THE BUTTE *by Thomas Thompson* 319

DUST STORM *by Max Brand* 368

SQUAW FEVER *by Bill Gulick* 382

THE AVENGING *by Jonathan Lord* 407

SCOUT DETAIL *by Ernest Haycox* 416

INTRODUCTION

I F THIS anthology of Western stories had been prepared and
published in 1920 or 1930 the reader could be reasonably
sure of finding certain familiar things in nearly every one
of the selections. For example:

1. The hero of nearly every story would be an iron-nerved
gentleman who was absolutely unfamiliar with the sensation of
fear. Even if he were being chased by sixty-seven men armed
with two guns and a knife apiece–a circumstance which would
cause most men in real life to shiver right out of their trousers–
the Western-story hero would just yawn and continue to lope
calmly along.

2. The Indians in the stories would be unthinking savages
who spent all of their time tracking down and killing white
men–doing their stuff for no reason other than blood-lust and
the joy of killing. You would practically never find the suggestion that sometimes Indian attacks were justified and pretty
much in the nature of self-defence.

3. The Western hero might sometimes kiss his horse, but
never his girl friend. (As a matter of fact, the girl in the average
Western story *circa* 1920 usually had so little to do that considerable interested speculation has been devoted to the questions
of why female characters were included in the first place.) . . .
At any rate, you'd certainly find that the male-female relation-
ships in Western stories were non-romantic, non-intimate, and
positively non-sexual. There were, of course, children in the
stories, sometimes, but these presumably arrived in some entirely
pure manner–perhaps astride storks.

4. The towns would be populated almost entirely with
wandering cowhands, gamblers, lawmen, gunmen, and saloon-
keepers. The less glamorous residents–the storekeepers, the
feed merchants, the town doctors, the lawyers, and so on–

would sometimes be mentioned in passing, but were rarely considered interesting and exciting enough to be given the stature of major characters, even though they may well have been the real backbone of the real Old West.

5. In general, the plots and characters would be enormously over-simplified—with the villain nearly always an out-and-out crook (the crooked banker out to steal the land or the crooked foreman out to steal the cattle), and the hero all too often an out-and-out angel who had no personal stake in the matter but helped defeat the bad guys because he was a good guy. Characters would rarely be understandable human beings whom circumstances and conflicting points of view had placed on opposite sides of the fence: villains were all-black, villainous in everything they said or did or thought, and heroes were all-white, entirely pure at all times.

These things, and others like them, were practically traditional in the Western story of some years ago—always excepting the yarns by the few writers who were ahead of their time—but, after a while, intelligent and thoughtful Western readers began to rebel against them because they were so obviously synthetic. More and more readers began to complain that, even in frontier life with men well-acquainted with bloodshed and sudden death a man is still going to get a frightened sensation in the stomach when people start pumping lead at him—many Indians were the victims of incredibly cruel and treacherous treatment by white men, and attacked wagon trains in the same way that you and I would defend our land against invaders—romantic and sexual activities formed as important a part of life in the Old West as anywhere else in the world—and a little more attention to storekeepers and farmers and other less-publicized figures of the Old West, and a little more attention to the subtleties of human behaviour and human relations, might be a sensible move.

And the result of this attitude on the part of readers—the result of the dissatisfaction with the stereotyped, or cornball, variety of Western story—has been the current story of the Old West, unarguably the Western at its best in history. To-day's better Western story goes far beyond the Class G movie level, the I - jest - happened - to - be - moseyin' - along - playin' - my -

guitar - Ma'am - and - I - overheered - yore - foreman - plottin' - some - rustlin' class: it portrays the Old West as it really was, and its people think and act like people.

The nice thing about it all, too, is that the current Western is even more interesting and exciting than the old-style horse opry. Perhaps it's because you can *believe* the modern Western yarn and its characters instead of having to keep fighting off the feeling that you're reading about a slightly ridiculous never-never land; or perhaps it's because the current Western, with its deeper probing of people and emotions, requires better writing and better writers and therefore means better stories. Whatever the reason, the fast-moving, plausible, completely enjoyable current Western has brought about a renaissance in the field, a new upsurge of popularity—one example of which is visible in the fact that every major Hollywood studio now regularly makes Class A Westerns featuring its top stars.

This book, a sampler collection of stories selected from the thousands published in recent years, covers nearly every locale and every type of human being within the Old West. You'll find Indian country and farming country, busy wideopen towns and the lonely desert, a young kid contemplating the owlhoot trail and an old prospector contemplating murder, a tired and cynical hired gunman and a man who never used a gun. Each of the stories is the current Western at its best.

A number of years ago, this writer lived briefly in an old house in a New Mexico town, just a short distance from the place at which Billy the Kid was killed. One of the rooms in the house had been a rendezvous for Wild West outlaws, and a scar on the bureau-top was reputed to have been made when Billy the Kid slammed his gun-butt down in a rage.

Outside the house, sleek new cars rolled along the highway, and people walked calmly back and forth on their twentieth-century pursuits, but that room was a world unto itself; it was still genuine frontier in there. That is the way it is with the stories in this volume, and perhaps that is their chief charm: they've a feeling of authenticity about them. I hope you'll agree that the opening paragraph of each story is a private doorway back in the colourful and rip-snortin' Old West. SCOTT MEREDITH

POSSE

By C. Hall Thompson

BILLY REO was dreaming again. The pain in the small of his back where buckshot had riddled the intestines seemed far away now and he was not lying in the loft of an abandoned barn; he could not smell the hay nor hear the rats squealing in the empty stalls below.

He was back in a town in the Panhandle and he was nineteen and had never watched a man die. A mob jostled along the main square. He could see the red, moustached faces of furious men and hear them yelling, 'Lynch the murdering greaser. Bust into the cell and string him up.'

Then he saw two townsmen come out through the jail door, dragging the Mexican boy between them. He heard the boy praying and moaning, and followed the mob across the dusty wide square to the big oak. The boy was crying softly and someone larruped the flank of the pony and it jolted out from under and the boy screamed only once before the hemp snapped his spine.

And, here in the barn loft, Reo could see the boy's face, twisted at a crazy angle by the knot under the left ear. Only now it was his own face; it was Billy Reo who danced there above the stiff white masks of the mob.

'No!'

He lurched to a sitting position.

The stab of fire along his back brought him full awake. Sweat wilted the blond bristles of his jaw. It stung his eyes. He sank back, breathing too hard.

Get hold of yourself, he thought. *Let them form their damned posse. They'll never find you here.*

They had never caught him before. In the ten years since he had drifted north into the territories, Billy Reo had killed four men. Riding from one gun town to the next, he had learned the lightning downsweep and rise of hand that could put three slugs into a man's belly before he sprawled in the dust. And the killing had been a safe, secret thing. People had looked at him and wondered, maybe, but no one had ever been able to prove his suspicions.

Safe and easy, his mind said. And this time was no different.

Only this time *was* different. This time it had been in a grubby saloon in Alamosa with a mob of witnesses right on the spot.

He hadn't figured the greenhorn to call his bluff. The greenhorn, a spindly kid named Reckonridge, had looked as if he never left mamma's side. Reo and Jack Larnin had idled into the bar to wash the red dust out of their tonsils and had seen this kid sporting a load of double eagles. It wasn't hard to talk up a game of deuces wild. It should have been easy to slip that deuce off the bottom when the pot was at its peak.

But Reckonridge had a quick eye and a temper to match. He had cursed and dropped one hand below the table. Reo never stopped to argue. A beer-blown blonde had screamed. The shots had sounded very loud and Reckonridge had gone over backward, still seated, with two small holes in his chest.

The saloon crowd had not moved. Elbow to elbow, guns level, Reo and Larnin had backed through swinging doors to the ponies at the hitch. They had swung up and wheeled west and, in that moment Reo had seen the long, loose-limbed man come running through the moonlight; glimpsed the lifting shotgun, the flash of a metal star against a black vest.

'Ride, Jack! Ride like hell!'

Slapping heels to the roan's flanks, he had bent low. But not low enough. He had felt the fire needles burn into his back almost before he heard the slam and echo of the double barrels. Somehow, he had kept the roan haunch to haunch with Larnin's pinto. Somehow, he had ridden.

Reo was sweating again. The blood-wet flannel shirt stuck to his back. His legs had a numbness that frightened him.

Witnesses, he thought. This time there was proof. This time, the man in the black vest would. talk. The citizens of Alamosa would swear in as deputies. Before daylight, the posse would lead out. Maybe even now . . .

'Damn,' he said hoarsely.

His head rolled from side to side. He could see the Mexican boy very clearly; the hard, implacable faces of the mob, the sudden, singing wrench of the rope.

'Billy.'

His body stiffened. A hand clawed for the pistol that lay by his hip. He caught the scrape of boots on the ladder; a light shaft cut up through the loft trap. Then the lean, flat-planed face and narrow shoulders came into view, one fist holding high the lantern, and Jack Larnin said, 'Easy, Billy. Just me.'

The gun hand relaxed.

Larnin set down the lamp. It was hooded so that only a thin yellow beam broke the darkness.

Reo's eyes narrowed. 'Well?'

Larnin stood tall above him. A rat rustled in the hay. Light shimmered on the dainty needlework of a spider's web. Larnin said, 'How's the wound?'

Reo looked at him. 'The wound's all right. I'm not thinking about the wound.'

The silent question hung between them. Reo felt sweat cold along his ribs.

Finally Larnin looked away, said, 'I went up along the rise. You can see Alamosa from there. It don't look good, Billy. They started already. I seen torches moving out of town; high, like they were carried by men on horseback.'

'Posse,' Reo whispered.

Larnin's boots shifted. 'You better let me take a look.'

'The hell with the wound!'

Reo hauled himself to one elbow. The effort cost him plenty. There was a red-brown stain where his back had crushed the hay.

'What're the chances?' he said.

Larnin shook his head. 'We got three, four hours on them,

Billy. But we was riding too hard to cover trail. We left signs a blind man could follow.'

Reo wet his lips. In the dark stillness now, a wind was rising and he could hear a voice praying high and shrill in Spanish and then cracking to dead silence.

Reo set his elbows, shoved himself erect. His teeth shut hard against the pain.

Larnin helped him. The numbness made his legs heavy and awkward. His insides burned. He held the pistol in a white-knuckled grip. He leaned against the wall, coughing for breath.

Larnin's face went uncertain. 'Listen, Billy.'

Pale eyes swung up. 'I'm listening.'

A minute passed. Their glances held. Then Larnin said, 'Maybe it'd be better if you didn't run. You need a doctor, Billy. If you just waited here . . .'

'For the posse?' Reo said. 'Sit here and wait for the mob to drag me out?' Fever made his stare too bright. 'Wait for the rope?'

'I'm only saying . . .'

The gun hand had lifted a fraction. 'You said it. Now forget it.'

'Sure, Billy, but . . .'

'But—you'd like to back down?'

'Billy, you got me wrong.'

The gun was level with Larnin's belt buckle now. 'Maybe,' Reo said. 'But you get me right. We're going to move. We're going to keep moving. They won't get me. Remember that, Jack. No mob'll ever get me.'

Wind soughed in the stalls below. A rat skittered into the hay.

Larnin nodded. All he said was, 'You still need a doctor.'

'We'll head for Monte Vista. There's old Doc Carson.'

Larnin frowned. 'We ain't got much money. The doc mightn't want to . . .'

Billy Reo's hands moved light and smooth with the gun, broke it and checked the cylinder, snapped the breech shut again. He looked at the gun for a long time, then said, 'He'll want to.'

Shadows followed them. The moon was high and cloud-pierced and, behind them now, the pale meadows were restless with shadows that might have been wind bending the tall grass; or the groping movements of a posse.

Reo tried not to look back. Turned north and west towards the far reaches of the San Juan range, his face set rigid against thought and the memory of a sun-bleached Panhandle town. The jogging of the saddle played hell with his back. He could feel the wounds seeping slowly: hot fingers clawed up from his belly and made breathing a torture.

Lifting gradually under them the land climbed toward distant foothills. The horses were wearing thin. The moon went down and winking stone-cold stars gave little light. Larnin took to shifting against the pommel, peering over his shoulder. Reo had drawn the Winchester from his saddle boot; he held it ready across his lap. Under the muffled dusty beat of hoofs, a Mexican tongue whimpered, *Madre de dios, socorro,* save me. *Madre de . . .*

'Shut up,' Reo said aloud. 'Shut up.'

Larnin glanced at him sharply. A white edge fringed Reo's lips. He shook his head dully.

'Nothing. I was . . . Nothing.'

Dawn was a pearl-grey cat paddling down from the westward mountains. A ground mist swirled rump-high to the ponies, made a cottony haze along the rim of Monte Vista. They reined in at the east end of the main street.

Reo felt dizzy. The numbness of his legs was worse.

'Jack. The poncho. In case we meet somebody.'

Larnin unstrapped the latigoes and slipped the oilskin over Reo's shoulders. It hid the dark clotted stain of the shirt.

'All right,' Reo said. 'Let's go.'

They didn't meet anybody. Monte Vista was curled up in sleep. A memory of stale beer and bought laughter drifted through dim saloon doorways. Even the red lights of the western skirt of town had gone dead. A dog hightailed across a side lane. Morning wind stirred the lazy dust.

The riders swung south along Don Paulo Street. Doc Carson's house was at the far end, grey, sand-eaten, set back in weeds.

They hitched the ponies in the shelter of a sad willow and walked around to the kitchen door.

Reo moved slowly. Each step sent pain splintering through his chest and stomach. In the shade of the back stoop, he leaned against the wall, sucking deep lungfuls of air. Larnin waited.

Finally, Reo said, 'Now.'

They didn't knock. The latch was up. The kitchen smelled of rancid coffee grounds. They went down the side hall. A thick, wet snoring led the way to the bedroom. Reo stopped on the doorsill. His palm rested lightly on the low-slung pistol.

The doc lay among crumpled quilts, fully dressed and booted. His string tie was undone and grey stubble matted his sunken cheeks. His mouth hung open. When he breathed out, a stink of whisky tainted the air.

Reo made a sign. Larnin crossed to the window and drew the blind. In the dark now, Reo leaned at the foot of the bed. Larnin stood just beside the pillow. Reo nodded, Larnin lifted the Colt and pressed the small muzzle under the hinge of Doc Carson's jaw.

Long bony fingers knotted in the patchwork. The doc's eyelids twitched and opened very slowly.

'Quiet,' Reo said. 'Nice and quiet, Doc.'

Carson sat up carefully, drawing back from the touch of the gun. 'Reo. What is this?'

Reo set a smile against the biting twinges of the wound. 'A professional visit, Doc.'

Carson let out a long sigh, but he kept watching the gun. Some of the liquor-haze cleared from his eyes. 'Law on your tail?'

The smile faded. 'A misunderstanding,' Reo said flatly. 'There was a kid. He didn't trust me. I don't like it when people don't trust me.'

The doc's stare wavered. The voice went shrill. 'Well, what do you want with me? I can't . . .'

Reo turned around and pulled aside the poncho. Carson whistled, swung his feet to the floor. 'Sit down,' he said. 'I'll look.'

For a second, Reo didn't move. Then he sat on the bed.

Carson said, 'I'll need light.'

Larnin looked at Reo and then brought a lamp from the washstand and set fire to the wick.

The doc peeled off Reo's shirt. Flesh tore where flannel stuck to the edges of the wound. Reo sat still, head down, sweating. Carson's fingers prodded; his loose mouth pursed. He straightened.

Reo said, 'So?'

Doc Carson scratched his jaw. 'It won't be no cinch, Reo.'

'You can do it?'

'There'll be a lot of pain.'

Reo said, 'You can do it.'

The doc went to the clothes chest. He uncorked a bottle, drank and swabbed his mouth with a shirt sleeve. At last he said. 'This is against the law. I never handle these things, unless . . .'

Reo said, 'You'll be paid.'

A smile cracked wet lips. 'Five hundred?'

Larnin's gun started to lift. 'You lousy cheating . . .'

Reo shook his head. Larnin stood still. Reo looked at the doc.

'All right. Five hundred.'

The smile broadened. Carson took a step forward.

'Not now,' Reo said flatly. 'Later. When this blows over.'

Carson said, 'Maybe you better get somebody else. I got nothing to ease the pain and . . .'

Abruptly, Reo stood up. His insides twisted and burned; nothing showed in his face. His hand hung over the thigh-thonged Colt. Carson went back a step.

'Like I told you,' Reo said, 'I don't like it when people won't trust me.'

The lamp wick flickered. Morning was a pale yellow crack fringing the dark blind. Somewhere a rooster crowed the day.

Doc Carson again tilted the bottle. The drink was a long one. He punched the cork home with his palm and said, 'I'll get the instruments ready.'

Reo sat down heavily. His head throbbed. He shut out the buzzing of his ears and looked up at Larnin. 'Circulate,'

17

he said. 'Ride out a ways. See if you can get wind of the posse.'

Larnin flicked a glance at doc.

Reo said, 'I'll handle him.'

Carson kept working over his leather case. The instruments chinked as if his hands were trembling.

'How long?' Larnin asked.

Reo swung his gaze to Carson.

'An hour,' Carson said. 'Maybe two.'

Reo's square blond face tightened. 'That long?'

'I told you. Probing for that shot won't be no picnic.'

Reo's breathing had picked up a beat. He managed to steady it and then he nodded at Larnin.

Larnin sheathed the gun and crossed to the hall. 'I'll be back.' The door closed.

The room was quite still. Reo could hear the rasp of his own lungs. He sat there, watching Carson spread bright tools on a towel on the bedside chair. Carson turned up the lamp wick and filled the washbasin with water from a cracked ewer. He rolled back his sleeves.

'On the bed,' he said. 'Belly down.'

Reo sat still. Their eyes held. Reo drew the Colt and lay down, right arm stretched wide, the gun in his fist. His cheek pressed the greasy pillow, eyes turned toward the lamp. Carson's hands moved over the instruments, forced a thin wood splint against Reo's lips. 'Bite when it gets bad.' Carson lifted a needle-fine probe, bent over the bed. 'This is it.'

The probe went deep. The splint snapped between Reo's teeth.

They were coming. The posse was riding down on him and he could not move. He lay there, watching the hoofs rear and crash down at his face. They did not hang him at once. They drove white-hot pokers into his back and dragged him over live coals and then the rope burned his neck. He was praying in broken Spanish and the mob laughed when the knot jerked taut under his ear . . .

It lasted an hour and twenty minutes. Then the blackness

went away. He could see the lamp, made pale now by the blaze of sun against the blind. The splint was gone. He tasted salt where his teeth had dug into the lower lip.

Stitches and plaster held him in a vice. Far off Monte Vista stirred with morning life. On the main drag, a pianola wrangled.

Doc Carson sat in the rocker by the window. 'Sixteen buckshot,' he was saying. 'Don't know how you ever got this far.'

Reo's lips burned. He licked them with a dry tongue. 'Jack?'

'Yeah.' Spurs chinked. 'Here, Billy.' Larnin brought him a tumbler of whisky.

'Watch it,' Carson said. 'Watch them stitches.'

Reo gained one elbow. His back seemed to tear apart, but the liquor helped. He looked up at Larnin. 'Any luck?'

Larnin took the glass and refilled it. 'If you'd call it that.'

He drank. Reo waited.

'I was up to the saloon. Ran into this Express rider. He'd passed a party on the east road.'

'And?'

'Posse,' Larnin said. 'Pony-boy says they was riding down a gunny. Lost his trail back in the meadows, then picked it up again. They're heading this way, Billy.'

'How far behind are they?'

'Twenty miles when he saw them; moving slow, asking questions at every cabin they passed.'

'Then we got time.' Abruptly, Reo swung his legs out of bed. His mouth twitched with pain.

Doc Carson jumped up. 'God A'mighty, man! Easy!'

Reo sat there, head low, hands clutching the mattress edge. 'We ride,' he told Larnin. 'We make the mountains. They'll never track us through shale and rock.'

Larnin said. 'Billy, maybe . . .'

'We won't go over that again,' Reo said thickly. 'We ride.'

'Ride?' Carson shrilled. 'Are you loco? Half an hour in the saddle and them stitches'll bust wide open. Your back'll be a sieve. And if you haemorrhage inwardly . . .'

Reo said, 'Shut up.'

19

'I tell you, it's one sure way to die.'

Reo's mouth paled. 'I can think of worse ways.'

'But, my money . . .'

'Shut up!' Reo caught hold of the bedstead and rose very slowly. The room pitched wildly, but he did not fall. 'I'll need a clean shirt, Doc.'

It took a long while to get dressed. Finally, teeth set against a rising inward ache, Reo faced Larnin. 'The horses?'

'All ready.'

Reo lifted his pistol from the tangle of red-flecked covers. He turned to Carson. His eyes showed no emotion at all.

The doc's loose mouth went to pieces. 'Listen, Reo.' It was a dry whisper. 'No hard feelings, eh? You know me. I'm a businessman. It ain't that I didn't trust . . .' Carson swallowed noisily and forced a smile. 'Ain't that right, Reo? No hard feelings?'

'Yeah.'

The gun went up fast and down. Carson saw it coming. He sidestepped too late. The barrel got him along the ear. He went down head first against the bed.

'Sure,' Reo said softly. 'No hard feelings.'

Larnin wet his lips. 'Look, Billy . . .'

The eyes stopped him. They were too brilliant and hard. 'It gives us time,' Reo said. 'It'll remind him to keep his lip buttoned.'

They went out through the kitchen. Reo waited in the warm shade of the stoop. Far up the street, a Mexican woman was stringing out wet wash. She did not look their way.

Larnin led the horses around. They had been fed and watered, but they didn't look rested. Reo frowned. There was no helping it. Trading for new mounts would only attract attention.

He caught the roan's stirrup and stepped up. The skin of his back stretched tight. Plaster cramped his ribs and he felt a wet ribbon run down his spine. He told himself it was only sweat, but he knew it was fresh blood. His jaw muscles corded. He gave Larnin the nod.

They rode along an alley to the south edge of town, then swung west. Reo sat with one hand resting on the butt of his Colt. Morning sun struck fire from the watchful slits of his eyes. They did not pass anybody. Far away, at the centre of Monte Vista, a school bell chimed, clean and cool sounding.

When they hit open ground, Reo turned once. He saw the main drag, pale and dusty under a yellow sky. Wagons rumbled up with kegs from the brewery. Grangers lounged and smoked outside the barber-shop and a fat woman waddled home with a basket of greens. There was no sign that anyone had noticed the passing of two strange riders.

The pain was a network of burning wires that jerked taut with every roll of the saddle. The wetness was thick along Reo's back now, soaking slowly into the bandages. He cursed Doc Carson for a bungler; he cursed a quick-tempered greenhorn and a man with a star pinned to his black vest. A nerve twitched his mouth.

'The hills,' he said. 'We make the hills and we're safe.'

Larnin frowned. 'It's a rough climb.'

Reo seemed not to hear.

'We make the hills and we're all right,' he said.

Larnin's frown deepened, but he didn't speak again.

Just before noon, they hit the first spur of the San Juans. Larnin hadn't been wrong. The going was steep and treacherous with tangleweed and shale. The horses didn't help. Reo's roan was whiteflanked and frothing at the bit. It walked head down, labouring against sun and the steady rise. Its feet were no longer sure.

Larnin was in the lead when they came on to the ledge. The pitching trail hung like the rungs of a ladder to the mountain face. The ledge was less than five feet wide with sheer wall to the left and, on the right, a drop of jagged rock to the next bench, thirty feet below.

Larnin heard the sudden slither of hoofs. Behind him, the roan shrilled and Reo yelled, 'Jack!' He swung in the saddle, saw the roan already plunging over the rim, pawing for a grip. Reo twisted violently, trying to jump clear, but his right boot heel snagged the stirrup.

Man and horse went down together. Their screams echoed high above the rattle of shale, pierced the billow of rising dust. A few pebbles danced in their wake and the screaming stopped.

Larnin back-tracked on foot. It took time. Dust had settled; the lower bench lay still under the blistering sun. He saw the roan first. It had struck the ledge head-on; its neck was snapped and twisted at a foolish angle.

'Jack.'

It wasn't more than a whisper. Reo lay against a boulder, legs stuck out straight before him, arms folded hard across his belly. The tear wasn't only skin-deep any more. There was a hot, wet feeling in his chest.

The grit-streaked face went crooked when Larnin tried to lift him. The legs wouldn't move at all. He tried to speak and the wetness welled into his throat. A bubble of red broke past his lips, trickled down into the blond beard. Larnin let go of him. Reo sat there, choking back the wetness, his eyes on Larnin. After a long time, he said, 'So this is it.'

Larnin did not answer. Uneasily now, his glance moved down the long ramp of the spur. He took a deep breath. 'Listen, Billy . . .'

The pale eyes didn't blink. 'Go on. Say it.'

Larnin's mouth worked. 'I didn't have nothing to do with this, Billy. I never done no killing. We were friends. All right. I helped you while I could. But now . . .' The narrow jaw tightened. 'Now I want out, Billy.' He started to turn away.

'All right,' Reo said. 'You want out.'

Larnin stared at the gun in Reo's fist. 'Billy, you're crazy.'

'I told you once. Whatever happened, it'd never be the posse. The mob'll never take me.'

Slowly, the meaning got to Larnin. He shook his head. 'I don't like it, Billy. I don't want your murder on my hands. You got a gun. You can do it yourself.'

'Maybe,' Reo said. 'Only I can't be sure. It ain't easy to put a bullet through your own head. At the last minute, I might lose nerve.' His gaze switched down to the blanched eastward flats. His voice went sharp. 'Then they'd come with their goddam rope. They'd . . .'

It ended in a coughing fit. Bright red drained down his chin. The gun hand didn't waver.

'I'm not sure, Jack. You're going to do me a favour. You're going to make me sure.'

'Billy . . .'

'That's how it is.' The muzzle came belly-high on Larnin. 'It's me or you, Jack.'

They looked at each other. Then Larnin's bony fingers went down and closed on the Colt butt and the long barrel came up, clean and shining in the sun.

The posse came into Monte Vista at high noon. They rode wearily. Stetsons tilted against the glare, wetting grit-caked lips. The tall loose-limbed rider sat straight, scanning the dusty main street. The silver star winked against his black vest.

They were passing the telegraph office, when a man came running out. He wore a deputy's star. He waved a slip of yellow paper.

'You Rob Tucker? Sheriff down Alamosa way?'

The tall man nodded.

'Still riding the tail of that Reo fella?'

Tucker's eyes narrowed. 'You got news?'

The man held out the yellow slip. 'They sent that on for you. Said you'd pass this way, maybe want our help.'

Tucker smoothed the paper on his thigh. Riders nudged close. 'I'll be damned,' Tucker said.

The deputy laughed. 'That's what I says to my wife, "That Reo's did it again." Looks as if your hunting party's over, Sheriff. Seems like that Reckonridge boy is going to live, after all. Come to, early this morning, and said he wouldn't press any charges. Admitted he was starting to draw when Reo fired. Ain't much use arresting Reo when the victim hisself says it was self-defence.' The grin widened. 'Honest boy, that Reckonridge. Sounds like a nice kid.'

'Yeah,' Tucker said. 'Nice kid.'

The riders were silent, then something like a sigh of relief went among them. They hitched ponies and ambled off to the cool shade of the nearest saloon. Tucker dismounted and lit a cigarette. For a long moment, he stared at the match flame. He flung the match to the dust. 'The luck of some sidewinders!'

The deputy nodded. 'You had a long ride. You're wore thin.'

'Can you figure it?' Tucker shook his head. 'Here's this Reo suspicioned of murder in four counties and just when we think he's pinned down, ready to bring to trial, out he slides by the skin of his teeth.'

The deputy frowned. Then a thought made him smile. 'Say, I got some stuff up to the office. Curl the hair on your chest.'

Tucker stared at the dead match. 'The luck,' he said. 'The luck always rides with him.' Then he shrugged and grinned back. 'Like you say. It was a long ride.'

They went off along the dry, hot boardwalk. The sheriff's office was at the east end of the main drag. Their backs were turned to the distant San Juan range. They didn't notice the shadows against the sun, the black, picket-winged birds that hovered for a long time above a mountain ledge and then circled down with a slow final grace.

★ WELL OF ANGER ★

By Morgan Lewis

JOE GATES put his paint cow pony through the creek and let him walk up the rise beyond. He was a tall, dark boy of fifteen, thin from overwork, and this day he had been in the saddle since sun-up.

He could plainly hear the sound of Eliphalet Sawyer's axe and see its red gleam in dying light as the homesteader notched logs for his house. This camp, with its covered-wagon body on the ground for a tent, its cookstove under stretched canvas and the four big horses picketed nearby, was only a dot in the immensity of rolling range.

The man rested his double-bitted axe on the log as Joe came up. He was a pleasant young giant with merry blue eyes in a strong brown face fringed by a silky chestnut beard. He was naked to the waist and the light glinted on the curled hairs of his chest.

He wiped sweat from his forehead with a brown forearm and said, 'How is thee, Joe?'

Joe wearily grinned and slumped sideways in the saddle. 'Tired.'

'The trouble still continues?'

The boy nodded unhappily. 'This drought is givin' Gans his chance. We're busy every day hazin' back the stock that he drifts over on to us at night. With the range all burned to blazes, we need every bit of grass we've got.'

Eliphalet considered this. 'Why doesn't thy Father talk to him?' he asked in his slow, deep voice.

Joe grinned wryly. 'Talk to a knotheaded mule? When Luke Gans wants something he just goes after it an' there's no stoppin' him; he's got a tough crew to back him up.'

The big man nodded, wiped his hands on his brown homespun pants and made two more cuts in the log.

'That is enough for to-day,' he said, and rolled it across a litter of chips to the half-completed walls of his house.

This was the first time Joe had seen him with his shirt off, and he marvelled at the man's build and the way the great muscles slid under the milk-white skin. He no longer grinned at the man's speech, but he remembered when Eliphalet had first come to the ranch in early spring to tell pop that he had filed on land across the creek. Pop had been stiff—the land was open range, although they had always used it—but Eliphalet was so friendly and pleasant it was hard not to like him.

After he had gone, pop had said, 'I reckon he's a Quaker. You took note of how he talked? I hear there's a settlement of 'em over beyond Dusty Forks. He must've struck out for himself.'

That had been six months ago. Now Eliphalet had part of his land fenced and planted to corn and his house half up, but he had worked a full fourteen-hour day to do it.

He rested his axe against the logs, picked up a water jug and offered it to Joe.

'That creek water's too muddy,' Joe said. 'Why don't you get it from Big Spring?'

'I carried home a jugful last Sunday, but it does not last for ever.' Eliphalet's blue eyes twinkled. 'Why did thy father build his house a mile from Big Spring?'

Joe grinned. 'He'd have started a war if he'd tried to take Big Spring—it's on open range.... Say, mom wants you for dinner to-morrow. It's Sunday, in case you've forgot.'

'Thy mother is kind, Joe. Thank her for me.' Eliphalet tilted the jug to his lips, and muscles writhed in his awesome arms.

'Gee-e-e.' Joe made the word long drawn out. 'You're built like—like a bull.'

The big man lowered the jug and wiped his mouth with the back of his hand. 'Muscles are not everything, Joe. It is what a man carries in his heart and his head that counts.'

'Maybe,' Joe said, 'but if I had muscles like yours I'd catch Luke Gans alone sometime and break him in little pieces.' His two hands showed exactly how it should be done. 'Well'—he gathered the reins—'I need sleep. See you to-morrow.'

Riding the mile to the ranch, he drowsily thought of Eliphalet and his strength. Why, there wasn't a man in the county that would be able to stand up to him in a fight. It made him feel good to have a friend like that. It gave him a feeling of confidence and safety.

Abby had on her new brown dress for dinner. She was just nineteen; and her hair was black, and curled softly like ma's. Joe noticed how bright her dark eyes were when she looked across the table at Eliphalet.

He tremendously admired the Quaker's table manners. Not once did Eliphalet put his knife in his mouth, and he was nice and polite and bragged up everything he ate. When ma said a certain thing had been cooked by Abby, he bragged it even more, until the colour came up into Abby's smooth cheeks.

'You know,' Joe said in a wondering tone, 'we were out this morning and there wasn't a head of Gan's stock on our range.'

'Prob'bly giving us a day off to rest up,' pop said with grim humour. He was dark and lean, with the beginning of a bald spot at the crown of his black head. He had worked hard with rope and saddle all his days and his shoulders under the blue shirt were slightly stooped.

'I do not see,' Eliphalet said gravely, 'why a man should want land that belongs to another. Has he not range of his own?' Joe liked to hear him talk. He used words kind of funny, different from the folks hereabout.

Pop gripped the fork upright in his dark fist. 'You ever see a rancher figured he had enough?' Pop shook his head. 'He's big and he wants to be bigger; he wants to be king. He's already crowded out a couple of two-bit ranchers on the other side. One of 'em,' he said slowly, 'was kind of weak-kneed. Gans went in and slapped him around until he was glad to quit.'

'He beat him?'

'Well,' pop said, 'the feller's wife did the drivin' when they left. He wasn't in any condition to see.'

'Now, John,' ma said reprovingly, 'you promised there wouldn't be any talk of trouble. Can't you forget Luke Gans for just a minute?'

'I'd be glad to,' pop said, 'if he'd forget me.'

Joe knew what he meant. Gans was the kind that never let

up. If one thing failed, he would try another, and each thing he did would be tougher. Pop never rode out, now, without his Colt at his hip and a rifle in the saddle boot. The thought sent coldness through him and ruined his appetite, until ma brought in the pie.

It was surprising the easy way Eliphalet fitted into the family. The first time ma had invited him pop had objected, because he was opposed to nesters, but ma had said, 'It is hard for a young man to live alone. It wouldn't be Christianlike not to ask him.'

Since then he had been here almost every Sunday, but he wasn't pushing and never came unless invited. And he always brought fresh vegetables from his garden, riding up on one of his big plough horses with a blanket for a saddle.

Toward evening he and Abby took his jug and walked the mile downslope to Big Spring. Pop had gone to sleep, slumped down in his big chair, his rope-hardened hands crossed on his flat stomach.

Joe wandered out to the porch where ma had gone for a breath of air. He was idly watching the tiny figures at the spring when a man topped a rise and rode toward it.

Even at this distance something struck him as familiar, and he got the glasses. 'Ma,' he said, taking a deep breath, 'Luke Gans is down at the spring!'

Ma looked nervously into the room where pop slept. 'Don't wake your father,' she said. 'After all, the spring is on open range; he has as much right there as we have.'

'Well,' Joe said, 'I'll go see what he wants, anyway.' He went out to the corral and got his horse. Riding down, he thought confidently, *If Gans tries to push Eliphalet around, he'll get his head knocked off.* The thought did him a world of good and he was feeling fine when he reached the spring.

Luke Gans was a square, blocky figure in overalls and checked shirt with a red bandana around his neck. He sat his big bay like a rock, quirt dangling from wrist, and the bay's nose was not six inches from Eliphalet's face.

As Joe arrived, Eliphalet grasped the reins close under the bay's chin and forced him back. 'There is room for thy horse, friend,' he said mildly, 'without seeking the ground where I stand.'

Gans' heavy face went a brick red and his stone-grey eyes

flared. 'Let loose my bridle, you damned nester!' he yelled. He leaned forward in the stirrups and brought the heavy quirt down with a full-arm swing.

Joe's stomach congealed; it became a solid lump of ice that crowded against his heart and took his breath. The lash cut across Eliphalet's shoulder and back, and its sound blended with Abby's scream.

For a moment the Quaker's big body swayed. He took a step forward, his fists knotted like hammers. *Ah,* Joe thought, *Gans picked on the wrong man this time: Eliphalet will haul him off his horse and beat him to a pulp.* A sudden wave of savagery swept through him. 'Smash him!' he said, and did not recognize his own voice.

But Eliphalet paused. A deep breath ran out of him and his hands loosened. 'There was no need for that, friend,' he said in a shaken voice.

'Keep your hands off my bridle,' Gans said, 'or you'll get more!' His eyes flicked to Abby. 'That's the way to handle nesters.' He settled his big hat on his head and rode off.

Abby made a small stifled sound. She looked with eyes strained wide at Eliphalet. She saw the red line where the quirt had cut seeping through his shirt, and her white hands balled at her breast. 'He struck you,' she said in a small voice, 'and you did nothing—nothing!' Her face worked, but her eyes were bright and dry. 'He beat you with a whip! What—what kind of man are you?' Her voice broke on the last word, and she turned away and walked upslope through the slanting red light with bent head.

Eliphalet made a half gesture with his hand and let it drop. He stared without sound after Abby, and his face was the saddest Joe had ever seen.

And then embarrassment touched Joe. He could no longer bear to look at him. He turned his horse and rode after his sister. Going home, shadows, like hungry wolves, ran swiftly over the land. He felt vast loneliness and fear. He had witnessed the destruction of an idol and the full measure of Gans' brutality. Long after he was in bed he heard Eliphalet come slowly to the house, get his big horse and ride off into the night.

When Joe went by Big Spring next morning, the jug was still

there, smashed against a rock where some careless hoof had knocked it. The glittering pieces were trampled into the mud.

It was three days before Joe could bring himself to ride down to the homestead. But he had to see Eliphalet; he had to know. It was as though a death had occurred in the ranch house. Mom was unusually quiet, and Abby went about her work, tight-lipped. Mornings her eyes were red, as though she had not slept. There was a solid, heavy weight in Joe's stomach.

The paint pony splashed through a shallow pool in the practically dry creek bed and went slowly up the other side. Joe had to see the big Quaker, but he dreaded it.

The house was no further along than when he had last seen it and, for a moment, he thought Eliphalet had gone. Then he saw the well. It was near the house and not deep, but water flowed in it clear and bright. Gee, Eliphalet was lucky. Pop had gone down twenty feet for their well.

Eliphalet came round the corner, and Joe felt shocked. He was worn and haggard looking and the merriment had gone from his blue eyes. They seemed to have deepened and grown darker.

Joe slid off his horse and stood, feeling young and awkward. 'Still working hard, Joe?' the big man asked.

He shook his head. 'Hasn't been a Gans steer on the place since last Sunday. I can't understand it.' Then the question that had been yeasting inside him came out with rush, 'Gee, why did you take it? Why didn't you come back at him?'

Eliphalet dragged a sleeve across his face. He said in a dull voice, 'Friends do not believe in fighting.'

'Friends?' Joe's voice was scornful. 'Gans hasn't got a friend in the world.'

'The Society of Friends,' Eliphalet explained wearily. 'They do not believe in laying hands on a man in violence.'

Joe stared. Pop had said something about this, but Joe hadn't taken much stock in it. Now he was confronted by the stark reality of a man who didn't believe in fighting. 'But—but s'pose somebody takes a swing at you?'

' "A soft answer turneth away wrath." '

'Well, gee–' Joe was confused. You couldn't very well argue with the Bible, but something was wrong. 'It didn't turn away Gans' wrath. Don't you see,' he argued desperately, 'There's times when you just have to poke a fella in the nose?'

Eliphalet sighed. 'That is true; there are times when anger takes thee by the throat and reason departs. Later thee is sorry, but the harm is done.' He gazed off into the distance where Dry Forks lay hidden by the earth's bulge and Joe got the feeling he was far removed from this time and place.

'It's tough out here,' Joe said. 'Pop says so, and I reckon he's right. Why, if a fella doesn't stand up for himself, every saddle bum in the country will cuff him around.'

'Thee has thy way, Joe,' the big man said, 'and I have mine.' There was a finality in his voice that shut off further discussion. 'To-morrow I start drawing firewood from the hills. I will bring thy father a load.'

Joe nodded and stepped into the saddle. He rode home with the weighty feeling still in his stomach.

Joe raced his pony in off the range just before noon as Eliphalet was unloading his wood. 'Hey, pop!' he yelled. 'Pop! Gans is fencing; he's coming right down the line!'

Pop turned from helping Eliphalet and a surprised, pleased look came over his face. 'I've always hated bobwire,' he said, 'but this is one time I'm glad to see it go up.'

Eliphalet dragged the last pole from the wagon and let it drop. 'This means he will leave thee in peace?'

Pop nodded. 'No other reason for him to fence. Now his stock won't keep driftin' over on to us. It must be,' he said slowly, as though trying to figure it out, 'that he's decided we're too tough and has quit. He–'

Pop broke off as a sound came faintly like a far-off shot. It came again and again, the sound of shots . . . or of someone pounding. He swung on his heel and strode around the house.'

When Joe came up with him he was staring downslope. A crew of three men had moved in by Big Spring and were driving posts. Even without glasses Joe could see that they were fencing the spring. In back of them was a wagon loaded with fence posts.

Pop said in a bleak, bitter voice. 'I should've known better than to think Gans would quit.'

'Is not Big Spring on thy land?' Eliphalet asked, beside him.

Pop's face was grim. 'Open range,' he said. 'We've both used it. Now that water holes are dry and the creek's run out, he figures to grab it and put me over a barrel.'

'This means no water for thy stock?'

'None at all,' pop said. 'There's just one way to fix this.'

He went into the house. When he came out he was carrying the rifle. Joe watched in a kind of tight fascination as he methodically shoved shells into it.

'Thee is not going to shoot men in cold blood!' Eliphalet protested.

'You tend to your business, Sawyer,' pop said, 'and I'll tend to mine.' He shoved in the last shell.

Eliphalet was sweating. He said, 'But that would be murder. There are other ways—'

Pop gave him a level look. 'You didn't do so well the other night.' He bellied down on the ground.

Joe breathed shallowly off the top of his lungs as he watched the rifle steady. This was bad trouble; it had never come to shooting before.

Two men were riding up on the left but pop paid them no heed; he levelled the rifle at the men down by the spring and pulled trigger.

The three jumped apart and wheeled as the top post on the loaded wagon jumped and skittered off. Pop levered in another shell and dust spurted a yard from the man with the sledge. He jumped again, dropped his sledge and ran for the wagon.

And then a shout arose from the two riders and they spurred toward the house. Pop stood up, rifle cradled in his arm. 'Look at him run.' There was vast contempt in his voice.

Joe turned. He hadn't seen Eliphalet leave. Now the Quaker was on one of his big horses, heading for his homestead. He had kicked the animal into a lumbering run.

'That boy smells trouble,' pop said, 'and he doesn't want any part of it.' He shrugged. 'Well, no fight of his,' and turned as the two horsemen pounded into the yard.

Joe's throat went suddenly dry–Luke Gans and Sheriff Bob Merril, of Dusty Forks. The sheriff said, 'Howdy, Gates.' He was a small compact man with eyes as arresting as gun muzzles.

Pop just nodded, his eyes flicking from the sheriff to Gans, sitting smugly in the saddle.

'Doing a little target practice?' Merrill was noted for never raising his voice; his reputation with a gun made it unnecessary.

'Just settin' my sights on the spring,' pop said.

'Don't do it again,' Merril said quietly. 'Gan's foreman, Boots Hardy, has filed homestead rights there.'

Pop sucked in his breath. He was stunned for a moment. Then fury flooded into his face and he swung on Gans. 'You robber!' he yelled. 'You're out to steal my water!'

Merrill kicked his horse between them. 'You can fight all you please over free range, Gates,' he said, 'but Hardy's filed legally. I'll have to back him up.'

Pop's hands clenched, but he was licked. Gans had made a move that put the sheriff on his side, and there wasn't a man in the country that would shoot it out with him,

'I reckon,' Gans drawled, 'now you'll be tame as your Quaker friend.'

Pop was breathing hard. He said, 'Get off that horse and I'll quick show you different.'

Gans just grinned and wheeled his horse.

'I'm sorry,' Merrill told pop. 'It isn't a job I like, but that's the way it is.' He rode after Gans. The two men conferred, then the sheriff headed back for town and Gans went on down to the spring.

Pop stared after them and the look on his face frightened Joe. Never before had pop looked beaten. He had taken the worst of his troubles with chin up, but now his shoulders sagged and the lines of his face were deeper cut. Years of hard, bitter work were being swept away by one man's greed. His stock could not live without water. Joe remembered seeing a disabled steer die of thirst and shuddered.

The pounding resumed down at the spring and Joe felt a new, dreadful fear. Pop was desperate; that sound would drive him crazy. His big hands were clamping the rifle until the knuckles showed white. He might lose his head and start shooting.

'Pop,' Joe faltered. 'Pop–' And then he heard the pound of hoofs and saw Eliphalet returning, the big horse lathered. 'Hey, pop,' he said loudly, 'here's Eliphalet back!' and felt deep relief at this break in the tension.

Eliphalet slid off beside them. 'Thee has failed, John Gates? They are taking thy spring?'

Pop didn't answer, but there was a smouldering light in his black eyes. 'They've homesteaded Big Spring,' Joe explained. 'Gans got the sheriff to side him.'

Eliphalet nodded, as though not surprised. 'That is wrong. It may be within the law, but it is wrong.' He dragged air into his deep chest. 'We will have to steal it back for thee.'

Pop gave him a bitter, impatient glance. 'Sure, we'll just hook on block 'n' tackle and haul it up on my land.'

Eliphalet said in a steady voice, 'If I get thy spring back, will thee promise there will be no shooting?'

Pop had started to turn away. Now, at the sincerity in the big man's voice he swung back. He put his eyes on Eliphalet and he studied the big brown face. 'Sawyer, if you can get that spring back, I'll throw away my gun–that's a promise. But I don't reckon you can.'

'Thee will see,' Eliphalet said calmly. . . . 'Joe, fetch spade and crowbar.'

That's queer equipment to steal a spring with, Joe thought as he loped off. He slowed at the house, where ma stood in the doorway, hands nervously clasped over her apron. 'Hey, we're going' to steal Big Spring back!' he informed her.

Ma turned into the room. 'Abby', she said quickly, 'go with them. They are less apt to start trouble with a woman along.'

But there was no sign of Abby when Joe got back to the wagon. He threw tools on to the sideless floor boards and sat sideways beside pop, with his legs dangling.

'How far down the slope does thy land lie?' Eliphalet asked as they jolted along.

Pop pointed to a narrow bench that broke the slope a hundred yards from the spring. 'Far side of that bench.'

Gans and his crew came into clearer sight as the wagon rolled closer. They already had a section of posts set and the wire strung.

'Not wasting any time,' pop said grimly.

Eliphalet stopped the team on the level land and got down. 'Wait here,' he said, and strode on down to the fence. Joe saw him take a slender forked stick from his boot top.

Gans and his crew stared curiously, but Eliphalet paid them no heed. He took the two ends of the stick in his hands with the point of the V pointing toward his body, and moved along the fence. Opposite the spring he turned and came upslope, not straight, but on diagonal, as though some invisible force were guiding him. He came up on to the bench and across it. Where the slope resumed, the stick bent in his big hands and pointed down.

'A water dowser,' pop murmured wonderingly. 'I've heard tell of 'em but I never took much stock.'

Eliphalet ground his heel into the earth and shoved the stick back into his boot. 'Here is thy spring,' he said.

Joe took a deep, quavery breath of pure excitement. This he would have to see. He lugged spade and crowbar over to the spot and Eliphalet started to dig. He was still scooping out topsoil when Abby stopped her horse beside them.

A red blouse was tucked into her divided skirt and her hair was plaited and wound about her head against the jar of riding. She sat her horse and watched, a coolly impersonal look in her eyes.

Eliphalet met her glance. He nodded and kept on digging, but Joe saw colour seep into his neck. He worked steadily while the sweat began to roll off him. At hardpan he used the bar to pry chunks of it loose.

'Let me take a turn at that,' pop said, and Eliphalet climbed out, the wet shirt clinging to his great shoulders, and watched while pop dug. Presently he took his stick and approached the hole at right angles. 'About four feet down,' he said.

Joe had distinctly seen the wood writhe and bend. He reached out with a grin and took it, but in his hands it was just a piece of dead wood.

'Some have the power, and some have not,' the Quaker told him gravely.

Pop continued to dig, working furiously, grunting with each shovelful, and Joe felt his driving excitement as the hole grew deeper. Abby maintained her cool look, but the little pulse in her throat, that showed when she was angry or excited, was throbbing.

Pop stopped for a breath and Eliphalet took over. Pop got out and stood on the edge, breathing heavily. Wet hair was plastered on his forehead and he had skinned a knuckle on the rough side wall.

Presently, as the hole went deeper, a tiny doubt crept into Joe's mind. There was no sign of water, not even a slight muddiness. The ground was hard and dry, as though the drought had baked clear down into it. Aw, how could a man trace water underground with just a little stick anyway?

Pop said in a sceptical voice, 'You're past four feet now.'

Eliphalet climbed out. Water ran from him and his face was dark red. He took the stick and came to the hole again, moving it from side to side, watching it closely. Then he jumped back into the hole, whirled the bar overhead and drove it deep into a corner.

Water spouted as though he had knocked the cork from a jug and Joe whooped. He struck again and again, enlarging it, and water gushed in a steady flow. Before he climbed out, it was swirling almost to his boot tops.

Pop stared with unbelieving eyes. 'An' all the time,' he murmured, 'it was on my land, if I'd known how to find it!'

And then Joe gave another whoop at this sudden breaking of strain. He capered on the edge of the new spring and whooped like an Indian while Abby's horse danced in excitement.

Gans' crew stopped their work to stare, and Gans, struck by a sudden thought, walked over to Big Spring.

'Thee had best leave,' Eliphalet said, 'and give tempers a chance to cool.'

Pop stared. 'Why? I don't see—'

Eliphalet jerked a thumb toward the fence. 'His spring is gone.' He turned and started downslope.

Pop slapped his leg. 'Well, I'll be– Wait a minute, boy. I'll go with you.'

Eliphalet turned. He shook his head. 'Remember thy promise, John Gates.' His glance rested on the Colt at pop's hip. Then he went striding down the slope, his big boots kicking dust from the grass.

Joe looked at pop for permission, got his worried nod and loped after Eliphalet, but his eyes went beyond the big man and across the fence.

Gans had made his discovery, and now turned, his face black and bonehard with anger. He came toward the fence as Eliphalet approached from the other side, and Joe felt a dryness in his mouth. The Quaker had made a fool of the rancher before his crew. Gans had gone to the trouble of having his foreman file and fence on dry ground.

Eliphalet paused and said, 'We have taken thy spring, but there is–'

Gans gave a great yell, as though his anger was too great to contain. He ran at the fence and put his hands on it and came over in a leap. He had been blocked, and that was the one thing his arrogant nature could not stand. He ripped his overalls on a barb and a flap hung down as he came at Eliphalet. He was cursing steadily in a crazy kind of voice.

Fright yelled through Joe. Eliphalet wouldn't fight; this man would beat his face off; he would kill him. 'Look out!' he yelled, his voice a thin bleat of fear.

And then Gans reached his man and aimed a great sweeping blow at the head. Eliphalet swayed away from it, but the rancher's hard-knuckled fist ploughed along the side of his face. He staggered, took another blow on his arm, then his hands shot out.

Twice he slapped Gans, open-handed, once on either side of the face, with full-arm swings. They cracked with a heavy, meaty sound.

The blows stopped Gans and dazed him so that he swayed on his feet like a sledged steer. Eliphalet bent forward and clamped his hands on the man's hips. The shirt split down his back as he lifted Gans over his head. He took five steps, said, 'Thee has no business on this side, friend,' and pitched him over the fence.

Gans struck on his back, and the wind went out of him with a deep rushing sound. He lay in the dust under downpouring sunlight, and the colour washed out of his face, leaving it grey. Presently he slowly rolled on his side and drew up his knees. The effort to get breath into his lungs made a deep groaning.

Wire pinged as Eliphalet went over the fence. He knelt beside Gans and helped him to sit up. 'Twice thee struck me,' he said. 'Once with the whip and once with the fist; it was more than mortal flesh could endure.'

Joe stared. This was a queer ending to a fight. He looked sideways at the idling crew and saw them exchange glances. The man with the sledge spat on his hands and went back to work.

Joe was still wondering when Eliphalet helped Gans to his feet and the two walked off along the fence. Eliphalet again had the forked stick in his hands. Joe turned and went slowly uphill. The big man's actions sorely puzzled him. It now looked as though he were finding water for Gans.

Pop was standing by the wagon, an uncertain, irritable look on his face. But there was nothing uncertain about Abby. She stood by her horse, her eyes shining and her lips softly parted. Joe sat on the wagon and waited.

When Eliphalet came, he moved slowly, as though this day had wearied even his great strength. He was dirty and sweaty; his torn shirt hung loosely upon him, and Gans' fist had left a red streak along his face. He said, 'I have found Gans a spring.'

Pop shook his head. 'I don't understand. Now the trouble will begin all over again; we're right back where we started.'

'No,' Eliphalet said, 'no. There will be no more trouble. Luke Gans' new spring also arises on thy land.'

Pop stared. Then, as the full significance came to him, the worry and the look of pressure left his face. He made a half-turn away from Eliphalet and swung back. 'It's a small thing to say I'm obliged, Sawyer.' He took a deep breath. 'I give you my word I'll never shut him off from water so long as he acts decent. I reckon that's what you want?'

Eliphalet nodded. He looked down at his big hands. 'Once before, in Dusty Forks, a man raised his hand against me and I struck him to the ground. The Society put me on probation, and now I have again laid violent hands on a man.' He shook his head. 'In some the flesh is stronger than the spirit. It takes long for a man to know himself, to find where his course lies.' There was hint of sadness in his voice.

And then Abby left her horse and came to him. 'Is that such a bad thing?' she asked. There was a warm, bright light in her eyes, and stood directly before him.

He looked at her steadily, but her eyes did not drop and their light seemed to grow and spread until it touched him and he smiled.

'Why, no,' he said. 'It is not bad at all.'

Pop touched Joe's arm and they went over to Abby's horse, but all he said was, 'Joe, I reckon this horse will have to carry double.'

As Joe swung up behind him he heard Abby say, 'I haven't seen your house yet, Eliphalet.'

At the top of the slope he looked back. The wagon was rolling toward the log house set in the new planting, and Abby's red blouse was a bright, hopeful spot of colour.

TWO-FACED PROMISE

By Bill Gulick

CAPTAIN THADDEUS BRADLEY, engineer in charge of the survey party, was in his tent writing a letter to his wife when the lanky, saturnine-faced, Steve Conners, appeared in the entryway and said, 'The Indians are waiting.'

Captain Bradley laid aside his pen, donned his hat and followed the scout across the camp to where the saddled horses waited. Mounting, they forded the shallow river and rode across an open park where the grass grew rich and green, Conners slouching loose and relaxed in the saddle, Bradley holding his short, stocky figure stiffly erect to ease the dull throb of pain in his right side. It was nearly noon. The late September sun stood straight overhead, warm even at that high altitude, and veiling cedar and pine on the upper slopes of the foothills in a translucent haze. Silence rode with the two men for a while, then the captain said, 'Can we trust him?'

'Maybe.' Conner lifted his shoulders in a shrug. 'Chief Qualchee is an educated Indian. Mission school. But that doesn't guarantee anything. Some Indians don't learn to lie till white men teach 'em.' The scout gave Bradley a quizzical look. 'How does he strike you?'

The captain considered for a moment. Problems of engineering could be measured by the tangible yardstick of facts, but long ago he had learned that men must be measured by less tangible things-a gesture, a tone of voice, a quiet glitter of the eye.

He said slowly, 'A man who has the best interests of his people at heart.'

'That,' Conners said dryly, 'puts us right back where we were.'

'You think the only feasible pass is to the south-west?'

'It's big country. I could be wrong.'

The implication was clear enough: there might be other passes through the mountain range to westward, but Conners did not regard it as likely. The captain knew that Conners was a man whom years in the West had taught caution. That was at once a virtue and a fault. The captain's thoughts started circling again, like a terrier chasing its own tail. The final decision must be his. The matter resolved itself to this: either Chief Qualchee was to be trusted or he was not. It was as simple, yet as difficult as that.

Thaddeus Bradley was a man driven by a single dream. For years he had fought an indifferent Congress, a sceptical President and an openly hostile Secretary of War in a stubborn and continuing battle to make that dream a reality – and in the end he had won the grudging victory of a small appropriation and a commission to lead a survey party westward from Saint Paul to Puget Sound. The money was spent now and no hope of getting more. The men were weary and disgruntled. He was tired. An old injury suffered in the Mexican War had returned to plague him and make every minute in the saddle torture, but the job was nearly done. With the early mountain winter weeks away, only a single rugged range lay between the party and its goal. But railroads did not climb mountains. Somewhere there had to be a pass, a low, gentle grade relatively free of snow, or the entire survey was worthless.

He thought of the commission which had been given him months before. ' ... empowered to search out the most feasible northern route for a railroad to the West, to treat with the Indian tribes encountered and set aside lands for them to the end that permanent peace may be insured. ...' It was a bit of irony that the only known pass through the mountains lay in a country jealously claimed by one of the strongest Indian tribes in the West. Well, the wording of the commission made the choice simple. The railroad came first; peace second.

The Indians were camped at the edge of the park a few miles south of the river. Chief Qualchee waited, a tall impassive man whose dignity clothed his powerful body with a quiet grace that no white man's raiments could ever have achieved. Dismounting, Captain Bradley studied him as they went into the council lodge, seated themselves and commenced the long ceremony of pipe-smoking which always preceded important discussions, trying to read whatever truth was in him.

41

'You brought the paper?' the Indian said at last, staring straight at Bradley.

'I have it here in my hand. Do you wish it read to you?'

Qualchee waved it away. 'The white man's words always stand on straight legs but sometimes the hand that writes them lies.'

'My words and my hand are one.'

The Indian inclined his head slightly. 'Good. Then the bargain is done. South of where the river runs—this shall be our land, as it always has been. When the beast that spits fire comes, it will not eat our land. It will turn northward and cross the mountains at the place I have agreed to show you.'

'There is a pass to the north-west?'

'I have said it.'

Captain Bradley's eyes went to Conners' face, and found it stony, expressionless. Whom was a man to believe? A white scout who admitted that his knowledge of the country was limited? A partly civilized savage who might best serve his people by lying?

He said quietly, 'We will sign the treaty.'

They had recrossed the river and were riding into camp before Conners spoke. His eyes probed the irregular horizon line to the north-west. 'Winter comes early in the mountains. If the pass ain't there, there'll be no turning back.'

The jolting of the saddle had made the pain in Captain Bradley's side start throbbing again, a pulsing, tearing pain that forced him to breathe in shallow gasps. 'I know,' he said shortly.

He called the men together and spoke to them briefly. 'I've signed the treaty. From now on the land south of the river belongs to the Indians. I want no trespassing—for any reason. Qualchee has promised to join us to-night. We'll start for the mountains to-morrow.'

Afterwards, he went to his tent and rested on his cot for an hour. When the pain had lessened somewhat, he arose and went back to the unfinished letter to his wife, which he planned to give to the expected army dispatch rider from the east who was due that afternoon. He read over what he had written, then picked up his pen.

...I signed the treaty with the Indians to-day. Perhaps it was a mistake. I'm sure Conners thinks so and I'm sorry for that, for he is the only man in the party who seems to be in sympathy with what I am trying to do. It was not an easy decision to make. If the best pass lies in Indian country south of the river, then that is the route the railroad should take—even if it means war. But the die is cast. Qualchee says that there is an easier and better pass to the north-west. I am risking the success of the entire project on the supposition that he is a man of honour. If his word is good...

He heard a horse clatter into camp and the voices of men raised in greeting. A moment later the dispatch rider, a slight, wiry figure with dust powdering the blue of his faded uniform, appeared in the doorway of the tent. He saluted, then handed the captain a packet of letters.

'You'll start back as soon as you eat?' Captain Bradley said.

'I'll wait till dark. Too many Indians around to suit me.'

'They're peaceful.'

'Perhaps, sir. But I'll still wait till dark.'

Captain Bradley thumbed quickly through the letters, putting aside those from his wife and saving them until he had finished what was bound to be more unpleasant reading. The official letters contained the usual complaints. The government would honour no more drafts for supplies and pack animals and he would be held personally responsible for any further debt incurred. Sentiment in Congress was changing, swayed by the fiery, eloquent Secretary of War, Jefferson Davis, who, being a Southerner, favoured the southern trans-continental route for the railroad. It was thought that a compromise might be reached and a central route through the Rockies decided upon. This, Captain Bradley thought angrily, despite Fremont's abysmal failure to penetrate those mountains in his expedition of a few years ago!

A shadow filled the tent doorway and he looked up to see the thick figure of George Joslyn, one of the party's civilian teamsters. 'What is it?' the captain said impatiently.

Joslyn was a heavy, morose man, slow of thought and action, a man drawn into himself by a secret dream that set him apart from the others. He did the job he was paid to do but no more; whatever free time he had to himself he spent in pursuing the will-o'-the-wisp of his private dream. That dream was gold.

As part of his personal effects, he had brought along from Saint Paul a miner's pan, a pick and a short shovel, and each time the party crossed a likely looking stream he somehow found time to dig a few shovelsful of sand, squat by the water's edge and test it. The other men had been interested at first, then, as his efforts showed little results and they learned the unpleasant fact that prospecting for gold was hard work, the interest gave way to amusement, and, finally, to indifference—none of which affected George Joslyn in the least. He continued to search, to dig, to dream.

There had been a time when Captain Bradley had cherished the hope that Joslyn would make a strike. Gold would bring people west. Gold would assure the success of the northern railroad route. Gold would pay the mounting deficit of the survey party—a deficit which now promised to make him a pauper. But time was running out, and the only gold he sought now was the hope that somewhere to the north-west he would find the vital pass.

'Captain,' Joslyn said with blunt directness, 'I'm quitting. I'm not going on with the party.'

'The word,' Bradley said quietly, 'is deserting.'

'Call it what you want, I'm through.'

'You have a reason, I suppose?'

'If I do, it's my own affair.'

Bradley gazed up at the man, trying to read what lay behind the uncomfortable expression in the heavy face. At last he said, 'I'm busy now, Joslyn. I'll talk to you later.'

His face was troubled for a moment after the man had gone, then it softened as he opened the letters from his wife, letters written months before and a wide continent away. They were cheerful letters for the most part, but here and there a phrase crept in that brought worry to his eyes.

. . . a hard winter here in Massachusetts. The snow still lies in the hill pasture and feed for the cattle is scarce. . . . Esther has

a bad cough. I'm sure it will be all right when spring comes, but, oh, it's so long in coming. . . .

He looked up from the letter and his eyes found the mellow sunlight sparkling on the clear surface of the river and the lovely park beyond. He thought of the vast, empty stretches of fertile park and meadow and wide reach of plain he had crossed since leaving Saint Paul, good land needing only the touch of the plough to make it productive. Then he thought of the bleak New England hills where he had been born and the stone-cluttered valleys where farmers tilled so frugally during the few months of the growing season. Tired, worn-out, sour land.

He sat for a long while gazing out across the camp, then he picked up the pen and started writing again.

The dispatch rider just brought half a dozen letters from you. I can't tell you how welcome they are. Though I know you're doing your best to conceal it. I can sense that you're worried and discouraged. I know the farm is poor. I know it's hard to live on what little money I am able to send you, but if you can bear up a little while longer my job here will be done, then I will come for you. You ask if this is not a terribly lonely land. At the moment it is, my dear, but it will not be long. When the railroad is built—as it surely will be—the people will come and the land will prove fruitful as the East never has. This is land of great promise.

He wrote steadily on while the afternoon sun moved slowly across the sky toward the jagged blue line of peaks on the western horizon.

An hour before sunset he stopped writing and got up and went out of the tent. Men sprawled about the camp, dozing and talking and waiting hungrily while the cook prepared the evening meal. Seeing Conners, the captain said, 'Has Qualchee come?'

'No.'

'He promised to be here by dark.'

'What's his promise worth?'

So Conners has lost faith too. The feeling of being completely alone made the captain look at the scout with a rising anger, then the anger died and became resigned acceptance. No words could inspire faith when the willingness to believe was gone. 'Have you seen Joslyn?' he said shortly.

'Couple of hours ago. He was headin' toward the river with his pick, shovel an' pan. Guess he's gone pokin' around in the hills.'

Captain Bradley frowned. He walked down to the river and stood on the north bank for a time, thinking of Joslyn and his morose, stubborn dream. Growing apprehension came to him. He picked his way across the river on the flat boulders, searched for a moment along the south bank and presently found the clear, deep print of a boot in the moist sand. His sign. It led south across the park, south into forbidden land toward the rising foothills, which were turning blue now with growing dusk.

'The fool!' muttered. 'The damned fool!' ...

He found George Joslyn just as the last pale glow of daylight was fading from the sky. He found him in the bend of a stream a few miles south of the river—lying still and unmoving on his face with the chill water gurgling around him and an Indian hunting arrow protruding from the centre of his back. He had not been dead long, for his body was not yet stiff, but the quiet murmur of the stream, the still rustle of pine on the slope above, told no tales of how he had died or whose hand had bent the bow.

Captain Bradley turned the body over on its side, staring with fascination at the sharp, barbed point protruding from beneath the breast bone and the red, green and white feathers bound to the arrow's notched end. He stood up. Near-by lay the pick, the shovel and the miner's pan Joslyn had carried across half a continent. In a sandbar not far away was a fresh excavation, and just beyond Joslyn's outstretched hand lay a buckskin bag, half full of a substance that gleamed dull yellow as Captain Bradley poured it out in his hand.

He stood for a long while staring down at the nuggets in his palm. George Joslyn had made his strike at last. There was no doubt of that. Gold. Nugget gold. That meant that somewhere near by lay a vein capable of enriching many men. Capable of turning a nation's eyes west.

A coyote on the crest of the hill lifted his lonely cry into empty space; after a while an answering wail floated back through the gathering twilight. Slowly Captain Bradley tilted his hand and let the gold spill out. He up-ended the buckskin sack and threw it into the water. Stooping, he picked up gold pan, shovel and miner's pick and tossed them far out into the forest. Then without a glance at the dead man, he limped slowly downstream. Once he paused, thinking he had heard a small movement in the hillside above him; he listened for a moment, and then, hearing nothing, gave a brief laugh and walked on. . . .

Full darkness had fallen by the time he reached camp. 'Find Joslyn?' Conners asked.

'Joslyn,' the captain said, 'has deserted.'

He went to his tent, lit a candle and sat down to finish the letter to his wife. He had been writing for only a few minutes when he was aware of a quiet step outside. He looked up to see the tall figure of Chief Qualchee standing in the entry of the tent.

'I am here,' the Indian said.

He held a blanket wrapped around him against the growing chill of night. Captain Bradley gazed silently at him for a while, then he said, 'You will lead us to the pass?'

Perhaps it was the captain's imagination again, but he thought a brief glint illumined the dark eyes, a wordless communication that pierced all barriers of race and colour and showed him the soul of Qualchee. The Indian said softly, 'Would Qualchee speak with a forked tongue and let the straight words of the white man shame him?'

Then he was gone and the entryway lay black and empty. The captain stared at the spot where the Indian had stood. There on the dusty ground lay a hunting arrow. The captain picked it up. The head was sharp and barbed. The feathers bound to the notched end were red, green and white.

Captain Bradley shivered and gingerly laid the arrow on the improvised desk across his knees. He picked up his pen, chewed thoughtfully at its end for a moment and then, the faintest ghost of a smile touching his lips, started writing.

. . . Qualchee came, as he promised he would. He says he will lead us to the pass to-morrow. Somehow I have confidence that he will. He impresses me as a man of honour. . . .

By A. B. Guthrie, Jr.

THERE were five men in the back room of the Moon Dance bar—three ranchers, a hay hand and a cattle buyer—all idled by the rain that was beating outside. They had quit their pinochle game, the cards and chips lying forgotten on the green table, and were listening to old Ray Gibler who'd started on one of his stories.

Then Ray saw me and grinned and held out his big hand. 'How, Tenderfoot.'

'I'll listen,' I said to Ray. I took off my slicker.

'I was just talking. Ought to be making tracks.'

One of the ranchers said, 'You ain't gonna ride herd on no dudes to-day.'

'My woman's probably on the hunt for me.'

'I'll buy a drink,' I said.

Ray gave me his wide grin again. It made deep wrinkles in his leathery cheeks. 'I don't like to get in the habit of refusin'.'

I yelled to the bartender for a round. 'What was this about a skunk?'

'Well, I'll tell you—'

Ray doodled the ice in his ditchwater highball with one horny finger. . . .

It was Shorty, the sheepherder, had the skunk, and it happened right here, right in this bar, and there was rooms overhead just like now, only you boys wouldn't remember it, being still slick-eared.

Shorty was new to the town then, but it didn't take us long to find he was all sheepherder. Had a fine, steady thirst and a free hand with money. He had been herding for George I. Smith for five-six months when he decided he couldn't stand thirst nor prosperity any longer. He came to town, a sawed-off, humpy feller with a mop of black hair and a habit of talking to himself, like all herders.

He got fired up good the first day and kep' the blaze going maybe a week, while his whiskers stooled out and his clothes got dirtier and dirtier, and a man meeting him was careful to get on the wind side.

He slept all one day under the hitch rack in back of the Moon Dance Mercantile Company, and when he woke up that night he was just as dry as he was broke, which is as dry as a man can get. He tried moochin' drinks, going from one place to another, but he'd run out of credit, too, and all he got was a bad eye and good advice from the men who had his money.

I was right here, on business you might say, that night when Shorty came in and asked if the roof didn't never leak.

Whitey Hanson said, polishing a glass, 'It's leaked plenty. I set 'em up for you three or four times. Git out!'

Shorty tried to argue. 'My money, you got it.'

'Ah-h. Why'n't you git back on the job?'

There was a couple of curly wolves in the bar, along with Whitey and Shorty and me. Anyhow, they figured they was curly. One of them was Rough Red Rourke and the other Stub Behr. Seeing Shorty, they moseyed over. '*Ba-a-a,*' Red said in his ear, loud enough to bust an eardrum.

'Way round 'em!' Stub yelled.

Red grabbed Shorty by the shoulder. 'Them pore ewes are missin' you, sweetheart.'

Together they ran Shorty limp-legged through the door and pitched him in the street. Shorty got up slow, talking to himself, and dragged off.

Whitey Hanson thought that was good stuff. He said thankee to Red and Stub and poured drinks on the house.

Must have been a couple of hours later—anyhow along towards midnight—when Shorty showed up again, and not alone neither. He had a skunk with him, carrying it along by the tail so it couldn't do business. Old-timers have seen that trick worked many a time in days before saloons got to be hideyholes for spooners. Of course we didn't know the skunk was Shorty's pet.

Red saw him first and a big, drunk smile came on his face.

He couldn't see the skunk on account of Shorty was carrying it on the off side. 'Hey, Stub,' he said, 'look what I see.' Then he hollered, *'Ba-a-a-a!'* at Shorty, so loud the roof shook.

He made for Shorty, and Shorty saw him and a look came on his face. He swung the skunk around. 'By damn!' he said.

Red stopped like he'd been butted by a bull. Stub was trying to slip out of sight.

'Way round 'em!' Shorty said, and pointed the skunk and held it low, so's its front feet almost touched the floor. 'Git out, both you! Git!'

He hazed them around towards the door, still holding the skunk low, business end to. It takes an awful brave man to face up to a skunk. Red and Stub wasn't that curly. They got.

Shorty closed the door after them and headed for the bar like a trout for a hopper. This was the business he had come for. He held the skunk up. To Whitey he said, 'Set 'em up or I set 'im down!'

'Sure, Shorty, sure. Don't set 'im down. Nice work, Shorty.' Whitey came from behind the bar and stretched his arm away out and shook Shorty's loose fist. 'Them fellers couldn't buffalo you, Shorty.'

Some of the rest of us ambled up, not too close, and told Shorty he sure did shine. Shorty said, 'Wasn't nuthin'. Wasn't nuthin'.'

'It sure was, Shorty. Sure was.'

I reckon all that glory was too much for Shorty. He wasn't used to compliments, but just to hearing sheep bleat and bartenders say hell no, they wouldn't trust him for a drink and why didn't he go to work. Yep, it must have been too much for him. Anyhow, he dropped the skunk.

Whitey jumped the counter like an antelope and tore out the back. Tubby Adams got squoze so hard in the doorway he swore his pants wouldn't fit for a month, being way big in the waist and way short in the leg. It must have taken us all of five seconds to clear out, leaving Shorty and his skunk in the saloon—with the whisky.

Well, we got together outside, still breathing hard, and held a rump session by the front door. Whitey was there, of course, and me and two or three cow hands and the printer for the

Messenger, who was celebrating on account of getting the paper out just one day late. We couldn't see inside; Whitey always kept the shades drawn and the place dim-lit.

'Boys,' Whitey said, hearing a cork pop, 'we got to get him out of there.'

One of the cow hands—Pete his name was, Pete Gleeson—said, 'I could open the door just a crack and shoot the skunk if I had sump'n to shoot him with.'

'I can't have the place stunk up,' Whitey said quick. 'I got think about my customers. I gotta think about the hotel. Ain't anyone wants to drink or sleep in a stunk-up place.' He gave us an anxious look.

'I couldn't guarantee to shoot him dead first crack,' the cow-poke said.

'I figure the place is already stunk up,' I told Whitey.

He put his nose to the keyhole. 'Maybe not. I can't smell nothin' yet. Maybe that skunk's used to Shorty.' He raised his voice. 'If you don't come out, Shorty, I'll have to get the law.' He waited for an answer. 'I'll get the sheriff.'

From inside we heard Shorty holler, 'Way round 'em, Shep.'

'That settles it. I will get the sheriff,' Whitey said. 'You fellers stand guard.' He moved off down the street, making for the jail.

After a while he came back, bringing Sheriff McKenzie with him. I had an idea he had been chewing McKenzie's ear off on the way.

'All right, Sheriff,' Whitey said when they came up to us.

McKenzie gnawed on his moustache. 'Now, Whitey, let's augur on this. What you want me to do, anyway?'

'Get Shorty and the skunk outta my place of business, that's what,' Whitey told him. 'And no stink!'

'It's a big order, Whitey, a mighty big order,' the sheriff said.

Whitey never did like the sheriff much. 'The taxes I pay, looks like you would have an idea.'

'Your paying taxes don't seem to help me much right now.'

'You got a reputation as a fast man with a gun. Anyhow, you used to have. But watch you don't hit my new mirror.'

McKenzie chewed his whiskers some more. 'I don't know. I wouldn't say I was *that* fast.'

Tubby Adams said, 'Try persuadin'. Looks like Shorty would feel plumb agreeable by now.'

The sheriff walked up to the door. 'This here's the law, Shorty. This here's the sheriff. You gotta come outta there, Shorty. Best come peaceful. Best not make a stink.'

What he got back was a song, or a piece of it. It sounded real pretty there in the dark.

> *'He's a killer and a hater!*
> *He's the great annihilator!*
> *He's a terror of the boundless prairie.'*

'Don't look like I'm doin' any good,' McKenzie said, turning around to us. He tried it again. 'I don't want no trouble, Shorty. You gonna make me come in and git you?'

This time Shorty answered, 'Yah.'

The sheriff backed away. 'This is serious, sure enough.' He kept bitin' his whiskers and got an idea. 'We'll just throw open the door and let the skunk come out by hisself.'

We all looked at each other. It wasn't for nothin' we had put McKenzie in the sheriff's office, you bet. McKenzie put his hand on the knob while the rest of us got ready to light out. Only the knob wouldn't turn. Shorty wasn't as dumb as you might think.

'You get any smell?' Whitey asked.

McKenzie put his snout to the keyhole. 'Yep.'

'Oh, hell!'

'Rotgut,' the sheriff said. 'The stink of plain rotgut. Nothin' else. Reckon that skunk's ashamed of his equipment by comparison.'

Tubby hitched his pants. 'Long as you won't let anybody shoot that woods pussy, ain't nothin' to do but starve Shorty out.'

'Starve 'im out!' Whitey bawled. 'Starve him out, you damn' fool! You think he'll want to eat?'

'I hadn't give proper thought to that,' Tubby answered.

The printer swallowed another hiccup. 'Have to wait till the well runs dry.'

Whitey clapped his hands to his head.

'I could use a drink myself,' the sheriff put in.

Come to think of it, all of us could. From here on we began to think deep.

I called the boys away from the door so's Shorty couldn't hear. 'Ain't there a way to poison skunks? What they eat, anyhow?'

'Chickens,' Tubby answered. 'Damn 'em!'

'I hear tell they eat frogs and snakes,' the printer said.

While we were thinking frogs and snakes, Shorty began on another tune.

> 'Drink that rotgut, drink that rotgut,
> Drink that redeye, boys;
> It don't make a damn wherever we land,
> We hit her up for joy.'

'A frog now,' Tubby said while he scratched his head with one hand. 'Or snakes. Then there's the poison.'

'I guess it ain't no trouble for you to put your hand on a frog or snake any old time,' Whitey said.

'My boy's got himself a collection. I don't figger he'd mind partin' with a frog or a snake.' Tubby licked his mouth. 'Not in a good cause, anyway.'

'It might work,' the printer said. 'Worth tryin'.'

So Tubby said he'd get a frog, and Pete Gleeson—that was the cow hand—said he'd rout the druggist out and get some strychnine.

By and by they came back, Tubby holding a little old frog that was still mostly tadpole and Pete bringing powdered strychnine in a paper bag.

'First,' said Sheriff McKenzie, taking charge of things, 'we got to poison the frog. Pry his mouth open, one of you.'

We gave the frog a good pinch of poison, with a drop of water for a chaser, and nosed him up to the crack and tried to goose him in. No go. That frog wouldn't budge.

After a while we found out it was because he was dead already.

'The frog idea ain't so good,' the sheriff said. 'Even with a live frog, it wouldn't work. A frog moves by hoppin'. How's he gonna hop *under* a door? Just bump his head, is all. Sump'n quick and slithery would be the ticket, like a snake.'

'And don't poison him inside,' I said. 'Poison him out.'

' 'Nother thing,' Pete Gleeson put in. 'Roll 'im in something sticky first, like flypaper.'

You can see we was all thinkin' dry and hard.

Tubby went back to the house and got a garter snake, and Pete waked the druggist up again to get a sheet of flypaper. The druggist came along with him this time, figuring it wasn't any use to try to sleep.

Tubby and the sheriff didn't mind handlin' the snake.

The strychnine clung fine to the flypaper stickem, and the stickem clung fine to the snake. You never saw a snake like that one! All powdered up pretty, with a kind of a flounce around the neck where the strychnine was extra thick. You would have thought it was going to a wedding.

It could still crawl, though. Tubby pointed it at the crack and let go, and it slipped inside slick as butter.

Shorty was singing 'Red Wing' now, only you could tell he had already sung his best and didn't have much class left in him.

'How long,' asked Whitey, 'does it take strychnine to work?'

The druggist chewed the question over with himself and came out with, 'Depends.'

'We'll give 'er plenty of time,' Whitey said. 'I won't open the place till mornin'.'

'We done a lot of thinkin' for you,' Tubby said, looking at Whitey sad-eyed. 'Got a frog, too, and a snake.'

'All right. All right, I'll set 'em up in the morning.' Whitey talked as if it hurt him.

So we all dragged away, figuring, of course, to be on deck come opening time, which we were.

Whitey had the sheriff with him again, and there was all the rest of us, plus quite a crowd who'd heard about the doings.

'Might have to break the door down,' Whitey say. 'I can't unlock her if she's locked from inside.' He turned to McKenzie, 'Sheriff, do your duty.'

The sheriff waited a while, as if to show he wasn't taking orders from the likes of Whitey. Then he up and turns the knob and the door swung open.

It was just like we'd left it, the place was, except for a couple of empty bottles. No Shorty. No skunk. No snake. No nothing. It was just like we'd left it, except Whitey's new mirror was busted all to hell, which made us feel awful sorry for him. Business took up as usual.

Ray drained his glass. 'I was tellin' the boys before you came in it was a stinkless skunk. Been separated from his ammunition, you might say, though we didn't know it, of course. The place didn't smell a bit worse than it does now.'

'You mean the skunk ate the snake and went off and died, and so Shorty left?' I asked.

'Oh, no. That wasn't the way of it at all. What happened was we cured Shorty. He had picked up his skunk and lit out. Never touched a drop afterwards. He said he'd seen snakes plenty of times while drinkin', but by grab when he saw one with frostin' on it, it was time to quit.'

LONESOME RIDE

★   ★

By Ernest Haycox

JOHNNY POTTER had only squatted himself in the cabin's doorway for a smoke when he heard Plez Neal's footsteps rattling along the stony trail in a rapid return from town. Plez came across the sooty shadows of the yard and made a mysterious motion at Johnny. He said, 'Come inside.'

Johnny followed Plez into the cabin and closed the door. A third partner, Thad Jessup, lay on a bunk, stripped to socks, trousers and iron-stained undershirt. He had been half asleep but his eyes opened and were instantly alert.

'Buck Miller's in town again,' said Plez Neal. 'He's huddled up with that saddle-faced barkeep in the Blue Bucket. They were talking about me—I could tell.' He went over to a soapbox to fill his pipe from a red tobacco can.

'Add those three other fellows that drifted in yesterday,' said Thad. 'There's your crowd. They smell honey.'

'They smell us,' said Plez. 'Now we're sittin' ducks, not knowin' which way we'll be flushed.'

'How'd you suppose they know we're worth a hold-up?' asked Thad.

'Talk of the camp. I wish we hadn't let that damned dust pile up so long.'

Johnny Potter sat hunched over on the edge of a box, arms across his knees. He spread out his fingers and stared at them while he listened to the talk of his partners. Both Plez and Thad were middle-aged men from the Willamette who had left their families behind them to come here and grub out gold enough to go back and buy valley farms. He was the youngster who had a good many more years to throw away than they had; he didn't dread the loss of the dust as they did, but he understood how they felt about it. He riffled his fingers through the ragged, curling edges of his hair and once he looked toward the fireplace, beneath whose stones lay $20,000 in lard cans. His eyes were flashing blue against the mahogany burn of his skin; he was one of those slender young men whose face had a listening silence on it. In the little crevices around his features boyishness and rough knowledge lay uneasily together.

'We've made our stake,' said Thad. 'We could pack and pull out.'

'Won't do. We've got some protection in camp. On the trail we'd be easy marks.'

'But,' said Thad, 'if we stay here we'll get knocked over. It's a Mexican standoff. If they want us they'll get us. Just a question of how and when.'

There was a silence, during which time Johnny Potter decided his partners had no answer to the problem. He straightened on the box and made a small flat gesture with both hands against his legs. 'The three of us would travel too slow, but one of us could travel light and fast. I'll take my horse, and your horse, Plez. To-night. With a head start I can outrun that crowd and get into The Dalles with the dust in four days.'

'Why two horses?' asked Plez.

Johnny nodded toward the fireplace. 'That stuff weights around a hundred pounds. I'll change horses as I go.'

Plez said, 'We'll cook up some bacon and you can take bread. You can make cold camps.'

'I got to have coffee,' said Johnny. 'Pack the dust in the two sets of saddlebags.'

Thad said, 'If they're watchin' us, they'll notice you're gone in the morning.'

'While you're packing,' said Johnny, 'I'll drop in at the Blue Bucket and play sick. To-morrow you tack a smallpox sign on the cabin. They'll think I'm in bed.'

Plez thought about it, sucking at his pipe. 'Johnny, it's two hundred miles to The Dalles. If they pick up your tracks you're a gone chicken.'

'Fall of the dice,' said Johnny and opened the door and stepped into a full mountain darkness. Cabin lights and campfires glimmered through the trees and along the gulch below him, and men's voices drifted in the windless air. He took trail to the creek bottom, threaded his way past tents and gravel piles thrown back from bedrock, and came upon Canyon City's shanties wedged at the bottom of the ravine. The sound of the saloons reached out to him. He turned into the Blue Bucket, stumbling slightly; he saw a few friends at the poker tables and nodded to them in a drawn and gloomy manner, and he made a place for himself at the bar beside Pete Hewitt. The saddle-faced barkeep was at the far end of the counter, talking to a man whose face Johnny couldn't see at the moment. The barkeep broke off the talk long enough to bring Johnny a bottle and glass, and went back to his talk. Johnny took his cheer straight and poured another. The barkeep was at the edge of his vision; he noted the man's eyes roll toward him.

Pete Hewitt said, 'What the hell's the matter with you, Johnny?'

'I ache, I'm hot, I'm cold, I feel terrible.'

'Ague. Get good and drunk.'

Johnny eased his weight on the footrail, swinging enough to have a look at the man with the barkeep. It was Buck Miller, no question—big nose, face the colour of an old grey boulder, a set of rough and raking eyes. Johnny called the barkeep back to pay for his drinks. He said to Hewitt, 'I'm goin' to bed and I'm not getting up for a week.'

Leaving the saloon, he remembered a chore and dropped into the Mercantile to buy caps for his revolver; when he came from the store he noticed Buck Miller in the doorway of the Blue Bucket, staring directly at him. Short gusts of sensation wavered up and down the back of Johnny's neck, as he travelled the stony gulch back to the cabin. 'No question about it,' he thought. 'He's got his mind made up for that dust.'

Plez met him in the yard's darkness and murmured restlessly, 'Come on.' He followed Plez along the creek to a corral which boxed in a bit of the hillside and found the horses packed to go. He tried his cinches and patted the saddlebags. There were two sets of bags, one behind his saddle and one hooked to a light rig thrown over the spare horse. Plez said, 'Bacon and bread's in your blanket roll. Coffee too-but get along without it, Johnny. A fire means trouble.'

'Got to have coffee, trouble or no trouble.'

'Tobacco and matches there. It's Thad's rifle in the boot. Shoots better than yours.'

Johnny Potter stepped to his saddle, taking hold of the lead rope. Thad whispered, 'Listen,' and the three of them were stone-still, dredging the night with their senses. A few stray sounds drifted up the slope; a shape passed across the beam of a campfire. 'Somebody around the cabin,' whispered Thad. 'Get out of here, Johnny.'

Plez said in his kind and troubled voice: 'Don't hold no foolish notions. If you get in a vice, dump the damned dust and run.'

Johnny turned up the ravine, reached the first bench of the hill, and paralleled the gulch as it ran northward toward the wider meadows of the John Day, two miles distant. He was tight with the first strain of this affair; he listened for the sound of a gun behind him, he made quick search of himself for things done right or done wrong, and presently he fell down the hill into the John Day and saw the dull glittering of the creek's ford ahead of him.

He held back a moment. There were lights along the valley, from other diggings and other cabins, and the trail was well travelled by men going to and coming from Canyon City. At this moment he neither saw nor heard anybody and left the shadows of the hill and soon crossed the creek. The racket of his horses in the water was a signal soon answered, for, looking behind him, Johnny saw a shape slide out of the canyon shadows and come to the ford. Johnny swung from the trail at once and put himself into the willows beside the river.

He waited, hearing the rider cross the water and pass down the trail perhaps two hundred feet and there stop and remain motionless for a full three minutes. Suddenly Johnny understood he had made a mistake; he had tipped his hand when he had gone into the store to buy the caps. It wasn't a thing a sick man would do.

The rider wheeled and walked his horse toward the ford. His shadow came abreast Johnny and faded, but at the creek he swung again and came back, clearly hunting and clearly dissatisfied. It was time, Johnny guessed, to use a little pressure; drawing his gun, he cocked the hammer and sent that dry little sound into the night. The rider whipped about, immediately racing over the ford and running full tilt toward Canyon City. He would be going back for the rest of Miller's bunch.

Johnny came out of the brush and went down the trail at a hard run, passing cabins and campfires and sometimes hearing men hail him. He followed the windings of this rough-beaten highway as it matched the windings of the river, he watched the shadows before him; he listened for the rumour of running horses behind him and once—the better to catch the tom-toms of pursuit—he stopped to give the horses a blow and to check the saddlebags. The lights of the diggings at last faded, and near midnight he reached another cluster of cabins, all dark and sleeping, and turned from the valley into the hills. Before him lay something less than two hundred miles of country, timber, rough mountain creases, open grass plains and rivers lying deep in straight-walled canyons.

He slowed the horses to a walk and wound through the black alleys of these hills while the night wore on and the silence deepened; in the first paling dawn he stopped at a creek for a drink and a smoke and went on steadily thereafter until noon found him on the edge of a timber overlooking a mead-owed corridor through these hills. Out there lay the main trail which he watched for a few minutes; then he staked the horses, cooked his coffee and curled on the needle-spongy soil to rest.

It was less than real sleep. He heard the horses moving, he came wide awake at the staccato echoes of a woodpecker, and drifted away again, and moved back and forth across the border of consciousness, straining into the silence, mistrust-ing the silence. He woke before sunset, tired. He threw on the gear and moved the horses to the creek and let them browse in the bottom grasses while he boiled up another pot of coffee. Afterwards he returned to the edge of the timber and, as long as light lasted, he watched the trail which was a wriggling pale line across the tawny meadows below. He had to take that trail for the speed it offered him, but when he took it he also exposed

himself. Thus far he had been pretty secure in the breadth of
the country behind him—a pinpoint lost within a thousand square
miles of hills and criss-cross gullies. Ahead of him, though, the
trail squeezed itself narrowly through a bottleneck of very rough
land. Buck Miller knew about that—and might be waiting there.

Under darkness he moved over the flats to the trail and
ran its miles down. He stopped to water at a creek and later,
well beyond the creek, he paused to listen and thought he heard
the scudding of other horses, though the sounds were so abraded
by distance that he could not locate them. Riding west, he saw
the ragged rising of hills through the silver gloom; the trail
went downgrade, struck the gravelled bottom of a dry wash,
and fell gradually into a pocket at the base of the hills. His
horse, seeing some odd thing, whipped aside, going entirely
off the trail. A moment later it plunged both forefeet into a
washout, dropped to its knees and flung Johnny Potter from the
saddle.

He turned in the air, he struck, he felt pain slice him through,
the odour of blood was in his nostrils and his senses ran out
like the fast tide, leaving him dumb on the ground. Then
the pain accumulated into one rolling shock wave and revived
him with its acute misery. He turned and he sat up, moving
fast to confirm or throw aside his fears. His left leg burned
from hip to ankle and he kicked it out straight with a rough
wish to know the worst. Nothing wrong there. He tried his
right leg, he moved his arms, he stood up. He was all right.

He couldn't get rid of his haste. All through the preceding
night a loneliness had worked its way with him and had made
him feel that every shadow concealed trouble; the same loneliness
now gave him the notion that listening ears were everywhere
around him and that men were rushing towards him. He crouched
in the washout and ran his hands along the down horse's front
legs and discovered the break. He wanted a smoke, risk or no
risk, and he filled his pipe and lighted it close to the ground.
Then he brought in the lead horse—which had strayed out toward grass—transferred the gear to it from the down horse.
When he was ready to travel again he put a bullet into the
head of the down horse, the report shouting and rumbling and

rocketing away in all directions, filling the world with a tremendous racket, and travelling on and never seeming to end. It appeared to follow him and point him out when he rode forward.

The trail fell into a black pocket, reached a creek, and swung with the creek around a long bend, bringing the North Star from Johnny's right shoulder point to a spot in the sky directly before him. In the first streaky moments of dawn he found himself in the bottom grasses and the willow clumps of Bridge Creek near its junction with the John Day. The ridges rose to either side of him and he sat a moment motionless in the saddle and felt naked under such exposure; it would be a better thing to get out of this meadow land and to lose himself in the rough and treeless stringers of earth which made a hundred hidden pockets as they marched higher and higher over the mountains toward central Oregon. But that was the slow way, and he had not enough knowledge of the country to leave the trail and thus, his restless nerves pricking him into action, he went down the creek bottom at the best gallop he could kick out of his horse and reached the still more open bottoms of the John Day.

He hunched his shoulders, listening for a shot and expecting it. He pushed his horse along and tried not to realize that he was asking too much of it. A fine sweat broke over his face like an itch and he reached deep for wind. It was a wonderful thing to at last see the trail rise up from the river through a notch and go directly into the broken land. As soon as the ridge permitted him, he went up its side and got into another draw; he pressed on, climbing and turning and searching the land until he felt his horse lag. Thereupon he changed his course until he reached a ridge from which he saw the trail visible in the ravine below. He fed the horse and put it on picket in a gully and lay down to rest.

Through his curtain of sleep, broken as it was by strain and weariness, he heard the clear running sound of horses below. He reached for his rifle, rolled and crawled to the rim of the ridge all in a motion, and saw four men swinging along the trail below him; the lead man's head was bent, carefully reading signs, and in a moment this man signalled for a halt and swung his horse around, bringing his face into view—that dark skin and big boney nose sharp in the sunlight. The four made a close group on the trail while they talked. Their words lifted toward Johnny:

'No,' said Buck Miller, 'we've gone too far this way. The kid left the trail back there where the ridge began. He went the other side. We'll go back and pick up his tracks.'

'He's tryin' to fool us,' said another man. 'He may be settin' behind a rock waitin' for us to walk right into his shot.'

'He's just a kid,' said Buck Miller. 'He'll run—he won't stand and fight. All he wants to do is keep ahead of us and get to The Dalles.'

The other man wasn't convinced. He said. 'You go back and pick up his tracks while I ride this way a couple miles. If I don't see anything I'll cut over the ridge and find you.'

'No,' said Buck Miller. 'If I see anything moving ahead of me I'll shoot it—and it might turn out to be you. We'll stick together. When we locate the kid we can box him in. He ain't far ahead. He's got two horses and the dust weighs enough to slow him down.'

The other man said, 'He's got the advantage and I don't like it much. He can watch us come and he's above us.'

Miller shook his head. 'If it was a hard customer we were trailin', I'd say you were right. But he's never shot a man. That makes a difference, Jeff. It's a hard thing to pull the trigger if you ain't done it before—and while he's makin' up his mind about it, we'll get around him. I figure we can bring him to a stop. Then one of us can slip behind and get above him. I can hit him, the first bullet, anywhere up to four hundred yards.'

Johnny Potter drew his rifle forward and laid its stock against his cheek. He had Buck Miller framed in the sights, with no doubt left in his mind; it was a matter of kill or be killed—it was that plain. Yet he was astonished that Buck Miller knew him so well; for he had trouble making his finger squeeze the slack from the trigger. It was a hard thing to kill—and that was something he hadn't known. 'Well,' he thought, 'I've got to do it,' and had persuaded himself to fire when the group whirled and ran back along the trail. He had missed his chance.

It would take them a couple of hours, he guessed. He sat still, sweating and uncomfortable, watching them disappear around the rough bends of the ravine; he swung his head back and forth to clear it and he rose reluctantly and went to the horse, pulling up the picket. With Miller behind him, he had a chance for a clear run on the trail, and maybe he could set a trap. He figured it out in his mind as he rode directly down the ridge's side into the trail and galloped westward. They were careless in the way they boomed along; they had no particular fear of him—which made the trap possible, maybe.

He came to a creek and turned the horse into it; he dismounted and dropped belly flat in the water at the feet of the horse, and he drank in great strangling, greedy gusts, rooting his face and head through the water like a hog snouting up acorns from the earth. He had to pull himself away from that luxurious coolness and felt the coolness go away as he travelled on. The canyon began to grow both narrow and crooked, and the hills rose more steeply around him. Somewhere ahead of him the canyon would run out and the trail would then move directly up the face of the hills. When he took that he was an open target. Meanwhile the creek, coming closer to its source, fed a thicker and thicker stand of willows and presently he left the trail and he put the horse well back into the willows. He walked a few yards away from the horse, parted the willows and made himself a covert. He took a few trial sights with the rifle down the trail, and sat back to wait. He closed his eyes, gently groaning. Canyon City was maybe a hundred miles behind him and The Dalles a like distance ahead. It was well into the afternoon when he heard the small vibrations of their coming. He turned on his stomach and brought the gun through the willows, took another trial sight, and had the muzzle against the bend when they came around it, riding single file and riding carelessly. They had convinced themselves he wouldn't stop to fight. They came on loosely scattered, the lead man watching the trail and Buck Miller bringing up the rear.

Miller was the man he wanted and he had terrible moments

of indecision, swinging and lifting the gun to bring it on Miller; but the other three made a screen for Miller and at last Johnny took a sure aim on the lead man, now fifty feet away, and killed him with a shot through the chest.

He dropped the rifle and brought up his revolver as he watched the lead man fall and the riderless horse charge directly up the trail. The other three wheeled and ran for the shelter of the bend. Two of them made it, but Johnny's snap shot caught the third man's horse, and it dropped and threw its rider into the gravel. The man cried as he struck and his arm swung behind him in an unnatural way; he got to his knees and turned his face—bleeding and staring and shocked —toward Johnny. He tried to get to his feet, he shouted, he fell on his chest and began to crawl for the bend on one arm.

Johnny retreated into the willows, got his horse and came into the trail at a charging run. The fallen man made no move; the other two were sheltered behind the point of the ravine. Rushing along the trail, away from them, Johnny overtook the riderless horse, seized its reins as he passed by, and towed it on. He was presently around another turn of the trail and thus for a moment well sheltered; but in the course of a half mile the trail reached a dead end, with the bald rough hills rising in a long hard slant; and up this stif-tilted way the trail climbed by one short switchback upon another. He took to the switchbacks, coming immediately out of the canyon. Within five minutes he was exposed to them against the hillside, and waited for a long-reaching rifle bullet to strike. He looked into the canyon, not yet seeing them. He shoved his horse on with a steady heel gouging. He rode tense, the sharp cold sensations rippling through him; he jumped when the first shot broke the windless, heated air. The bullet, falling short, made its small 'thut' in the ground below him. He kept climbing, exposed and at their mercy, and having no shelter anywhere. He heard the second shot strike, still short, and he turned and, from his increased elevation, he saw the two crouched behind the point of land. They were reloading. The third man was still motionless on the trail.

He kept climbing, his horse grinding wind heavily in and out. He tried a chance shot with his revolver and watched both men jump aside though he knew the bullet came nowhere. They were both aiming, and they fired together. It was the foreshortened distance of the hillside which deceived them and left their bullets below him again. By that time he had reached a short bench and ran across it, temporarily out of their sight; then the hill began again and the trail once more began its climbing turns, exposing him. At this higher level he was beyond decent shooting and he noted that the two had abandoned their rifles and were bending over the man lying on the trail. He stared at the crests above him, some of the tension going out of him, and he let the horse drop to a slightly slower gait. An hour later he reached the top of the hill and faced a broken country before him; bald sagebrush slopes folded one into another and rocky ravines searched through them.

He dismounted and gave the horses a rest while he sat down on the edge of the hill and kept watch on the two dark shapes now far below. They hadn't come on. From his position he now had them on his hip unless they backtracked through this slashed-up country and took another ridge to ride around him. As long as he stood here they couldn't climb the open slope. He stretched out, supporting his head with a hand. His throat was so dry that the flesh seemed brittle and he breathed with tremendous effort and couldn't get enough air. The memory of the cold creek recently tasted became a distant memory, an aggravation; he closed his lids and felt gritty particles scraping across his eyeballs—and suddenly he felt a sharp stinging on his cheek and jumped to his feet. He put a hand to his cheek and drew a short bit of sagebrush from his skin. He had fallen asleep and had rolled against the sagebrush.

The two men were at the creek, resting in the shade of the willows—no doubt waiting night. He rose to the saddle of the borrowed horse and started along the ravine which curled around a bald butte. Near sundown the ravine came out to the breakoff of this string of hills and he saw the slope roll far down into a basin about a mile wide, on the far side of which lay a dark rim. Beyond the rim the high desert ran away to the west and the north; through the haze, off to the west, he saw the vaguest silhouette of snow peaks in the Cascades. He descended the slope as sunset came on in flame and violence.

Darkness found him beside a seepage of water in a pocket of the high sagebrush land. He fed the horses half the remaining oats, ate his bacon and bread and built a fire to cook coffee. He killed the fire and made himself a little spell of comfort with his pipe. Haze covered the sky, creating a solid blackness; the horses stirred around the scanty grasses. He rose and retreated twenty yards from where his fire had been and sat against a juniper. He got to thinking of the two men; they knew he was somewhere in this area—and they no doubt guessed he'd camp near water. If he were in their boots, he decided, he wouldn't try to find a man in this lonesomeness of rolling earth; he'd lay out on some ridge and wait for the man to come into view. The trail—the main trail to The Dalles—was a couple miles west of him.

He seemed to be strangling in water; he flung out a hand, striking his knuckles on the coarse-pebbled soil, and then he sprang up and rammed his head against the juniper. He had been sleeping again. He walked to the seepage and flattened on his stomach, alternately drinking and dousing his head until coldness cleared his mind; then he led the horses to water and let them fill, and resumed his ride, following little creases he could scarcely see, toward a shallow summit. An hour later he came upon the main trail and turned north with it.

The country rose to long swells and fell into barren hollows which he marked more by the feel of the trail than by any decent view; nothing broke the shadows except an occasional upthrust of rock ledge. Having been once over this route he knew the deep canyon of the Deschutes was in front of him, with a wooden toll bridge, but of its exact distance from his present location he had no idea. Around midnight he identified the blurred outline of a house ahead of him—a single wayside station sitting out in the emptiness—he left the trail to circle the station at a good distance. By daylight he found himself in a rutty little defile passing up through a flinty ridge and here, at a summit strewn with fractured rocks, he camped his horses in a pit and crawled back to the edge of the trail, making himself a trench in the loose rubble. The defile was visible all the way to its foot; the plain beyond was in full view. Two riders were coming on across the plain toward the ridge.

He settled his gun on the rocks and, while he waited, he slowly squirmed his body against the flinty soil, like an animal gathering tension for a leap. They were still beyond his reach when they came to the foot of the defile and stopped and then, in tremendous disappointment, he saw that they would not walk into the same trap twice. They talked a moment, with Buck Miller making his gestures around the ridge. Afterwards Miller left the trail and travelled eastward along the foot of the ridge, away from Johnny, for a half mile or so before he turned into the slope and began to climb. The other man also left the trail, passing along the foot of the ridge below Johnny.

Johnny crawled back into the rocks and scrambled in and out of the rough pits and boulder chunks, paralleling the man below him. He went a quarter mile before he flattened and put his head over the rim, and saw the rider angling upward. Johnny retreated and ran another short distance, gauging where he'd meet the man head-on, and returned to the rim. He squeezed himself between two rocks, with the aperture giving him a view of the rider so slowly winding his way forward. He looked to his left to keep Buck Miller in sight and saw Miller slanting still farther away as he climbed. He returned his attention to the man below him and pulled his rifle into position; he watched the man's eyes sweep the rim. Suddenly, with a fair shot open to him, Johnny stood up from the rocks—not knowing why he gave the man that much grace—and aimed on a shape suddenly in violent motion. The man discovered him and tried to turn the horse as he drew. Johnny's bullet tore its hole through the man's chest, from side to side.

The pitching horse threw the man from the saddle and plunged away. Johnny gave him no more thought, immediately running back toward his own horses. Miller, having reached the crest of the ridge half a mile distant, paused a moment there to hear the shot, to orient it—and to see Johnny. Then Miller ran down the slope, toward the toll bridge, toward The Dalles. Johnny reached his animals and filled his pipe and smoked it while he watched Miller fade out of sight in the swells of land to the north. Now he had trouble in front of him instead of behind him—for there was no other way to reach The Dalles except by the toll bridge. But the odds were better—it was one and one now. When he had finished his pipe he started forward, plodding a dusty five miles an hour along a downhill land under a sky filling with sunlight. The trail reached a breakoff, with the river running through a lava gorge far below. He took the narrow trail, winding from point to point.

Rounding a last bend and dropping down a last bench, he found the bridge before him—a row of planks nailed on two logs thrown over waters boiling violently between narrow walls. There was a pack string on the far side and four men sitting in the dust. Coming to the bridge he had a look at the men over the way, and the shed beyond the house, and the crooked grade reaching up the hill behind the bridge. He went across and met the tollkeeper as the latter came out of the house.

'Two dollars,' said the tollkeeper.

'Can you fill that nose bag with oats?'

'All right.'

Johnny Potter pushed the horses on to a trough and let them drink. He waited for the man to furnish the oats and went to a water barrel with a cup hanging to it. He drank five cups of water straight down. When the man brought the oats Johnny scattered a good feed on the ground for the horses. He paid his bill, watching the packers, watching the shed, watching all the blind corners of this place.

'Man pass here little while ago?'

The tollkeeper nodded and pointed toward the north. Johnny looked at the hill before him, the long grey folds tumbled together and the trail looping from point to point and disappearing and reappearing again. The sight of it thickened the weariness in his bones. 'How long into The Dalles?'

'Ten-twelve hours.'

Johnny said. 'You know that fellow ahead?'

The tollkeeper said most briefly, 'I know him.' Then he added, 'And he knows me.' But this was still not enough.

'You know him?' he asked.

'Yes.'

'Well, then,' said the tollkeeper, and felt he had said everything necessary.

That made it clear, Johnny thought. Since Miller knew that the tollkeeper knew him, he probably wouldn't risk a murder so near witnesses. It was his guess he could climb the canyon without too much risk of ambush; it was only a guess, but he had to go ahead on it. A hopeful thought occurred to him. 'That pack outfit going my way?'

'No. South.'

Johnny mounted and turned to the trail. Half an hour of steady riding brought him to a series of blind short turns above which the grey parapets of land rose one after another; and the sense of nakedness was upon him once more as he watched those parapets and hugged the high side of the trail. The sun came fully in and the condensed heat sucked moisture out of him until he felt dryness again glueing his throat tissues together. His muscles ached with the tension of waiting for trouble and his nerves were jumpy. When he reached the summit, long afterwards, he faced a country broken into ridges with deep canyons between; he gave the horses a half-hour's rest, and stood on his feet to smoke, much too weary to risk lying down. He returned to the saddle feeling that he weighed three hundred pounds.

In the middle of the burning afternoon he reached the beginnings of a great hollow which worked its way downward between rising ridge walls. The road went this way, threading the bottom of the hollow and curving out of sight as the hollow turned obediently to the crookedness of the ridges. He followed the road with his doubt growing, meanwhile watching the ridges lift above him, and studying the rocks and the occasional clusters of brush. Three miles of such travelling took him around half a dozen sharp bends and dropped him five hundred feet. He thought, 'This is a hell of a place to be in,' and considered backing out of the hollow. But his caution could not overcome his weariness; the notion of extra riding was too much and so he continued forward, half listening for the crack of a gun to roll out of some hidden niche in the hills above him. The road

70

curved again and the curve brought him against a grey log hut a hundred yards onward, its roof shakes broken through in places, its door closed and its window staring at him—not a window with its sash, but an open space where a window once had been.

He halted. He drew his gun and he felt the wrongness of the place at once. Why, with the cabin showing the wear and tear of passing travellers, should the door be closed? He kept his eyes on the window square, realizing he could not turn and put his back to it; a rifle bullet would knock him out of the saddle long before he reached the protection of the curve. Neither could he climb the steep ridge and circle the cabin, for on that slope he would be a frozen target.

He got down from the horse and walked forward, the gun lifted and loosely sighted on the window square. The clinking between the logs, he noticed, had begun to fall away but the logs—from this distance—didn't appear to have spaces between them large enough to shoot through. At two hundred feet he began to listen, knowing that if Miller was in the place he'd have his horse with him. He heard nothing. He pushed his feet forward and began to fight the entire weight of that cabin. It shoved him back; it made him use up his strength; it was like walking against a heavy wind.

The sun had dropped behind the western ridge and quick shadows were collecting in the hollow; he felt smaller and smaller underneath the high rims of the ridges, and the empty window square got to be like an eye staring directly at him. His stomach fluttered and grew hollow.

He called out, 'Hello—anybody in there?'

His voice rolled around the emptiness. He stooped, never taking his eyes from the window square, and seized a handful of gravel from the road, walnut-sized chunks ground out of the roadbed by the passing freight teams. A hundred feet from the cabin he heaved the rocks at the window square. He missed the opening but he heard the rocks slap the log wall, and suddenly he heard something else—the quick dancing of a disturbed horse inside the cabin. He jumped aside at once and he straightened his aim on the squared window. A shadow

71

moved inside the cabin, and disappeared. Johnny broke into a run, rushing forward and springing aside again. He had thought there could be no moisture left within him after his brutal day, but he began to sweat and his heart slugged him in the ribs. Energy rushed up from somewhere to jolt his muscles into quickness. A gun's report smashed around the inside of the cabin and its bullet scuttered on the road behind Johnny. He saw the shadow moving forward toward the window. He saw Buck Miller stand there, Miller's face half concealed by his risen arm and his slowly aiming gun.

Johnny whipped his shot at the window, jumped and dodged, and fired again. Buck Miller's chest and shoulders swayed; the man's gun pulled off and the bullet went wide. Johnny stopped in his tracks. He laid two shots on that swinging torso and saw his target wheel aside. He ran on again and got to the corner of the house, hearing Miller's horse thrashing about the cramped enclosure. Johnny reached the door, lifted the latch and flung it open; he was still in quick motion and ducked back from the door to wait out the shot. None came.

He held himself still for ten or fifteen seconds, or until a great fright made him back away from this side of the house and whirl about, half expecting to find that Buck Miller had gotten through the window and had come around behind him. He kept backing until he caught the two sides of the cabin. He stepped to the right to get a broader view of the cabin through the doorway, and presently he saw a shape, crouched or fallen, in the far corner. He walked toward the doorway, too exhausted to be cautious. The figure didn't move and when he reached the doorway he found Buck Miller on his knees, head and shoulders jammed into the corner. He looked dead.

Johnny caught the horse's cheek strap as it got near the doorway; he pulled it outside and gave it a slap on the rump, then stepped into the cabin and went over to Miller. He moved Miller around by the shoulders and watched him fall over. Miller's hat fell off and he rolled until he lay on his side. This was the fellow who figured that he, Johnny Potter, would run rather than stand up and kill a man. He thought, 'How'd he know that much about me? He was right—but how'd he know?'

He was sick and he was exhausted; he turned back through the doorway and leaned against the casing a moment to run a hand over his face and to rub away the dry salt and caked dust. His horses were three hundred feet up the road. His knees shook as he walked the distance, his wind gave out on him and he stopped a little while; then he went on and pulled himself into the saddle and started on through the growing twilight.

Even now, knowing he was safe, he found himself watching the shadows and the road with the same tension. It wouldn't break—it had been with him too long, and he reached the hill and rode down a last grade into The Dalles near ten o'clock at night with four days behind him and the watchfulness screwing him tight. Wells Fargo was closed. He had to get the agent's address and go to find him and bring him down to the office; he leaned against the desk while the dust was weighed out and took his receipt. He found a stable for the horses, and from there went to the Umatilla House and got a room. He walked into the bar; he had one whisky quick, and took another to the steam table and ate a meal, and finished with a third whisky. Then he went to his room, took off his boots and laid his gun under the pillow. He flattened on the bed with nothing over him.

He thought, 'Well, it's done and they can buy their damned ranches.' He lay still and felt stiffness crawl along his muscles like paralysis, and his eyelids, when he closed them, tortured him with their fiery stinging. The racket of the town came through the window and a small wind shifted the curtain at the window. He opened his eyes, alert to a foreign thing somewhere in the room and searching for it. Finally he saw what troubled him—a small glow of street light passing through the window and touching the wall of the room. The curtain, moved by the wind, shifted the shadow back and forth on the wall. Saddle motion still rocked him and, soothed by this rocking, he fell asleep. It was not a good sleep; it was still the tense and fitful sleep of the trail, with his senses struggling to stay on guard, and quite suddenly the strongest warning struck him and he flung himself out of bed, straight out of his sleep, seized the revolver from beneath the pillow, and fired at the wall.

The roar of the gun woke him completely and he discovered

he had put a bullet through the shadow which slid back and forth along the wall. He stared at it a moment, reasoning out his action, as he listened for somebody to come up the stairway on the heels of the shot. But nobody came; apparently this hotel was accustomed to the strange actions of people out of the wild country. He put the gun on the dresser and rolled under the covers and fell so deeply and peacefully asleep that a clap of thunder could not have stirred him.

PRIDE IN HIS HOLSTERS

★ ★

By Robert W. Lowndes

E was tired of the streets. He rode into Sacaton and the name of the town was something to roll on the tongue, but the glare of the single street was the same. Same saloons, same mercantile, barber shop and hash joints, same line of ponies and rigs hitched on both sides of the street; same boardwalk. And his mission here was the same.

He dismounted, hitched and went into the saloon marked LEARY'S, his eyes widening to accommodate themselves to the dimness there. Men at the bar looked up and saw his bright red shirt, saw the wolf-like leanness of him, saw the well-worn holsters on his hips and the guns they contained, and knew him for what he was. Gunman and hired killer; flip-and-toss expert; prideful, the kind that would be sure the other man had a square shake.

He looked around, caring naught for the stares, until his eyes rested on a stocky man sitting alone in a booth to the rear; he strode over and slid in across the table from this one. The man's voice was soft, his hands that had once known calluses from a rope and branding iron were soft; his midriff was beginning to bulge. But there was no softness in his eyes; they looked out at the gunman like the eyes of a lizard, small, unblinking, set in deep pouches. The man said, 'Talbot?'

'Yeah. You're Jennings.'

The other nodded. 'You got my message then. Know what you're here for.' It wasn't a question.

The bartender came up and put a bottle on the table, shoved shot glasses before both of them. Talbot shook his head. 'I'll take beer,' he said. 'You know my terms.' That wasn't a question, either.

He saw the frown creep across the big cowman's face and knew what Jennings was going to say.

Jennings said it. 'I don't like to pay half in advance.' He made a gesture with his hands. 'Suppose—'

'Tough luck, tough luck for both of us,' Talbot cut in. 'Tougher on me than you; you'd still be alive and maybe there'd be a cartwheel left on me you could get back. And if you didn't, you could squeeze the dough out of someone else.'

Jennings started to take exception and the gunman stood up. 'There are other gents who'll do your dirty work.' He started to get out of the booth but the other held out a pudgy hand. 'All right.' He reached into his pocket and took out a billfold. 'Two hundred and fifty in advance. You don't have to worry about the law so long as Reardon draws first; I own the law.'

'Nice thing to have in your vest pocket. Hell, man, what do you need me for? A frame is cheaper than what I'm costing you and props up your law to boot.' There was no anger in Talbot's tones. He'd seen these things too long to care, but he liked to bait the kind of man who'd hire a killer to get rid of someone who stood up to him. And he could spot Jennings' kind with a glance; you could see the greed as clearly as if it had been branded on his forehead.

He got up then, his beer untasted, and stuck the bills into his pocket.

'You'll hear from me later,' he said and walked out without a backward glance.

He lay on the bed in the cheap hotel room, looking up at the ceiling, and ran over in his mind the information he'd picked up about Johnny Reardon. It was what he had expected; a solid, hard-working man with a will of his own and determination that had brought him up from a drifter to respectability. Wouldn't give an inch when he knew he was in the right; wouldn't turn down a call for help from anyone so long as he had anything to give. Yeah, this was the kind that men like Jennings had to get rid of; you couldn't buy them and you couldn't scare them.

Reardon had one weakness Talbot knew he could use. A temper that flamed when he thought he saw something crooked, particularly in card games. Someone opined that Reardon's father had been shot by a card sharp and that accounted for Johnny's touchiness on this score, but it didn't matter how this had come about. The weakness was there, lurking underneath and waiting to come out, and that was all that Talbot needed. Reardon would be in town to-night, in on a stud game.

He slept then, easily, until the light went out of the sky and the glare was gone from the streets. Soft coal-oil lamp-light spilling out of the saloon across from his hotel awakened him. He got up and doused cold water on his face, went downstairs and into a hash joint.

When he came out he heard a woman's voice calling 'Smoke Talbot,' and turned around to see her standing in the doorway of the mercantile. He walked across the street and the years seemed to run backward quickly as he came up to her. He looked into Ann Seward's face and the thought of how much he had changed and how little she had was a disturbing thing.

'Still singin', Ann?'

She nodded. A smile crossed her face, the smile he'd known before, as she added, 'But not for long, Smoke. I'm getting married next month.'

'You should have hit me on the head, Ann. You should have knocked me cold and brought in the sky-pilot. Why didn't you tell me?'

She looked at him levelly and shook her head. 'Do you think you would have stayed, Smoke? Young as I was then, I knew better!'

His eyes dropped as he realized the truth in her words; no, he wouldn't have stayed long. He wondered briefly why she wasn't bitter, but another thought crowded this out. A trace of hunger he hadn't realized was in him touched the edges of his words as he said, 'You always said you'd name him Pete, Ann. Did you?'

She nodded and he realized that there was a change, after all, something around the eyes that made her look more mature. The thought came to him that she pitied him.

Ann said softly, 'He looked a lot like you, Smoke.'

Talbot's mouth was suddenly dry. 'Is he—'

'There was a flu epidemic that winter; I had it, too. For a long time I wished the doctor had come a little later. Now I'm glad, Smoke. Someone needs me, someone who's had a hard time and understands a woman like me. I haven't kept anything from him, Smoke, and he still wants me for his wife.'

He said harshly, harsh as the thoughts that crossed his mind, 'You're marrying Johnny Reardon.'

'Yes. Don't go up against him; he'll kill you.'

He smiled then, a lean smile that had no humour in it. He looked at her and shrugged slightly. 'He might not; I'm pretty fast.'

'He'll kill you because he has something to fight for and something to live for. You haven't; all you have is pride in your gunspeed. That isn't enough.'

'Suppose he doesn't?'

'Then I will.' She said it quickly, then turned away. He watched her walk down the street and something tugged at him, something urged him to go after her. Then the pride in him rose and beat down the weariness, smothered what he wanted to say. He stood for a while, looking out on to the street, then went into Leary's. . . .

Hired gunman and killer. Smoke Talbot studied his cards and said quietly, 'I'll keep these.' He looked at Reardon across the table from him, and the faces of other men like him who had gone down before Talbot's guns kept coming into his mind. Reardon met his eyes, looked at the stack of chips that had grown in front of the gunman in the past hour; the others had dropped out and only Talbot and the rancher seemed to be left in the place. 'I'll have two,' he replied just as quietly.

Talbot pushed a stack of chips out on to the table and Reardon called him. Talbot put his cards down and said matter-of-factly, 'Four kings.'

Reardon caught Talbot's hand firmly as he started to rake in the chips. 'That would make an extra king in the deck, wouldn't it?' He held Talbot's right hand and said, 'Don't try a sneak, gunwolf. The law may be bought and paid for here, but there's some things it can't afford to overlook.'

Talbot smiled coldly. 'Let go of me, Reardon. I give any man a square shake.'

Reardon nodded. 'Yeah, your word's good on that, even if

you do deal crooked.' He gathered up the chips and Talbot smiled.

There was an ache in Talbot's right palm and he knew what would cure it. He said, 'You name the place; I'll be there.'

Reardon said, 'Out in front, at noon.' He stood up and put on his hat. 'Better spend as much as you can to-night, because you won't need any money after to-morrow.'

Talbot watched him go and the realization was sharp in him that Reardon knew what was afoot, that he hadn't waited for the showdown planned. He looked around and saw Jennings beckoning him from a back booth. He nodded, got a bottle from the bar and joined the heavy man.

'Why didn't you get him when the time was right?' Jennings wanted to know. 'I told you I own the law.'

'Might have known you'd be here watching your investment.' Talbot said. 'Better walk wide of me after tomorrow, mister, because I might get a touch of sunblindness and mistake you for a snake. Of course, your law would hang me if they got me, but that wouldn't help you any.'

'You muffed it,' the cattleman said angrily. 'You sure damned well muffed it!'

'For your special information,' Talbot replied quietly, 'I don't shoot under tables. And you'd better not have a stake out anywhere around to-morrow, because I'm touchy about such things. I might shoot wild and hit the wrong person.'

Jennings' lips twitched as he advised Talbot to clear out as soon as the job was done. . . .

Flip-and-toss expert. The usual crowd was watching as he started down the street in the noonday sun. He recognized Jennings and saw the man with the star on his shirt across from the rancher. And he knew Ann would be watching.

Prideful. He could tell from the way Reardon wore his guns, from the way the man's hand had grasped him that he, too, could shoot. He started toward the other and the weariness in him was almost alive; it wasn't in his hands, in his arms, in his eyes. But it was there and he thought, Some day it will swallow me. There was no fear attached to his thought, only a certainty.

He saw Jennings out of the corner of his eye, saw the man standing there, licking his lips. Then it was as if a thread had snapped and he was outside of his body, watching with the others. He knew his hand had dropped to his holster in that draw that had beaten the fastest; knew his arm was bringing the gun up before Reardon; knew as well that the shot was high even as he squeezed the trigger. He heard the whine of Reardon's bullet as it passed him, saw the man's gun drop out of his hand as Talbot's slug knocked him backward.

He had time to think: He'll recover, with the nurse he's got. Then his gun was swinging rapidly and Jennings was sinking down, clutching his middle even as the sound of the shot came to his ears.

Talbot felt himself running, zig-zagging as he made for cover. Something slammed into his back and drove the breath out of him. He tried to turn, to lift his gun again, but he knew he was falling. Somehow, somehow his thoughts were sharper than the dust in his nostrils.

Then the sun began to go out, and he knew he wouldn't be tired any more. . . .

A MAN CALLED HORSE

By D. M. Johnson

HE was a young man of good family, as the phrase went in the New England of a hundred-odd years ago, and the reasons for his bitter discontent were unclear, even to himself. He grew up in the gracious old Boston home under his grandmother's care, for his mother had died in giving him birth; and all his life he had known every comfort and privilege his father's wealth could provide.

But still there was the discontent, which puzzled him because he could not even define it. He wanted to live among his equals—people who were no better than he and no worse either. That was as close as he could come to describing the source of his unhappiness in Boston and his restless desire to go somewhere else.

In the year 1845 he left home and went out West, far beyond the country's creeping frontier, where he hoped to find his equals. He had the idea that in Indian country, where there was danger, all white men were kings, and he wanted to be one of them. But he found, in the West as in Boston, that the men he respected were still his superiors, even if they could not read, and those he did not respect weren't worth talking to.

He did have money, however, and he could hire the men he respected. He hired four of them, to cook and hunt and guide and be his companions, but he found them not friendly.

They were apart from him and he was still alone. He still brooded about his status in the world, longing for his equals.

On a day in June, he learned what it was to have no status at all. He became a captive of a small raiding party of Crow Indians.

He heard gunfire and the brief shouts of his companions around the bend of the creek just before they died, but he never saw their bodies. He had no chance to fight, because he was naked and unarmed, bathing in the creek, when a Crow warrior seized and held him.

His captor let him go at last, let him run. Then the lot of them rode him down for sport, striking him with their coup sticks. They carried the dripping scalps of his companions, and one had skinned off Baptiste's black beard as well, for a trophy.

They took him along in a matter-of-fact way, as they took the captured horses. He was unshod and naked as the horses were, and like them he had a rawhide thong around his neck. So long as he didn't fall down, the Crows ignored him.

On the second day they gave him his breeches. His feet were too swollen for his boots, but one of the Indians threw him a pair of moccasins that had belonged to the half-breed, Henry, who was dead back at the creek. The captive wore the moccasins gratefully. The third day they let him ride one of the spare horses so the party could move faster, and on that day they came in sight of their camp.

He thought of trying to escape, hoping he might be killed in flight rather than by slow torture in the camp, but he never had a chance to try. They were more familiar with escape than he was and, knowing what to expect, they forestalled it. The only other time he had tried to escape from anyone he had succeeded. When he had left his home in Boston, his father had raged and his grandmother had cried, but they could not talk him out of his intention.

The men of the Crow raiding party didn't bother with talk. Before riding into camp they stopped and dressed in their regalia, and parts of their victims' clothing; they painted their faces black. Then, leading the white man by the rawhide around his neck as though he were a horse, they rode down toward the tepee circle, shouting and singing, brandishing their weapons. He was unconscious when they got there; he fell and was dragged.

He lay dazed and battered near a tepee while the noisy life of the camp swarmed around him and Indians came to stare. Thirst consumed him, and when it rained he lapped rainwater from the ground like a dog. A scrawny, shrieking, eternally busy old woman with ragged greying hair threw a chunk of meat on the grass, and he fought the dogs for it.

When his head had cleared, he was angry, although anger was an emotion he knew he could not afford.

It was better when I was a horse, he thought—when they led me by the rawhide around my neck. I won't be a dog, no matter what!

The hag gave him stinking, rancid grease and let him figure out what it was for. He applied it gingerly to his bruised and sun-seared body.

Now, he thought, I smell like the rest of them.

While he was healing, he considered coldly the advantages of being a horse. A man would be humiliated, and sooner or later he would strike back and that would be the end of him. But a horse had only to be docile. Very well, he would learn to do without pride.

He understood that he was the property of the screaming old woman, a fine gift from her son, one that she liked to show off. She did more yelling at him than at anyone else, probably to impress the neighbours so they would not forget what a great and generous man her son was. She was bossy and proud, a dreadful sag of skin and bones, and she was a devilish hard worker.

The white man, who now thought of himself as a horse, forgot sometimes to worry about his danger. He kept making mental notes of things to tell his own people in Boston about this hideous adventure. He would go back a hero and he would say, 'Grandmother, let me fetch your shawl. I've been accustomed to doing little errands for another lady about your age.'

Two girls lived in the tepee with the old hag and her warrior son. One of them, the white man concluded, was his captor's wife and the other was his little sister. The daughter-in-law was smug and spoiled. Being beloved, she did not have to be useful. The younger girl had bright, wandering eyes. Often enough they wandered to the white man who was pretending to be a horse.

The two girls worked when the old woman put them at it, but they were always running off to do something they enjoyed more. There were games and noisy contests, and there was much laughter. But not for the white man. He was finding out what loneliness could be.

That was a rich summer on the plains, with plenty of buffalo for meat and clothing and the making of tepees. The Crows were wealthy in horses, prosperous and contented. If their men had not been so avid for glory, the white man thought, there would have been a lot more of them. But they went out of their way to court death, and when one of them met it, the whole camp mourned extravagantly and cried to their God for vengeance.

The captive was a horse all summer, a docile bearer of burdens, careful and patient. He kept reminding himself that he had to be better-natured than other horses, because he could not lash out with hoofs or teeth. Helping the old woman load up the horses for travel, he yanked at a pack and said, 'Whoa, brother. It goes easier when you don't fight.'

The horse gave him a big-eyed stare as if it understood his language—a comforting thought, because nobody else did. But even among the horses he felt unequal. They were able to look out for themselves if they escaped. He would simply starve. He was envious still, even among the horses.

Humbly he fetched and carried. Sometimes he even offered to help, but he had not the skill for the endless work of the women, and he was not trusted to hunt with the men, the providers.

When the camp moved, he carried a pack, trudging with the women. Even the dogs worked then, pulling small burdens on travois of sticks.

The Indian who had captured him lived like a lord, as he had a right to do. He hunted with his peers, attended long ceremonial meetings with much chanting and dancing, and lounged in the shade with his smug bride. He had only two responsibilities: to kill buffalo and to gain glory. The white man was so far beneath him in status that the Indian did not even think of envy.

One day several things happened that made the captive think he might some time become a man again. That was the day when he began to understand their language. For four months he had heard it, day and night, the joy and the mourning, the ritual chanting and sung prayers, the squabbles and the deliberation. None of it meant anything to him at all.

But on that important day in early fall the two young women set out for the river, and one of them called over her shoulder to the old woman. The white man was startled. She had said she was going to bathe. His understanding was so sudden that he felt as if his ears had come unstopped. Listening to the racket of the camp, he heard fragments of meaning instead of gabble.

On that same important day the old woman brought a pair of new moccasins out of the tepee and tossed them on the ground before him. He could not believe she would do anything for him because of kindness, but giving him moccasins was one way of looking after her property.

In thanking her, he dared greatly. He picked a little handful of fading fall flowers and took them to her as she squatted in front of her tepee, scraping a buffalo hide with a tool made from a piece of iron tied to a bone. Her hands were hideous—most of the fingers had the first joint missing. He bowed solemnly and offered the flowers.

She glared at him from beneath the short ragged tangle of her hair. She stared at the flowers, knocked them out of his hand and went running to the next tepee, squalling the story. He heard her and the other women screaming with laughter.

The white man squared his shoulders and walked boldly over to watch three small boys shooting arrows at a target. He said in English, 'Show me how to do that, will you?'

They frowned, but he held out his hand as if there could be no doubt. One of them gave him a bow and one arrow, and they snickered when he missed.

The people were easily amused, except when they were angry. They were amused, at him, playing with the little boys. A few days later he asked the hag, with gestures, for a bow that her son had just discarded, a man-size bow of horn. He scavenged for old arrows. The old woman cackled at his marksmanship and called her neighbours to enjoy the fun.

When he could understand words, he could identify his people by their names. The old woman was Greasy Hand, and her daughter was Pretty Calf. The other young woman's name was not clear to him, for the words were not in his vocabulary. The man who had captured him was Yellow Robe.

Once he could understand, he could begin to talk a little, and then he was less lonely. Nobody had been able to see any reason for talking to him, since he would not understand anyway. He asked the old woman, 'What is my name?' Until he knew it, he was incomplete. She shrugged to let him know he had none.

He told her in the Crow language, 'My name is Horse.' He repeated it, and she nodded. After that they called him Horse when they called him anything. Nobody cared except the white man himself.

They trusted him enough to let him stray out of camp, so that he might have got away and, by unimaginable good luck, might have reached a trading post or a fort, but winter was too close. He did not dare leave without a horse, he needed clothing and a better hunting weapon than he had, and more certain skill in using it. He did not dare steal, for then they would surely have pursued him, and just as certainly they would have caught him. Remembering the warmth of the home that was waiting in Boston, he settled down for the winter.

On a cold night he crept into the tepee after the others had gone to bed. Even a horse might try to find shelter from the wind. The old woman grumbled, but without conviction. She did not put him out.

They tolerated him, back in the shadows, so long as he did not get in the way.

He began to understand how the family that owned him differed from the others. Fate had been cruel to them. In a short, sharp argument among the old women, one of them derided Greasy Hand by sneering 'You have no relatives,' and Greasy Hand raved for minutes of the deeds of her father and uncles and brothers. And she had had four sons, she reminded her detractor—who answered with scorn, 'Where are they?'

Later the white man found her moaning and whimpering to herself, rocking back and forth on her haunches, staring at her mutilated hands. By that time he understood. A mourner often chopped off a finger joint. Old Greasy Hand had mourned often. For the first time he felt a twinge of pity, but he put it aside as another emotion, like anger, that he could not afford. He thought: What tales I will tell when I get home.

He wrinkled his nose in disdain. The camp stank of animals and meat and rancid grease. He looked down at his naked, shivering legs and was startled, remembering that he was still only a horse.

He could not trust the old woman. She fed him only because a starved slave would die and not be worth boasting about. Just how fitful her temper was he saw on the day when she got tired of stumbling over one of the hundred dogs that infested the camp. This was one of her own dogs, a large, strong one that pulled a baggage travois when the tribe moved camp.

Countless times he had seen her kick at the beast as it lay sleeping in front of the tepee, in her way. The dog always moved, with a yelp, but it always got in the way again. One day she gave the dog its usual kick and then stood scolding at it while the animal rolled its eyes sleepily. The old woman suddenly picked up her axe and cut the dog's head half off with one blow. Looking well satisfied with herself, she beckoned her slave to remove the body.

It could have been me, he thought, if I were a dog. I'm a horse.

His hope of life lay with the girl, Pretty Calf. He set about courting her, realizing how desperately poor he was both in property and honour. He owned no horse, no weapon but the old bow and the battered arrows. He had nothing to give away, and he needed gifts, because he did not dare seduce the girl.

One of the customs of courtship involved sending a gift of horses to a girl's older brother and bestowing much buffalo meat upon her mother. The white man could not wait for some far-off time when he might have either horses or meat to give away. And his courtship had to be secret. It was not for him to stroll past the groups of watchful girls, blowing a flute made of an eagle's wing bone, as the flirtatious young bucks did.

He could not ride past Pretty Calf's tepee, painted and bedizened, he had no horses, no finery.

Back home, he remembered, I could marry just about any girl I'd want to. But he wasted little time thinking about that. A future was something to be earned.

The most he dared do was wink at Pretty Calf now and then, or state his admiration, while she giggled and hid her face. The least he dared do to win his bride was to elope with her, but he had to give her a horse to put the seal of tribal approval on that. And he had no horse until he killed a man to get one....

His opportunity came in early spring. He was casually accepted by that time. He did not belong, but he was amusing to the Crows, like a strange pet, or they would not have fed him through the winter.

His chance came when he was hunting small game with three young boys who were his guards as well as his scornful companions. Rabbits and birds were of no account in a camp well fed on buffalo meat, but they made good targets.

His party walked far that day. All of them at once saw the two horses in the sheltered coulee. The boys and the man crawled forward on their bellies, and then they saw an Indian who lay on the ground, moaning, a lone traveller. From the way the boys inched eagerly forward, Horse knew the man was fair prey—a member of some enemy tribe.

This is the way the captive white man acquired wealth and honour to win a bride and save his life: he shot an arrow into the sick man, a split second ahead of one of his small companions, and dashed forward to strike the still groaning man with his bow, to count first coup. Then he seized the hobbled horses.

By the time he had the horses secure, and with them his hope for freedom, the boys had followed, counting coup with gestures and shrieks they had practised since boyhood, and one of them had the scalp. The white man was grimly amused to see the boy double up with sudden nausea when he had the thing in his hand....

There was a hubbub in the camp when they rode in that evening, two of them on each horse. The captive was noticed. Indians who had ignored him as a slave stared at the brave man who had struck first coup and had stolen horses.

The hubbub lasted all night, as fathers boasted loudly of their young sons' exploits. The white man was called upon to settle an argument between two fierce boys as to which of them had struck second coup and which must be satisfied with third. After much talk that went over his head, he solemnly pointed at the nearest boy. He didn't know which boy it was and didn't care, but the boy did.

The white man had watched warriors in their triumph. He knew what to do. Modesty about achievements had no place among the Crow people. When a man did something big, he told about it.

The white man smeared his face with grease and charcoal. He walked inside the tepee circle, chanting and singing. He used his own language.

'You heathens, you savages,' he shouted. 'I'm going to get out of here some day! I am going to get away!' The Crow people listened respectfully. In the Crow tongue he shouted 'Horse! I am Horse!' and they nodded.

He had a right to boast, and he had two horses. Before dawn, the white man and his bride sheltered beyond a far hill, and he was telling her, 'I love you, little lady. I love you.'

She looked at him with her great dark eyes, and he thought she understood English words—or as much as she needed to understand.

'You are my treasure,' he said, 'more precious than jewels, better than fine gold. I am going to call you Freedom.'

When they returned to camp two days later, he was bold but worried. His ace, he suspected, might not be high enough in the game he was playing without being sure of the rules. But it served.

Old Greasy Hand raged—but not at him. She complained loudly that her daughter had let herself go too cheap. But the marriage was as good as any Crow marriage. He had paid a horse.

He learned the language faster after that, from Pretty Calf, whom he sometimes called Freedom. He learned that his attentive, adoring bride was fourteen years old.

One thing he had not guessed was the difference that being Pretty Calf's husband would make in his relationship to her mother and brother. He had hoped only to make his position a little safer, but he had not expected to be treated with dignity. Greasy Hand no longer spoke to him at all. When the white man spoke to her, his bride murmured in dismay, explaining at great length that he must never do that. There could be no conversation between a man and his mother-in-law. He could not even mention a word that was part of her name.

Having improved his status so magnificently, he felt no need for hurry in getting away. Now that he had a woman, he had as good a chance to be rich as any man. Pretty Calf waited on him; she seldom ran off to play games with other young girls, but took pride in learning from her mother the many women's skills of tanning hides and making clothing and preparing food.

He was no more a horse but a kind of man, a half-Indian, still poor and unskilled but laden with honours, clinging to the buckskin fringes of Crow society.

Escape could wait until he could manage it in comfort, with fit clothing and a good horse, with hunting weapons. Escape could wait until the camp moved near some trading post. He did not plan how he would get home. He dreamed of being there all at once, and of telling stories nobody would believe. There was no hurry.

Pretty Calf delighted in educating him. He began to understand tribal arrangements, customs and why things were as they were. They were that way because they had always been so. His young wife giggled when she told him, in his ignorance, things she had always known. But she did not laugh when her brother's wife was taken by another warrior. She explained that solemnly with words and signs.

Yellow Robe belonged to a society called the Big Dogs. The wife stealer, Cut Neck, belonged to the Foxes. They were fellow-tribesmen; they hunted together and fought side by side, but men of one society could take away wives from the other society if they wished, subject to certain limitations.

When Cut Neck rode up to the tepee, laughing and singing, and called to Yellow Robe's wife, 'Come out! Come out!' she did as ordered, looking smug as usual, meek and entirely willing. Thereafter she rode beside him in ceremonial processions and carried his coup stick, while his other wife pretended not to care.

'But why?' the white demanded of his wife, his Freedom. 'Why did our brother let his woman go? He sits and smokes and does not speak.'

Pretty Calf was shocked at the suggestion. Her brother could not possibly reclaim his woman, she explained. He could not even let her come back if she wanted to—and she probably would want to when Cut Neck tired of her. Yellow Robe could not even admit that his heart was sick. That was the way things were. Deviation meant dishonour.

The woman could have hidden from Cut Neck, she said. She could even have refused to go with him if she had been *ba-wurokee*—a really virtuous woman. But she had been his woman before, for a little while on a berrying expedition, and he had a right to claim her.

There was no sense in it, the white man insisted. He glared at his young wife. 'If you go, I will bring you back!' he promised.

She laughed and buried her head against his shoulder. 'I will not have to go,' she said. 'Horse is my first man. There is no hole in my moccasin.'

He stroked her hair and said, *'Ba-wurokee.'*

With great daring, she murmured *'Hay-ha,'* and when he did not answer, because he did not know what she meant, she drew away hurt.

'A woman calls her man that if she thinks he will not leave her. Am I wrong?'

The white man held her closer and lied. 'Pretty Calf is not wrong. Horse will not leave her. Horse will not take another woman, either.' No, he certainly would not. Parting from this one was going to be harder than getting her had been. *'Hay-ha,'* he murmured. 'Freedom.'

His conscience irked him, but not very much. Pretty Calf could get another man easily enough when he was gone, and a better provider. His hunting skill was improving, but he was still awkward.

There was no hurry about leaving. He was used to most of the Crow ways and could stand the rest. He was becoming prosperous. He owned five horses. His place in the life of the tribe was secure, such as it was. Three or four young women, including the one who had belonged to Yellow Robe, made advances to him. Pretty Calf took pride in the fact that her man was so attractive.

By the time he had what he needed for a secret journey, the

grass grew yellow on the plains and the long cold was close. He was enslaved by the girl he called Freedom and, before the winter ended, by the knowledge that she was carrying his child. . . .

The Big Dog society held a long ceremony in the spring. The white man strolled with his woman along the creek bank, thinking: When I get home I will tell them about the chants and the drumming. Some time. Some time.

Pretty Calf would not go to bed when they went back to the tepee.

'Wait and find out about my brother,' she urged. 'Something may happen.'

So far as Horse could figure out, the Big Dogs were having some kind of election. He pampered his wife by staying up with her by the fire. Even the old woman, who was a great one for getting sleep when she was not working, prowled around restlessly.

The white man was yawning by the time the noise of the ceremony died down. When Yellow Robe strode in, garish and heathen in his paint and feathers and furs, the women cried out. There was conversation, too fast for Horse to follow, and the old woman wailed once, but her son silenced her with a gruff command.

When the white man went to sleep, he thought his wife was weeping beside him. The next morning she explained.

'He wears the bearskin belt. Now he can never retreat in battle. He will always be in danger. He will die.'

Maybe he wouldn't, the white man tried to convince her. Pretty Calf recalled that some few men had been honoured by the bearskin belt, vowed to the highest daring, and had not died. If they lived through the summer, then they were free of it.

'My brother wants to die,' she mourned. 'His heart is bitter.'

Yellow Robe lived through half a dozen clashes with small parties of raiders from hostile tribes. His honours were many. He captured horses in an enemy camp, led two successful raids, counted first coup and snatched a gun from the hand of an enemy tribesman. He wore wolf tails on his moccasins and ermine skins on his shirt, and he fringed his leggings with scalps in token of his glory.

When his mother ventured to suggest, as she did many times,

'My son should take a new wife, I need another woman to help me,' he ignored her. He spent much time in prayer, alone in the hills or in conference with a medicine man. He fasted and made vows and kept them. And before he could be free of the heavy honour of the bearskin belt, he went on his last raid.

The warriors were returning from the north just as the white man and two other hunters approached from the south, with buffalo and elk meat dripping from the bloody hides tied on their restive ponies. One of the hunters grunted, and they stopped to watch a rider on the hill north of the tepee circle.

The rider dismounted, held up a blanket and dropped it. He repeated the gesture.

The hunters murmured dismay. 'Two! Two men dead!' They rode fast into the camp where there was already wailing.

A messenger came down from the war party on the hill. The rest of the party delayed to paint their faces for mourning and for victory. One of the two dead men was Yellow Robe. They had put his body in a cave and walled it in with rocks. The other man died later, and his body was in a tree.

There was blood on the ground before the tepee to which Yellow Robe would return no more. His mother, with her hair chopped short, sat in the doorway, rocking back and forth on her haunches, wailing her heartbreak. She cradled one mutilated hand in the other. She had cut off another finger joint.

Pretty Calf had cut off chunks of her long hair and was crying as she gashed her arms with a knife. The white man tried to take the knife away, but she protested so piteously that he let her do as she wished. He was sickened with the lot of them.

Savages! he thought. Now I will go back! I'll go hunting alone, and I'll keep going.

But he did not go just yet, because he was the only hunter in the lodge of the two grieving women, one of them old and the other pregnant with his child.

In their mourning, they made him a pauper again. Everything that meant comfort, wealth and safety they sacrificed to the spirits because of the death of Yellow Robe. The tepee, made of seventeen fine buffalo hides, the furs that should have kept them warm, the white deerskin dress, trimmed with elk teeth, that

Pretty Calf loved so well, even their tools and Yellow Robe's weapons—everything but his sacred medicine objects—they left there on the prairie, and the whole camp moved away. Two of his best horses were killed as a sacrifice, and the women gave away the rest. They had no shelter. They would have no tepee of their own for two months at least of mourning, and the women would have to tan hides to make it. Meanwhile they could live in huts made of willows, covered with skins given them in pity by their friends. They could have lived with relatives, but Yellow Robe's women had no relatives.

The white man had not realized until then how terrible a thing it was for a Crow to have no kinfolk. No wonder old Greasy Hand had only stumps for fingers. She had mourned, from one year to the next, for everyone she had ever loved. She had no one left but her daughter, Pretty Calf.

Horse was furious at their foolishness. It had been bad enough for him, a captive, to be naked as a horse and poor as a slave, but that was because his captors had stripped him. These women had voluntarily given up everything they needed.

He was too angry at them to sleep in the willow hut. He lay under a sheltering tree. And on the third night of the mourning he made his plans. He had a knife and a bow. He would go after meat, taking two horses. And he would not come back. There were, he realized, many things he was not going to tell when he got back home.

In the willow hut, Pretty Calf cried out. He heard rustling there, and the old woman's querulous voice.

Some twenty hours later his son was born, two months early, in the tepee of a skilled medicine woman. The child was born without breath, and the mother died before the sun went down.

The white man was too shocked to think whether he should mourn, or how he should mourn. The old woman screamed until she was voiceless. Piteously she approached him, bent and trembling, blind with grief. She held out her knife and he took it.

She spread out her hands and shook her head. If she cut off any more finger joints, she could do no more work. She could not afford any more lasting signs of grief.

The white man said, 'All right! All right!' between his teeth.

He hacked his arms with the knife and stood watching the blood run down. It was little enough to do for Pretty Calf, for little Freedom. Now there is nothing to keep me, he realized. When I get home, I must not let them see the scars.

He looked at Greasy Hand, hideous in her grief-burdened age, and thought: I really am free now. When a wife dies, her husband has no more duty toward her family. Pretty Calf had told him so, long ago, when he wondered why a certain man moved out of one tepee and into another.

The old woman, of course, would be a scavenger. There was one other with the tribe, an ancient crone who had no relatives, toward whom no one felt any responsibility. She lived on food thrown away by the more fortunate. She slept in shelters that she built with her own knotted hands. She plodded wearily at the end of the procession when the camp moved. When she stumbled nobody cared. When she died, nobody would miss her.

To-morrow morning, the white man decided, I will go.

His mother-in-law's sunken mouth quivered. She said one word, questioningly. She said, '*Eero-oshay?*' She said, 'Son?'

Blinking, he remembered. When a wife died, her husband was free. But her mother, who had ignored him with dignity, might if she wished ask him to stay. She invited him by calling him Son, and he accepted by answering Mother.

Greasy Hand stood before him, bowed with years, withered with unceasing labour, loveless and childless, scarred with grief. But with all her burdens, she still loved life enough to beg it from him, the only person she had any right to ask. She was stripping herself of all she had left, her pride.

He looked eastward across the prairie. Two thousand miles away was home. The old woman would not live for ever. He could afford to wait, for he was young. He could afford to be magnanimous, for he knew he was a man. He gave her the answer. '*Eegya,*' he said. 'Mother.'

He went home three years later. He explained no more than to say, 'I lived with Crows for a while. It was some time before I could leave. They called me horse.'

He did not find it necessary either to apologize or to boast, because he was the equal of any man on earth.

THE GHOST LODE

By William Brandon

THE desert lay like a rug at the foot of the gaunt, grey mountains. The shadows of the night ran from it and dissolved in the ivory daylight, and waking quail talked sleepily from their mesquite roosts. The rising sun opened a golden fan across the sky, and the quail moved out in vast, softly whirring clouds and settled to the ground to feed.

Sunlight touched the mountain peaks a mile above and fell like a gilded curtain from the rims and cliffs and ridges to the deep, green canyons, where little dun-coloured deer with velvet antlers paused to lift their heads and watch. Now the sun stood on end on the edge of the world, and glittering rivers of sunlight raced across the land, melting the last of the cold night air, breathing the heat of the day.

An old man and two burros threaded their way through the chaparral. The landscape all about them was splashed with the vivid paint of countless flowers, masses of scarlet ocotillo and yellow paloverde and the giant incandescent yucca that the *paisanos* called the candle of God. On the higher mesas great seas of field flowers ran in rainbow waves before the morning wind.

From time to time the old man killed a quail with a rusty shotgun. The muzzle blast of the gun echoed for minutes, it seemed, in the immensity of space. The quail fled rustling through the brush, chirping in terror, but they did not fly.

The old man's eyes were bright and lively. A stubble of silver beard masked his face. His clothes and his ragged hat were streaked with sweat and dust. He wore a length of rope for a belt. He talked to the blue quail as he killed them and stuffed them in his pocket.

'Shake your topknot at me, will you. . . . Look there, now, your breast all tore up. Wasn't that a bum shot, though? . . . You'll sing for me in the skillet, mister. That ain't a bad go, is it?'

The burros stopped suddenly, heads up and ears wigwagging, and refused to go on.

'Now, what in tarnation?' the old man said. 'The day ain't hardly started yet—you going to begin making trouble already? Hey, get along now!'

The burros were named (after a pair of minstrel men of the old man's youth) Hasdrubal and Hamilcar. They looked frail under their packs. They heaved their grey, moth-eaten flanks in unison. Their eyes were wan and philosophical. The old man swatted Hasdrubal's bony rump with the shotgun, but the burro only humped his back and hiked a leg to kick.

'All right, baby, all right, we'll see. Old Dad will see what you're scared of, and it blamed well better be something.' He called to a quail perched on a flower-covered cactus, 'Cordonisito, what do you see yonder?'

The little quail looked at him with disconcerting directness, his topknot dangling over one eye, and then hopped down to the ground and disappeared.

The old man walked ahead, looking here and there. He peered through the brush, and saw a man sitting on the ground only a few feet away, watching him.

'Why, holy smoke!' the old man said. He spoke out sternly, but without moving from behind the greasewood that screened him, 'Hey, you, young fella!'

The young man looked at him, smiling, but did not answer. He was hatless. His hair was black and shaggy. He sat in an attitude of complete exhaustion, his legs sprawled out, his shoulders bowed, his hands resting palm up in the dust. His smile did not waver and his watching eyes scarcely seemed to blink.

The old man swallowed. Everyone knew there were creatures out here that could take any form they pleased. The young man smiled on, never moving. After a time the old man said suddenly, 'By golly, boys, I believe he's dead.'

He walked up cautiously to the black-haired young man and touched him, and the young man swayed and fell on his side. But he was not dead. One arm moved, and the black head, after a moment, turned a little, as if to nuzzle into the warm comfort of the sand.

97

The old man knelt over him and felt the fast, faint beat of his heart, and brought his hand away smeared with black blood. He pulled off the young man's shirt and saw a gunshot wound through his body. The bullet had smashed into his lower ribs and come out the small of his back, where it had left a gaping purple eruption. The smile on his face, the old man saw now, was a frozen grimace of pain. The expression in his eyes was the fixed, tranquil stare of coma.

He was as good as dead already, the old man knew, but he thought he would do what he could for him. He brought the packs from his burros, made a fire and boiled water, cleaned the two wounds of dirt and pus and bits of shattered bone, and bound them up. He rolled out his own bed for the wounded man and staked up a trap for a sunshade.

'You might as well die in style, boy,' he said. 'That's more'n most of us will get.'

When he straightened the young man out on the blankets he found the leather bags of gold. There were two of them, flat saddlebags, strung by thongs to the wounded man's belt. When the old man opened them he poured from each a double handful of ore samples.

'Well, now,' the old man said, in a whisper of awe.

The bits of rock were of a richness he would not have believed possible. Why, dirt like this, he thought would assay five hundred fine straight from the pick and shovel. It wasn't ore, it was solid gold!

He looked from the gold to the wounded man with a totally new interest and excitement. The boy's breath whistled faintly in his throat and his half-closed eyes smiled mysteriously at the tarpaulin overhead.

'This tells a story,' the old man said, 'And don't I wish I knew it?'

He studied the ore for a long while, and kept it before him while he ate his noon meal of quail and coffee. The lode it had been dug from would surely be the richest strike in the world. The old man had found pay streaks in his time, but never anything to come close to this. He had dreamed all his life of something like the fabulous, free milling-ledge these samples must represent.

He returned the samples to the two saddlebags finally, and stowed them deep in one of his packs.

The wounded man's lips moved to a taste of water.

'Where'd you find it, son?' the old man asked softly.

He listened, and heard only the laboured breathing. It was weaker, he thought. Very likely the boy would not live till sundown. The old man settled himself and stayed close by, with the thought that the boy might possibly come to himself for a minute before he died, and talk.

The sun filled the world with white, quivering, smothering heat, and the dazzling colour of the flowered desert danced and leaped, while the quail all about cried incessantly, 'He's got the gold! He's got the gold!' The sun sat upon the mountains like a pot of burning brass. Evening shadows stole across the flats and the sun slid suddenly from sight. Rails of gold and silver stretched across the sky and slowly faded away, and the afterglow flared in the east. The old man made up his fire again.

He tried feeding the wounded man with a spoonful of broth cooked from the bones of the quail.

The boy swallowed the broth and feebly worked his tongue.

The old man said coaxingly, 'What's that? What's that you say, son?'

'... Bill Jones ...'

'Sure, sure; go on. Bill Jones, you say? Pleased to know you, Bill. My name's Ben—Ben Sandy, they call me, although that ain't my name, but that's no matter; Crazy Ben Sandy some folks say when they want to get my goat. They think any man's crazy who will live and die out here. You got something else to say, Bill? You locate something up in the hills, did you, Bill? Seems to me I seen some high-grade ore. You remember, son? Can you remember?'

Bill Jones said nothing. His eyes were entirely closed now and his sunburned face looked like death, but the old man touched his pulse and felt it drumming madly on.

The old man sighed. Death was standing by, nevertheless, and would surely step into the camp before morning. But Bill Jones had spoken once. He might, still, talk again.

It was easy enough to cipher out a great part of the story, the old man thought. Bill Jones had gone prospecting in the mountains with a partner. They had made this strike, this bonanza pocket of infinite riches, enough to make any man lose his senses. Rich enough to give you a fortune for every day's work, rich as the Ghost Lode itself. So they had no more than located it before they had turned suspicious of each other, crazy with gold madness as they would have been. They had fallen into a row, and one of them had gone for the other with a gun. Bill Jones had killed his partner, but he had gotten a bullet through him while he was about it. He had lived long enough to wander this far (from where?) and now he, too, was dying.

That Bill Jones had killed his partner the old man was reasonably certain, because Bill Jones was carrying the samples with him. The saddlebags of ore would naturally have gone to the victor.

Night fell. Coyotes yapped in the hills, and a cactus rat worked tirelessly near by on his house of cholla joints. The burros came close to the fire to doze. Stars flowed in glittering streams across the sky. The mountains towered among the stars, black and gigantic and silent.

The Ghost Lode returned to the old man's thoughts, and an uneasiness ran through his bones.

The story of the Ghost Lode had been old before Ben Sandy was born. No one had ever found it. No one ever saw anything of it except a load of pure raw gold, alike enough, the old man supposed, to the samples Bill Jones had been carrying. Although there would be a good deal more of it, he guessed, hundreds of pounds, a burro-load or so, enough to be a fortune in itself. But the story, as it was told, held that no man could live to bring in the Ghost Lode gold.

The Ghost Lode led men to death. Worse, it led them to murder, which meant they lost their souls before they lost their lives. Its bewitched gold went eternally from hand to hand, the story related, and to possess it was to die. But, so the story said, you could possess it only by killing the previous owner. That was where you lost your soul. After that you missed your way, your mules sickened and died, your water gave out, and then the next man found you. And when the gold from the Ghost Lode set his brain on fire, then it was your time to die, and the gold travelled on.

Plenty of men had dropped out of sight in these mountains. Ben had known many. Who was to say the Ghost Lode was a myth? The old man had once been young enough to laugh at the story. The young are natural sceptics. When you are young you think death itself a myth. But the old man had been too long alone, with time for thought, and he had seen too many strange things.

There had been a girl once, a long time ago, and the old man had almost married her, but she had died of the smallpox. Now, he had seen her many times since, in the desert. She would come running toward him and stop a little way off and then hold out her hands, and then she would be gone. In his own head? Maybe, but Hamilcar and Hasdrubal saw her, too. They would stop stock-still and watch.

The burros saw her as the burros heard the voices that the old man heard. The voices, the scattered words of people from days long gone, people the old man had known or people the desert only had known, the voices dwelt for ever in certain secret places. Who would prove they were only the wind? ...

The old man wakened with a start. The fire was dead and the stars were dim. Bill Jones was talking in a hoarse and fretful whisper. The old man moved on his aching legs and bent close to listen.

'... old Bill Jones ...

'All right, Bill. Go ahead. Tell me what you want to say.'

The wounded man opened his mouth and drew in a long, shuddering breath.

'Now he's dying,' the old man thought angrily. But a thread of pulse still clung to life. The old man crouched beside him waiting, and presently fell asleep again.

In the morning Bill Jones was still alive. He was young and well-muscled and strong, and so death was having a long wait for him, but it was impossible, the old man thought, that he could last through the day.

'Sure can't be no Ghost Lode,' the old man told his burros. 'He's dying fast enough of his own self without any help from me.'

Hamilcar drew back his lips and wheezed through yellow teeth.

'I'm doing the best I can to keep him alive,' the old man pointed out. 'Ain't that so? You never knew me to do harm to anyone yet, did you? Not my style, boys; you know that. But I sure wish he'd come to for just five minutes.'

He would have liked to stay on in camp, in case Bill Jones should talk again and say something worth hearing, but his water was running too low. He had used a lot of it for the wounded man. He took the burros and packed on to the mountains to refill his kegs.

He followed Bill Jones's back trail as long as he could make it out. It wandered erratically across the dreamlike desert gardens, among the fantastic flowers. At one point he found a discarded canteen. Then the trail skirted a mesa, through a broken country slashed with blood-red gullies, and here the last traces of tracks disappeared.

Later, on the mesa, he killed another mess of quail. The birds did not run from him through the grass, but flushed and sailed away over fields of waving poppies. It was unusual for these birds to fly, back here where they were never hunted.

The wide tableland was split across its middle with a deep arroyo, as though by the stroke of a giant axe. The arroyo ran to the base of the mountains, where its wash, strewn with boulders and a vast float of rubble, angled into a shallow stream. The creek was now more dry than wet, but the old man found water enough in its potholes.

He returned along the arroyo clear to the flats and went back to camp by a different route, hoping to cut further sign of Bill Jones's trail. He saw nothing.

He was a hundred yards from his camp when he heard Bill Jones's voice raised in a yell. The old man broke into a frantic run, and pounded into camp out of breath and with his blood booming in his ears.

The wounded man greeted him with delirious exuberance. His face was a bright red and his eyes gleamed like fire.

The old man dropped to his knees beside him. He gasped, 'What's that you say, Bill? What was you saying, boy?'

'... *Old Bill Jones ... had two daughters and a song* ...'

The boy was singing. His voice rolled lustily across the stillness of the afternoon.
'Old Bill Jones had two daughters and a song,
One went to Denver and the other went wrong ...'
The old man, after a time, got up and brought him a drink of water. Bill Jones knocked the cup aside. The water flew glistening through the air.

'... *His wife she died in a poolroom fight,*
But still he sings from morning till night ...'

Bill Jones groaned and his back stiffened in a convulsion of agony. The old man reached out and held his shoulders. He could see the boy's red-rimmed eyes filming over.
The old man said desperately, 'Bill, the gold, the gold you got, son, where was that? Where was it, boy?'
Bill Jones turned his face away. The black tip of his tongue protruded between his teeth. His body strained to move, as if he wrestled some enormous unseen opponent. He choked for breath, and a pink film of blood appeared at the corner of his mouth.
'All right, son,' the old man said in resignation. 'I won't trouble you no more.'
He continued to grip the young man's shoulders and hold his body still. The black head dropped back and the knotted muscles relaxed.
'Go peaceful; don't be scared,' the old man said. 'It's just eternal rest, and that ain't a bad go, is it?'

Presently the old man stood up, rubbing his hands on his pants. He hobbled away, mumbling to himself, to tend to the burros. He dug out the saddlebags suddenly and poured out the gold to look at it once more.

'No Ghost Lode,' he said. 'Just a plain, damned, lost strike.' The samples winked dully, enigmatically. 'The richest strike in the world,' the old man said bitterly. 'Old Ben Sandy, with the richest strike in the world. I've got it right here in my hand and I don't know where it is.' He put the gold away again, with a savage emphasis, and went on with his work.

He looked down at Bill Jones. The young face was no longer feverish. The skin was as yellow as wax. The bloodshot eyes were blank.

'Dead enough,' the old man said. 'Besides everything else I've got to dig you a grave.'

He closed the boy's eyes and crossed his hands over his chest. He checked for a pulse automatically, and he was astonished to find it running gently on.

He was still alive when evening came. If anything, he was a little stronger. It was a sure thing, the old man thought, that he couldn't get any weaker, not if he was going to insist on hanging on to life the way he was doing. The old man made his supper and fed Bill Jones again with broth and water, and changed the bandage on his wounds. While he was about it he undressed him and washed him down and wrapped him in blankets. Then he went through his clothes, in the hope that he might find some lead on the location of the strike. It would be enough, he thought, if he could get a general idea of where it was. He found a few nondescript personal belongings, a handsome silver watch, and a notebook.

The notebook contained a pencilled test log, evidently a record of face sampling taken at the strike. The old man could read it clearly enough. It indicated a narrow outcrop, apparently without much lateral extension, but within its short confines immensely rich. The old man could almost visualize it. But there was nothing in the notebook that gave a hint of its location.

He sat for a long while in thought. He got the bags of samples and took them close to the fire and gazed at them by the hour, as if they might sooner or later speak to him and tell him where they came from. At last he went to sleep.

In the morning Bill Jones was asking for water.

The old man hustled to him, half awake, with a drink. He said, 'Bill, can you hear me? Can you hear me, son?'

The wounded man sipped at the water and laboriously swallowed.

'Look at me, son. Look here. Look at me. Can you hear what I'm saying?'

The young man's eyes opened and moved with an infinite effort. The old man's heart pounded with excitement.

'That gold, son, that ore you was carrying.' The old man stopped to lick lips and get his breath. The boy was looking at him, he understood him, he thought; he was going to be able to talk. 'Can you remember where you found it? The gold. That gold.'

Bill Jones moved his lips.

The old man gave him another taste of water. 'Do you remember, boy? Do you remember where you got it?'

Bill Jones tried to speak. The old man waited breathlessly.

Bill Jones said clearly enough, 'I don't know.'

'Of course you know!' the old man exploded. 'You had it on you, boy!' The old man restrained his impatience. 'I'm talking about those samples, son. Where'd they come from? Where was it?'

The old man waited, gripping his trembling hands together.

Bill Jones said in a dry whisper, 'Don't know.'

'You picked 'em up, didn't you?'

'Don't know. Don't know where it came from.'

'You got to know! Would you lay there on your deathbed and lie to me?'

Bill Jones closed his eyes and seemed to sleep. The old man reached out to shake him awake, but the eyes would not open.

'You can't take a gold mine with you when you're dead, can you?' the old man demanded, enraged. 'Listen, boy; listen to me. Wake up and listen to me.'

Bill Jones slept on. The old man got up and stumped across the camp. He saw the watch and the notebook. He sat down and took the watch apart to make sure no clue was hidden within it. He leafed furiously through the notebook.

He yelled at the wounded man. 'A dozen words, that's all I wanted! So you give me a lie!'

He got up and flung the notebook away, and a blue quail, pecking at the ashes of the fire, scampered off, calling shrilly, 'Queet, queet, queet!'

The old man shouted after it, 'Run, blame you!'

He was struck by a sudden shift of thought.

These quail always ran. You could trot after one and shoot at him ten times and he wouldn't fly. They stayed on the ground because in this remote country they didn't know about hunters and guns. The killers they knew were hawks, which came from above and from which they customarily hid on the ground. When, rarely, you found quail that flushed, it usually meant the country had been recently hunted. When they were hunted enough they got in the habit of taking to wing. They learned, after a while, that running was not good enough to get away from a gun.

But the quail on the mesa had flushed.

'Why, that's it,' the old man thought, in such excitement that he could not speak. 'That's it, sure.'

He was immediately certain that someone had been camped on the mesa lately and had killed the birds there regularly, day after day. He was as sure of it as if the birds themselves had told him.

And there was the arroyo, where the earth was split open, revealing a cross-section of ancient benches and river-beds and decayed rock, that was where they would have been prospecting from a camp on the mesa. It all fit together. The strike was bound to be some place along the arroyo.

The old man bawled at the burros in a great voice, 'Boys, I've got it!' Hasdrubal gave him a sceptical look. The old man whooped at him, 'It's enough to go on, ain't it? You bet your boots it is! Hellsfire, I'll walk right dab to it!'

He started away with the burros, scarcely aware that he had packed them. He ran back to the camp for the two bags of samples.

He howled at the sleeping Bill Jones, 'Sure, keep it to yourself, son! Old Dad ain't as dumb as you thought!'

He was filled with derision for the pitiful, greedy efforts the wounded boy had made to conceal his treasure. Did he think he could show Ben Sandy ore like that and keep him from smelling out where it came from?

The old man laughed and hugged Hasdrubal round the neck as he stumped along.

He said, 'Would of been a sight better of him to of told me, wouldn't it? All I done for him, and then he'd lie and try to cheat me. We got around him, didn't we? Didn't we, boys?'

The burros slanted their ears at him, and jogged on in their quick and dainty walk.

On the mesa the quail flew up and sailed away as before, and the old man shouted with glee to see them. He promised himself that he would buy the mesa and fence it in and feed these birds for ever at his own expense.

He had thought he would push on straight to the wash, but when he reached the country rock of the arroyo rim he decided to make camp there, for the first thing. His legs were uncommonly tired. They trembled at each step. He would set up camp here, and then go to the wash and prospect up this far and be all set to turn in when he got here.

There was no point in looking for the site of Bill Jones's camp or the body of his partner. What with lions and coyotes and buzzards the dead partner could easily be scattered over half the mesa by now. He might find their workings or markers in the arroyo, and he might not. The thing to do was work the whole arroyo, prospect, the float and the open bedrock, and before too many days he'd be sure to hit the spot. There was plenty of time, now that he was certain the strike was some place along here.

He clambered down the arroyo wall to a hardpan bench and crouched there and got his breath.

There was a delicious sense of anticipation that made him almost want to prolong the actual work of discovery. He took out the gold and looked at it, and time passed while he waited, unmoving, in a madness of inactivity. He laughed aloud at every plumed quail that whirred into the air above the poppies. He stood up at last, but his legs still shivered like stems of grass.

He laughed again and sat down on the bench, suddenly yawning. He hadn't rested long enough. But his legs continued to tremble even though they were stretched out at ease, and he could no longer hide from the truth. It was not weariness, but fear.

The boy's fever had gone this morning. Chances were, if he had pulled through this far, that he might live. That was part of the fear.

'He ain't got a chance of living,' the old man said contemptuously, but he did not convince himself. 'All right!' he said furiously. 'If he lives, what happens to me? I let him go on and claim the whole thing and hog it for himself, do I?'

That was a still greater part of the fear, and he felt a hundred times better for having spoken it straight out. He looked around boldly at the silent rocks and the silent, brilliant flowers.

'Is there any laws says I'm bound to go on taking care of him?'

He remembered then that he had not even left water beside Bill Jones.

Was that murder? Had it been in his mind all day that he would commit murder for the strike he now knew he could find? Had he intended deliberately to leave the boy to die? He told himself he hadn't thought of Bill Jones at all, but the back of his mind, which had been thinking secretly of little else, told him coldly that was a lie.

Murder, and that was, at last, the whole fear.

The old man said plaintively, 'Suppose I go back and take care of him and he pulls through? What do I get for it? He's made it plain enough what I'll get from him—not a thing. So what do I owe him?'

He poured out the ore samples and lifted them in his hands. They called to him with the deep glorious music of their colour. They enveloped his senses, they offered a vision of a cool, desirable world in payment for all the burned-out years of his life.

The boy would die easily. He was weak enough already; he

would die as easily as going to sleep. That thread of pulse would quit, that was all. It might be stopping at this instant.

Why should he keep Bill Jones alive and let Bill Jones take the strike from him?

The old man jumped to his feet and threw the samples out into the arroyo. He grabbed up the rest of them from the ground and hurled them away with all his might. They rattled against the rocks and brush like so many common pebbles. He made his way back up to the mesa. He said to the burros, 'Come on, boys. Bill Jones will be wanting a drink.'

The burros moved off, and then stopped in their tracks, and the old man saw a brown-haired girl in a gingham dress coming toward him through the flowers.

She stopped and looked at him with a sweet, grave smile. She said, 'Ben, think of this grass. You're such a fool sometimes.'

The old man looked at the poppies and the grass under his feet, and a quail flew up, madly beating his way free of a snarl of grass. The poppies were a little jungle of feathery stems and the clumps of panic grass were each a tangled mat.

His eyes had been full of gold and he hadn't thought of the grass. He had dreamed that the flying quail meant there had been a camp here, because he had been thinking of nothing but the gold and some way of finding it. But it was the grass and the poppies, of course, that forced the quail to fly. They couldn't run through this thickly grown stuff. There had not been a prospector's camp on the mesa. There was no more reason, now, to think the lode was located in the arroyo. He had been wrong.

The girl was gone. A breeze swept across the mesa and the poppies bent before it, and the old man thought suddenly of the Ghost Lode. Throughout the day the Ghost Lode had been shut away from his mind as if by magic. He was stricken with a startling feeling of dread at the memory of how near he had been to murder. He moved on, hurrying the burros along.

Bill Jones was still sleeping when the old man reached the camp. He slept solidly through the night, and in the morning woke up feeling stronger and hungry, and able to talk.

His name, it happened, was not Bill Jones, which was neither here nor there to the old man; he would be Bill Jones to him for good. He was a college student. He had been spending his spring vacation on the Daly ranch the other side of the mountains, and he had taken a couple of horses and packed across the mountains to see the area.

In the mountains he had come upon a prospector who had apparently been injured in a fall. The man had broken his back and was paralysed from the waist down. He was more dead than alive. He had said nothing, except to sing endlessly the song about Old Bill Jones. He had been carrying the two bags of ore samples and the notebook.

In a fit of delirium he became suspicious, seemed to fear that he was going to be robbed, and got hold of a gun and went to blazing away with it. Bill Jones tried to take the gun from him, and the prospector died of the effort of the fight. But during the struggle he shot Bill Jones through the body. Later, the boy's animals got away from him, and after that he didn't know anything that happened until he came to in the old man's camp. He guessed he had tried to walk, and he had naturally gone the easiest way, down-hill, which had led him to the desert.

'Ghost Lode,' the old man said.

'I brought his gold with me,' Bill Jones said. 'You can have it if you want it. If you ask me, I'd say it's got a curse on it.' He grinned diffidently. 'I've been having the damn'dest dreams about it.'

'I know,' the old man said.

'It weighed me down,' Bill Jones explained, as if it was necessary to make the dream absolutely clear. 'It piled up on me, like I was dead and buried. Seemed like it was there for a week so I couldn't hardly breathe, but now it's gone.'

'I know,' the old man said.

THE TRAP

By Roe Richmond

JOE DODD wondered who was going to break first. None of them could hold out much longer with the grub gone and the water going fast. He shifted, craned his sunburnt neck and looked around at the other six men on that flat hilltop. Shaded as it was by brush and boulders the heat was terrible in the daytime. And at that altitude the nights were freezing cold. They had a fortune in gold dust, but it wouldn't buy food or water or passage off this bleak hill in the Gallatins. The end of the road for the seven survivors of the Sudbrack gang.

It was afternoon now and the sun beat upon that small pinnacle with savage searing fury, blinding their eyes and frying their brains.

The slow gurgle of Ostrander's breathing came from the deepest shade by the drying seep of water. Their suffering was as nothing to Oz's with that bullet in his chest. From time to time the lank Skinner McKeel glanced sourly in the direction of the dying man, begrudging Ostrander every drop of water, hating him for making that noise when he breathed.

Big Boguson heaved back from the rimrock on the opposite side, spitting tobacco juice and bulling toward them. 'Just a question of time. I say make our move while we got the strength.'

'That's what I say too,' Kid Cater declared, his voice cracking dryly, his boy's face inflamed under the bronze stubble.

Sudbrack stared coldly at them. 'No,' he said with quiet authority, and Dodd could see the two men shrink under his pale eyes. 'What I say is still what counts here.'

The lean Ackeret nodded in jerky agreement. 'Can't leave Oz. Or carry him out.'

'He's dead,' Skinner McKeel said, with a disgusted gesture. 'He's already—' He broke off as Sudbrack's bleached eyes flickered at him.

111

Joe Dodd said nothing, still wondering which man would be the first to break. Kid Cater maybe, for the Kid was going crazy with all that gold in his possession and no place to spend it on women and whisky. Boguson perhaps, because big Boge wanted to rear up and make a fight of it, no matter how hopeless the odds. There was McKeel too, wanting to finish Ostrander off, and Ackeret, edgy and highstrung by nature.

Nothing would crack Sudbrack, and Joe Dodd himself had to hang on to the end of this caper.

They had been plundering the gold-mining camps of the Beaverhead, Alder Gulch and Virginia City, until that last stage hold-up roused the Vigilantes into driving them out. Skinner McKeel had turned his guns loose on the driver, guard and passengers, swearing that he'd been recognized and couldn't afford to leave any survivors to identify him. Boguson and Kid Cater opened fire along with him. That cold-blooded massacre brought the whole country out after them.

Sudbrack had led them in eastward flight with an evergrowing force on their heels, hoping to reach the Big Horn Basin in Wyoming, but Joe Dodd had known they would never make it. On the run for a week, swapping or stealing horses when their mounts wore out, they had ridden the final relays to death in the Gallatin Mountains. Bogged down on foot and surrounded by posses, they had forted up on this blunt hillock three or four days ago. An upland wilderness in the Bozeman Peak area, tangled with timber and brush, slashed with crooked canyons, studded with boulders and outcrops. The Vigilantes were all around them, but hadn't struck their trail or started closing in as yet. But as Boguson said it was simply a matter of time—unless the hunters tired of the chase and went home to their diggings.

Scratching the filthy sweated stubble on his jaws, Joe Dodd contemplated rolling a smoke and decided against it. Tobacco sometimes eased hunger, but it would certainly increase thirst. He licked his lips painfully, but his tongue was too dry to ease the split chapped surfaces.

Boguson lumbered back to the opposite rim to study the landscape below, hopeful perhaps that the enemy was closing up to get it over with. Down by the spring Ostrander was moaning now, a rasp on their flayed nerves, and McKeel eyed him with naked malevolence. Sudbrack, hunched calm and impassive against a pinon, watched both Boguson and McKeel with his strange colourless eyes. Kid Cater lay on his stomach staring at the swollen moneybags that were so utterly worthless here, and Dodd wondered what sensuous visions were colouring and maddening the Kid's mind.

Ackeret rolled toward Dodd, eyes and cheeks sunken in his gaunted face. 'Can't stand much more of this, Joe.'

Dodd shrugged his rangy shoulders. 'Got any other ideas, Ack?'

Ackeret slackened back hopelessly, with a ragged-sleeved forearm across his wasted features.

When Dodd felt Sudbrack's glance touch him, he turned to the outlaw leader. 'What you think, Sud?'

'One chance. That they get sick of it and pull out.'

'About what I figure.'

You're pretty smart for a kid. Who'd you run with before, Joe?'

Dodd smiled. 'Never was out before.'

'You catch on quick,' Sudbrack said. 'And you take it calm.'

Skinner McKeel whirled on them. 'Too damn calm if you ask me!'

'Nobody asked you, Skin,' said Sudbrack mildly.

'I still got a right to talk, Sud,' said McKeel. 'I been thinkin' it ain't natural. A punk like him so cool and easy.'

Dodd grinned. 'You want me to bust out cryin', Skinner?'

McKeel's attempt to spit was a dry failure. 'You will before this is done, punk! I'm goin' to get me a drink.'

'No, Skinner,' said Sudbrack. 'You'll drink when we do.'

McKeel's voice rose: 'How much longer we goin' to waste water on that stinkin' corpse?'

White fire flared in Sudbrack's eyes as he started to get up, and McKeel was already wilting when Ostrander's faint choked voice came to them: 'He's right, Sud. Better off dead. Let Skin shoot me.... Or gimme a gun.' The effort set off a spasm of coughing that racked through them all.

Sudbrack, on his feet in one smooth motion, looked at McKeel for a long chilling moment and went on to kneel beside Ostrander. 'We aren't cashin' in yet, Oz,' he said gently. 'Always hope as long as a man's got one chip left.'

'It ain't worth it,' Ostrander panted, rolling his balding head on the blanket. 'It takes—too long.'

'Can't ever tell.' Sudbrack wet a bandanna and wiped the blood from Ostrander's fever-parched mouth. 'You might be glad some day.'

Skinner McKeel watched the scene with murder in his vulture-face, and Joe Dodd shifted over to clear the gun on his right thigh. McKeel caught the motion and wheeled with a snarl: 'Don't be gettin' ideas, sonny!'

'I won't,' Joe Dodd said. 'Just makin' sure nobody else did.'

'Come to think of it, who brung us up on top here like treed coons?'

'Why, we just kinda drifted up, the way it seemed to me.'

McKeel shook his high, small, evil head. 'To me, it seems like you was leadin' the way, boy.'

Dodd lifted his shoulders indifferently, but Ackeret sat upright in sudden tense anger. 'Could you pick a better place, Skin?'

'You two sidin' each other?' McKeel glared from one to the other. 'You joined up late, I recollect, and you always was cosy-like.'

'Recruits have to stick together,' Joe Dodd said easily, rising to his rangy height in case the wildness in McKeel boiled over, and Ackeret stood up beside him.

At that moment big Boguson returned from making a circuit of the small rock-girded summit. 'They're comin' up all around.' There was a kind of grim satisfaction in his hoarse tone. 'Ain't spotted us yet but they got a notion.'

Kid Cater jumped up, slim and lithe with his reckless grin flashing. 'It's about time. They'll get a bellyful of it before they ever take this hill!'

'Yeah, that's just dandy,' Ackeret said dryly. 'More fun than we ever had on Idaho Street, Kid.'

Joe Dodd laid a big hand on Ackeret's thin shoulder. 'Buck up, Ack.'

Ackeret shook the hand off. 'Don't worry about me. I've smelt as much powder as you have, Joe.'

Sudbrack left the wounded man's side and listened gravely to Boguson's report, as the men gathered up their carbines and extra shell belts to take the positions previously assigned. Sudbrack gave them a swallow apiece from his big canteen and said quietly:

'Don't fire until I give the word. Don't do anythin' to give our position away. They may pull out, even if they figure we're up here. They know it'll cost 'em plenty to get to us.'

'They can starve us out,' Skinner McKeel grumbled.

'Maybe. But don't forget they aren't eatin' or sleepin' too well either. And they're losin' money every day they're away from their claims, and some of them maybe are losin' their wives or women. We're used to this business where they aren't. In a lot of ways we're still better off than they are.' Sudbrack gazed into the west, where the blazing golden sun hung in the molten blue above the Tobacco Roots. 'If they don't come before sundown, I've got a hunch they won't come at all. So whatever you do, boys, don't show yourselves and don't start shootin' until I tell you to.'

With the casual precision of a small military unit in combat, the tattered, bearded, sun-blackened men moved to their respective positions and settled down to wait as comfortably and alertly as possible.

The tiny hillcrest was roughly triangular, the narrow apex pointing east, the broad base fronting on the west. The eastern approach, almost sheer in spots, was too steep for any general attack from that direction. Skinner McKeel had been posted at this peak. Once the fighting started, a sharpshooter of his quality could wreak terrible havoc along both flanks of the hillside.

Kid Cater held the north-west position, and Sudbrack himself the south-west. Any large-scale frontal assault would have to come up the long gradual slope from the west, in which case both men could cover their flanks. Joe Dodd was stationed at the centre of the western rim, with Boguson at his left and

Ackeret on his right. Joe studied these positions thoroughly, visualizing the showdown ahead. Once he had them firmly fixed, his mind went back along the flaming history of the Sudbrack band.

So cleverly had Sudbrack operated that it was a long time before the miners realized they were being victimized by one highly-organized outfit. For two years the crimes were seen as isolated and haphazard misdemeanours, committed by various prospectors or gamblers driven to desperation by the loss of their claims or pokes. The few victims who were left alive seemed totally unable to describe or identify the robbers. But gradually a pattern emerged, becoming clear when old Bill Dodrill and his partner, left for dead, lived long enough to give the first real clue to the identity of the bandits. Joe wondered how many innocent men the Vigilantes had strung up the past several years.

In their way, the Vigilantes were as ruthless as the outlaws. A suspect was named in meeting, quite possibly out of pure spite, and after an elementary investigation his cabin was posted with the dread warning: '3-7-77,' over a skull-and-bones design. The dimensions of a grave: three feet wide, seven feet long, and seventy-seven inches deep. Then, if the man didn't leave within twenty-four hours, he was taken out and hanged in public. And everyone seemed satisfied that justice had been done.

But the hold-ups and murders went on.... Until that final slaughter of all the stage coach occupants by Skinner McKeel and Boguson and Kid Cater. Recalling it still made Joe Dodd retching sick. He was thankful he had never thrown down on a helpless man, never fired a shot except in self-defence.

Far down the slope there were sounds of movement, and occasionally Joe Dodd glimpsed a blurred form. But the posse seemed to be circling instead of climbing. Time dragged and the fiery ball of the sun hung motionless above the Tobacco Mountains, and the heat was enough to scorch all sanity from a man's brain and shrivel his insides to cinder-ashes. How long would it be before Cater cut loose a shot, or Boguson bellowed out in bull-like defiance, or Ackeret cracked screaming mad under the strain?

Glancing to his left, Joe could see Boguson and Sudbrack, and turning to the right brought Ackeret and Cater into view. Only Skinner McKeel was out of sight behind him, along with the dying Ostrander, and there was no telling what McKeel might do. But Sud would keep an eye on Skinner, on all of them, in fact. Sud was quite a man. With a different quirk of nature, he might have been a great man.

Now the sun was lowering and reddening at last, dipping nearer the Tobacco Roots, and it looked as if no attack was coming before sundown. The Vigilantes could be waiting for darkness, but more likely they were falling back to make camp, or moving out altogether before the light failed. Joe Dodd had an idea Sudbrack's prediction was right, as usual: *If they didn't come up this afternoon, they'd pull out for home.*

Ackeret stirred on his right, and Joe glanced over that way. Ackeret looked at him in a queer, haunted, questioning way, and Joe Dodd nodded, as if in reassurance.

A few minutes later a low cry from Cater froze Joe Dodd, even as he turned to see Ackeret up and moving, clambering over boulders and crashing through brush toward the open slope below. Kid Cater dropped his carbine and took after Ackeret, pistol in hand and running hard.

Joe Dodd got up, leaving his rifle on the ground, and moved toward Boguson, who was cursing over his levelled carbine. 'No, Boge! Let him go, let the Kid take him. A shot'll bring 'em all up here.'

Boguson hesitated, his barrel wavering, then swore and lined it again. 'You're crazy as he is! I'll stop the son—'

Joe Dodd had drawn in stride and now he smashed the long steel barrel down on that large intently-aiming head with wicked force. Boguson's knees bent and the rifle clattered down, and still the big man wheeled and lunged ponderously at his assailant. Joe struck again, feeling the shock all the way up his arm, and this time Boge grunted, sagged and pitched forward.

Joe caught him and held that massive bulk up against himself like a shield, as he saw Sudbrack coming with his carbine ready. A gun blasted on the hillside below, and Joe wondered whether Ackeret or Cater had taken that bullet.

'Drop it, Sud!' Joe pushed his gunhand through between Boguson's left arm and body, holding it steady in spite of the vast dead weight on him. Sudbrack showed only the mildest of surprise.

Sudbrack's pale eyes flicked from Joe's muzzle to his own barrel. 'A slug from this might go through both of you—at this range.'

'You wouldn't have time to fire. Let it drop, Sud.'

Sudbrack let the rifle fall. 'I don't get this, Joe.'

'Drop your belt now. I'll tell you when I've got time.'

Sudbrack slowly shook his head. 'They'll never hang me, Joe.' His right hand streaked for the holster.

Holding low, Joe Dodd fired, the .44 slashing Sudbrack's legs from under him, tumbling him awkwardly to earth. Unable to support Boguson's weight any longer, Joe shouldered the senseless hulk off and watched it topple backward. Sudbrack was lying where he had fallen, conscious but inert from shock. . . . Joe turned his back to the sun and looked across the hilltop for McKeel.

Skinner was coming all right, lank and loose and deadly. He was already passing the little spring, and he had a bead on Joe Dodd and the Skinner never missed with a Colt. Not at this distance. . . . Joe tried to bring his barrel to bear, knowing he was a dead man, but when McKeel's gun flamed it went straight into the dirt. Joe Dodd triggered but McKeel was abruptly gone, floundering on his hands and knees as the slug screamed overhead, and only then did Joe realize that Ostrander, good old Oz, had somehow stuck out a boot and tripped McKeel as he went by.

Skinner McKeel fired once from the ground, the vicious breath of it in Joe's face as he threw down from the recoil and thumbed another shot at the kneeling man. McKeel heaved upright, teetered back a few steps, jerked forward and fell full on his face.

'Thanks, Oz,' called Joe Dodd. 'I'll remember that.'

'Pleasure—kid,' panted Ostrander, grimacing in an attempt to smile.

Joe turned to see what was going on behind him, and saw Ackeret standing over Sudbrack and Boguson, the big man still in a senseless sprawl. Joe walked to them, smiling at Ackeret. 'I was afraid the Kid had you, Ack.'

'He was so surprised when I whirled around he never got off a shot.' He grinned faintly, hefting the gun he had taken from Sudbrack.

Sudbrack looked up at them without emotion. 'Where's the posse?'

'Comin' up. Be here in a minute,' Ackeret told him.

The pale eyes swerved to Dodd. 'Maybe you've got time now, Joe?'

'It was the double-cross, Sud. But we had reasons.'

'I had it comin' anyway. I just wish you hadn't shot so low.'

'Remember Bill Dodrill? He was my dad, Sud. And his partner was Ack's father.'

Sudbrack nodded sombrely. 'You boys did a good job on us. Nobody but Skinner suspected, and he was suspicious of everybody.... I don't deserve any favours but I'm askin' one. Finish the job, Joe—or give me a gun.'

Joe Dodd thought it over, and nodded at Ackeret. 'Reckon you rate that much, Sud. Give him back his gun, Ack.'

Ackeret did so unhesitatingly, and they turned away from Sudbrack without any fear whatever of getting bullets in the back. There was a muffled explosion behind them, and Joe Dodd winced as he felt Ackeret shudder at his side.

Silently, the crimson of the low sun at their backs, they walked to the spring to get a drink and comfort old Ostrander and wait for the Vigilantes to come up and join them.

★ THE MAN AT GANTT'S PLACE ★

By Steve Frazee

WITH the time at hand for the actual break, Lew Gantt was a little nervous. He did not return to the wild-horse corral after dinner to continue replacing posts that old Stump had chalked as unsound. Work was all there ever had been around this place—fix something before it busted, get ready for winter, get ready for summer, scatter grass seed from heck to breakfast, push yourself into old age by trying to look ahead so blamed far.

Lew was seventeen and one day. He had waited the one day so Stump could not say it was because of his birthday. He went down to where Stump was watching Railroad Costigan lead a big, wall-eyed bay gelding around the breaking corral.

Stump did not ask why Lew was loafing. He did not even look at his son, and that made Lew more uneasy. Old Stump just stood there watching Railroad and the bay, and after a while he said, 'Try a blanket on him, Railroad.'

The gelding did not like the blanket, and Costigan had a devil of a time. The way to break was to top 'em off and show 'em who was boss, and get things done without a lot of fooling around. But no, Lew's father would rather get six mounts half gentled in two weeks than break a whole corralful in a week; he did everything that way.

Old Stump had just been too long up here in the hills, looking down at Revelation Valley, where they did things with a bang. He was pretty old, all right—anyway past forty, Lew figured. He studied his father from the side. Not a very big man at all, but he was pretty tightly put together. He didn't care much what he wore, even a patch on the seat of his pants. His mouth was sort of tight, and he did not use it much. He shaved every morning. He never leaned or sprawled all over things, like Lew was doing right now. He favoured a bench to sit on, or a stool.

Chairs with backs made men without backbones, Stump always said.

Lew knew plenty about his father, and none of it was very interesting. Lew put both feet on the ground.

'Work him until he'll carry the blanket,' Stump said. 'Don't rush him. There's going to be a good saddle horse.'

Don't rush nothing! Stump had been here when he could have taken up the choice part of Revelation Valley, where the Mexican Spur had its home ranch now; but no, he had to settle up here in the hills where there was water one year and not much the next year. He let the cattlemen run over him, even let them range some of their stuff up here without saying boo about it. If he saw a critter that was loaded up on larkspur, down and bloated and dying, he took his knife and tried to save it. Generally he never even bothered to tell anyone.

'What is it, Lew?'

'Uh–I–' The old man was looking at him like he knew just what Lew was thinking. Aw, it was just that slow way of his when he threw a study on anything. 'I'm leaving, Stump. I got to do something besides fix fences and make little dams and fool around with horses, and besides . . .' Lew let it drift away like smoke.

Stump never let anything drift. 'Besides what?'

You couldn't tell old Stump about things he had never felt, of the wishing rock in the pines where Lew sat sometimes at night, looking at the twinkling pinpoints in the valley, wondering what everybody was doing down there; about his clothes and the beat-up wagon when he went to Revelation for supplies, and saw the cowboys thundering down the street, yelling and shooting, plunging off their horses in front of the Valley Saloon; about the time the four fancy women from Arbor's Dance Hall passed Lew on the street, looking at him with the merest brush of interest that died before it really lived, telling him that they figured him in a class with the nesters from the range east of town. Stump wouldn't understand those things at all.

'I'm riding out,' Lew said.

Stump put out his hand. 'So long, son.' They shook hands, and Stump turned back to the corral.

Lew spun away and went to the house. Lew's mother was sitting in the big rocker with brass-capped arms, looking out the bay window at Gantt Creek and the pines with sunlight on them. She wasn't much for sitting. Nobody who stayed around old Stump did much sitting, Lew thought bitterly, except Odalie, and she was only a brat sister. He heard Marian in the kitchen.

'I'm leaving, Ma,' Lew said.

Mrs. Gantt did not seem surprised, and that nettled Lew a little. 'Where are you going?'

'Down in the valley for a spell. If I don't like it there, maybe I'll drift on west a few hundred miles.' He had not intended to add the last, because his vague plans extended no farther than the valley, but now that it was out, it sounded pretty good. Some of the riders who brought horses up to Stump had told Lew of far places that old Stump didn't even know about. Why, out there on those distant ranges, where a man wasn't known just as Stump Gantt's boy. . . .

'We packed your things, son.'

Lew blinked. Marian came on into the living-room with a sort of scared smile on her face. Anyway, there was one person around here who thought it was bad that he was going so far away. Marian was a pretty girl, with her mother's slenderness and dark good looks, but she was just another sister.

'Well, I'm going,' Lew said. He wanted to tell his mother how crazy it was for all of them to stay up here in the hills and work themselves old for Stump. But his mother did not look so old right then. In fact, she did not look a heck of a lot older than Marian. She sure was a healthy, strong woman, to look so good after putting up with old Stump all these years.

'I guess I'll get my stuff.' Lew went upstairs to his room. Odalie was there, her face buried so deeply into his pillow that only her red pigtails showed. 'What the devil are you—' She raised her head and he saw that she was crying, so instead of finishing by asking what she was doing in his room, he said—'bawling about, Odalie?'

'You're going away!' she wailed.

'Well, cut it out. I'm only going a couple thousand miles, and maybe in a few years I'll come back.'

'A few years!' Odalie began to wail louder.

'I'll bring you back something.'

Odalie rolled over and looked at him. She sniffed a little. 'What?'

'A parasol.'

'I want a saddle.'

Lew considered. He probably would be in the chips when he returned. . . .

Odalie saw his hesitation, and began to screw up her face.

'All right!' he said. 'A saddle.'

'With silver trimmings?'

'I make no promises about that.'

Odalie began to laugh. 'You look just like Pa when he says that!' She wiped at her tears with the bends of her wrists, then laughed some more.

She sure was a pug-nosed, scheming little brat. Lew scowled at her, and then he grinned. 'Where's my warbag?'

'It's in there,' Odalie pointed at a flat leather bag lying on a chair. 'So's your noisy old six-gun that Pa wouldn't let you wear.'

Lew looked disgustedly at the bag. 'That thing!'

'Ma says that folks who carry their belongings in warbags don't know where they're going. She says–'

'I know what she says. I know what everybody around here says! That's why I'm going away for keeps.'

'You said you'd be back, with my saddle–with the silver trimming.'

Lew shook his head. Sisters, parents–they gave you nothing but arguments. Odalie trailed him downstairs. Marian was standing by Mrs. Gantt, and Marian was getting ready to bawl. Lew gave them each an awkward hug. He would have hugged Odalie, but she made a face at him and ran out the back door.

Mrs. Gantt looked at Lew the way she had when he was a little boy. 'Stay decent, stay clean, Lew.' She looked at him a moment longer and then started toward the kitchen. 'Come on, Marian. Let's finish the dishes.'

Lew threw his sprung saddle on old, rough-coated slow Ranger, the only horse he had ever owned. Stump did not even look away from the breaking corral when Lew rode past, but Railroad stared at the black bag behind the saddle, and then over to the bars and asked Stump something.

'He's going out to try on a new pair of britches,' Stump said. 'Put the saddle on the gelding now, Railroad.'

'Good luck, Lew!' Railroad called.

Lew waved. Over in the pines Odalie was jumping up and down on the wishing rock, yelling his name. He waved at her, then turned toward the valley.

Mrs. Gantt and Marian cleaned up the dishes in silence, then Mrs. Gantt went to the back door and called Odalie in from the wishing rock.

'Go down the trail after Lew, Odie. When you get near the gyp rock caves, watch Ranger's tracks carefully until—'

'I know, Ma! He'll stop and switch his plunder from that suitcase into his dirty old warbag, and hide the suitcase in one of the caves.'

Mrs. Gantt smiled on the thin line between laughter and tears. 'Bring the suitcase back, Odie.'

Marian said. 'At least, he didn't ride away looking like a saddle bum, even if nobody but us saw him.'

Down at the corral, Stump's brown, clean-shaved face showed no change, except that his mouth was a little tighter. From the corner of his eye he saw Odalie running down the trail, but mainly he watched the baby gelding circling nervously with the saddle on its back.

'Ride him, Railroad.'

Slim and wiry, Costigan stopped in mid-stride. 'What?'

'I said ride him!'

Railroad's eyes went sidewise, toward the valley.

'You don't mean that, Stump.'

'No, I guess I don't.' Stump Gantt walked away toward the upper meadow.

Railroad called after him. 'Never was a kid that was any good didn't pull his picket pin a few times!'

Gantt went on walking. Railroad resumed his patient circling of the corral, now and then speaking to the bay in a soothing voice, and all the time thinking of the days when he was seventeen down in Arizona Territory, many years before. He made a dozen trips around the big corral before he noticed the gelding was no longer humping or pulling sidewise in an effort to get from under leather.

Railroad stopped then, facing the emerald flatness of the distant valley, looking far beyond the purple ranges. He was glad that his guns had long ago been laid aside. Here was the only place he had ever been at home, at peace. If he were seventeen again . . . if he were seventeen and knew what he knew now . . . life would be awful dull.

Free with fifty dollars in his pocket, Lew strolled the main street of Revelation. Now that he was here, all the things he had longed to do when he was not free to do them did not have the same appeal. He would be a little cautious about what he did first, sort of get the feel of things. There was no rush.

He saw Mexican Spur horses in front of the Valley Saloon, and four of five Short Fork horses before the Green Grass Saloon. There was not a single nester wagon in town. It was time the danged nesters learned they couldn't move right in on cattle range. They claimed to have legal right, but Lew did not take much stock in that; in fact, he knew only the superficial facts about the trouble that was shaping up, but his sympathy was with the cowmen, so he did not need to have many facts.

Gaunt, blistered Custer Wigram, owner of the Spur, came from the Valley as Lew was passing for the third time. He bunched pale brows at Lew and said, 'Howdy, kid. What's Stump doing in town in the middle of the week?'

'He ain't here, Mr. Wigram.'

Wigram sized the youth up once more. Lew's levi's were new, but he had soaked them for a week in mild lye water to take away their give-away blueness. He was wearing the long barrelled .44, for which he had traded a month's work at Wigram's hay ranch the year before.

'Oh,' Wigram said in a long breath. 'You're out on your own now, huh?'

'Yeah.'

Townspeople passed. Four cowboys drifted from the Green Grass to the Valley. They all spoke with deference to Wigram. Lew did not mind at all being seen talking on equal terms to the biggest rancher in the country.

'How does it look out there?' Lew nodded east.

Wigram shook his head. 'We overlooked a thing or two when we settled here. Then we didn't work together.' His eyes strayed toward the west hills. 'A few days ago four farmers filed on the very ground Joe Hemphill's home ranch stands on.'

Hemphill owned the Short Fork. Lew cursed to show concern. Not used to profanity, he overdid it. 'That won't stand, will it?'

'I don't know.' Wigram shook his head dubiously.

'You ought to run every nester out of the country right damn now!'

The Spur owner smiled vaguely. 'That would be quite a drive— now. You want a job, Lew?'

Lew's heart leaped. Never be over-anxious, Stump always said. 'Well . . . my horse ain't too good with cows.'

'All you'll need him for is to ride to Spur. I want some range stuff broke.'

That was a wet slap. Break horses! There was no fun in that, not doing it Stump's slow way, the only method Lew understood.

'Your old man says you're about as good as Costigan.'

'Huh.' Stump had never mentioned that to Lew.

'No, thanks, Mr. Wigram. I don't much care for that kind of work.'

The corners of Wigram's eyes crinkled. 'Too much like home, huh?' Then he started up the walk. 'Ride over if you change your mind.'

The youth swung his gun belt around and went into the Valley. Spur and Short Fork riders at the bar were talking about the nesters. There was a pause until Shindy Lemons said, 'Aw, that's only Stump Gantt's boy from the west hills. C'mon over, Lew, and have a drink.'

Lew was awkward at the bar, not sure just what to do with his hands. He saw the others watching him closely, and knew they were guessing it was his first drink of whisky. It was. No rush about it. He took his time.

'Hmm!' a cowboy said. 'Old Stump sure must run a still up there.'

They all laughed. Lew tossed a coin on the bar. 'Have one around on me.' It was the thing to do, but he sure didn't like to see the money go into the till. There were better ways to spend money, and while the whisky was loosening social tightness inside him, he still didn't think it was worth good gold that he had been a long time saving. He had a drink on four others, and he could honestly say that, other than a sort of warm pushing behind his eyes, the whisky did not seem to affect him.

Before it was his turn to buy again, he thanked the cowboys and strolled over to a poker game in the corner. Confidential Pete, the houseman, was having a bad time with Buck Hodel, the Spur foreman, and a slim stranger dressed in grey. Ivers, the liveryman, and two cowboys were in the game, too.

'Jump in, kid, and get your feet wet,' Hodel said. He was a broad, black-browed man, about half drunk at the moment. He had a pretty bad temper, they said.

'No rush,' Lew said. 'I like to see where the power is before I jump.'

'You sound just like your old man,' Hodel said.

The stranger in grey smiled at Lew. It was hard to figure that one out. He was a handsome devil, grey eyes, curly brown hair and a clean grin. His face was brown and so were his hands, and he wasn't dressed quite like a gambler, not the kind old Railroad talked about, leastwise. But he was dressed just a little better than a range hand, too.

Lew watched the game. One of the cowboys won a small pot. The stranger won a big one when the houseman bucked into a full house with two pair. After a while Lew got things figured out. The man in grey was merely having a big lucky streak, and the others were letting him draw too cheap when they should have been raising the devil.

At least that was the way Railroad Costigan would have figured it, and Lew had spent many an evening playing poker for fun with Railroad.

This beat drinking whisky. Lew itched to get into the game,

but he waited a while, watching how they played, before he bought forty dollars' worth of chips.

Confidential Pete hesitated before he shoved the stack across. 'You sure you know how to play this, Gantt?'

'I learn fast.'

Pete grunted, 'I don't want your old man on my neck after you lose your money.' He was half afraid it was Stump's money.

Lew grinned. 'Worry about the man who owns this dump getting on *your* neck after I take *his* money.'

The stranger laughed. 'You'll do, Gantt. Smoky Cameron.' He put out his hand as Lew settled into a chair beside him.

'Lew Gantt.' The name had a fair sound, at that Cameron's hand was hard, with work bumps there, all right, but not the dry-raspy kind. He had not worked recently, Lew figured.

Lew drifted along for about a half-hour, like someone who wanted to make his forty bucks last a long time. And then on a pot that Hodel opened for five dollars, five men stayed. Lew was the last one. He raised five. One of the cowboys dropped out. Everybody else stayed. They drew cards. Ivers took one. He cursed. Before he tossed in his hand he spread it to show how he had missed a flush. Nobody paid any attention. They were all watching Lew, who had not drawn any cards.

'Beginner's luck!' one of the cowboys muttered, and threw away his hand.

Hodel bet five dollars, scowling at Lew. The houseman stayed, and raised five more. When it came to Lew he met the raise and pushed in all the chips he had.

'Never try to bluff a dumb kid,' Pete said. He tossed his hand away.

Cameron got out with a laugh, and that left it up to Hodel. He scowled and grunted and tried to read Lew's face, and at last threw his hand away with a curse. 'What have you got you're so proud of?'

Lew pushed his hand into the discards. 'You didn't pay to see, Hodel.' Lew had been bluffing.

'I think he was pulling a whizzer,' Cameron said good-humouredly.

'He's too dumb for that!' Hodel growled. But still he was not sure. It showed in his eyes, and it would keep eating at him. The next time he would call anything, Lew figured. And that was just what happened an hour later. Hodel was still far ahead of the game, and Lew had made steady little winnings, so he now had about two hundred dollars.

He got a full house, queens over sixes, on the deal. When the smoke cleared there was about two hundred dollars in the pot, with only Lew and Hodel left. The Spur foreman had drawn one card, and Lew was sure he had filled something. Hodel pushed out chips to match everything Lew had. His face went splotchy red when he saw the full house. He slapped a Jack-high straight on the cloth and pushed his chair back savagely.

'You're just too damned lucky, Gantt, or else–'

'Else what?'

'–or you're too slick for this game. You'd better get out now.'

Cameron said, 'Don't push on the lines, Hodel. The kid's been lucky, and played good poker.'

Hodel's face swung like a club at Cameron. 'You keep that little thing under your nose quiet, tinhorn. I ain't just sure about you anyway.'

'Is that a fact?' Cameron rose. 'Just what is it you aren't sure about?'

Lew had his chance to get from under, but he wasn't letting anyone carry the load for him. 'It's a free country, Hodel. Get out yourself if you don't like the way I play'. An instant later he thought that maybe the whisky had not been quite as harmless as it seemed.

'Why, you little west-hills pup!' Hodel kicked his chair away. He was a blocky, solid man, and it was his boast that he could lick any man in the valley.

Confidential Pete's voice was a lost squeal. 'No trouble in here, boys. No trouble in here!'

Across the room a Spur rider said to the bartender, 'No Sammy. Just lay your little white mitts on the cherrywood and watch the fun.'

'I guess,' Hodel said, 'I'd better slap some manners into you, Gantt.' He flung aside a cowboy who was struggling to rise with his feet entangled in the balingwire braces of his chair. Hodel walked through the space toward Lew.

Lew went around the table. He was hot-scared, but he was not going to run.

'Stay back, Hodel,' he said.

The Spur foreman made a lunge. Lew kicked a chair in front of him and went farther around the table. Hodel crashed over the chair and fell. He came up insane with anger.

'Stay back, Hodel.' Lew kept the table between them. He saw it coming then. He could almost smell the brimstone scent of it.

Hodel went for his pistol.

He was not fast. No one in the Revelation country was fast with a gun. Lightning draws were merely something men like Railroad talked about. But Buck Hodel was faster than Lew Gantt, who had never drawn his .44 quickly, except in secret practice against old Railroad.

The explosion almost deafened Lew. He did not hear or feel the bullet, and he did not know where it went until someone told him afterward. He smelled the great bloom of dirty-grey powder smoke that obscured the middle of Hodel's body. Lew had drawn by then, and now he shot, trying to aim through the rising murk and hit Hodel in the right leg to knock him flat. Instead, he shot Hodel through the side. The man twisted back and fell into the check rack.

Lew had to step to one side to see through the acrid fumes. Hodel was lying there, his mouth open with shock. Lew Gantt stared. He was scared to death, and sick.

Smoky Cameron was against the wall, off to one side. His gun was in his hand and his eyes were on the Spur and Short Fork men.

'Was it fair?' he asked.

After a moment grizzled Rip Goodwin said, 'Yeah, it was fair.' He sent a sullen, wicked look at Lew. The cowboys went over to Hodel.

With his gun still in his hand, Lew started to run. He would get Ranger. He would ride as fast as he could, clear out of the country. He had killed a man, and a deadly fear was riding him and urging him to get away quickly.

Cameron caught him at the door. Lew clubbed his gun and tried wildly to beat the man away, but Cameron caught his wrist and hurled him against the wall.

'Where you going, Gantt?'

After a while Lew stopped struggling. He stared at Cameron. The man was calm and friendly. 'I know,' Cameron said. 'You want to run from here to the Pacific. I know how you feel. Put that gun away and sit down there in a chair.'

Lew obeyed, gaining control from Cameron's quiet voice. The man in grey went back to the poker table. He scooped Lew's chips into his hat. He stood there a while looking steadily at Confidential Pete, and after a few moments Pete took his hand from his coat pocket and added a fistful of yellow chips to the hat. Cameron found two more in the pocket.

'Them are mine!' Pete protested. Cameron dropped the chips in the hat.

'Interest on a filthy trick,' he said. Pete slunk away.

About then Lew heard Hodel curse weakly and say something to Goodwin. A breath of terror went out of Lew.

The sheriff came in with Plug Riddle, the druggist, who was also the doctor for men and horses. A lot of people streamed in, crowding close to Hodel, then turning to stare in surprise at the boy in the chair by the door.

Riddle said loudly. 'If he don't get complications or something, he may be all right in a month or so.'

Lew stood up, and his legs held him without shaking. He wanted to tell Hodel he was sorry, but just then Wigram came over, a savage, calculating look on his face. 'For a punk button, you sure messed things up, didn't you?'

'He started it.'

Wigram turned away and went to the bar. Cameron came up and handed Lew a canvas sack. 'Five hundred and twenty-five.'

Lew wanted to throw the gold through the window. He wished he had never left home. No matter whose fault this was, it made him sick again to see blood dripping as they carried Hodel out.

Sheriff Nate Springer was a big, slow-moving, chunky man who surveyed everything thoughtfully from green eyes almost buried under his brows. Stump said he got that way from figuring how to stay in office the rest of his life.

'I don't figure to make a fuss,' the sheriff told Lew, 'but you better come down to the office with me.'

Wigram turned around at the bar. 'Let's hear what you got to say right here, Springer.'

'He said his office.' Cameron took Lew's arm and hustled him outside, and a moment later Springer followed, relieved because he had not been forced to argue the matter.

They did not go inside. Springer kept his office neat, and he did not like dirt on the oiled floor or things moved out of place on his desk.

Springer said. 'You'd best get on back home right away, Gantt—and stay clear of town for quite a spell.'

'What for? I didn't start anything.'

'I don't like trouble here.'

'It wasn't my fault!' Lew said.

'Nobody said it was. Go on home.'

'You want to run me out of town just because I'm only a kid, but you don't say nothing about running the others out because Spur and Fork elect you.'

Springer nodded slowly. 'That's right as far as it goes. Also, I don't want to have more grief when some drunk cowboy sees you around and jumps you.'

'I'll take care of myself.'

'That's what I'm afraid of,' Springer said quietly. 'Stump Gantt's likely to have enough trouble on his hands, without his son trying to be a gun fighter.'

'I don't want to be a gun fighter, and I didn't start anything, so I don't see what right you got to tell me to beat it.'

The sheriff looked at Cameron. 'It's still the best thing for you, kid.'

That was what Lew was mainly tired of, someone telling him what he ought to do.

'You ordering me to go?' he asked.

'No, but I sure suggest it strong.' Springer sighed. He turned away and went into his office.

'I wasn't figuring to stay anyway,' Lew said to Cameron. 'Now I might.'

Cameron asked casually, 'What are you planning to do with the money?' Lew was still holding the sack.

'Half of it is yours. If you hadn't picked the chips up, I wouldn't have any money at all. And I think you had me beat that first hand I won, when I shoved in everything I had.'

'Yes,' Cameron said, 'I knew you were bluffing.' He smiled briefly. 'It would have saved a lot of trouble if I'd busted you right there.'

'Yeah,' Lew said, thinking of the way Hodel had looked on the dirty floor. 'I don't much care about this money now.'

'I'll be glad to ease half of your conscience.'

They went behind the livery stable to divide the gold.

'You drifting out?' Lew asked. He'd go along with Cameron if Cameron asked him. 'You won't stand much chance to get a job here now—after siding in with me to-day.'

'You may be right,' Cameron said vaguely. 'But I thought I'd look the ranches over and see what I could stir up. I sort of like this country.'

'Huh! It ain't much.'

Cameron gave him a grave look. 'Maybe you've lived too close to it to see its good points, Lew.'

A short time later Lew watched Cameron ride away on a leggy claybank that was a jim-dandy. Lew thought of old Ranger there in the stable. He had enough money now to make a trade for a good horse, but he hated to part with Ranger. No need to rush things. Maybe later, when Cameron returned from looking for a job nobody would give him, the two of them could ride away together.

Lew put a hundred dollars in the bank. He did not know just why he did, unless it was because Stump was always saying a man ought to save something out of every chunk he made. The banker was glad to take the money. He asked a lot of questions about how Stump was, and you'd have thought old Stump was a big wheel around the valley.

In two days the draw game in the Green Grass took everything Lew had in his pockets. He walked past the bank several times before he went in to get his hundred dollars. The banker was just as polite as before.

When Lew went out the nesters were coming into town. There was quite a bunch of them. Judging from the rifles and shotguns on their wagon seats, a man could say they were ready for trouble if it came.

Lew studied the farmers pretty closely. They were clean, quiet, going about their business as if they figured to be in the country a long time. A few days in Revelation taught Lew that the town was not against the nesters. Maybe the farmers did have some right on their side.

A nester named Cranklow, a raw-boned, sun-blistered man with a square jaw, said hello to Lew, and the youth remembered him from the times Cranklow had been to the ranch to talk to Stump about grass seed and dams. Cranklow stopped to talk, but Lew just said hello curtly and went on toward the Green Grass.

Lew was pretty lonely right then, and it occurred to him how he would have felt if someone had been short with him for no reason. A lot of people had talked to Lew, but generally only to ask how he had become so fast with a pistol.

He was cleaned out in three hours, losing his last twenty dollars when he tried to run a busted flush past the houseman's two pairs. He was hungry when he reached the street. At noon he had eaten well, but now, knowing he was broke, he was hungry ahead of time. He stood there wondering what his mother would have for supper that night.

Three cowboys from two-bit outfits were lounging at the hitch rail, watching the farmers leaving town in a body.

The devil could take the whole works, he thought angrily. He did not want anything to do with nesters, and cattlemen wanted nothing to do with him since he shot Buck Hodel. The thing to do was get as far away as possible from this two-bit valley and find a good riding job where nobody knew he was Stump Gantt's kid from the west hills, or that he had shot a man. Something deep inside him warned him that he was not thinking straight, but he was too flushed with resentment to pay any attention.

To heck with Smoky Cameron, too. Cameron had taken half of the five hundred and not even asked Lew to ride out with him. Lew Gantt was on his own. He did not owe anyone anything. He could do as he pleased. He was . . .

Pitching hay at a nester place two days later for a dollar a day and all he could eat. The whole deal had been Cameron's idea, after he returned from riding the ranches and reported no jobs available. Cameron was pitching hay right alongside Lew. The weather held good. For a month they moved from place to place. Lew kept his eyes open and learned a lot.

The last place was Jemmie Cranklow's, on Little Elk, smack in the middle of what had been Spur range. Cranklow had put in a pile of work. He was figuring on planting winter wheat, and building a canal to water his upper eighty.

'This is as good farmland as any in the valley,' Cameron explained. 'It's even more sheltered.' He put up a shock of hay to Cranklow's youngest boy on the rack. 'The thing is these people have made legal filings. Some of the ranchers don't even own the land where their buildings are. Wigram got wise two years ago and protected himself, but Hemphill waited too long. Now he'll have to compromise or lose the very land he lives on.'

Lew looked sidewise at Cameron's grey clothes. 'You know quite a bit about this valley, don't you?'

'I do.' Cameron hoisted a shock that made the fork handle creak. 'You favour law, don't you?'

'I guess I do. What happens, though, if there's a big fight?'

'There won't be,' Cameron said. 'Not on this side of the valley. The farmers are too strong here now.'

Lew couldn't seem to get his fork into shocks just right for a long time. Stump had been throwing grass seed around in the west hills since before Lew—or even Marian—was born. He owned rock claims, timber claims, placers, five homesteads that had fizzled—just about everything that was worth a dime over there. Come to think of it, Stump had been building something slowly in the west hills. A man could run cattle there now, not like it used to be on this side, of course, but still the west hills would stand grazing. Spur and Short Fork were already running stuff over there.

The cowmen were beat on this side, but over there—just one man standing between them and all the range.

'My father has got legal claim to everything he holds!' Lew said.

'I know. So have the farmers over this way.'

Sheriff Springer had it figured out. That's what he had meant when he said Stump was going to have trouble. Wigram said he had overlooked something, and then he had glanced toward the west hills.

'I was at your father's place after I left Revelation,' Cameron said casually. 'I never saw so much good solid craftsmanship in everything around there.'

'My father does things right!' Lew was darned sure of that now, having seen plenty of work that wasn't done well.

In the shadowy bunkhouse at Stump Gantt's horse ranch the owner and Railroad Costigan looked at each other past a dim lamp on the table between two Walker Colts that were shiny-worn.

Costigan's face was as brown and wrinkled as a frost-rotted apple. 'They might be a little afraid of him, Stump. It wasn't luck when he shot Hodel. They might want him out of the way.'

'Cameron's with him.'

'Cameron has to go prowling at times.'

Gantt shook his head. 'He's on his own. It's got to be that way. We've got to let him make his own decisions, Railroad.'

He shook his head sadly. 'I never thought it would come down to this again. I guess I've just been blind to everything you've been doing here, Stump, scattering seed, making those little rock dams.... Of course, it's been only the last year or two that the results began to show up.'

Stump nodded sombrely. 'They still call 'em the "dry hills," but Wigram and Hemphill have seen, and Springer saw it long ago.'

'Springer won't be no help.'

Stump smiled. 'When did we ever ask the law for help?'

'Maybe I'm getting old,' Railroad said. 'Maybe I've slipped since I been here, but it seems to me this is one time when the law ought to work. You've spent the best part of your life here,

Stump, raising a family, building up a range that no one wanted, putting every dime into developing something. Now–'

'That makes it all the more worth fighting for. I didn't want the fight. I hoped they'd learn from what was happening over east, but now a fight is all that's left.'

'Wigram is ordinarily a reasonable man.' Railroad picked up . the other gun. 'Joe Hemphill isn't much on fighting.'

'Wigram is desperate now. I offered to lease the west hills. I made him a good offer. Hodel was the one who made him stiffen when he was about to come around. Wigram knows he's been beat over east. He knows it too late, and it rankles all the more to think he let the west hills get away from him. He's carrying Hemphill, too. Joe don't want the fight. Joe was the one who stopped Wigram from burning out nesters years ago, when the cowmen might have made it stick.

'Now Wigram is working on Hemphill by telling him what a terrible mistake that was. They're both ruined unless they get the west hills, and Hemphill's ruined any way you figure it, because Wigram will ease him out later if they win. I've let them run a few cattle over here, Railroad. They let me take a beef whenever we needed meat. The hides have always been right there on the fence for anyone to see. I got the worst of it, of course, but I wanted to see just how well the west hills would stand up under grazing. They'll stand it, but we'll have to watch the dry years and cut herds–and there will never be a time when my range will stand one-third of the cows Spur and Short Fork have.'

Costigan picked up both guns. His eyes had a young look in his old brown face. 'A man never changes, Stump. I thought maybe you had, since the old days in Arizona, but you're just the same inside.' He scowled. 'How about Emily and the kids?'

'Emily got sore when I tried to edge around to sending her away. She knows what we both know, Railroad–nothing is any good to you unless you get it the hard way and hold it the same way against all comers.'

Stump hesitated at the door, looking at the warm lights of the house. When Cameron, that young United States Marshal, had been here, he and Marian had looked at each other with the same expression springing in their eyes that Stump remembered from long ago, when he first saw Emily.

Stump looked toward the valley. It was overcast to-night, with a threat of rain, and the lights down there were not visible. Why didn't Lew come back? He must know by now how things were shaping up. But if he did not come back, he was still a boy that Stump Gantt was mighty proud of. Stump's mouth was sort of loose when he thought that perhaps he should have hinted that to Lew now and then, but such things came hard to Stump.

Stump's mouth was tight when he turned again toward the room. 'You and me both know how easy it is to stop a fight before it gets started.'

Railroad's eyes were wicked and narrow. Both Walkers were in holsters on his hips, and he was standing there with something on his mind that made him look as wound-up and dangerous as he had been in the old days. Stump and Railroad had ridden much of the West together as young men, and Railroad was the only man Stump had ever known who could actually use two guns with quick accuracy. There was a cold spot on Costigan's conscience; he had never worried about killing men who asked for it.

'Yeah,' Railroad said. 'Blast a rattler's head and all you got left is a lot of sickening twisting and humping. The trouble is all gone.'

'Hodel is up and around,' Stump said slowly. 'He's been making talk about Lew, and about the west hills, too. It struck me that you might figure to go down and take Hodel and Wigram.'

'Did it?' Railroad stood there, thin and wrinkled, wearing the tough, blank look Stump had almost forgotten.

'You wouldn't figure to come clear,' Stump said. 'You think you've lived a long time, but the older we get the better we like the thought of getting still older. We both want to live to see Lew running this place, see the girls married off to decent youngsters, with you and me having time to fool around with blooded horses, like we've always wanted.'

'Sure,' Railroad said. 'I've thought of all that. I've also thought that we ain't got much chance, waiting for them to come after us.'

Stump had never been one to try to make words change facts. He said, 'That's right. But we've got to stay with the law all the way. That's the way this place was built, and that's the way I want to leave it. We've got the right to defend ourselves, but we can't go out and start killing before we're attacked.'

After a while the tenseness went out of Railroad. He sat down on a bench and he was just an old man wearing two pistols that were out of date. 'I wish Lew would come back,' he muttered.

'Maybe he will.' Stump peered again at dark mist over the valley. He shut the door quietly and went toward the house. Before he crossed the flagstone porch he straightened his shoulders and composed his face, so Odalie, at least, would not know what he was thinking. With him and Railroad gone, Emily would still be in legal possession of most of the west hills, Wigram knew that, and he also knew that women could not run a horse ranch. After doing half his work by violence, Wigram would do the other half legally, letting shock and necessity wear Emily to the point of selling everything at his price.

It was worry about Lew that made Stump feel scared and helpless. They would figure to take Lew first. He went inside. Emily read his face, and then glanced toward the bedroom where Marian was waging a battle to get Odalie down for the night.

'Has the rain start–' Emily asked.

'Pa! Lew's going to bring me a silver-mounted saddle, just my size, and a real Navajo bridle!' Odalie popped out of the bedroom.

'Is that a fact?'

'It ought to be. I've told you about ten times,' Odalie said. 'When's Lew coming back?'

'When he gets ready. Get to bed, Odie.' Stump looked at his wife. 'It's fixing to rain, all right.'

Blocking the bedroom door, Marian turned her head to look at her parents. There was a starkness in the room as the first drops began to fall.

In the mow of Cranklow's barn Lew shook hay from his blankets and prepared to go to bed. 'I'm going home tomorrow,' he told Cameron.

Standing by the ladder, fully dressed, Cameron was silent as the rain hit the roof in a steady whisper. Then he said. 'It's too far now, Lew, too far across the valley and up through the rocks to the west hills.'

'I don't think I get you, Cameron.'

'You wouldn't get there, Lew.'

After a while Lew asked, 'Wigram?'

'In a day or two I'll need your help. We can keep this thing from ever starting, maybe. Will you stay with me, Lew?'

'I don't know what you're going to do.' Lew decided he did not know much about Cameron at all. The man had a habit of riding out almost every night, and never saying where he went.

'Believe me, you can help your father more by staying with me and helping me than by getting waylaid on your way home.'

'I'll stay two days.'

'Wear your gun,' Cameron said. He went down the ladder. Ten minutes later Lew heard him head the claybank toward Revelation.

The slender little man rode into the yard while Lew was still eating breakfast. The others had finished, but Lew was having one last stack of pancakes when he heard the man ask, 'How do you get to Stump Gantt's place?'

Cameron's voice was casual. 'How'd you happen to get so far north of the road, stranger?'

Lew took his gun belt off the peg by the wash bench and strapped it on before he went out. If the man looked at him at all it was merely a side flick of eyes like black chips. 'I got off the track last night,' the fellow said. 'Where at is this Gantt place?'

'What do you want with Stump Gantt?' Cameron asked.

Whew! Cameron sure didn't mind asking personal questions.

The man didn't mind answering either. 'That old cutthroat gave me a rasping on a horse I bought from him a few months back. I aim to get some satisfaction.'

'You waited quite a while to squawk, didn't you?' Cameron glanced at the man's mount, a deep-barrelled bay with a beautiful saddle. 'That the horse?'

'Yeah.'

Lew was walking forward stiffly, so mad he could hardly see. 'You're a dirty liar, mister,' he said. 'My father never cheated nobody in his life, and you're another dirty liar when you say that horse ever came from his place.'

'Easy, Lew!' Cameron said.

It was too late. The man swung his face toward Lew, and the boy got his first full glimpse of the stranger. There was a deadly sort of blankness in the face, a frozen look of concentration in the black eyes. Lew realized he had stepped full-on into something pretty stout. It did not make any difference. Nobody was lying about old Stump while he was around.

'You call me a liar?' the man asked.

'Twice,' Lew said. 'What do you want to do about it?'

The man stretched thin lips across rows of teeth that were small and brown and strong. 'You know I can't take that kind of talk, sonny.'

Lew was not angry now. The thing fell into place in his mind. If he had used his head at all a minute before, he would have seen how raw and direct the whole plant was. He ought to back out right now. Native pride would not let him. He sensed that this little man would not make any of Buck Hodel's mistakes.

'Kid ...' the man said casually, and went for his pistol. It was all too fast for Lew. He saw the fellow's gun come clear. He heard the ear-stunning roar, and saw the man spin clear around and almost fall. And then the stranger was standing there, grey-faced, his gun on the ground, his right arm hanging heavily, with blood sopping all around the elbow.

Cameron's pistol was in his hand, and a cloud of stinking, acrid smoke was drifting away from it. Lew Gantt had not even got his pistol out of the holster.

'It had moss all over it, Martin,' Cameron said.

The black eyes glittered in the cold-grey face. 'Who are you?' Martin asked. 'How do you know me?'

'I'm Smoky Cameron.'

'Ah ...' the fellow said in a long breath. 'I can feel a little better about this now.' His eyes grew blank. Pain and shock dropped him. His cheek slashed along the hard earth. His hat came off and showed a bald spot at the back of his head. At the

141

wrinkled crook of his right coat sleeve bits of bone from his shattered elbow showed in the bloody fabric.

Lew sensed some of it, just enough to know that he was far out of his class, that years of experience separated him from complete understanding. He knew that he was just a greenhorn who had tried to sit in a high-rolling game. The feeling was heightened when, after Cameron dressed Martin's wound and put him on his horse, Martin went without another glance at Lew.

Lew heard him tell Cameron, 'I sort of got sucked into something, didn't I?'

'You hired out once too often.'

It took a good deal of self from Lew's thinking. Sure, they were afraid enough of him to send a killer to drop him and help clear the way to the west hills, but that did not make him feel important. It did not scare him, either. It made him more anxious to go home and ask Stump what he could do to help. To-morrow his promise to Cameron would be up.

Worry ran the sharp points of restlessness through Lew as he waited for Cameron to return. He offered to start digging the canal for Cranklow.

'Too rainy, Lew,' the farmer said. 'You just lay low to-day, and trust your friend.'

Cameron came back through the rain that night. He took care of the claybank and ate his supper. He did not have much to say, other than that he had taken Martin to Revelation and turned him over to Sheriff Springer.

'What's the charge?' Cranklow asked.

'No charge. Just holding him. He couldn't go anywhere with that arm, anyway.'

Lew felt that a mighty wall of violence was building in the valley, with him not able to understand all the details. When he and Cameron were crossing the rain-greased yard on their way to the haymow, Lew said, 'I've decided not to wait the other day. I'm going to start for home to-night.'

Cameron did not answer until he was in the mow, struggling out of wet boots. 'To-morrow. We'll win or lose the whole deal to-morrow.'

'Is that all you want to say?'

'Yeah.'

Lew sat down on his blankets. 'Who hired that Martin?'

'I don't know,' Cameron said.

It was still raining when they rode out before daylight. Lew figured they would go toward Spur, but they went down-valley instead. Where the roads forked a mile from town, Sheriff Springer was waiting under the cottonwoods. He looked gloomily at water darkening the skirts of his rig, and he showed no enthusiasm for what lay ahead. His slicker rattled as he turned his horse toward Short Fork. There were tracks of five or six horses already in the muddy ruts.

'You were right, Cameron,' Springer said. 'I got the word that it starts from Short Fork.'

'Wigram has got to push Hemphill all the way, but he's pushing a dead horse now. How's Martin?'

'Plug Riddle was taking his arm off when I left. You'd a done him a favour to kill him instead of that.'

The Short Fork yard was full of horses. A poker game was going on in the bunkhouse. The four men lounging out of the rain on the wide front porch of the main building paid little attention to the riders drifting in through the misty drizzle until Lew and his companions were right at the gate. Then someone said, 'Oh, oh!' and went quickly into the house.

Custer Wigram was on the porch by the time the three dismounted. The bleak planes of his face were white with anger. Hemphill came out and stood beside him. He was a stocky man with a big shoulder reach and a pugnacious face that said he was willing to tackle the devil and give him odds; but that only went as deep as his face, which right now was flushed, and more stubborn than determined.

Buck Hodel and Rip Goodwin, followed by nine or ten others, came from the bunkhouse. Hodel was a little pale, Lew observed, but otherwise he seemed all right.

There ought to have been some better way to get things stopped than this, Lew thought. His stomach felt like it was flat against his backbone.

Cameron went out in front of his horse. 'You're not taking a gang to Stump Gantt's to-day, Wigram—or any other day.'

Wigram looked at Springer. 'How'd *you* get into this?'

'First, because the U.S. marshal here asked me; second, because he's right.' Springer unbuttoned his slicker. He removed it and let it drop in a stiff heap over a puddle of water. Under his corduroy coat he was wearing an old black sweater, with his gun belt buckled over it, and the trim, curving handle of his .45 right in handy reach.

He looked pretty solid and dangerous, Lew thought, and wished he could make some kind of gesture, too; but all Lew could do was gulp at dry cotton in his mouth and try to hold a poker face.

'You're licked, Wigram,' Cameron said. 'You know it. To start what you want to start you're going to have to kill us three, and you'll have to do it before Hemphill, a man who no longer owns a cow or piece of land in the valley.'

Wigram swung his gaunt head toward Hemphill, who stared at the floor of the porch.

'So that's why you backed out!' Wigram said.

Hemphill raised his head. 'By God, I've had about enough of your abuse, Wigram! Sure, I sold out! What right I had from use of the land here I relinquished to four farmers. I told you two years ago we couldn't beat this thing.'

'You chicken-livered, gutless—'

'Shut up, Wigram, or I'll knock the blisters off that skinny face of yours!' This was a personal affair now.

Even in his rage Wigram realized that. 'What'd you do with your cattle?'

'That's none of your business,' Hemphill said.

'Buck Hodel, your own foreman, took an option on them, Wigram,' Cameron said. 'Does that give you an idea of what might have happened to you, if you'd been lucky enough to grab the west hills?'

All Wigram's rage seemed to evaporate, but it was worse than ever inside him, Lew figured, as he watched the Spur owner pace deliberately from the porch and start toward Hodel.

'Is that the truth, Buck?' Wigram asked.

'Just a minute!' Cameron's voice was a hard crack in the tension as men moved away from Hodel, as Spur and Short Fork began to separate. 'Lew here has a little business with Hodel first. Hodel is the one who sent for Trey Martin to come in here and kill Gantt.'

Hodel was set like a spring. 'That's a dirty lie.'

'It all came out of Martin—this morning while Plug Riddle was taking his arm off without chloroform.'

Lew saw on Hodel's face that Cameron had bluffed through to the truth. The Spur foreman's mouth loosened. His eyes flicked from side to side. He was alone with hostile men.

'What do you want to do with him, Lew?' Cameron asked in a flat tone.

For a moment Lew did not want to do anything, and then he gathered thoughts about Hodel from here and there, and the feel of watching men helped, and he brought everything into a great cold lump that resembled reason, which said that he must kill Buck Hodel in the name of justice.

He started slowly toward Hodel. The second time would be easy. Hodel was scared tight, so desperate that he would try to do everything at one time—and be wild and helpless. Lew Gantt was cold and sure. For the first time he understood the intangible factors that old Railroad Costigan always claimed were the real weights in a pistol scrap—complete disregard for life; don't think, just shoot.

For three slow steps Lew Gantt was as impersonal as death, a stocky youth with a tight mouth and blue eyes knife-cold with blankness. He was geared to kill, and the rest was nothing but obedience. Then he stopped. The reasons he had summoned fell apart before the trapped look in Hodel's eyes. Habit and training made Lew weigh the forces that pushed him. He remembered the fine green lines of evil in Trey Martin's face. A man could become another Martin too easily.

'I think,' he said slowly, 'you better get clean out of this country for good, Hodel.'

'I'll go,' Hodel said.

Cameron made a little nod and something quick ran across his face. He was saying that Lew had done the right thing.

Springer's eyes were pale points under the cliffs of his brows.

He did not look at Lew. The tension of a waiting mountain sat in Springer, and Lew wondered why the sheriff did not realize that the backbone of the fight was broken.

Wigram said, 'The kid is soft, Buck. But I can't let you go.'

'Yes, you will,' Springer said suddenly. 'It's time I got my spoon into this mess. Hodel is drifting. I'm arresting you, Wigram.'

Wigram thought a moment. 'What for?' he challenged.

The cone of interest now ran its point between the bulky sheriff and gaunt Wigram, but Lew observed that Springer was only half watching Wigram. And then, standing there in the rain beside the tepee of his yellow slicker, Springer drew his gun. The thick fumes of black powder smoke hung in the damp air.

Across the yard Hodel's mouth dropped open. The pistol bearing on Lew fell into a puddle, and then Hodel went down in the mud like a head-shot beef.

Springer looked angrily at Lew. 'You can't turn your back on a man like that. Don't you ever learn nothing?'

'I slipped, too,' Cameron said.

Wigram only glanced at Hodel. 'You can't arrest me, Springer.'

'I know it,' the sheriff said. 'You're bad beat, though. You got your choice of clearing out or going to Stump Gantt on his own terms if you figure to run cows in the west hills.'

'Dead as hell,' a Short Fork rider said, turning Hodel over.

'I get paid for it,' Springer said bitterly. 'Let's get out of here.'

The sheriff did not like the mud on his floor, or the way Cameron pushed things aside to sit on a corner of the desk. But he did his best to cover up his feelings. 'You put me in for another term, Cameron. Considering the farmer vote that's come in the last two years, I wouldn't have made it this fall.'

'Nobody *dragged* you out to Short Fork this morning,' Cameron answered.

'Uh-huh.' Springer looked at Lew. 'I guess I earned my votes all right.' In a curiously sombre voice he asked Lew: 'Do you know what it might have meant if you'd gone over the hump and killed Hodel when you started to?'

'I guessed. It wouldn't have been so good for me.'

'Maybe you did learn something down here,' Springer said.

'Maybe you crossed the line between being a kid and a man. You can go back to Stump now and see how much he's changed.'

Cameron's face was dead sober. 'You may find that your old man has learned a lot since you been gone.'

Springer knew Mark Twain, too, but he had never heard him so aptly quoted. The sheriff forgot the muddy tracks. He made little noise but he was laughing all the way down when Cameron and Lew stepped outside.

'Tell your sis—tell your father—I'll be up in a few days,' Cameron said. 'Don't forget the rig for that pig-tailed demon. She told me all about it when I was up there. I see just the answer in Bixler's saddle shop every time I go past.'

'Yeah. That's where Odalie saw it. I couldn't buy a second-hand saddle blanket now, let alone a silver-trimmed rig.'

'Try the bank,' Cameron said. 'When I start splitting with a man in a poker game I'll know I'm not fit to make an honest living. You must have about two hundred and fifty bucks left.' He gave Lew a little shove, and then went back into Springer's office.

For a while Lew stood on the walk with his hat brim drooping lower in the rain. From the corners of his eyes he saw them watching him from inside. It would take a little time to straighten out and sort some of the things which he had learned. But there was no rush.

This rain was going to be mighty good for the grass in the west hills. Lew Gantt went slowly up the street toward Bixler's saddlery.

CAMPAIGNING COWPOKE

By Clark Gray

THE two Ferguson boys operated a three-hundred-cow ranch they had inherited from their daddy. The ranch bordered the Canadian River in the Texas Panhandle. The entire place was fenced with six wires and cedar posts. Most of the grass was open; the river gave abundant water and wintertime shelter in the breaks. It was a nice layout, and the Ferguson boys tended to business and made a nice living.

They were lean and friendly young men. Having been brought up with cattle, they knew how to work their calves at the right time to avoid screw-worm infestation. They gentled their old mother cows and kept their fences up and had the horses as tame as pet dogs. Every year they sold about two hundred and thirty weanling calves as stockers to the neighbours. Their cull cows, some forty a year, were thrown in with a larger herd and trailed to the Abilene, Kansas, railhead.

The steady one was Dave. Dave was tall and blond, with brown sober eyes. He had married early, a girl as steady and sober as himself. Already they had two saucer-eyed, unsmiling children. Dave stayed at home and tended the mother cows while Red trail-drove to Abilene.

Red wasn't wild in the sense that he drank or gambled or shot up people. He was no hard case. He was freckled and blue-eyed, with a lithe, well-muscled body. But Red believed that along with work, a man was entitled to his fun.

That was why Red wintered over in Abilene and didn't get back to the home stomping-grounds in Roan till the following June. And that, too, was why Ellie Jones threw Red over.

'Ellie,' Dave told Red over the supper table on the day of his arrival home, 'has got herself engaged to Sheriff Tom Blake. What in blazes kept you so long, Red?'

Red stuffed a forkful of fried round steak into his mouth and grinned. He had a grin that could charm the ears off a sow. 'Ever been in Abilene in wintertime, Dave? The floating population's all gone then. Only the gamblers and the barkeeps left. And the girls.' He winked. 'I got myself a job in a feed store and spent the winter making friends.'

Dave shook his head and sighed. 'You've lost Ellie while you've been tom-catting around. You can't expect a girl like that to wait for ever, Red. And you won't get her back. Tom Blake will make trouble if you try.'

'Tom Blake,' Red opined, 'is too old for Ellie. And too fat. Ellie wouldn't like a lazy husband, Dave.'

Dave shrugged. His sober eyes had a far-away look, the look of a man weighing his responsibilities. Then he smiled and punched Red affectionately on the arm.

'We've always stuck together, Red. I reckon we always will. I think I know how you feel about Ellie. You let me know how you come out.'

Red bought a box of lemon drops at Roan Mercantile. He got a barbering job, and about eight o'clock he was walking up the boardwalk toward Lawyer Jones's house with his lean shoulders swaying jauntily and his Stetson hat cocked a little to one side. He didn't anticipate any trouble with Ellie, for he had been courting her off and on since they'd been in the eighth grade together. He knew Ellie like an old shoe. Often of late he'd caught himself wondering why he didn't marry her and get it over with.

He found Ellie on the front-porch steps and right away he began making up his lost ground. It was a thing Red was good at. Before long he was sitting pretty close to Ellie, there on the step in the moonlight. That was when Sheriff Blake came stalking through the picket gate and up the plank walk.

'Heard you were back in town,' Tom Blake greeted. Blake was a paunchy man ten years older than Red and Ellie. He halted before them and put his hands on his hips and scowled. Moonlight carved out the black outline of a holster at his side. It sparkled bluely off the handcuffs hanging from his belt. 'Get out of here, Red.'

Red Ferguson grinned at Ellie. His voice was a trifle cool. 'Maybe he thinks I'm his dog.'

'Get moving.' Tom Blake said. 'Ellie's engaged to me.'

Red unwound his lean body and came slowly to his feet, still grinning.

He said, 'Now, Tom, I came here on a friendly visit. I reckon it's up to Ellie to tell me when to leave.'

'All right.' Tom Blake turned gruffly to Ellie. 'Tell him to scat, hon!'

Ellie Jones's pretty face turned from one man to the other. She was a small, dark girl dressed in white. She touched her hair with a dainty hand, an instinctively feminine gesture, Red thought. Now, being a lawyer's daughter, Ellie had been very properly brought up. She knew how to cook and sew and keep household accounts, which was the correct field of knowledge for a nice young girl. But it appeared to Red that she was not above a little feminine enjoyment of this kind of thing. She smiled sweetly and impartially.

'You're my guests.' Her voice had a silky touch of command, and she patted the porch step on either side. 'Sit down, both of you.'

Stubbornly Tom Blake shook his head. He was a big man with a one-track mind. 'I ain't going to do it. I came here to visit my future wife, not to listen to some jakeleg cowpuncher.' He glowered at Red. 'I got a notion to teach you some manners, bucko.'

Red Ferguson shifted a little on his feet. He was still smiling; his mop of hair was a little mussed in the moonlight. He had known he'd have to make this decision about Tom Blake sooner or later. Cheerfully he made it now.

'It ain't polite to refuse that kind of invite, is it, Tom? Leave your gun with Ellie.'

He heard Ellie suck in her breath sharply, but he ignored it. Turning, he stalked around the house and out the gate into the alley. He heard Tom Blake's gruff voice as the sheriff ordered Ellie into the house. Presently Blake joined him in the alley. Blake's shoulders looked blocky as hams in the shifting light of the alley.

'Bucko,' he said, 'I'm going to cut your face up so you won't want to see Ellie for a while.'

'Come ahead,' Red said, and when Tom Blake charged Red hit him in his soft stomach, burying his fist to the wrist.

He heard Blake's grunt of dismay; then Blake half spun away and Red saw him grasping for something at his belt. Red thought of the handcuffs, but he didn't believe it. Then he couldn't help but believe it, for he caught the shine of them as Blake got them free and hefted them to strike.

Red ducked, but not far enough. The slashing cuffs caught him on the back of the neck, driving him to his knees and flinging an array of gaudy lights across his vision. He tried to get up, and he sensed that Tom Blake was striking again with the steel cuffs. . . .

He awoke on an iron cot, in a barred cell. He came erect, groaning, feeling pain in his face. He prodded gingerly at his nose, and there was a deep cut there. Then a shadow fell across him.

'Come on,' a voice said.

Red looked up to see Tom Blake standing outside the bars. Blake was freshly shaved; he was smoking a cigar.

Red said wryly, 'You meant it, didn't you—about cutting me up?'

'Come on,' Tom Blake said. 'I want to see you in my office.'

Red got up painfully and followed Blake through the cell door, down the corridor. A half-dozen deputies loafed outside Blake's office. They stared curiously, but at Blake's curt words of dismissal they drifted off. Inside the office Blake sank into a swivel chair and put his spurred boots on top of his desk.

'Set,' Blake said.

Red Ferguson sat. He took note of a few things. The deputies, for instance, who had been loafing in the corridor. The bagged canvas seat of Blake's swivel chair. The long scratch marks on Blake's desk where the sheriff had raked his spurs. The foul scent of stale cigars that filled the room.

Red said, 'You must spend a lot of time here.'

Tom Blake knocked cigar ash on the floor. 'Red, I could book you for disturbing the peace. I ain't going to do it—this time. But you'll have to behave from here on out. Understand?'

Red said, 'I understand all right, Tom. I never knew you was afraid of competition.'

'I ain't.' Tom Blake grinned around his cigar. 'I know how to handle it.'

Red Ferguson touched his chin. There was another cut place there, where the cuffs had struck after he had lost consciousness.

'You sure do—Tom, ain't there an election this fall?'

Blake's eyes narrowed. 'What about it?'

Red Ferguson tried a tentative smile. It hurt his mouth, but he kept on smiling anyway. He said, 'I don't think you do enough work, Tom. You set there in that swivel chair and smoke cigars and let your deputies run around on your chores. And you've got twice as many deputies as any sheriff in Roan ever had before. That ain't good. Costs the county too much.'

He turned and went out, leaving Tom Blake staring at him. He got his horse and rode home.

Dave was shoeing a pony in the cattle pens when Red rode by on the way to the house. Red didn't stop, but he saw Dave lower the pony's forefoot to wave, saw Dave's mouth drop open at the sight of his cut-up face. At the house Red went to his room and began to sponge the dried blood from his face with a wet towel.

Dave came in. Red saw that his brother's face was dark with anger. Dave had gone to his own room and got a gun. The gun strapped at Dave's lean hip did not look natural there.

'Who did it?' Dave said.

Red looked at Dave over the towel without speaking for a moment. He dabbed cautiously at his eye. Dave asked harshly:

'Was it Blake?'

Red put down the towel. 'Dave, it was Blake. But I'll square this in my own way. I'm going to run for sheriff.'

Dave sat down heavily on the bed. He shook his head. He glanced up at Red and studied him as if he were a queer species of critter, then shook his head again. For the first time Red noticed with a pang that Dave really looked like an older brother, with the worried eyes, the little lines of age on his cheeks, everything.

Dave said, 'That's a damned crazy thing to do!'

Red nodded. 'Would you rather I'd take after him with a gun?'

'But suppose you win?' Dave protested. 'You might actually get elected.'

'I damned well aim to get elected.'

Dave got up and walked to the window, hands behind his back. Red poked at his face with the towel and watched Dave's hands clasp and unclasp, and he was sorry that he'd had to upset Dave.

'Red, I'll be glad when you marry Ellie and settle down,' Dave said wearily.

'One thing at a time, Dave. When's the closing date for filing?'

'Couple days.' Dave sighed. 'You won't have much time to campaign. The primary's less than a month off.'

'Then I won't meet him in the primary. I'll file on the Republican ticket. That way I have till November to beat him.'

'The Republican ticket!' Dave turned and looked at Red, and he began to laugh. 'Boy, you been in Abilene too long. This here is Texas. You couldn't get elected flea-scratcher on the Republican ticket.'

Red grinned, not minding it when Dave laughed at him. 'You watch me.'

Dave said, 'I'll watch you, all right, Red. But hell, I kind of hate to vote Republican myself, even for you. It just ain't the custom in Texas.' Thoughtfully he knuckled his blond head. 'Look, you go see Phineas Jones, Ellie's dad. He's a Republican, if I remember right—the only man I ever heard own up to it. Go see what he says.'

Red did go to see Phineas Jones. He found him in his office, a starchy, prunelike little man with a stiff white collar. Jones became somewhat wistful when Red stated his business.

'I wish I could advise you to run on our ticket, Red. But the fact is you'd never live it down. People would laugh at you the rest of your life. Not that I wouldn't like to see you run, mind! I'm only thinking of your own good.'

Red said, 'How do I get on the ticket?'

'Hell, I can take care of that for you. There's not even enough

Republicans in the county to fill out the slate. If you want the sheriff's nomination, all you got to do is say so.'

'Will you help me campaign?'

'Sure.' An eager light replaced the wistfulness in Phineas Jones's face. 'I'll figure the issues for you. How do you feel about the tariff, Red? And you're for hard money, I take it?'

'I don't know if I'm for hard money or not,' Red said. 'I thought all money was hard, except paper money. I don't know about such things, Mr. Jones. All I know is that Tom Blake is a Democrat. That makes me a Republican.'

Phineas Jones sighed. 'I guess that's as good a reason as most folks have. All right, Red, I'll get you filed. You'll begin to campaign next week.'

Red found out about campaigning, and he didn't like the things he found out. He had thought vaguely about making speeches, about getting his picture in the Roan *Weekly Gazette*. But Phineas Jones laughed wryly at those ideas.

'The ways to campaign,' Jones said, 'is to go talk in person to every qualified voter in the country. Back him in a corner and argue with him. Convince him you're the man for the job.'

Red blinked his dismay. 'All of 'em! There must be hundreds!'

'Two thousand three hundred and forty-two,' Jones said. 'I can cross a couple hundred party regulars off the list, because they'd vote Democratic if the devil himself was a candidate.' He sighed. 'I wish there was some Republicans like that in Texas.'

Red grinned. 'What'll I tell the others?'

'I'll work it out for you. But remember this, son. It ain't so much what you say as it is the way you say it. You got to turn on the personality. You got to shine.' Phineas Jones turned to spit into a big brass cuspidor, and he did not look happy.

Red spent the next few days in Phineas Jones's office, memorizing the gist of what Jones wrote out for him on long legal sheets of paper. The duties of a county sheriff, his own qualifications, the aspects in which Tom Blake had failed to do a good job. Phineas Jones even went out and did a little snooping for him at the courthouse and the bank, and he came back with some facts that made Red grunt in surprise. Red copied down the facts with grim pleasure.

The Sunday night before he was to start campaigning he went to see Ellie with a handful of roses from the picket fence around the home ranch.

Ellie came to the door with a smile. The smile disappeared and her eyes darkened when she recognized him.

'You came to see Father?'

Red shook his head and extended the roses with a grin. 'I came to see you, Ellie. Can I come in?'

She bit her lip and stared a long moment at the half-healed cuts on his face. Suddenly her eyes filled with tears.

'Oh, Red! Why did you have to pull a gun on Tom?'

Red lost his grip on the roses and almost dropped them. 'Why did I what?' His voice was harsh.

'Pull that derringer out of your hat? Tom wouldn't have hurt you like that if you'd fought fair.'

Red said grittily, 'Tom told you I pulled a derringer?'

She nodded in silent misery. 'He had to tell me, Red. He didn't want me to think he'd used the cuffs on you without cause.'

Red felt a sudden sharp pain in his hand; he realized he was gripping the roses so tightly a thorn had pierced his thumb. He said gently, 'And you believe him?'

'Of course.' There was a kind of pride in the erectness of her shoulders. 'Tom may have his faults, Red. But lying isn't one of them.'

'Isn't it?' Red took the roses and separated them in his hands, staring at them without seeing them, sorting his bitter thoughts. At length he sighed.

'Ellie, you're a nice girl, and you think nice things about people. But you don't know the truth about Tom Blake. I hope I can show you the truth before you marry him.'

Red began to campaign next morning. He strapped his warbag behind his saddle and rode toward the far end of the county, stopping at every farmhouse on his way. To every voter he told his story.

Tom Blake, Red said grimly, had fifteen deputies on the county pay roll. Never in the history of Roan County had any sheriff before Blake hired more than seven. What did those extra eight deputies do? Red asked. He left it to the voter to remember the way those deputies hung around the courthouse.

And where, Red argued, did Tom Blake get the money in his bank account? Red pulled out the figures Phineas Jones had given him and read them off. A bank account of five thousand dollars. A new house in town that cost three thousand if it cost a nickel. A ranch south of Roan. Blake had acquired these things since he had become sheriff. Could it be that Blake was taking kickbacks from his deputies?

These were telling arguments, because they were true. It was also true, Red suspected, that too many drunks had been rolled in Roan saloons lately. But he had no proof of that.

Sometimes Red got a promise of votes. More often the man would say:

'Maybe so, Mister. But my pappy and grandpappy would turn over in their graves if I voted for a Republican.'

Red would grin then. 'Don't you believe in voting for the best man?'

'Sure,' the voter would answer. 'But if he was a Republican, how could he *be* the best?'

Red stayed out for a month in that section of the county, seeing some eight hundred voters. He grew gaunt with the constant travel and the irregular hours. His stomach became upset now and then from eating strange food, and he found it a little harder to maintain his cheerful grin. It was late July when he got back into Roan to find that he had been right about the drunks.

'It's been a regular crime wave,' Phineas Jones reported. 'A man don't dare take more'n three drinks or he wakes up in the alley with his pockets empty. It's hard to prove it on Tom Blake's deputies, but they're always hanging around.'

'Do you suppose,' Red said, 'that those deputies are kicking back part of that to Blake?'

'Hell, yes, I suppose it,' Phineas Jones snapped peevishly. 'Rolling drunks is a crime, ain't it? How else would them deputies get away with it without Blake's knowledge and permission? And Blake wouldn't give that permission without a good reason. And money is a damned good reason.'

Red said, 'How's Blake taking the campaign?'

Phineas Jones looked embarrassed. 'He's laughing like hell, Red. He thinks it's funny to have a Republican running against him. Matter of fact, I think that's another reason why he's letting his deputies roll so many drunks. It's sort of a taunt, you might say. But he could go too far. If we could only get some proof about those kickbacks—'

'How's Ellie?' Red asked.

Phineas Jones took out a stubby pipe and stuffed it with slender old fingers. 'Red, you know the girl as well as I do, maybe better. She got engaged to Blake while you was prowlin' around Abilene. It might have been to show you she was independent—I don't know. Anyway, she's got her pride up now, and neither you nor I can help her there.'

Red said, 'All right. I'll head south next week.'

He spent three days helping Dave cut out and sell some two hundred weanling calves. He found that Dave, too, knew about the drunks. 'Them deputies,' Dave said, 'ain't Texas boys, Red. You can tell by listening to 'em talk. There's a different accent for every man of 'em.'

Red grinned. 'It ain't polite to listen to a man's accent, Dave. Some folks are kind of shy about letting on where they come from.'

'That's what I was getting at.' Dave's usually placid face was lined with worry. 'Red, did you ever stop to think about where Tom Blake gets his deputies?'

Red looked up at Dave sharply. He said, 'No, Dave, I never did think about it. But I'm thinking about it now.' He slapped Dave on the shoulder with the flat of his hand. 'You ain't as simple as you look, son.'

Red rode south and spent two more months campaigning. He found that the temper of the populace was changing. News of the goings-on in Roan had spread out into the rural areas, where Tom Blake's vote-getting strength was greatest, among the church-going, God-fearing people.

'I can't figure it,' one leather-faced old cattleman told Red. 'Tom Blake's a religious man. Him and me are deacons in the same church. I can't believe he's a part of this small-time skul-duggery. But if he ain't, how come nobody's been arrested?'

Red Ferguson nodded understandingly. 'Most politicians put up a front, I reckon. Tom Blake is a deacon because it gets him votes. But pretending to be pure don't change the actual smell of a man, does it?' His young jaw hardened. 'You'll see an honest job done, if I'm elected.'

He began to feel that he was making progress after that. Not much, but a little. Tom Blake, he decided, wasn't playing his cards close enough to his vest. Blake was over-confident, counting too much on a solid Democratic vote.

The feeling grew as the weeks passed and the first frosts of October put a chill in the clear morning air. Voters talked a little less of party loyalty now. They began to ask more pointed questions about Tom Blake. Some of the questions Red couldn't answer, for he had no absolute proof. If he only had proof–The thought sent him into deep concentration one night as he sat beside his lonely campfire with his back propped against his saddle.

Next day Red reached the little railroad community of Blackbird, in the south end of the county. There he went to the brick railroad station. He wrote two telegrams. The first read:

Sheriff Tom Blake, Roan, Texas.
Your list and description of Roan County deputies received. Incomplete investigation shows rewards outstanding for at least six of your men. Will arrive Roan to make necessary arrests within few days. Your claim to rewards on these men acknowledged.– TIM O'SHANTER, *Texas Ranger.*

Red kept a copy of the telegram and gave another copy to the station agent for immediate dispatch. Then, grinning, he re-read his second telegram:

Sheriff Tom Blake, Roan, Texas.
Arriving Roan to-day on 3:22 northbound.   –O'SHANTER.

Red gave his second telegram to the station agent. 'Keep this one till you hear from me, will you, Mister?'

The station agent was a burly man with one ear half shot away. His lips moved as read the second telegram.

'And keep your mouth shut,' Red added. 'This here is confidential business.'

The agent folded the second telegram and put it carefully in his pocket. His mouth was grim. 'I come from Kansas, Ferguson. A Mississippi Democrat shot off this ear during the war. Anything else you need?'

Red's blue eyes crinkled in a sympathetic smile. Then he nodded. 'You might ask the agent in Roan to see that one of Blake's deputies gets hold of this first telegram. Accidental-like, you know. Can you trust him to do that?'

'I reckon. He's my son.'

Red grinned and paid the man. He left Blackbird at a gallop, heading directly home.

He arrived in town shortly after noon next day. As he crossed the tracks and turned his pony's nose toward the business district, he heard a gunshot. The figure of a big man cut through the cottonwoods and across the sandy street three blocks ahead at a dead run. Sunlight flashed from the handcuffs at the figure's belt.

Red Ferguson saw the running man duck into Phineas Jones's office building, and he grinned and swung his pony around toward the railroad station. The action had started a little quicker than he'd figured. Dismounting, he spoke quickly to the youth behind the counter.

'Get in touch with your pa. Have him send on that other telegram to Blake. When it comes through, you deliver it yourself to Phineas Jones's office, pronto. Got it?'

The youngster nodded solemnly. His eyes were big with excitement and curiosity, but Red had no time for explanations now. He ran back to his pony at a lope.

By the time Red had reached Phineas Jones's office building, the deputies had gathered. They stood in the middle of the street under the cottonwoods, all fifteen of them. Fifteen dark-faced men, some tall, some short and fat, some light and some dark, but all alike in the guns they wore and in the grim determination in their eyes. Red halted before them.

'Tom Blake around?'

The tallest of the deputies nodded. 'Up in Jones's office.'

Red took a look around. The street seemed empty, but it wasn't. There were faces peering out of windows and around doors and behind blinds all up and down Main Street, from the mercantile and the barbershop and the saloon and the blacksmithy and the bank.

Red lit a cigarette and puffed out the match. 'Something wrong, boys?'

The tall deputy shook his head. 'You go up and find Blake, Ferguson. Tell him we want to see him.'

'What about?'

'That,' the tall deputy answered coolly, 'is private. But you tell Blake it won't be private long, if he don't come out.'

Red shrugged. 'Okay, boys.' He moved to the hitchrack and dismounted and went up the stairway to Phineas Jones's office.

He found Phineas seated in his swivel chair, with Tom Blake standing over him. Phineas's mouth was opening and closing soundlessly; he was very pale. Tom Blake was talking, his big voice booming through the room, which was why he hadn't heard Red's entry. Blake's gun was on his hip.

'You started it,' Blake was roaring. 'You and that damned redhead cowpuncher, with that fake telegram. Now end it!'

Red grinned and tiptoed across the room and lifted Blake's gun from its holster. He flipped the gun to Phineas Jones as Blake whirled with a startled oath. Phineas caught the gun skilfully and turned it on Blake, and a little colour returned to his prunelike face.

Red said, 'A little trouble with the boys, Tom?'

Blake licked his lips. He lifted his right hand to the handcuffs in his belt, then after a thoughtful moment dropped it.

'Damn you to hell, Ferguson! One of my deputies took a shot at me!'

Red grinned. 'Lucky I got back to town. I'll fix everything for you, Tom.'

Still grinning, he went to the window. Outside he saw that the deputies had scattered a little, behind the shelter of the horse trough and the cottonwoods in the middle of the street. The boy from the railroad station was coming up the boardwalk with a yellow envelope in his hand now.

Red spotted the tall deputy staring at him from the mercantile porch. He cupped his hands around his mouth and shouted:

'Blake claims you boys owe him some money. Says he only wants to collect what's coming to him.'

He heard Tom Blake's inarticulate curse, but he ignored that. He watched the bafflement, and the anger, twist the gaunt face of the deputy.

'That dirty lying son!' the deputy shouted hoarsely. 'That cooks him with me, Ferguson. I won't cover up for him no more. I paid him ten per cent of my salary, and so did the rest of the boys. When that wasn't enough, we went out in the alleys and got more. Send the penny-pinchin' coyote down, or by Ned, we're comin' after him!'

The sigh that came up from the town then was plainly audible. Behind the doors and windows and curtains voices spoke excitedly to one another. Out of the corner of his eye Red saw Ty Corbett, the newspaper editor, break from the bank and run at a crouch across the street toward the office of the Roan *Weekly Gazette*.

At that moment there came a knock on Phineas Jones's door, and Red turned to see Tom Blake sputtering helplessly under the gun in Jones's gnarled hand. Jones himself was scratching his head in pop-eyed bewilderment.

'Red, I don't savvy how you done it! Or how you're going to keep Blake from getting killed!'

'You will, Phineas.'

Red went to the door and took the telegram the youth handed him. He read it aloud.

'*Arriving Roan to-day on 3:22 northbound.*   –O'SHANTER.'

Grinning, Red crumpled the telegram and tossed it out the window. He watched the wind catch the yellow paper as it fell past the cottonwoods to strike on the far side of the street. There was a little scuffle in the sand over there; one of the deputies made a dive for the telegram and got it and ran quickly back behind the horse trough.

Red turned to Phineas. 'How's Ellie?'

Phineas Jones's eyes were brooding. He shook his head with a sigh. 'All right. She broke it off with Blake, here, a couple days ago. Confound it, Red, I don't know what in blazes you've done, but—'

'I've done nothing,' Red said, 'but send a couple innocent telegrams from a man that doesn't exist.' He grinned. 'You know, Phineas, it's a funny thing about snakes. Snakes don't trust each other. Every snake among 'em thinks that the other snakes are going to act like snakes.' He eyed Tom Blake gravely. 'Ain't it so, Tom?'

He moved to the window before Tom Blake could answer. Down in the street he saw the group of deputies clustered around the tall one, who had the wrinkled telegram in his hand. They were conferring excitedly, arguing. A moment later they separated, and as Red Ferguson faced back toward the room he heard the rapid beat of galloping hoofs heading out of town.

Red wasn't smiling now as he advanced toward Tom Blake. Being an easy-going, soft-hearted young man, he felt a little sorry for Blake. But he didn't let that sorrow change his mind.

'Tom,' he said, 'I reckon you know this finishes you here. Everybody in Roan heard that deputy admit kicking back part of his salary to you. I'm going to boot you out of town, Tom.'

Tom Blake's cheeks seemed to cave in. But the man still had bluster. 'You can't run me out of town, Ferguson. Just because a lying deputy spouts some crazy tale—'

'We could call a grand jury,' Red interrupted calmly. 'We could let them decide whether the deputy was lying. Take your choice, Tom. A penitentiary sentence—or leave town.'

Tom Blake's heavy face was mottled with red splotches. But his eyes darkened with defeat, and he dropped his glance, and his voice, when he spoke, was sullen.

'My property?'

'I'll sell it at a sheriff's sale,' Red said, 'and send you the money.'

Nobody was on the street when Red and Tom Blake came out of Phineas Jones's office and crossed toward the courthouse, where Blake's horse stood at the hitch rail. But Red knew that the eyes behind the doors and windows and curtains were still there. He could feel them, and he had no doubt from the rigid whiteness of Tom Blake's face that Blake felt them, too. Blake walked with his eyes straight ahead and unseeing, like a man walking toward the gallows.

Red waited gravely until Tom Blake got into his saddle. Then he said:

'I think you'd be happier outside of Texas, Tom.'

Tom Blake nodded bitterly. His lips made a thin, bloodless line. He turned his horse and rode out of town.

The election went off very smoothly. It was true that Blake's name was still on the ballot, but Blake was no longer a resident of Roan County, and everybody knew it. Of eighteen hundred and thirty-two votes cast, Red Ferguson received eighteen hundred and thirty-two.

Phineas Jones became wildly enthusiastic. 'We had to disgrace a Democrat to do it,' he said, waving his pipe, 'but we finally elected a Republican in Texas! This is the beginning, boy! With you in office we can build an organization now. Some day we'll put Texas in the marching columns of the Grand Old Party, and you and I will be responsible. Don't that make you feel proud, boy? Think of being the father of all those good Republicans!'

Red Ferguson grinned. 'I don't want to be the father of a whole stateful of Republicans, Mr. Jones. Ellie says she only wants to have three.'

FEAR IN THE SADDLE

By H. A. DeRosso

T RAVIS awoke and lay a while, listening to the sounds coming from the corral. In his mind's eye he could see the restless pacing of the roan. It seemed that the animal was never still. In one way this might be a good thing, for this constant fitfulness could tire the animal, thus making the job ahead a trifle easier. But just thinking about it turned Travis cold at the pit of his stomach.

Travis rose and dressed. He cursed a little, quietly and disgustedly, while he cooked his breakfast. It seemed that his appetite was gone. His throat clogged and he doubted that he could get anything down. He kept thinking about what he had to do this morning.

Down in the corral the roan still paced.

Though there was no taste to it, Travis forced some food into himself. Then he built a cigarette and sat with his legs stretched out to savour an after-breakfast smoke. He told himself there was nothing better than a cigarette after eating but he knew this was just an excuse. It helped prolong the time before he went to the roan.

Finally, he rose to his feet, full of disgust with himself. This was not the first time he had tried to break a horse. He had been doing this for ten of his twenty-five years. This was his livelihood. He had ridden the buckers in Calgary, Pendleton, Cheyenne. He was one of the best riders in the business. He had topped tougher broncos than this wild roan he had captured a month ago. But all that lay in the past, he realized sickeningly. This was something altogether different.

He decided it was no good standing here, thinking about it. The thoughts only tormented him. The thing to do was to get it over with.

The roan heard Travis coming and abruptly stopped its pacing.

It turned to face Travis, ears cocked, all tense and waiting. The roan snorted once, then was quiet, watching Travis crossing to the corral.

Travis stopped and stared through the bars and as he looked he thought he felt a pain in his right thigh where his leg had been broken. But that had happened over a year ago and more than one doctor had pronounced the leg healed. Still the pain persisted as Travis stood there. He knew it was only in his mind but it felt real enough. Travis began to sweat.

Realizing that the longer he stood here the harder it would be to get started, Travis clenched his teeth and stepped into the corral. The roan emitted a loud snort and paced nervously to the far end of the enclosure.

Travis shook out a loop in his rope. He did not have too much trouble with the roan. By now the animal had grown accustomed to being roped and snubbed and saddled. Travis had been patient with the horse. He had taught it first to become used to a halter, then a blanket on its back, then the saddle, and finally weights on the saddle. Now it was time to ride the roan and Travis felt weak and sick inside.

The roan was snubbed tight to a post which Travis had sunk into the ground at one end of the corral. The horse stood docilely enough, its tension apparent only in the way it flicked back its ears.

Travis stood undecided. He told himself he could not be too careful. This abandoned ranch he had selected for his job was in an isolated part of these mountains. No one ever passed by here. A man could not be too careful with a wild horse when he was by himself. However, Travis had to be alone. The shame was so great in him he could not endure the thought of displaying his cowardice to another.

As Travis contemplated the roan, he began to feel that he should try a weight on the roan again to-day. Perhaps the horse was not yet ready to be ridden. He had to be careful about that because he was alone. Travis thought, and then he flushed with disgust and mortification. He knew this was just another excuse to put off riding the roan.

Travis could feel the muscles of his thighs quivering as he

quietly loosened the snap holding the roan snubbed. For a wild instant Travis hoped the roan would jerk away from him so he could not mount, but the animal stood quietly, not flicking a muscle.

Travis sucked in his breath and then he was going up into the saddle. The roan reacted swiftly. Even before Travis touched the seat of the kak the animal was going up in the air, its back arching. However, Travis' boots found the stirrups and he stayed on.

The roan kept its back arched and began crowhopping across the corral. This manoeuvre would never have sufficed to unseat Travis in the past. But he instantly envisioned himself being hurtled through the air and then striking the ground and the roan bearing down on him and the forehoofs rise, flailing, to come crashing down on him as he cowered helplessly on the ground with a fractured leg. He was alone, his mind shrieked at him. He had to unload of his own will. He had to pile off of his own choosing if he did not want to be trampled again. There was no one around to drive off the roan and drag him away as there had been in Calgary. Panic filled Travis' throat. He could not get off the pitching horse soon enough.

He hit the ground on both feet and the momentum of it carried him forward and down but he spread his hands before him and saved himself from going flat on his face. You've got to get out of here, his mind screamed at him. You've got to run before he tramples you. Travis was on his feet in half a second and streaked for the corral bars. Terror shrieked in his brain. He went through the bars so fast he sprawled on the ground, his cheek scraping the dirt. For a moment he lay there, breathing hard, all aquiver and sick with fear, afraid to rise and afraid almost to hope that he was safe. But the height of the panic soon passed and Travis rolled over and sat up.

He stared at the corral and saw the roan on the far side, watching him. It came then to Travis that the horse had made no effort to trample him. The instant he had quit the saddle the roan must have stopped bucking. It was not even breathing hard. It stood there with ears cocked forward, looking at Travis as if it understood what had gone on in his mind.

Travis put his face in his hands and shuddered. He could have wept with helplessness. . . .

Travis lay on his bunk, blowing cigarette smoke up at the ceiling. The quivering of his insides had stopped and fear seemed a distant and alien thing to him now. He supposed it was because he had knocked off for the rest of the day and would not have to face the job until the next morning.

He told himself there was no compulsion about this thing except what he himself wanted to do. It was not necessary for him to follow the rodeo circuit to earn his keep. He could do all right in some other line of business. It was not even a question of being unable to ride a horse. The broken ones he could ride without a qualm. It was the buckers that turned him hollow and quivering inside, but he did not have to stick to bronc-riding for a living.

I guess I'll quit, he thought, puffing slowly on his smoke. It wouldn't be too hard to give a reason. I can say that I'm all busted up inside and that the doctors have told me never to top a bronc again. . . .

But he felt ill and miserable at the thought of quitting, for, despite what he might tell others, he himself would know he had quit because he was afraid. He was yellow.

Travis turned his face to the wall and cursed with a studied, frustrated vehemence. He was yellow, his mind kept whispering to him. He just didn't have any guts any more. . . .

Travis awoke before dawn. He lay a while in his bunk, listening for sounds from the corral, but they did not begin until the break of day. Then, because he could not stand hearing them and because he wanted to get an early start, Travis jumped out of bed.

After breakfast, he went outside. The morning was clear and cool. There was a stiff breeze coming down from the mountain, stirring the tops of the pines and cedars and raising occasional small swirls of dust in the corral.

The roan was staring wistfully out through the bars at the timbered slopes and pitches. It seemed immersed in this study

167

and paid no attention to Travis as he came down from the house.

Travis stopped and watched the roan a while. The horse still did not face Travis, though surely it must have heard the jingle of his spurs as he had come up. The roan just went on staring with a longing that was apparent to Travis.

He found himself thinking, It's a shame to coop him up like this. He never hurt anybody. He wants to be out there, free and wild like the wind. He should be turned loose. . . .

Then the feeling came to Travis that this was just the old excuse taking another turn. There was always something popping into his mind that would allow him to get out of riding the roan. It was the cowardice working in him.

Travis was quite angry with himself when he stepped into the corral.

He roped the roan and snubbed it to the post. The horse was quite difficult this morning and there was a fine film of sweat on Travis' face by the time he got the animal tied to the post. The roan would not stand still. It knocked the saddle off three times before Travis got it cinched on. Travis was getting angrier all along.

'I don't like this any more than you do,' he growled at the horse. 'but it's something that has to be done. If you'd just go along with me, we'd get it over with that much faster. Now you stand still or I'll take a whip to you.'

The instant that Travis released the snap the roan jerked away. Travis grabbed for the lines but the roan moved so fast and hard that the reins were ripped out of Travis' grip. Snorting loudly, the roan whirled and raced to the other end of the corral.

Cursing savagely Travis went after the roan, but before he was within ten feet of the animal it broke wildly past him, spraying him with grit and dust kicked up by its pounding hoofs. Travis got his rope.

He shook out a loop and advanced on the roan. For an instant the horse bared its teeth, while its ears flattened against its head. A shrill, angry snort emitted from it and then the roan broke. It seemed to hurtle straight at Travis and he had a swift, terrifying vision of going down under those churning hoofs, but at the last instant the roan swerved, and as it pounded past him Travis dropped the loop over the animal's neck. The roan fought all the way back to the snubbing post but Travis finally got it tied again.

Travis was breathing hard. The roan kept shying and snorting and Travis realized it was no use trying to do anything with the horse until it had calmed down.

He was angry again, at himself and at the horse. If things had not gone wrong he might have had the ordeal over with by this time, he might have had the roan broken by now. Instead, he still had to start, and as he waited, watching the roan, he could feel the first tentative flutters of fear in his thighs and in his belly. He knew that in a little while he was going to feel sick again and this knowledge almost made him weep with anger.

He edged in on the roan and caught the halter and began patting the horse's neck. 'I'm not going to hurt you, boy,' he told the roan, all the while stroking its neck. 'It's just something that's got to be done. Can't you understand? I've just got to top you. For myself. Can't you see? Why do you keep fighting me?'

The roan quieted. The wicked, perverse glint seemed to go out of its eyes. Now it stood there almost still.

'We're going to get along all right together. I know we are,' Travis said with an assurance he certainly did not feel. He kept stroking the roan's neck.

The roan was very still now. It seemed relaxed and no longer vigilant. Continuing to stroke it with his right hand, Travis released the snap with his left, and before the roan realized that once more it was free, Travis had vaulted up into the saddle.

The roan whirled around twice as it pulled away from the post. Travis had both feet in the stirrups and this time he had a good seat and for the instant he was almost overwhelmed with confidence.

He could feel his body sway with the old ease and effortlessness with the first harsh movements of the roan and Travis almost sang with joy. The roan kicked up its hind end and then reared sharply. Then it started whirling again, raising a great cloud of dust that almost gagged Travis, but he went along with it, sticking like a burr to the saddle, exulting all the while.

Abruptly the roan changed tactics. Its back arched and it began hopping stiff-legged across the corral. With each try the horse seemed to go a trifle higher and come down a trifle harder. The jolts began to jar up Travis' spine. He felt the joy, the assurance ebb from him.

It was not a question of sticking in the saddle any more, he thought. He was sure he could do that, but there was something wrong inside him. His belly seemed full of pain. It was as if the jolts had torn something loose in there and it kept bouncing up and down, agonizingly, with each movement of the roan. The doctors had lied, Travis knew now. He was not well. He was all torn up and busted inside. He could feel something break loose and rise up to gag in his throat. He could no longer breathe. He was a sick man and he had no business on a bucking horse.

The roan had reached the other end of the corral and now it swerved up against the poles, seeking to scrape Travis off the saddle. Travis saw the bars come at him and he waited for no more. He threw himself wildly out of the kak. He hit the ground badly and went sprawling. However, he recovered quickly and was half-way to his feet when the roan hit him. It was so sudden and unexpected that at first Travis had no idea he had been struck. He left himself being barrelled along over the ground and only then it occurred to him that the roan had turned on him. Panic clogged Travis' throat. Luckily, he had been knocked toward the side of the corral, and as the roan, squealing with rage, came smashing back Travis rolled to safety beneath the bottom bar.

Travis lurched up on his knees, trembling with fear and fury. His face was all wet but he did not know if it was from sweat or tears or blood. His thigh ached furiously and for the moment he was afraid that his leg had been broken again.

The roan smashed up against the side of the corral once more. Then the horse put its head down between its front legs and went bucking frenziedly around the enclosure. Travis raised a fist and brandished it at the roan.

'I'll fix you,' he shouted. 'I'll show you if you can get away with this. I'll fix you for good!'

He jumped to his feet, raging with defeat and frustration, and went at a run up to the house. He got his Winchester and ran back to the corral.

'Damn you,' he screamed at the roan, 'see how you like this!'

He had the sights lined up with the roan's head when the sudden thought struck Travis and he froze there. The roan had stopped bucking. It stood, startled and wild, head flung up, in the middle of the corral. Travis knew he could not miss, but the thought he had just experienced caused him to hold his fire.

He was all right inside. There was nothing wrong with his belly, there was nothing loose in him, there was nothing clogging his throat any more. It had been panic that had caused the pain and had thrown him off the roan. You're really yellow, Travis, his mind said to him. . . .

'I'm not yellow,' he screamed aloud at himself. 'It's that damn devil in there. He scraped me off. I'm not yellow.' He was almost sobbing now. The rifle fell from his shoulder. 'How can I be yellow after all the tough broncs that I've topped?'

The misery and shame combined with the rage that still remained in him. 'Damn you,' he cried at the roan and began to slide between the poles into the corral. 'I'll show you if I'm yellow. I'll show you if I can't ride you. You scrape me off again and I'll put a slug through your brain!'

He ran up to the roan in a frenzy and made a grab for the reins but the horse whirled and galloped away. Half-blind with fury, alternately cursing and sobbing, Travis snatched his rope and went after the roan. He cornered it and dropped the loop over its neck and then, hand over hand, he went swiftly up to the lunging, plunging animal.

The roan started to rear but Travis had a good hold on the hackamore and he stubbornly refused to let go. The roan snorted and swung away, but Travis, raging, hung on. He made a wild, leaping grab for the saddlehorn and caught it and went up into the saddle. The roan, squealing with fury, was pitching and lunging even before Travis hit the kak. The jolt of it cracked his teeth together but he stayed on and caught up the lines and found the flapping stirrups with his boots.

The roan was in the full grip of its fury as it went bucking savagely across the corral. Travis did not expect to stay on. He had never thought the roan to be so mean and savage. Those other attempts had been picnics compared to this try. He fully expected to be thrown at any instant.

171

Realizing that defeat was imminent, the rage in Travis grew. As the jolts jarred him, he began to scream, 'Go on, pitch me off. Throw me. Throw me and I'll put a slug in your brain!'

He was sobbing with anger. Stinging tears ran down his cheeks. He thought it might be blood but he knew better. It was only his cowardice that made him think it was blood pouring out of his nose and mouth.

'Pitch me off,' he screamed at the roan. 'Throw me. The gun is ready for you, you damn devil. Throw me!'

The roan aimed for the side of the corral but Travis saw it coming and at the last instant he swung his leg out of the way and stayed on the roan with only one foot in a stirrup to support him. The horse smashed with insane fury against the poles and rebounded and Travis settled back in the kak again. His spurs raked the roan's flanks.

'Throw me,' he shouted, knowing that he did not have long to go. 'Pitch me off, you red devil. You'll throw me only once more. I promise you that!'

The wetness on his face tasted like blood, but again he was certain it was just his cowardice playing tricks on him. He knew he would never conquer his fear. Once he went off the roan he knew he would never mount another bucker. Travis was crying openly now.

'Throw me,' he shouted. 'What are you waiting for? Throw me and get a slug in your head. Come on, throw me!'

The roan squealed and reared high and for a breathtaking instant trembled there, then it came crashing down on its back. But Travis had sensed this coming and he'd kicked free of the stirrups and was down on the ground as the roan crashed on its back. It was instinct more than anything else that sent Travis back into the saddle as the roan righted itself and lunged up on its feet. It started to rear again and Travis raked hard with the spurs and sawed on the lines and this time the roan did not crash over backwards. It came down on its four hoofs and started crowhopping.

'Throw me,' Travis screamed. 'Pitch me off, you devil. Go ahead and throw me!'

Now it dawned on Travis that the jolts were not so hard any

more. The roan's fury seemed to have diminished. Its stiff-legged hopping was being done in a half-hearted manner and Travis could not believe that he had triumphed.

The roan tried two more desultory hops and then brought up still, its legs spraddled and its foam-flecked flanks heaving. Travis could hear the whistling of the roan's breath and he lifted a hand to wipe some of the sweat off his face, and it was then that he noticed it was really blood that was pouring out of his nose....

Travis awoke and saw that it was evening. He rose, fully clothed, from his bunk and went outside. He was still sore from the effects of his ride but it was a welcome stiffness. For the first time in more than a year he felt at peace with himself.

He walked slowly down to the corral. The roan was standing listlessly as if it, too, were fully spent and Travis supposed that it really was. Travis stood and stared at the roan and he began to feel something inside that he just could not put into words. He guessed it was gratitude but then he started to think it was more than that.

The roan turned its head once and looked briefly at Travis. Then it averted its gaze and just stood there. It no longer was a proud, untamed animal. Its spirit was broken like Travis' had almost been broken. The roan would make a good mount, Travis thought, but its fight was gone for ever.

Thinking thus, Travis wondered if it had really been worth it.

THE SOUND OF GUNFIRE ★

By John O'Reilly

HE rode into town on a sunless day with the sky as grey as the streaks in his hair, and he swung out of the saddle where a group of rannies were talking in front of the saloon. He wasn't much over thirty-five, despite the grey hair, and he had a tanned, bony face, slightly haggard, and strange-looking eyes. They were grey, too, and completely blank and expressionless, and they didn't waver or move when he sidestepped the other men and walked through the batwings.

'I'm looking for McCord,' he told the barkeep. 'This his place?'

There was a big sign outside the saloon which said *McCord's,* and a couple of *No Credit* notices signed with McCord's name behind the bar. The keep stared at the grey-haired man for a moment, then guffawed and slammed a dirty hand on the bar.

'No education, huh?' He jerked a thumb at the signs. 'Can't you read, pard?'

The man reached forward, took hold of the bartender's shirtfront, and pulled him across the bar. His expressionless eyes stared straight ahead. 'You can't read when you're blind, mister. Get McCord.'

He released the keep and listened to his footsteps move down the length of the saloon. A minute later he heard two pairs of feet returning, and one of them moved into position next to him.

'Nice to meet you, McCord,' he said softly.

The man next to him had a deep, harsh voice, 'How do you know I'm McCord?'

'Easy,' the grey-eyed man said. 'You fit your description. Tall, maybe six-four, heavy, smooth-shaven.'

'The keep told me you were blind.'

'I've been blind for years,' the stranger said. 'Enough years so it doesn't matter . . .'

'When I talked to the barkeep, I smelled his stinking rotgut

174

breath right in my nose, which makes him slightly taller than I am—say six-three. His head didn't touch the drape when he walked into your room in the back but I heard the drape rustle up high when you walked out—so you're taller. Heavy, too—easy to tell that by the way your feet hit the floor. And smooth-shaven—you rubbed your jaw a minute ago, and I heard a rasping sound instead of the soft one you get when you stroke hair.'

'You're guessing,' the other man said.

'I don't guess about things like that,' the blind man said. 'A schoolteacher I used to know told me it's called the law of compensation—Nature providin' that when a man loses one sense another gets twice as strong. That's the way it is with me—I can hear things no one else can hear. That's why I know you're rolling a smoke on heavy brown paper. White paper has a softer sound.'

McCord shook his head. 'Very interesting, mister,' he said. 'Very interesting. You learn something every day.' He paused. 'But what I want to know is, what's it got to do with me?'

'I'm just startin' my qualifications, McCord. Fact is, I rode into town to do a job for you.'

'What kind of job?'

The blind man leaned forward. 'I hear tell,' he said, 'that you want Johnny Hale dead.'

McCord's hand jerked, and his whisky glass tumbled to the floor. It shattered loudly, and there was silence for a minute. Then McCord said: 'You're crazy.'

'Sane as any gunfighter,' the blind man said. 'My price, McCord, is one thousand dollars.'

'I tell you you're crazy,' McCord said hoarsely. 'And even if I did want somebody killed, what kind of hired gun would *you* make? A blind man—you wouldn't even know where to shoot.'

The grey-eyed man laughed, a laugh as unhumorous and un-emotional as his eyes. 'McCord,' he said, 'I've been listening to your clock on the wall there ever since I came into this place. You've probably never noticed it, but the pendulum makes one sound when it swings to the right, and another when it swings to the left.' His gun flashed in his hand, and a bullet tore the pendulum neatly off its mount. 'It was swinging right that time.'

He laughed again. 'How about it, McCord?'

There was another dead silence. Then McCord said, chokingly, 'Out. Get out, don't come into this place again.'

Smiling gently, the blind man walked out of the saloon.

Johnny Hale's office was an airless little room just beyond the schoolhouse, a desk and two chairs in back of a rusty-hinged door with *Sheriff* scrawled on it in crude black letters. The blind man went there directly, his nostrils twitching slightly as he approached the desk. 'Hale around?'

'Me,' the man behind the desk said. He didn't sound like much more than a button, maybe a few years over voting age. It was the way the blind man had figured he would sound, from his description: unruly sandy hair, kid's face with a couple of freckles on the bridge of his nose, wide grin. 'What can I do for you?'

'Nothing much,' the blind man said. His long fingers found the empty chair and sat down. 'I just thought we ought to meet, seein' I've been volunteerin' to kill you.'

Hale's breath whooshed out in a rush. 'Say that again.'

The blind man smiled. 'I've just been down to McCord's saloon, tellin' McCord my price to put a bullet in you is a thousand dollars. Cheap, too, considerin' the prices some hired guns draw.'

Hale jumped to his feet and came around the desk. He thrust his face close to the blind man's. 'What is this, mister—some kind of joke?'

'No joke a-tall,' the grey-eyed man said casually. 'Word's pretty general all around this territory that McCord is out to get you, and I just sorta thought I'd get *my* bid in. Honest shootin' work is scarce these days, Johnny.' He paused. 'Want to make a counter-offer on McCord's gizzard, son?'

He could feel Hale staring hard at him. 'I'll counter-offer you right into the hoosegow in a minute,' the Sheriff said slowly. 'I don't need any hired gunnies to do my work for me. I'll get McCord before he gets me—but I'll do it legal.'

'Got grounds, Johnny?'

'None of your business,' Hale snapped. He paused. 'Well, maybe it is, if you're with McCord.' His hands slapped the leather of his holsters. 'Mister, I'm so close to pinnin' cattle-stealin' on McCord that you'd better make your play right now, if you're going to make it at all. Couple more days, and you'll have to take your pay out of McCord's pocket while he's hangin' from the end of a rope.'

The blind man grinned. 'Easy, son, easy–don't get your temper up. Right now everything's still in what you might call the negotiation stage.' He got to his feet, his hands away from his sides. 'I'm sure glad you're close to the proof, Johnny. Your ideas on the subject are no secret around town, you know, and it would be kind of embarrassin' if you were accusin' the wrong guy.'

Hale swore. 'McCord's behind all the cattle-rustlin' in the last couple of months, all right; I'm not the kind of hombre who talks without reason.'

The blind man smiled again, and walked to the door. 'That's what I kinda figgered,' he said. Then he turned.

'Guess you've noticed by now that I'm a sort a nosy bird,' he said. 'One more question, son: you happen to have your own ranch?'

Hale stared at him. 'Huh? Me? No, course not–sheriffin's my full-time job. It's all I can do hangin' around town keepin' things orderly.'

'That's what I figgered, too,' the blind man said. His blank eyes stared at the Sheriff for a moment. 'Well, so long, son–maybe I'll be seeing you again soon.'. . .

He thought it would come the moment he passed the schoolhouse, which was still lighted, but the pressure against his eyes lessened and he knew the light had gone out just as he reached it. Then he stopped. The light footsteps he had heard leaving the schoolhouse were running toward him, and when he heard a girl's voice say, 'Bill! Bill Reynolds!' – the same voice, grown-up now, but with the familiar quality of sweetness–he knew it was Lorna Stone.

He turned and said, 'Been a long time, hasn't it?'

She was in his arms and her lips touched his before she answered. 'Almost eight years,' she said. 'Eight years – but you came right away.'

'Us blind fellers ain't kept too busy, Lorna,' he said softly. 'Anyway, I wanted to know if you grew up the way I figgered....' He heard the swift intake of her breath. 'Your–your eyes, Bill. How can you...?'

'Lots of ways, Lorna,' he said. 'That perfume, for instance–not the strong, smelly stuff some gals wear–but soft and gentle and just right. And the fact that you're at the schoolhouse–takes courage to take a job as unpopular as book-learnin' out here.' He reached out and touched her hair. 'And your hair's long and soft, and probably just as red as when–I used to be able to see it. You're a beautiful girl, Lorna.'

Her voice was strained when she answered. 'Johnny–Johnny Hale, the boy I'm going to marry–he says I am.'

The blind man's face lost its smile. 'I've just been talkin' to him, Lorna–and I'm afraid your letter was right. That boy *is* usin' his mouth too much....'

'Then you think–'

'That McCord *isn't* behind the rustling?' he finished for her. 'No Lorna, I think Hale's right about that. But he's still talkin' too much.' He paused. 'Lorna, there's something I've got to tell you....'

There was a sudden sharp crackling sound in the brush down the road. He said rapidly, 'I'll have to save it. Lorna, honey, get into that schoolhouse and stay there until I come for you. Quick!'

She started to protest. 'Bill–' she said.

'Inside. You wrote that I was the only friend you could turn to. Inside, before you don't have any at all.'

When she entered the schoolhouse, he started to walk forward. Might as well get under way, and over.

The shot came just when he knew it would–the moment he stepped away from the darkened schoolhouse into the area which pressure on his eyes told him was lighted. For a moment he felt wild, muscle-stiffening fear, the way he had felt as a kid when owlhoots killed his mother and dad and fired the bullet which left him alive but blind, and then it passed away. He fell on to his stomach, and his gun leaped forward in his hand.

He fired twice rapidly in the direction of the sound, and heard footsteps running. Then another shot snapped back at him, close, and he knew the other had found cover and was trying to finish his work. He grinned crookedly and leaped back into the darkness.

We're on even ground now, he thought—*maybe not so even, at that. Any fool ought to know better than to tangle with a blind man in the dark, but he won't.*

He waited until another shot came, hitting not so close. Then calmly, methodically, the way a man does a thing he has done often before, he fired again—and heard the familiar coughing, gasping shout. The sound of a dying man, choking off into silence.

Casually, the blind man reached out and felt along the ground until he found a fist-sized rock. He flipped it into the air and listened to it land in the soft earth a few feet away.

A bullet whanged metallically against the rock.

So it wasn't over. He fired carefully at the sound, and heard another body drop.

There was a long silence, and he realized that the men across the road were beginning to understand that a gun battle in pitch darkness with a blind man was suicidal. They were firing by guess-work; he was right at home. The blind man heard soft, rapid whispers—three voices—and they began to run toward him. They came from different directions.

He caught one of them with a bullet in the stomach, and then the other two were upon him. He brought his knife into play.

It was the colour of silver and had a long razor-sharp blade, and it came from the blind man's sleeve and moved upward with a tearing movement into the body of the nearest man. The man started to curse and then bubbles of blood cut off his voice, and he made a sound deep in his stomach and rolled over on one side.

The other man twisted out of the way of the knife, and his back fell against the blind man's right hand. The blind man stiffened the hand and pulled it upwards. He rabbit-punched twice, and the man slumped to the ground without a sound.

Calmly, the blind man got to his feet and shot him three times through the chest.

He took a deep breath. 'I never do fight fair with killers,' he said, and bent down beside the man he'd shot. The man was still alive; thick gasps gurgled through his lips.

'McCord?' the blind man asked.

The dying man didn't answer for a minute. Then his voice, McCord's voice, said, spitting the words out: 'Go to hell.'

'Not me,' the grey-eyed man said. 'That's where you're going, McCord, any minute now.' He paused. 'Why'd you jump me tonight?

The thick gasps continued; no answer.

'McCord,' the blind man said again. 'You're checking out soon. Why don't you tell me?' And then he stopped: McCord wouldn't be answering anyone again.

The blind man sighed and reloaded his gun and cleaned his knife and put them away. Nobody had come at the sound of gunfire. This was on the edge of town, and it wasn't surprising about anybody else—but Johnny Hale should have shown better sense.

Some hombres aren't as smart as a weak-minded cayuse, the blind man thought sadly, and he opened the schoolhouse door and called Lorna. 'I was going to tell you about this,' he said, 'but maybe I'd better show you.'

Johnny Hale was at the little cook-stove in the room adjoining his office when Lorna and the grey-eyed blind man entered, and he whirled and let the pan clatter to the floor.

'Don't you ever investigate shooting, Johnny?' the blind man asked.

'Shooting?' the Sheriff said, 'I—didn't hear any shooting.'

'Son,' the blind man said, 'your ears would have to be as useless as my eyes to keep you from hearing the shooting that just went on.'

'Your eyes?' Hale said. 'What's wrong with ...'

'Now let's not act damn silly, son,' the grey-eyed man said, gently. 'It doesn't take much to spot a blind man. I was kind of curious when you didn't say anything when I felt around for a chair, but that, I know now, was because one of McCord's boys beat me to your place and told you about me.' He sighed.

'You know, it sure would have been more convincing for you to have come running out just before—but I guess you were too sure things would go right to bother.'

He heard Hale slump heavily in a chair. 'I won't even try to figger out what you're talkin' about.'

'Ain't hard to figger, Johnny,' the blind man said. 'Puttin' it in black and white, there's just two things I don't like: outlaws, and people who try to kill me or get me killed.' He rolled a smoke with his left hand and kept his right close to his holster. 'It just looks to me like you fit in both those classes.'

Hale's answer came in a harsh, bitter voice. 'I kind of figured you were a mite loco when you first came in here. Now I'm beginning to think it's a lot more than a mite.'

The blind man shook his head sadly. 'Aw, now, Johnny,' he said, 'you shouldn't go calling people names when you know it isn't so. Listen, son, and tell me if I'm shootin' close to the target.

'I first began to figure somethin' was funny when Lorna wrote and told me she was scared of trouble because you'd been tellin' everybody around town that McCord was behind the rustlin', and McCord was tellin' everyone around town he was going to get you. Hell, Johnny, that wasn't as smart a scheme as you thought.'

'You're still talkin' loco,' Hale said.

'It'll made sense soon. Your scheme wasn't so smart because, in a wide-open town like this one, a feller like McCord doesn't go around threatenin' things for months without doin' something about it—and a sheriff doesn't accuse a man of rustlin' unless he's got plenty of proof.

''Course, you and I know why you started that talk. You figgered if everybody thought you and McCord was enemies, nobody'd ever connect you together on the cattle-stealin'. Later on, I guess, when there wasn't too much left to rustle, you planned to say you found you were wrong, and apologize.' He spat. 'Sure must've been awkward when a professional gun like I said I was come up to McCord and offered to do a job on you....'

'Lorna,' Hale cut in, his voice suddenly thin and high. 'You brought this crazy man here. Tell him he's wrong; tell him he'll get in trouble spreading stuff like this....'

181

The blind man felt Lorna's fingers pressing more tightly on his arm. 'No, Johnny,' she said, slowly, 'I'm afraid I can't. I think he's right. I think now that I've known it from the start...'

'All right,' Hale said. His words were coming faster now, feverishly, hysteria in them. 'If you want to stick with your blind boy-friend there, go ahead—but I tell you he's crazy. Everything he's said is guesswork....'

And then the blind man stepped closer. 'It's not guesswork, Johnny,' he said. 'If you want to fool a man who can't see and has to rely on other senses, you better take baths more often. You told me before that you stay round town and haven't a ranch of your own—but the stink of cattle is all over you.

'Where did you get it if you haven't been rustling with McCord?'...

Young Hale was fast, the blind man knew that the moment he heard the slap of hand against leather. He pulled his own gun and, fanning his shots, jerked the trigger three times. He heard his bullets thud into flesh before Hale's first came, awry and heading for the side wall, and he knew Hale would be dead before he hit the floor.

He turned to the red-headed girl. Her body was warm and trembling against him.

'I'm sorry, Lorna,' he said. 'It would have happened to him sooner or later, anyway.'

He put his arm gently around her waist. 'I'll take you home,' he said, 'You'll feel better later on....'

'No,' she said. 'Not home. There's nothing for me here. I'm going back with you.'

They walked out into the clear night air, farther and farther away from the echoes of the sound of gunfire—and he wanted to tell her that he could not let her come, that he could not let her saddle herself with a blind man. But then she kissed him and he forgot all about it, and somehow the subject never came up after that.

SERGEANT HOUCK

By Jack Schaefer

SERGEANT HOUCK stopped his horse just below the top of the ridge ahead. The upper part of his body was silhouetted against the sky line as he rose in his stirrups to peer over the crest. He urged the horse on up and the two of them, the man and the horse, were sharp and distinct against the copper sky. After a moment he turned and rode down to the small troop waiting. He reined beside Lieutenant Imler.

'It's there, sir. Alongside a creek in the next hollow. Maybe a third of a mile.'

Lieutenant Imler looked at him coldly. 'You took your time, Sergeant. Smack on the top, too.'

'Couldn't see plain, sir. Sun was in my eyes.'

'Wanted them to spot you, eh, Sergeant?'

'No, sir. Sun was bothering me. I don't think–'

'Forget it, Sergeant. I don't like this either.'

Lieutenant Imler was in no hurry. He led the troop slowly up the hill. The real fuss was fifty-some miles away. Captain McKay was hogging the honours there. Here he was, tied to this sideline detail. Twenty men. Ten would have been enough. Ten and an old hand like Sergeant Houck.

With his drawn sabre pointing forward, Lieutenant Imler led the charge up and over the crest and down the long slope to the Indian village. There were some scattered shots from bushes by the creek, ragged pops indicating poor powder and poorer weapons, probably fired by the last of the old men left behind when the young braves departed in war paint ten days before. The village was silent and deserted.

Lieutenant Imler surveyed the ground they'd taken. 'Spectacular achievement,' he muttered to himself. He beckoned Sergeant Houck to him.

'Your redskin friend was right, Sergeant. This is it.'

'Knew he could be trusted, sir.'

'Our orders are to destroy the village. Send a squad out to round up any stock. There might be some horses around. We're to take them in.' Lieutenant Imler waved an arm at the thirty-odd skin-and-pole huts. 'Set the others to pulling those down. Burn what you can and smash everything else.'

'Right, sir.'

Lieutenant Imler rode into the slight shade of the cotton-woods along the creek. He wiped the dust from his face and set his campaign hat at a fresh angle to ease the crease the band had made on his forehead. Here he was, hot and tired and way out at the end of nowhere with another long ride ahead, while Captain McKay was having it out at last with Grey Otter and his renegade warriors somewhere between the Turkey Foot and the Washakie. He relaxed to wait in the saddle, beginning to frame his report in his mind.

'Pardon, sir.'

Lieutenant Imler looked around. Sergeant Houck was standing nearby with something in his arms, something that squirmed and seemed to have dozens of legs and arms.

'What the devil is that, Sergeant?'

'A baby, sir. Or rather, a boy. Two years old, sir.'

'How the devil do you know? By his teeth?'

'His mother told me, sir.'

'His mother?'

'Certainly, sir. She's right here.'

Lieutenant Imler saw her then, standing beside a neighbouring tree, shrinking into the shadow and staring at Sergeant Houck and the squirming child. He leaned to look closer. She wore a shapeless, sacklike covering with slits for her arms and head. She was sun-and-windburned, dark yet not as dark as he expected. And there was no mistaking the colour of her hair. It was light brown and long and coiled in a bun on her neck.

'Sergeant! It's a white woman!'

'Right, sir. Her name's Cora Sutliff. The wagon train she was with was wiped out by a raiding party. She and another woman were taken along. The other woman died. She didn't. The village bought her. She's been in Grey Otter's lodge.' Sergeant Houck smacked the squirming boy briskly and tucked him under one arm. He looked straight at Lieutenant Imler. 'That was three years ago, sir.'

'Three years? Then that boy—'

'That's right, sir.'

Captain McKay looked up from his desk to see Sergeant Houck stiff at attention before him. It always gave him a feeling of satisfaction to see this great, granite man. The replacements they were sending these days, raw and unseasoned, were enough to shake his faith in the service. But as long as there remained a sprinkling of these case-hardened old-time regulars, the Army would still be the Army.

'At ease, Sergeant.'

'Thank you, sir.'

Captain McKay drummed his fingers on the desk. This was a ridiculous situation and the solid, impassive bulk of Sergeant Houck made it seem even more so.

'That woman, Sergeant. She's married. The husband's alive— wasn't with the train when it was attacked. He's been located. Has a place about twenty miles out of Laramie. The name's right and everything checks. You're to take her there and turn her over with the troop's compliments.'

'Me, sir?'

'She asked for you. The big man who found her. Lieutenant Imler says that's you.'

Sergeant Houck considered this expressionlessly. 'And about the boy, sir?'

'He goes with her.' Captain McKay drummed on the desk again. 'Speaking frankly, Sergeant, I think she's making a mistake. I suggested she let us see that the boy got back to the tribe. Grey Otter's dead and after that affair two weeks ago there's not many of the men left. But they'll be on the reservation now and he'd be taken care of. She wouldn't hear of it; said if he had to go she would, too.' Captain McKay felt his former indignation rising again. 'I say she's playing the fool. You agree with me, of course.'

'No, sir. I don't.'

'And why the devil not?'

'He's her son, sir.'

'But he's– Well, that's neither here nor there, Sergeant. It's not our affair. We deliver her and there's an end to it. You'll draw expense money and start within the hour.'

'Right, sir.' The sergeant straightened and made for the door.

'Houck.'

'Yes, sir.'

'Take good care of her–and that damn' kid.'

'Right, sir.'

Captain McKay stood by the window and watched the small cavalcade go past toward the post gateway. Lucky that his wife had come with him to this god-forsaken station lost in the prairie wasteland. Without her they would have been in a fix with the woman. As it was, the woman looked like a woman now. And why shouldn't she, wearing his wife's third-best crinoline dress? It was a bit large, but it gave her a proper feminine appearance. His wife had enjoyed fitting her, from the skin out, everything except shoes. Those were too small. The woman seemed to prefer her worn moccasins anyway. And she was uncomfortable in the clothes. But she was decently grateful for them, insisting she would have them returned or would pay for them somehow. She was riding past the window, sidesaddle on his wife's horse, still with that strange shrinking air about her, not so much frightened as remote, as if she could not quite connect with what was happening to her, what was going on around her.

Behind her was Private Lakin, neat and spruce in his uniform, with the boy in front of him on the horse. The boy's legs stuck out on each side of the small, improvised pillow tied to the forward arch of the saddle to give him a better seat. He looked like a weird, dark-haired doll bobbing with the movements of the horse.

And there beside the woman, shadowing her in the mid-morning, was that extra icongruous touch, the great hulk of Sergeant Houck, straight in his saddle, taking this as he took everything, with no excitement and no show of any emotion, a job to be done.

They went past and Captain McKay watched them ride out through the gateway. It was not quite so incongruous after all. As he had discovered on many a tight occasion, there was something comforting in the presence of that big man. Nothing ever shook him. You might never know exactly what went on inside his close-cropped skull, but you could be certain that what needed to be done he would do.

They were scarcely out of sight of the post when the boy began squirming. Private Lakin clamped him to the pillow with a capable right hand. The squirming persisted. The boy seemed determined to escape from what he regarded as an alien captor. Silent, intent, he writhed on the pillow. Private Lakin's hand and arm grew weary. He tickled his horse forward with his heels until he was close behind the others.

'Beg pardon, sir.'

Sergeant Houck shifted in his saddle and looked around. 'Yes?'

'He's trying to get away, sir. It'd be easier if I tied him down. Could I use my belt, sir?'

Sergeant Houck held in his horse to drop back alongside Private Lakin. 'Kids don't need tying,' he said. He reached out and plucked the boy from in front of Private Lakin and laid him, face down, across the withers of his own horse and smacked him sharply. Then he set him back on the pillow. The boy sat still, very still. Sergeant Houck pushed his left hand into his left side pocket and pulled out a fistful of small hard biscuits. He passed these to Private Lakin. 'Stick one of these in his mouth when he gets restless.'

Sergeant Houck urged his horse forward until he was beside the woman once more. She had turned her head to watch and she stared sidewise at him for a long moment, then looked straight forward again.

They came to the settlement in the same order: the woman and Sergeant Houck side by side in the lead, Private Lakin and the boy tagging behind at a respectful distance. Sergeant Houck dismounted and helped the woman down and handed the boy to her. He saw Private Lakin looking wistfully at the painted front of the settlement's one saloon and tapped him on one knee. 'Scat,' he said and watched Private Lakin turn his horse and ride off, leading the other two horses.

Then he led the woman into the squat frame building that served as general store and post office and stage stop. He settled the woman and her child on a preserved-goods box and went to the counter to arrange for their fares. When he came back to sit on another box near her, the entire permanent male population of the settlement was assembled just inside the door, all eleven of them staring at the woman.

'. . . that's the one. . . .'

'. . . an Indian had her. . . .'

'. . . shows in the kid. . . .'

Sergeant Houck looked at the woman. She was staring at the floor and the blood was leaving her face. He started to rise and felt her hand on his arm. She had leaned over quickly and clutched his sleeve.

'Please,' she said. 'Don't make trouble account of me.'

'Trouble?' said Sergeant Houck. 'No trouble.' He stood up and confronted the fidgeting men by the door. 'I've seen kids around this place. Some of them small. This one needs decent clothes and the store here doesn't stock them.'

The men stared at him, startled, and then at the wide-eyed boy in his clean but patched skimpy cloth covering. Five or six of them went out through the door and disappeared in various directions. The others scattered through the store. Sergeant Houck stood sentinel, relaxed and quiet by his box, and those who had gone out straggled back, several embarrassed and empty-handed, the rest proud with their offerings. Sergeant Houck took the boy from the woman's lap and stood him on his box. He measured the offerings against the small body and chose a small red checked shirt and a small pair of overalls. He set the one pair of small scuffed shoes aside. 'Kids don't need shoes,' he said. 'Only in winter.'

When the coach rolled in, it was empty and they had it to themselves for the first hours. Dust drifted steadily through the windows and the silence inside was a persistent thing. The woman did not want to talk. She had lost all liking for it and would speak only when necessary. And Sergeant Houck used words with a natural economy, for the sole simple purpose of conveying or obtaining information that he regarded as pertinent to the business immediately in hand. Only once did he speak during these hours and then only to set a fact straight in his mind. He kept his eyes fixed on the scenery outside as he spoke.

'Did he treat you all right?'

The woman made no pretence of misunderstanding him. 'Yes,' she said.

The coach rolled on and the dust drifted. 'He beat me once,' she said and four full minutes passed before she finished the thought. 'Maybe it was right. I wouldn't work.'

They stopped for a quick meal at a lonely ranch house and ate in silence while the man there helped the driver change horses. It was two mail stops later, at the next change, that another passenger climbed in and plopped his battered suitcase and himself on the front seat opposite them. He was of medium height and plump. He wore city clothes and had quick eyes and features that seemed small in the plumpness of his face. He took out a handkerchief and wiped his face and took off his hat to wipe all the way up his forehead. He laid the hat on top of the suitcase and moved restlessly on the seat, trying to find a comfortable position.

'You three together?'

'Yes,' said Sergeant Houck.

'Your wife then?'

'No,' said Sergeant Houck. He looked out the window on his side and studied the far horizon.

The coach rolled on and the man's quick eyes examined the three of them and came to rest on the woman's feet.

'Begging your pardon, lady, but why do you wear those things? Moccasins, aren't they? They more comfortable?'

She shrank back further in the seat and the blood began to leave her face.

'No offence, lady,' said the man. 'I just wondered—' He stopped. Sergeant Houck was looking at him.

'Dust's bad,' said Sergeant Houck. 'And the flies this time of year. Best to keep your mouth closed.' He looked out the window again, and the only sounds were the running beat of the hoofs and the creakings of the old coach.

A front wheel struck a stone and the coach jolted up at an angle and lurched sideways and the boy gave a small whimper. The woman pulled him on to her lap.

'Say,' said the man. 'Where'd you ever pick up that kid? Looks like–' He stopped. Sergeant Houck was reaching up and rapping against the top of the coach. The driver's voice could be heard shouting at the horses and the coach stopped. One of the doors opened and the driver peered in. Instinctively he picked Sergeant Houck.

'What's the trouble, soldier?'

'No trouble,' said Sergeant Houck. 'Our friend here wants to ride up with you.' He looked at the plump man. 'Less dust up there. It's healthy and gives a good view.'

'Now, wait a minute,' said the man. 'Where'd you get the idea–'

'Healthy,' said Sergeant Houck.

The driver looked at the bleak, impassive hardness of Sergeant Houck and at the twitching softness of the plump man. 'Reckon it would be,' he said. 'Come along. I'll boost you up.'

The coach rolled along the false-fronted one street of a mushroom town and stopped before a frame building tagged Hotel. One of the coach doors opened and the plump man retrieved his hat and suitcase and scuttled into the building. The driver appeared at the coach door. 'Last meal here before the night run,' he said.

When they came out, the shadows were long and fresh horses had been harnessed. As they settled themselves again, a new driver, whip in hand, climbed up to the high seat and gathered the reins into his left hand. The whip cracked and the coach lurched forward and a young man ran out of the low building across the street carrying a saddle. He ran alongside and heaved the saddle up on the roof inside the guardrail. He pulled at the door and managed to scramble in as the coach picked up speed. He dropped on to the front seat, puffing deeply. 'Evening, ma'am,' he said between puffs. 'And you, general.' He leaned forward to slap the boy gently along the jaw. 'And you too, bub.'

Sergeant Houck looked at the lean young man, at the faded Levis tucked into high-heeled boots, the plaid shirt, the amiable competent young face. He grunted a greeting, unintelligible but a pleasant sound.

'A man's legs ain't made for running,' said the young man. 'Just to fork a horse. That last drink was near too long.'

'The Army'd put some starch in those legs,' said Sergeant Houck.

'Maybe. Maybe that's why I ain't in the Army.' The young man sat quietly, relaxed to the jolting of the coach. 'Is there some other topic of genteel conversation you folk'd want to worry some?'

'No,' said Sergeant Houck.

'Then maybe you'll pardon me,' said the young man. 'I hoofed it a lot of miles to-day.' He worked hard at his boots and at last got them off and tucked them out of the way on the floor. He hitched himself up and over on the seat until he was resting on one hip. He put an arm on the window sill and cradled his head on it. His head dropped down and he was asleep.

Sergeant Houck felt a small bump on his left side. The boy had toppled against him. Sergeant Houck set the small body across his lap with head nestled into the crook of his right arm. He leaned his head down and heard the soft little last sigh as drowsiness overcame the boy. He looked sidewise at the woman and dimly made out the outline of her head falling forward and jerking back up and he reached his left arm along the top of the seat until his hand touched her far shoulder. He felt her shoulder stiffen and then relax as she moved closer and leaned toward him. He slipped down lower in the seat so that her head could reach his shoulder and he felt the gentle touch of her brown hair on his neck above his shirt collar. He waited patiently and at last he could tell by her steady deep breathing that all fright had left her and all her thoughts were stilled.

The coach reached a rutted stretch and began to sway and the young man stirred and began to slide on the smooth leather of his seat. Sergeant Houck put up a foot and braced it against the seat edge and the young man's body rested against it. Sergeant Houck leaned his head back on the top of the seat. The stars came out in the clear sky and the running beat of the hoofs had the rhythm of a cavalry squad at a steady trot and gradually Sergeant Houck softened slightly into sleep.

Sergeant Houck awoke, as always, all at once and aware. The coach had stopped. From the sounds outside, fresh horses were being buckled into the traces. The first light of dawn was creeping into the coach. He raised his head and he realized that he was stiff.

The young man was awake. He was inspecting the vast leather sole of Sergeant Houck's shoe. His eyes flicked up and met Sergeant Houck's eyes and he grinned.

'That's impressive footwear,' he whispered. 'You'd need starch in the legs with hoofs like that.' He sat up and stretched, long and reaching, like a lazy young animal. 'Hell,' he whispered again. 'You must be stiff as a branding iron.' He took hold of Sergeant Houck's leg at the knee and hoisted it slightly so that Sergeant Houck could bend it and ease the foot down to the floor without disturbing the sleeping woman leaning against him. He stretched out both hands and gently lifted the sleeping boy from Sergeant Houck's lap and sat back with the boy in his arms. The young man studied the boy's face. 'Can't be yours,' he whispered.

'No,' whispered Sergeant Houck.

'Must have some Indian strain.'

'Yes.'

The young man whispered down at the sleeping boy. 'You can't help that, can you, bub?'

'No,' said Sergeant Houck suddenly, out loud. 'He can't.'

The woman jerked upright and pulled over to the window on her side, rubbing at her eyes. The boy woke up, wide awake on the instant and saw the unfamiliar face above him and began to squirm violently. The young man clamped his arms tighter. 'Morning, ma'am,' he said. 'Looks like I ain't such a good nursemaid.'

Sergeant Houck reached out a hand and picked up the boy by a grip on the small overalls and deposited him in a sitting position on the seat beside the young man. The boy sat very still.

The sun climbed into plain view and now the coach was stirring the dust of a well-worn road. It stopped where another road crossed and the young man inside pulled on his boots. He bobbed his head in the direction of a group of low buildings up the side road. 'Think I'll try it there. They'll be peeling broncs about now and the foreman knows I can sit a saddle.' He opened a door and jumped to the ground and turned to poke his head in. 'Hope you make it right,' he said. 'Wherever you're heading.' The door closed and he could be heard scrambling up the back of the coach to get his saddle. There was a thump as he and the saddle hit the ground and then voices began outside, rising in tone.

Sergeant Houck pushed his head through the window beside him. The young man and the driver were facing each other over the saddle. The young man was pulling the pockets of his Levis inside out. 'Lookahere, Will,' he said. 'You know I'll kick in soon as I have some cash. Hell, I've hooked rides with you before.'

'Not now no more,' said the driver. 'The company's sore. They hear of this they'd have my job. I'll have to hold the saddle.'

'You touch that saddle and they'll pick you up in pieces from here to breakfast.'

Sergeant Houck fumbled for his inside jacket pocket. He whistled. The two men turned. He looked hard at the young man. 'There's something on the seat in here. Must have slipped out of your pocket.'

The young man leaned in and saw the two silver dollars on the hard seat and looked up at Sergeant Houck. 'You've been in spots yourself,' he said.

'Yes,' said Sergeant Houck.

The young man grinned. He picked up the coins in one hand and swung the other to slap Sergeant Houck's leg, sharp, stinging and grateful. 'Age ain't hurting you any, general,' he said.

The coach started up and the woman looked at Sergeant Houck. The minutes passed and still she looked at him.

'If I'd had brains enough to get married,' he said, 'might be I'd have had a son. Might have been one like that.'

The woman looked away, out her window. She reached up to pat at her hair and the firm line of her lips softened in the tiny imperceptible beginnings of a smile. The minutes passed and Sergeant Houck stirred again. 'It's the upbringing that counts,' he said and settled into silent immobility, watching the miles go by.

It was near noon when they stopped in Laramie and Sergeant Houck handed the woman out and tucked the boy under one arm and led the way to the waiting room. He settled the woman and the boy in two chairs and left them. He was back soon, driving a light buckboard wagon drawn by a pair of deep-barrelled chestnuts. The wagon bed was well padded with layers of empty burlap bags. He went into the waiting room and picked up the boy and beckoned to the woman to follow. He put the boy down on the burlap bags and helped the woman up on the driving seat.

'Straight out the road, they tell me,' he said. 'About fifteen miles. Then right along the creek. Can't miss it.'

He stood by the wagon, staring along the road. The woman leaned from the seat and clutched at his shoulder. Her voice was high and frightened. 'You're going with me?' Her fingers clung to his service jacket. 'Please! You've got to!'

Sergeant Houck put a hand over hers on his shoulder and released her fingers. 'Yes. I'm going.' He put the child in her lap and stepped to the seat and took the reins. The wagon moved forward.

'You're afraid,' he said.

'They haven't told him,' she said, 'about the boy.'

Sergeant Houck's hands tightened on the reins and the horses slowed to a walk. He clucked sharply to them and slapped the reins on their backs and they quickened again into a trot. The wagon topped a slight rise and the road sloped downward for a long stretch to where the green of trees and tall bushes showed in the distance. A jack rabbit started from the scrub growth by the roadside and leaped high and levelled out, a grey-brown streak. The horses shied and broke rhythm and quieted to a walk under the firm pressure of the reins. Sergeant Houck kept them at a walk, easing the heat out of their muscles, down the long slope to the trees. He let them step into the creek up to their knees and dip their muzzles in the clear running water. The front wheels of the wagon were in the creek and he reached behind him to find a tin dipper tucked among the burlap bags and leaned far out to dip up water for the woman, the boy and himself. He backed the team out of the creek and swung them into the ruts leading along the bank to the right.

The creek was on their left and the sun was behind them, warm on their backs, and the shadows of the horses pushed ahead. The shadows were longer, stretching farther ahead, when they rounded a bend along the creek and the buildings came in sight, the two-room cabin and the several lean-to sheds and the rickety pole corral. A man was standing by one of the sheds and when Sergeant Houck halted the team he came toward them and stopped about twenty feet away. He was not young, perhaps in his middle thirties, but with the young look of a man on whom the years have made no mark except that of the simple passing of time. He was tall, soft and loose-jointed in build, and indecisive in manner and movement. His eyes wavered as he looked at the woman, and the fingers of his hands hanging limp at his sides twitched as he waited for her to speak.

She climbed down her side of the wagon and faced him. She stood straight and the sun behind her shone on her hair. 'Well, Fred,' she said. 'I'm here.'

'Cora,' he said. 'It's been a long time, Cora. I didn't know you'd come so soon.'

'Why didn't you come get me? Why didn't you, Fred?'

'I didn't rightly know what to do, Cora. It was all so mixed up. Thinking you were dead. Then hearing about you. And what happened. I had to think about things. And I couldn't get away easy. I was going to try maybe next week.'

'I hoped you'd come. Right away when you heard.'

His body twisted uneasily while his feet remained flat and motionless on the ground. 'Your hair's still pretty,' he said. 'The way it used to be.'

Something like a sob caught in her throat and she started toward him. Sergeant Houck stepped down on the other side of the wagon and walked off to the creek and kneeled to bend and wash the dust from his face. He stood drying his face with a handkerchief and watching the little eddies of the current around several stones in the creek. He heard the voices behind him.

'Wait, Fred. There's something you have to know.'

'That kid? What's it doing here with you?'

'It's mine, Fred.'

'Yours? Where'd you get it?'

'It's my child. Mine.'

There was silence and then the man's voice, bewildered, hurt. 'So it's really true what they said. About that Indian.'

'Yes. He bought me. By their rules I belonged to him. I wouldn't be alive and here now, any other way. I didn't have any say about it.'

There was silence again and then the man spoke, self-pity creeping into his tone. 'I didn't count on anything like this.'

Sergeant Houck walked back to the wagon. The woman seemed relieved at the interruption. 'This is Sergeant Houck,' she said. 'He brought me all the way.'

The man nodded his head and raised a hand to shove back the sandy hair that kept falling forward on his forehead. 'I suppose I ought to thank you, soldier. All that trouble.'

'No trouble,' said Sergeant Houck.

The man pushed at the ground in front of him with one shoe, poking the toe into the dirt and studying it. 'I suppose we ought to go inside. It's near suppertime. I guess you'll be taking a meal here, soldier, before you start back to town.'

'Right,' said Sergeant Houck. 'And I'm tired. I'll stay the night, too. Start in the morning. Sleep in one of those sheds.'

The man pushed at the ground more vigorously. The little pile of dirt in front of his shoe seemed to interest him a great deal. 'All right, soldier. Sorry there's no quarters inside.' He turned quickly and started for the cabin.

.   .   .   .

The woman took the boy from the wagon and followed him. Sergeant Houck unharnessed the horses and led them to the creek for a drink and to the corral and let them through the gate. He walked quietly to the cabin doorway and stopped just outside.

'For God's sake, Cora,' the man was saying, 'I don't see why you had to bring that kid with you. You could have told me about it. I didn't have to see him.'

'What do you mean?'

'Why, now we've got the problem of how to get rid of him. Have to find a mission or some place that'll take him. Why didn't you leave him where he came from?'

'No! He's mine!'

'Good God, Cora! Are you crazy? Think you can foist off a thing like that on me?'

Sergeant Houck stepped through the doorway. 'Thought I heard something about supper,' he said. He looked around the small room, then let his eyes rest on the man. 'I see the makings on those shelves. Come along, Mr. Sutliff. A woman doesn't want men cluttering about when she's getting a meal. Show me your place before it gets dark.'

He stood, waiting, and the man scraped at the floor with one foot and slowly stood up and went with him.

They were well beyond earshot of the cabin when Sergeant Houck spoke again. 'How long were you married? Before it happened?'

'Six years,' said the man. 'No, seven. It was seven when we lost the last place and headed this way with the train.'

'Seven years,' said Sergeant Houck. 'And no child.'

'It just didn't happen. I don't know why.' The man stopped and looked sharply at Sergeant Houck. 'Oh. So that's the way you're looking at it.'

'Yes,' said Sergeant Houck. 'Now you've got one. A son.'
'Not mine,' said the man.' 'You can talk. It's not *your* wife. It's bad enough thinking of taking an Indian's leavings.' He wiped his lips on his sleeve and spat in disgust. 'I'll be damned if I'll take his kid.'

'Not his any more. He's dead.'

'Look, man. Look how it'd be. A damned little halfbreed. Around all the time to make me remember what she did. A reminder of things I'd want to forget.'

'Could be a reminder that she had some mighty hard going. And maybe come through the better for it.'

'*She* had hard going! What about me? Thinking she was dead. Getting used to that. Maybe thinking of another woman. Then she comes back—and an Indian kid with her. What does that make me?'

'Could make you a man,' said Sergeant Houck. 'Think it over.' He turned away and went to the corral and leaned on the rail, watching the horses roll the sweat-itches out on the dry sod. The man went slowly down by the creek and stood on the bank, pushing at the dirt with one shoe and kicking small pebbles into the water. The sun, holding to the horizon rim, dropped suddenly out of sight and dusk came swiftly to blur the outlines of the buildings. The woman appeared in the doorway and called and they went in. There was simple food on the table and the woman stood beside it. 'I've already fed him,' she said and moved her head toward the door to the inner room.

Sergeant Houck ate steadily and reached to refill his plate. The man picked briefly at the food before him and stopped, and the woman ate nothing at all. The man put his hands on the table edge and pushed back and stood up. He went to a side shelf and took a bottle and two thick cups and set them by his plate. He filled the cups a third full from the bottle and shoved one along the table boards toward Sergeant Houck. He lifted the other. His voice was bitter. 'Happy home-coming,' he said. He waited and Sergeant Houck took the other cup and they drank. The man lifted the bottle and poured himself another drink.

The woman looked quickly at him and away.

'Please, Fred.'

The man paid no attention. He reached with the bottle toward the other cup.

'No,' said Sergeant Houck.

The man shrugged. 'You can think better on whisky. Sharpens the mind.' He set the bottle down and took his cup and drained it. Sergeant Houck fumbled in his right side pocket and found a short straight straw there and pulled it out and put one end in his mouth and chewed slowly on it. The man and the woman sat still, opposite each other at the table, and seemed to forget his quiet presence. They stared everywhere except at each other. Yet their attention was plainly concentrated on each other. The man spoke first. His voice was restrained, carrying conscious patience.

'Look, Cora. You wouldn't want to do that to me. You can't mean what you said before.'

Her voice was determined. 'He's mine.'

'Now, Cora. You don't want to push it too far. A man can take just so much. I didn't know what to do after I heard about you. But I was all ready to forgive you. And now you—'

'Forgive me!' She knocked against her chair rising to her feet. Hurt and bewilderment made her voice ragged as she repeated the words. 'Forgive me?' She turned and ran into the inner room. The handleless door banged shut behind her.

The man stared after her and shook his head and reached again for the bottle.

'Enough's enough,' said Sergeant Houck.

The man shrugged in quick irritation. 'For you maybe,' he said and poured himself another drink. 'Is there any reason you should be noseying in on this?'

'My orders,' said Sergeant Houck, 'were to deliver them safely. Both of them.'

'You've done that,' said the man. He lifted the cup and drained it and set it down carefully. 'They're here.'

'Yes,' said Sergeant Houck. 'They're here.' He stood up and stepped to the outside door and looked into the night. He waited a moment until his eyes were accustomed to the darkness and could distinguish objects faintly in the starlight. He stepped out and went to the pile of straw behind one of the sheds and took an armload and carried it back by the cabin and dropped it at the foot of a tree by one corner. He sat on it, his legs stretched out, his shoulders against the tree, and broke off a straw stem and chewed slowly on it. After a while his jaws stopped their slow slight movement and his head sank forward and his eyes closed.

Sergeant Houck woke up abruptly. He was on his feet in a moment, and listening. He heard the faint sound of voices in the cabin, indistinct but rising as the tension rose in them. He went toward the doorway and stopped just short of the rectangle of light from the lamp.

'You're not going to have anything to do with me!' The woman's voice was harsh with stubborn anger. 'Not until this has been settled right!'

'Aw, come on, Cora.' The man's voice was fuzzy, slow-paced. 'We'll talk about that in the morning.'

'No!'

'All right!' Sudden fury made the man's voice shake. 'You want it settled now. Well, it's settled! We're getting rid of that damn' kid first thing to-morrow!'

'No!'

'What gave you the idea you've got any say around here after what you did? I'm the one to say what's to be done. You don't be careful, maybe I won't take you back.'

'Maybe I don't want you to!'

'So damn' finicky all of a sudden! After being with that Indian and maybe a lot more!'

Sergeant Houck stepped through the doorway. The man's back was to him, and he spun him around and his right hand smacked against the side of the man's face and sent him staggering against the wall.

'Forgetting your manners won't help,' said Sergeant Houck. He looked around, and the woman had disappeared into the inner room. The man leaned against the wall, rubbing his cheek, and she came out, the boy in her arms, and ran toward the outer door.

'Cora!' the man shouted. 'Cora!'

She stopped, a brief hesitation in flight. 'I don't belong to you,' she said and was gone through the doorway. The man pushed out from the wall and started after her and the great bulk of Sergeant Houck blocked the way.

'You heard her,' said Sergeant Houck. 'She doesn't belong to anybody now. Nobody but that boy.'

The man stared at him and some of the fury went out of his eyes and he stumbled to his chair at the table and reached for the bottle. Sergeant Houck watched him a moment, then turned and quietly went outside. He walked toward the corral, and as he passed the second shed she came out of the darker shadows and her voice, low and intense, whispered at him: 'I've got to go. I can't stay here.'

Sergeant Houck nodded and went on to the corral. He harnessed the horses quickly and with a minimum of sound. He finished buckling the traces and stood straight and looked toward the cabin. He walked to the doorway and stepped inside. The man was leaning forward in his chair, his elbows on the table, staring at the empty bottle.

'It's finished,' said Sergeant Houck. 'She's leaving now.'

The man shook his head and pushed at the bottle with one forefinger. 'She can't do that.' He looked up at Sergeant Houck and sudden rage began to show in his eyes. 'She can't do that! She's my wife!'

'Not any more,' said Sergeant Houck. 'Best forget she ever came back.' He started toward the door and heard the sharp sound of the chair scraping on the floor behind him. The man's voice rose, shrilling up almost into a shriek.

'Stop!' The man rushed to the wall rack and grabbed the rifle there and held it low and aimed it at Sergeant Houck. 'Stop!' He was breathing deeply and he fought for control of his voice. 'You're not going to take her away!'

Sergeant Houck turned slowly. He stood still, a motionless granite shape in the lamplight.

'Threatening an Army man,' said Sergeant Houck. 'And with an empty gun.'

The man wavered and his eyes flicked down at the rifle. In the second of indecision Sergeant Houck plunged toward him and one huge hand grasped the gun barrel and pushed it aside and the shot thudded harmlessly into the cabin wall. He wrenched the gun from the man's grasp and his other hand took the man by the shirt front and pushed him down into the chair.

'No more of that,' said Sergeant Houck. 'Best sit quiet.' He looked around the room and found the box of cartridges on a shelf and he took this with the rifle and went to the door. 'Look around in the morning and you'll find these.' He went outside and tossed the gun up on the roof of one of the sheds and dropped the little box by the pile of straw and kicked some straw over it. He went to the wagon and stood by it and the woman came out of the darkness, carrying the boy.

The wagon wheels rolled silently. The small creakings of the wagon body and the thudding rhythm of the horses' hoofs were distinct, isolated sounds in the night. The creek was on their right and they followed the road back the way they had come. The woman moved on the seat, shifting the boy's weight from one arm to the other, until Sergeant Houck took him by the overalls and lifted him and reached behind to lay him on the burlap bags. 'A good boy,' he said. 'Has the Indian way of taking things without yapping. A good way.'

The thin new tracks in the dust unwound endlessly under the wheels and the waning moon climbed through the scattered bushes and trees along the creek.

'I have relatives in Missouri,' said the woman. 'I could go there.'

Sergeant Houck fumbled in his side pocket and found a straw and put this in his mouth and chewed slowly on it. 'Is that what you want?'

'No.'

They came to the main-road crossing and swung left and the dust thickened under the horses' hoofs. The lean dark shape of a coyote slipped from the brush on one side and bounded along the road and disappeared on the other side.

'I'm forty-seven,' said Sergeant Houck. 'Nearly thirty of that in the Army. Makes a man rough.'

The woman looked straight ahead and a small smile showed in the corners of her mouth.

'Four months,' said Sergeant Houck, 'and this last hitch's

done. I'm thinking of homesteading on out in the Territory.'
He chewed on the straw and took it between a thumb and
forefinger and flipped it away. 'You could get a room at the
settlement.'

'I could,' said the woman. The horses slowed to a walk,
breathing deeply, and he let them hold the steady, plodding
pace. Far off a coyote howled and others caught the signal and
the sounds echoed back and forth in the distance and died away
into the night silence.

'Four months,' said Sergeant Houck. 'That's not so long.'

'No,' said the woman. 'Not too long.'

A breeze stirred across the brush and she put out a hand and
touched his shoulder. Her fingers moved down along his upper
arm and curved over the big muscles there and the warmth
of them sank through the cloth of his worn service jacket. She
dropped her hand in her lap again and looked ahead along the
ribbon of the road. He clucked to the horses and urged them
again into a trot and the small creakings of the wagon body
and the dulled rhythm of the hoofs were gentle sounds in the
night.

The late moon climbed and its pale light shone slantwise
down on the moving wagon, on the sleeping boy and the woman
looking straight ahead, and on the great solid figure of Sergeant
Houck.

THE LAST SHOT

By *Frank O'Rourke*

JOHN BRANDON stopped that night in a stand of pines on the last, long slope above the Shovel valley, eating two sandwiches and drinking cold, flat coffee from his canteen. Darkness had settled when he spread one blanket under the pines and lay back, with the soft, grass-sweetened wind stirring the treetops above him, shaking the first dead leaves over his bed. His horse cropped grass with tired dignity about the perimeter of its stake rope. John Brandon thought of his younger brother and replaced this sad memory with the face of another man—the man he hoped to find in the town up this valley; and then, forcing body and mind into rest, he slept deeply through the early fall night.

He rode late the next morning, picking up a dusty wagon trail that brought him into the town of Bend during the noon hour. He stabled and cared for his horse in the livery barn on the north end of Bend's single business block, and followed the stableman into the dingy, unswept office. The stableman—an old, weathered man with the bright, inquisitive eyes of the small-town gossip spreader—carried a floating aroma of nitrogen and stale barn smells in his clothing. Brandon had to start somewhere and the stableman was nearest at hand. Brandon sat in the bigger of two wire-tied kitchen chairs and started to roll a cigarette.

'Quiet little town,' Brandon said.

'She is and she ain't.'

Brandon said, 'Been here long?'

'Ten years this winter.'

Brandon said, 'Then you know everybody, I reckon?'

'All the living and most of the dead,' the stableman said. 'You looking for somebody?'

'Why, yes,' Brandon said mildly. 'A pretty big fellow with curly black hair and a moustache. Nice-looking and wears good clothes with fine boots. Does that place him for you?'

'Sure,' the stableman said. 'That's Charley Cannady. Been here about six months, buying and selling stock and some land. A real nice fellow, Charley.' The stableman stared innocently at Brandon. 'Got business with him?'

'Yes,' Brandon said.

The stableman frowned. 'Hope Charley ain't in no trouble?'

'No trouble,' Brandon said. 'Where does he hang out?'

'Up to the hotel.'

'Thanks,' Brandon said. 'You care if I sit around awhile? My legs are tired.'

'Make yourself to home,' the stableman said. 'I got to see a fella. Anybody comes in, tell 'em I'll be right back.'

'Take your time,' Brandon told him. 'I'll hold the place down until you get back.'

He saw the avid curiosity rising in the stableman's eyes, that small lurking fear of any stranger riding into town and inquiring about a citizen in good standing; and with this fear lay the hope that something might happen to relieve the monotony. Brandon watched him step outside and walk from view. Alone in the musty office with horses moving lazily against stall boards behind the thin office wall, Brandon thought of the ten months he had spent in trailing one man, the work and time and grief compressed into those months. And now his man was no more than one block distant. Now he could take his time.

He heard boots on the board sidewalk; and then a man middle-aged and plump filled the street door of the office with his short, wide bulk. His eyes found Brandon and stared without interest as he said, 'Howdy.'

'Stableman's out,' Brandon said. 'Be back soon.'

'I'm Meagher,' the man said. 'Town marshal.'

Brandon saw the star then, half concealed by an open, sagging vest, and knew where the stableman had gone—directly to the marshal's office with information. Brandon wondered incuriously how many times this same tableau had been repeated in past years. He said quietly, 'My name is Brandon, Marshal. What's the trouble?'

'No trouble, Mr. Brandon.'

'He told you fast enough,' Brandon said.

Meagher reddened faintly and stepped into the office. He said, 'What's your business with Cannady?'

'My own,' Brandon said. 'But seeing you're the law, I'll make it plain. I plan on shooting him.'

Meagher did not show surprise. He said, 'Why?'

'He shot my brother,' Brandon said. 'I've been trailing him quite a spell.'

'How long?'

'Ten months,' Brandon said. 'Maybe you figure I'm foolish to tell you, Marshal. Here's my papers from down home. I'm deputized legally and got a warrant to bring him back. You can wire the sheriff there if you want proof.'

Meagher examined the faded, sharply creased papers and returned them. He said, 'You want him legal, I take it.'

'You read the warrant,' Brandon said.

'Dead or alive?'

Brandon said, 'You read the warrant.'

Meagher breathed gustily and took another step into the office. 'You got a warrant, but you don't figure on taking him back, do you? You want to shoot him right here?'

'I described my man,' Brandon said gently. 'Your errand boy verified it, and now you agree. He's here. I'll be seeing him.'

'All right,' Meagher said. 'He's been here six months and doing fine. Getting married next week, matter of fact.'

'Home-town girl?'

'Yes. He built a new house. All furnished and ready to live in. This will hurt the girl. She's a good girl.'

'Better now than later,' Brandon said. 'Will you tell him I'm in town?'

'Can't we do this legal?' Meagher asked heavily. 'Take him back to stand trial. If that was the only thing he done wrong, it might not be too late for him to square the debt.'

'I didn't need to ride in and tell you,' Brandon said. 'I could get him on my own. I just want to make it clear. My brother had no gun that night. Understand?'

'No gun? But—'

'I know,' Brandon said tonelessly. 'You know this Cannady. He's good with a gun. No use arguing, Marshal.'

'You won't change your mind?'

'No,' Brandon said. 'And I'll warn him. At six tonight, clear your street and send him out. I'll be here. I'll meet him.'

Meagher glanced at the gun on Brandon's right leg. 'You any good with that?'

'You been studying in ten minutes,' Brandon said bluntly. 'You knew before you asked. No, I'm no good with it.'

'Then why—'

'I want it that way,' Brandon said. 'I'm giving him a fair chance, more than he gave my brother. He can't back down and save face. You want to tell him or do I?'

Meagher was completely serious now. 'That's your job. I reckon I ought to stop you, but it wouldn't do no good. You'd just keep on till you got him.'

'A good guess,' Brandon said.

Meagher nodded and moved through the door, pausing on the sidewalk to look once more at Brandon's gun and shake his head with heavy bewilderment. Brandon waited in the office until the marshal's steps had died away to the south. They were replaced minutes later by the stableman's light, tapping feet; then Brandon stood quickly and faced the stableman in the door.

'That was fast work,' Brandon said, 'but let me tell you something. Just stay around here this afternoon, and stay away from my horse. I'll be back directly.'

Brandon passed the suddenly frightened man and walked south along Bend's short business block. The marshal's office and the jail were on the same side of the street and fifty feet or so south of the livery barn; and standing in a weather-worn rectangular shape on the opposite corner, three stories high and needing paint, was the hotel. Brandon crossed over and entered the lobby, hearing the clatter of dishes and talking voices from the adjoining dining room. Brandon took a faded, dried-out leather chair against the north wall and sat quietly until these sounds had nearly died away. The clerk watched him incuriously from behind a small desk.

Brandon said, 'Mr. Cannady in there?'

'I think so,' the clerk said. 'You want to see him?'

'Please,' Brandon said mildly.

'I'll tell him,' the clerk said. 'He's almost done with dinner.'
The clerk went into the dining room and returned immediately, saying, 'He'll be right out.' Brandon rose from the chair and moved closer to the connecting door, hearing boots scrape and chairs pushed back as the unseen men rose from their table and spoke together for a brief moment. One man left the dining room by the street door and another paused to exchange a pleasantry with the waitress and then entered the lobby. Brandon recognized his man.

'Cannady,' he said.

Cannady smiled and extended one hand. 'You wish to see me, sir?'

'Yes,' Brandon said. 'Don't you know me?'

Cannady frowned. 'Can't seem to place you.'

'My name is Brandon,' Brandon said. 'Does that help?'

Cannady was not wearing his gun at this noon hour, but one hand made an automatic, involuntary gesture toward his right leg. He stood alert and stiffly, understanding and remembrance masked behind sharp black eyes.

'Brandon?' he said then. 'I don't know any Brandons, sir. There must be some mistake.'

'Talk is a waste of time,' Brandon said. 'I'll be at the livery barn this afternoon. At six I'll step into the street. I expect you to do likewise from this hotel. Stop thinking about making a break. I've trailed you ten months. Run for it and you'll get no even chance next time.'

'Look here–' Cannady said.

'You hear me,' Brandon said stolidly. 'Make a break and I'll use a rifle on you in the hills.'

Cannady remembered him well enough, even though their meeting in the past had been a quick passage on the main street of Brandon's home town. It was through the close resemblance of Brandon to his younger brother that Cannady saw and compared and remembered. Brandon watched him search rapidly into the past and recall certain facts about the Brandons. As the marshal before him had done, Cannady glanced at the gun on Brandon's leg and noted that it was unpolished by use and riding much too high on Brandon's leg for a swift, accurate draw.

Cannady was remembering that the Brandons were peaceable men who no longer used guns in settling their quarrels; and, knowing this, he lost all fear.

Brandon said again: 'You hear me?'

'Certainly,' Cannady said. 'I will accommodate you at six with pleasure. I suppose it would do no good to repeat that your foolish brother pushed me into that fight?'

'I know how it happened,' Brandon said. 'Save your words. I'll see you at six.'

'I'll explain to our marshal,' Cannady said. 'I don't want interference.'

'No need,' Brandon said. 'I saw him.'

Brandon was inwardly pleased to see the sudden fear on Cannady's face at the mention of the marshal. No matter what it was, the hunt was finished. Brandon turned and walked from the hotel and north on the quiet street to the office of the livery barn. The stableman came from the alleyway, shaking straw from his thin shoulders, and pottered uncomfortably behind the desk.

'Swallow the talk,' Brandon said curtly. 'You wouldn't be having any more business around town, would you?'

'I reckon not,' the man said.

'Then do your work,' Brandon said, 'and keep your mouth shut.'

A man needed to go back, Brandon thought, and consider everything carefully before he went forth to finish anything. He had trailed Cannady for ten months with the memory of his younger brother clear in his mind; but now, in the last minutes before the end of the trail, it was only fair and wise to remember everything and make sure he was right. Brandon sat in the dirty office through the long afternoon, watching the town move sluggishly, thinking of his own home and the past.

South of here was another country in a sense, settled and done with the first wild rush of the bad ones such as Cannady. Brandon had almost forgotten how to draw his gun in the past five years except to use it to hammer staples and twist wire and shoot an occasional crippled animal. His own town had settled comfortably into the middle portion of any town's history, growing steadily with the addition of schools and churches and good people. Brandon had grown through the wild years, but his younger brother had come along too late for a real taste of this feeling, and the result showed up in him as it did in all the younger men on the range. Boys will be boys, the old-timers chuckled, watching the younger men ride fast and whoop it up on Saturday nights, taking their excess meanness out in fist fights that left them slightly battered but thoroughly cleansed of that wildness. A few men like Cannady still happened through the towns, though, and it was inevitable for the younger men to appraise them with a feeling of wonder and envy. Brandon's younger brother had been foolish to a certain degree, but he had never considered serious harm to any man.

Brandon had been hazing strays from the river bottom that week and had not ridden into town on Saturday night. His younger brother and the two hands left in late afternoon, after begging him half-heartedly to come along. They rode away in high spirits, dressed in their best, racing to a big night. Brandon watched them go and chuckled with the knowledge and stability of his thirty-five years.

He knew the pattern of their night before they made the first move: riding fast down the main street, yelling in sheer good humour, a couple of drinks at the Longhorn, and then the dance. And about five the next morning they would ride into Brandon's river camp with a great deal of unnecessary hullabaloo, waking him and retelling all the fights and flirtations and other gossip of the neighbourhood. Brandon's younger brother was interested in a town girl and would moon around for a day, thinking about her. Brandon knew the girl was an empty-headed little fool, but it was useless to give warning. His brother would discover it for himself in due time.

Five old friends rode into the river camp just after three o'clock, and they woke him without shouts or laughter. He sat up in his blankets and stared above the hastily kindled fire and missed his brother's face. They told him what had happened while he slipped into his boots and saddled his horse for the ride to town. His brother had been shot by a stranger named Charles Chambers. Brandon had seen Chambers in town a week ago, in the Longhorn, but had not spoken to the man. It seemed that Chambers had kept company with young Brandon's girl for several evenings prior to the Saturday night dance. Brandon's younger brother exchanged hot words with Chambers on the dance floor, and Chambers said, 'Shut up, kid. Grow up and then come around.' That was more than enough for a hotheaded fool, even though Chambers wore a gun and knew how to use it. Chambers escorted the girl to her home at midnight and Brandon's younger brother followed. His friends tagged along to watch the expected fist fight. Chambers was in the kitchen with the girl, his horse tied out back, his equipment ready for a long ride. Brandon's younger brother knocked on the kitchen door and shouted at Chambers to come out and fight like a man. Chambers told him to go away, and Brandon's younger brother answered that he was coming in. He was not wearing a gun. When he slammed the door open and stood in the doorway, Chambers lifted a shotgun from beside his kitchen chair and shot him. By the time the other young men reached the house, the girl was screaming and Chambers had gone.

Brandon rode thirty miles to town without speaking. He stayed with his brother until the inevitable happened and then did the only thing a man could do. He knew his younger brother had been foolish and rash, but he had not carried a gun and Chambers knew this. The county sheriff deputized Brandon and wrote out the warrant. Brandon went home and made arrangements for the future. His older brother and two uncles would take care of the ranch work, and the neighbours would help. Brandon started on the trail that night. He had ridden ever since, following the cold trace, the little clues, the gradually warming scent of his man. He had given himself a year; now two months were on the credit side of the ledger.

He had lost weight during this time. He had been a tall and somewhat bulky man, but he had sloughed off his excess weight until he was pared down to muscle and bone–a sober-faced man with a three-day growth of black whiskers partially hiding his square jaw and weather-darkened face. He wore the same heavy leather chaps he had started with, buckled above the knee and frayed from endless days of riding over all kinds of country.

Those chaps in this higher grassland were out of place, but sitting quietly in the sun-heated, smelly office Brandon made no move to remove them and give his legs the additional freedom needed at six o'clock.

People had gone about their daily business during the afternoon, talking on the street, going and coming, moving unhurriedly through the town. A few wagons rattled in from the west and south, and saddle horses lined the rail before the saloon adjoining the hotel. People were pretty much the same anywhere a man rode, he thought, living out their days in the same jobs and pleasures. This town of Bend was no different from his own town so far away; it would grow more in the next few years and add churches and schools and bigger houses. The marshal would put his gun away and walk the streets without fear of men like Cannady who changed their names to suit their purpose. That would be the best time for the town and its people, he thought, and for all towns and all people.

The marshal did not appear during the afternoon. Cannady came from the hotel at four o'clock and drove past the livery barn in a light buggy, turning north on the last side street toward an unseen house. He returned in an hour and entered the hotel. The stableman pottered around the barn, doing nothing and listening closely. After five o'clock, people began drifting downtown and gathering in the saloons and stores. They had got the news on the invisible grapevine and were waiting for the show. He would not disappoint them, Brandon thought grimly, but might surprise them.

Time was short now. He had reviewed everything and could not see a better way to end the hunt. He had been right from the beginning; his heart, beating steadily without excitement, told him that. He rolled a last cigarette and smoked it deliberately, watching the sun fall lower in the far west.

At exactly ten minutes of six, Brandon walked into the barn alley and said, 'Go into your office and stay there.' He waited until the stableman scuttled past him and ducked through the inner door. Then he went to his stall and patted his horse gently, murmuring, 'Easy, boy, easy.'

The horse nuzzled his shoulder while Brandon saddled and checked all gear twice. He led the horse into the alley, facing the rear door, and tied the reins in a loose slipknot to the last brace post beside the door. He was standing in deep shadow when he pulled the stubby, double-barrelled shotgun from its saddle holster. He inspected two shells and went on to a detailed and careful examination of the shotgun, snapping both triggers and checking the firing pins before loading both barrels and closing the breech. He cocked both triggers, grasped the shotgun by its carved pistol grip, and placed the stock under his arm, against his body, the butt pushed into his armpit, the forearm and barrels pressed firmly against his left leg. The sweat-stiffened wings of his leather chaps and his loose shirt sleeve hid the shotgun from front view. He had practised this many times and knew exactly how to hold the shotgun. He did not check his revolver in the awkward holster tied against his right leg.

Brandon walked slowly to the barn door facing the street and paused, looking north and south. He saw the stableman's expectant face framed in the office's one dirty window, jerking back quickly as Brandon looked his way. Brandon walked into the street, to the exact centre, and faced south; and at this moment Cannady stepped briskly from the hotel veranda and faced north in the centre of the street. Brandon estimated the intervening distance at about one hundred steps. The street was empty, but people stood behind every window and door, and one kill-hungry man was straddling the saloon roof.

Brandon walked twenty steps down the street and stopped just before he came abreast of the marshal's office. Meagher stood in his doorway, hands on hips, staring moodily at Brandon. He called in a gentle voice: 'You won't reconsider, Brandon?'

'Sorry,' Brandon said. 'Stay where you are.'

Brandon waited in this spot and saw Cannady laugh and move forward quickly, right arm hanging in a fixed arc at his side. In this moment, Brandon saw a girl come from the hotel and stand on the veranda. She was a slender and delicately-featured woman with dark hair, and she lifted one hand to her mouth and leaned stiffly against the weathered, knifewhittled railing in a position of fear. Brandon saw her, knew who she was immediately, and thought of the girl in his home town and of other girls who must be living in other towns, remembering Cannady and nursing the thinly healed scars of old, bitter memory. He could see them as they lived, forgotten by Cannady; but, watching this woman, he understood why Cannady had stayed on in Bend. She was the woman Cannady had searched for; and, having discovered something as good and decent as she was, he had pushed his old life behind and began a new one. But too late.

Brandon stood without arm movement, watching the distance between them decrease to sixty, fifty, nearly thirty paces. Then Cannady stopped, his face clear and bright in the first soft evening shadow. 'Make your play, Brandon,' he called sharply.

'Come on,' Brandon said. 'Come on.'

'An old trick,' Cannady said. 'I've come my half. Your turn now, Brandon. But I'll tell you something. Take five steps and stop. Then go for your gun.'

'All right,' Brandon said. 'I'll call that bluff. I knew you were a coward before. Now I'm sure. I'm wondering which step you'll draw on to catch me off balance. You wouldn't be thinking of that, would you?'

Brandon did not wait for words. He walked forward stiffly and, reaching his third step, tensed his left arm as his leg lifted and moved forward into the fourth step. He stopped suddenly and dropped into a crouch and swung the shotgun up from behind the leather chap, level with his hips, right arm coming across and steadying the barrels. He pulled both triggers at the apex of this swift movement, just before Cannady made his draw. Through the heavy simultaneous reports, the smoke, and the recoil, Brandon saw the buckshot sweep Cannady from his feet and smash him face down in the street's brown dust. The half-drawn gun spun from lax fingers as Cannady screamed. Behind Brandon, the marshal called hoarsely and came in a heavy angry rush, shouting: 'I knew you had something figured, you–!'

Brandon reloaded the shotgun as he turned to face the marshal. He said coldly, 'He won't die. I shot him in the legs.'

People were running into the street. The town doctor came through this thickening crowd with his black bag and dropped on both knees beside Cannady. The marshal spoke with a raging fury: 'A damned shotgun. Look at his legs. He'll never walk again. You know what buckshot does close up. He'll lose both of 'em. Brandon, you're under arrest. Drop that gun.'

Brandon lifted the shotgun and stopped Meagher's hand midway in its flight to the holster. Brandon said, 'Listen to me, Meagher. He shot my brother in the legs with a shotgun. My brother had no gun. My brother's alive, sure, with one leg. You can check on that, Meagher. I told you I would shoot him. I didn't say kill him. I didn't say what with. This is how I've wanted it for ten months; this is the way it had to be. He's no good, Meagher. He's a coward and a killer, and I want him like this for the rest of his life, and I hope he lives a hundred years.'

'I–' Meagher said, and turned away, head low on his chest. 'I believe you, Brandon. Everything else checked like you told me.'

'I'm riding,' Brandon said. 'You figure on stopping me?'

'No,' Meagher said. 'Not now.'

Brandon lowered the shotgun and stepped beside the doctor and the man, groaning now in the street's thick dust. Brandon said, 'Will he live?'

The doctor did not look up. He said, 'Of course he'll live, without the right leg, maybe part of the left. Get a stretcher, you fools. I've got to move this man.'

Brandon stepped back and watched them carry Cannady into the hotel. Only then did he turn and say, 'Walk along to the barn with me, Meagher.'

They pushed through an angry crowd of uncertain, babbling people, into the darkness of the barn alley. Brandon pushed the shotgun into its saddle holster and untied his horse. He said then, 'Thanks for understanding, Meagher.'

'I got to,' Meagher said. 'I got to thank you, too. I knew what he was when he came up the street. I've seen a lot of them in my time, Brandon. When they get ready to draw, they show a lot in their eyes.'

'*Gracias,*' Brandon said softly.

He mounted and leaned forward in the saddle, a last thought stirring and bothering his mind. He said, 'That girl he was marrying tomorrow. I hope you give her the straight of it.'

'I will,' Meagher said. 'That's why I'm thanking you.'

'You know her?' Brandon asked.

'My daughter,' Meagher said. 'You better ride, Brandon. He had a few friends in town. I got to get home.'

Brandon began words and shut them off deep in his throat. He rode from the back door of the livery barn, east from the town into open range, then south toward the distant rising ridges. Two hours later, stopping beside a small creek to blow his horse and listen, he drew the shotgun from his saddle holster and dropped it into the creek before riding on.

★ THE OUTLAWS ARE IN TOWN ★

By Bennett Foster

WHEN Lonny Kesh was a kid there were two kinds of people in Double Rivers: those who had money in the bank and those who hadn't. Lonny learned this well. He absorbed the knowledge with his turnip greens and pot liquor; it was beaten into his cringing back; he heard it at the meetinghouse when the text was First Samuel, 2:7.

'Damned blue-bellied Yankee! Him an' his bank! You, Lonny, git on with your ploughin'!'

So Lonny's father when Jud Collins passed by in a buggy. Old man Kesh had deserted from Joe Johnson's Army in the fall of '62, and any man with money was a Yankee.

'That stuck-up Mrs. Tawson was over today, talkin' about her Adele marryin' the Collins boy. She needn't turn up her nose just because they got money in the bank.' So Lonny's mother, snuff bulging her cheek, bare feet slapping on the dogtrot floor. 'Lonny! Where is that boy? I declare, I'll flail the daylights outen him!'

Weary of Georgia stock and corn row, of cotton sack and aching back, of nagging and slap and curse and drunken kick, Lonny ran away. He caught on with a freight outfit which carried him to Sanantone and there hired out to a livery barn. He cleaned alleyways and stalls, he groomed horses, he learned the location of cribs and bawdy houses, of gambling rooms and saloons, he heard the gossip. In Little Steamboat's crib, Lonny told Frank Banner that the rangers were in town. Frank Banner's name was in the ranger black book.

'I guess I'd better go,' Banner said. 'How about comin' with me, kid? Ain't you tired of forkin' hay?'

Banner had connections up in the Nations, where there was no law. He rode with the Lapman boys: Dock and Big Tobe, Blackjack and Sam Steves. So did Lonny. Lonny was along when the Denver and Southwestern train was stopped below

Trinchera Pass, over in New Mexico Territory. That was a water haul, with no man hurt or money stolen, and Dock was furious.

'I'll scout the next one myself,' Dock vowed. 'Then there won't be no slip-ups.'

It was a mistake for Dock to scout the Plainfield job; he was too well known. A ranger, in town to serve a warrant, saw and recognized Dock, and when the Lapmans rode in the place was organized. The ranger was on top of the bank with a rifle and there were deputies in the saloon, the hardware store and the butcher shop. They waited for Dock and Tobe to start into the bank before they opened up.

Blackjack was knocked from the saddle and Sam Steves was killed by the first volley. Frank Banner, covering the job from the bank steps, fought back, as did the two Lapmans. Lonny never cracked a cap; he was too surprised and scared to think of the gun on his hip. He fought the plunging horses and held on to their reins until Frank and Tobe and Dock were clear and mounting. He rode with them toward the edge of town. Some posseman with a good aim dropped Lonny's horse, but Lonny fell clear.

He might have caught what Sam Steves did, for he scrambled to his feet, bewildered by his fall, and the air about him sang with lead. Dock and Tobe went on, but Banner turned, caught Blackjack's horse and led it back. He emptied his six-shooter down the street, covering Lonny, and it was then that Frank was hit. Frank Banner sided Lonny out of town and they caught up with Dock and Tobe, and Banner cursed them for cowards, leaving a man like that.

Of course there was pursuit, but not too close. One posseman was dead, the hardware merchant was dying, the ranger had a hole in him and the rest were not too eager. They followed, but they did not press, and the Lapmans, with Frank Banner and Lonny, reached the live oaks north of Plainfield.

Lonny lost the others in the live-oak thickets, for his horse was slow and they would not wait. The last he saw of them, Frank Banner was sprawled forward in the saddle, astride only because he would not fall, while Dock led Banner's horse and Tobe rode behind. They disappeared into a thicket.

Lonny turned his own horse to the left, and where the brush was thickest, stopped, dismounted and hid there, holding his breath and feeling the blood pound in his temples while the posse went threshing by. He was still there when night came, but with the darkness he mounted and rode again.

Double Rivers was just as Lonny remembered it. There was Branch's store, the New York Store and Fienbaum's Mercantile; there was the Exchange Saloon, and the State Saloon and pool hall. The Baptist Church was on a corner, the Methodist Church pushed its steeple skyward a block north. The bank faced the Baptist Church, the saddle shop was next to the bank, while down the street a block were the livery barn and feed yard. Lonny, dismounting in front of Branch's store, was willing to swear that the same wagons were waiting to be loaded, the same horses tied to the hitch rails, as when he went away.

Old man Purcell, coming out of Branch's wagging his white beard, eyed Lonny, started down the street and then turned back.

'Too bad about your folks,' he quavered. Lonny's eyes were wide as they followed the feeble figure.

In the store, Carl Branch was behind the counter talking to Jud Collins, and neither of them looked a day older. Lonny waited diffidently until Branch, turning his head, stared at him through his glasses.

'You're Lonny Kesh, ain't you?' Branch demanded.

'Yes, sir.'

'Come back on account of your folks,' Branch stated. 'Too bad you didn't get here sooner. Two-three weeks might of made a difference. Well, we done all we could.' His hands fussed with a package on the counter. 'You back to stay?'

'Why, I guess so.'

Jud Collins picked up the package. 'That's all, Carl,' he said. He looked at Lonny, his eyes keen. 'Come over to the bank,' he directed. 'I want to talk to you.'

'Sure.' Lonny turned to follow Collins.

'Lonny!' Lonny halted. 'There's a little bill your folks had here,' Branch said apologetically. 'No hurry about it. Come in when you got time.'

'I will,' Lonny agreed, and followed Collins out of the store.

In the bank office Jud Collins sat behind his desk and folded his hands over a plump middle while Lonny, occupying a chair, kept his eyes lowered. Collins cleared his throat, rocked his chair and cleared his throat again.

'I don't hardly know how to begin,' he said. 'I'm sorry about your folks. Typhoid's a mighty hard thing to beat. Your maw died first an' your paw the next day. Mrs. Tawson nursed 'em an' we had the doctor. We didn't know where you were, so me an' Dolf Tawson looked after things. Your paw owed me a little money an' Dolf was the closest neighbour.'

'I'm obliged,' Lonny said. He felt no sorrow; his reaction was one of relief.

'I suppose you got word someway an' come back,' Collins said. 'What have you been doin', Lonny?'

'Punchin' cows. Yeah, I got word an' come back.' Lonny still kept his eyes lowered.

'Well'—the banker hung to the word while he studied Lonny— 'you've been gone quite a while. How old are you?'

'Nineteen. I've been gone three years.'

There was silence. Collins considered and then apparently reached a decision. 'Nineteen,' he said. 'Well, Lonny, what are you goin' to do? Like I said, your paw owed me some money. Are you goin' to hold a sale and clear out or did you have it in mind to stay and put in a crop?'

'Stay and put in a crop.' Lonny met Jud Collins' eyes. 'That is, if I can.'

Where could a man be safer? Who would look for one of the Lapman gang in a cotton patch?

'You was always good to work.' Collins unlocked his fingers and nodded slowly. 'I guess that's best.' He was musing, half to himself. 'Yes, likely that's best. All right, Lonny. I'll advance you seed money an' a little to go on. Dolf has been lookin' after things since your folks died an' he's moved the stock over to his place. Times are mighty hard an' cotton ain't worth much, but I reckon I can carry you. I'm carryin' everybody else.' His plump hands moved toward the clutter on his desk. 'We'll fix up a mortgage,' he said, 'for enough to cover what your paw owed an' what you'll need right now. An', Lonny–leave the money here in the bank. You can draw cheques on it.'

'Yes, sir,' said Lonny.

Sometimes in the following days it seemed to Lonny Kesh that he had never left Double Rivers. He cleaned and deepened the old well because the doctor told him to. He broke land, followed two mules, lines over neck and shoulder. He planted corn, and he dropped cotton seed in the furrows. He saw the small green plants push up, and walked along the rows, broad-bladed hoe in hand, chopping cotton.

Sometimes, in the cabin, he could almost hear his mother shrilling at him. Sometimes he could almost hear his father's whine and feel the strap across his shoulders. It was hard to realize that they were gone.

The neighbour folks were kind. Dolf Tawson had the mules, a milk cow and a brood sow. Lonny brought them home, the hog in the wagon, the cow tied on behind. Too, he brought home packets of garden seed that Mrs. Tawson gave him. Lonny planted the seed and his garden grew. The Rutherfords, to the south, were also kind. Mrs. Rutherford baked a pie and Cal Rutherford brought it over. Cal ran a few cattle and had punched cows. He visited with Lonny. Tawsons, Rutherfords, and all the rest were curious concerning his wandering years, but Lonny told them very little.

While he was planting cotton, Mike Groome, the deputy sheriff, stopped near the house and called him over. Lonny felt the gun he carried, rubbing cold and hard against his belly as he went to see what Mike wanted. He was panicked then and ready for anything, but Mike asked concerning the whereabouts of John Hance. Hance, Mike said, was suspected of stealing a cow. Lonny leaned against a post and visited awhile.

Being an officer, Mike was conversant with crime. He spoke of local offences and of the Lapman gang and Plainfield. 'They came ridin' in, bold as brass,' Mike said, 'an' the town was ready for 'em. Dock Lapman had been seen an' recognized the day before. There was a posse waitin' and they opened up before they ever got into the bank. Blackjack an' Sam Steves were killed right there.'

'Uh-huh,' Lonny agreed. 'I heard about it.'

'An' that ain't all.' Mike Groome would not be denied his tale. 'While the four of them was ridin' out, somebody shot one of the horses. The kid that was on it started to run an' the posse would of got him, only Frank Banner come back. Banner caught a horse an' helped the kid out of town.'

'Anybody recognize the kid?' Lonny asked. His heart was in his throat.

'No.' Mike Groome shook his head. 'Nobody knew him. The only way they knew Frank Banner was that they found him afterwards. He was hit when he brought the horse back for the kid, and the posse found him next day, shot through the head.'

'Then the posse caught up with them?' Lonny asked. Relief was flooding him. No one knew that Lonny Kesh had been with the Lapmans.

'Posse, hell!' Mike Groome exploded. 'It was the Lapmans. Banner was hurt an' they couldn't fool around. One of 'em shot him an' they went on their way. The posse never saw 'em again.'

When Mike Groome rode off, Lonny returned to the planter and sat down. He was weak; his very bones seemed liquid. The law was not looking for Lonny Kesh; the law was looking for Dock and Tobe Lapman and another man, a man no one had recognized. And Frank Banner was dead. The Lapman boys had killed him. Tobe or Dock had done that. After a time Lonny got up and put the lines over his neck. The mules went down the row and the planter clicked steadily.

Corn and cotton grew. Lonny kept the fields clean, first with the cultivator, then with his hoe. He went to town for supplies and found Carl Branch cordial, for Lonny had sold his horse and saddle and paid the debt at the store. He saw Jud Collins and spoke of how the crop was coming. There was still money in the bank; Lonny's chequebook showed a balance of eighty-seven dollars.

The cotton bloomed. Mrs. Tawson offered to supply Lonny with milk, for his cow was dry. The Rutherfords, en route to church, stopped by for Lonny. They drove a spring wagon and Lonny sat behind with Alice Rutherford, seventeen years old and blushing whenever Lonny spoke to her. The Rutherfords took Lonny home to dinner.

After dinner, while the womenfolks were redding up, Cal said: 'Heard some gossip after church today while you an' Alice were talking' to the preacher. Folks seem to think Jud Collins has extended himself too far an' give too much credit. I hope that ain't so.'

'Of course it ain't so!' Lonny was indignant, startled by the idea. 'You know that, Mr. Rutherford.'

'I sure hope not.' Cal considered the smoke rising from his pipe. 'Everybody around Double Rivers banks with Collins. If the bank was to go under, it would about clean us out.'

'Lonny,' Alice spoke from the doorway, 'Mother wants to know if you can use half a pie and some cottage cheese.'

'You bet I can,' said Lonny Kesh.

The cotton stalks turned brown and the bolls broke open, showing white wealth. Lonny Kesh worked in the field, picking, dragging his long cotton sack between the rows, dumping the sack in the wagon, hauling to the gin.

The crop would go half a bale to the acre, he thought, maybe more than that. With cotton at ten cents ... In the lamplight he figured on an envelope: ten cents, half a bale, twenty acres. The corn would run pretty slim. He looked at his chequebook and found a tiny balance. It would be bigger when the gin paid off. There would still be money when he paid his note.

Lonny drew two heavy lines below his figures and put his pencil down. Money in the bank! He had worked hard that day and all the days before, but he wasn't tired.

In the morning Lonny hauled the last of his cotton to the gin. When the load was weighed the gin man gave him a slip and stood to talk awhile.

'You're handlin' all your cotton through the bank, ain't you?' the gin man asked.

'That's right,' Lonny agreed. 'Why?'

'Nothin' much,' the gin man said, 'only there's an examiner down to the bank now. I heard Jud Collins was pretty worried. Folks say that the bank ain't in too good shape.'

'The bank's all right,' Lonny assured, and pulled off from the scales.

At the bank Lonny gave his gin slip to Jud Collins. Collins

was preoccupied. There was a stranger behind the counter working with Jud's son, he who had married Adele Tawson, and as Lonny watched the stranger carried a ledger into the vault.

'This is the last of the cotton, Mr. Collins,' Lonny said.

'That's good, Lonny.' Jud Collins fingered the gin slip. 'I'm glad you got it all in.'

'Looks like I'd have some money when the gin pays off,' Lonny ventured.

'Looks like you might. Excuse me, Lonny.' Jud started toward the vault. Lonny lingered a moment and then went out, frowning.

He had brightened by the time he reached Branch's store. He bought a box of candy and then, after deliberation, added two shirts and a pair of trousers. A man with money in the bank could afford to spend some on himself, and the candy was for Alice. Lonny left Branch's and, climbing to the wagon seat, clucked to the team.

He was cheerful as he left town, but along the home road his mood changed. He remembered how Jud Collins had acted in the bank; he remembered what Cal Rutherford had said, and the comments of the gin man. Lonny was depressed and moody when he reached the familiar gate. He drove in, unhitched and fed the mules, fed the eager sow and her brood, looked carefully at the milk cow and fed her too. She was sure springing. He got his packages from the wagon and walked on the house, entering through the dogtrot door. The room was dark, and Lonny, placing his burden on the table, fumbled for a match.

'Hello, Lonny,' a voice said in the darkness.

The match spurted into flame and then went out while Lonny stood stock still. 'Here, I'll light it,' the voice said. 'Kind of surprised you, didn't we?'

When the lamp glowed, Lonny could see Dock and Big Tobe, Dock grinning, Tobe's face vacuous as always. They were by the table, making themselves right at home. 'I remembered you talkin' about Double Rivers,' Dock said, 'so we come this way. We've got a job in mind.'

'A job?'

'Sure,' Dock nodded. 'We needed another man, didn't we, Tobe?'

Tobe did not answer. 'I'm hungry,' Tobe growled. 'How about some grub? I'll build a fire.' He slouched toward the stove and Dock sat down.

'Did you come straight here?' he asked, his eyes on Lonny. 'After we split up, I mean? We lost you, back there in them live oaks an' I never did know where you went.'

Tobe rattled the grates, and Lonny, recovered from the shock, moved to the cupboard. 'I came straight here,' he agreed, pulling out the corn-meal sack.

'An' nobody bothered you?'

'No.'

Tobe had the fire laid. He struck a match and put the stove lids back in place. Lonny mixed corn meal and salt and soda, added sour milk from a crock, and greased his pan.

'You're smart,' Dock said. 'Nobody would look for one of us in a cotton patch. Is that how you figured?'

'That's right.'

The fire was roaring. Lonny pulled up the draught and slid his pan of corn bread into the oven. He put the coffee-pot and a kettleful of greens on the stove.

'You hear that, Tobe? Lonny's smart. He came right here and he's been here ever since. Nobody's bothered him.'

'I heard it.' Big Tobe had rolled a cigarette. 'I'm goin' out to look at the horses.'

Lonny sliced salt pork, long and white and flaccid. Dock bestrode a chair, his arms resting on the chair back. He got up and stretched. 'I'll set the table,' Dock offered.

Big Tobe returned. 'Horses are all right,' he announced. 'We brought one for you, Lonny. Didn't know how you'd be fixed.'

'He's fixed good.' Dock laughed and put the last plate on the table. 'Turnip greens, corn bread, coffee and fat back. He's even got a nogging of milk; I took a drink of it when we come in. Candy, too, by grabs! Look here, Tobe.' Dock tore the wrapper from the candy box.

The meat began to sizzle in the heavy iron skillet and Lonny turned it. He had forgotten to stop by for the milk that morning and Mrs. Tawson had brought it over. The greens were steaming gently and the coffee-pot boiled. Lonny slid it back.

'Real good,' Dock continued around the candy in his mouth, 'but he's goin' to be better fixed. There won't be no slip-up on this job.'

'I heard Frank Banner died,' Lonny said.

The room was quiet save for the sound of the frying meat. Then: 'Yeah, he died,' Dock said.

'I heard they found him shot through the head.'

'That's right.' Dock's voice was heavy. 'We run into the posse an' they got him.'

'Oh,' said Lonny. 'Sit down. It's ready.'

The tightness left Dock's face as he pulled his chair to the table. Tobe sat beside his brother, reaching for another piece of candy. Lonny bent to the oven. The corn bread was brown and he filled a plate, placing it before his guests. He dished up greens, poured the coffee, forked the salt pork out on a plate.

'I'll make poor-man's gravy,' Lonny said, and picked up the milk. 'This job you've got in mind—how do you know there won't be no slip-up?'

Milk hissed in the hot skillet and Lonny stirred.

Dock had filled his plate and Tobe was already eating. 'Because,' Dock said, 'there won't be. They know you at the bank, don't they, Lonny?'

'I've got money there.' Lonny lifted the skillet, holding it with a rag, for it was fiery hot. He carried it in both hands toward the table.

'I knew it!' Dock laughed. 'I told Tobe. You see, there can't be no slip-up. They know you at the bank. Me and Tobe will go in with you an' they won't suspect a thing. It's easy money.'

'The Double Rivers Bank?' Lonny held the skillet poised to pour. 'Is that the job?'

'Sure.' Dock lowered a forkful of fried meat and stared at Lonny. 'What's the matter with you? Do you want to stay here an' live on pot liquor an' greens the rest of your life?'

That was Alice Rutherford's box of candy at Dock's elbow. The greens were grown from Mrs. Tawson's garden seed. The side meat came from a Rutherford hog. Little things for a man to remember, things like that. And, because Lonny had money in the bank, he and Dock and Tobe could walk in, unsuspected.

'Do you?' Dock snarled.

The gravy in the skillet was scalding hot; the skillet was heavy; the gun under Lonny's shirt was cold against his belly. Lonny Kesh made answer. The skillet swept in a circle, spewing gravy into surprised faces, the sweep ending in contact with Tobe's head.

At midnight Jud Collins, sleeping soundly after a hard day, was wakened by his wife. She shook him, demanding that he get up, and when sleep was finally dissipated he heard a pounding at the door. Nightshirt trailing over hastily donned trousers, carpet slippers slapping the floor, lamp in one hand and shot gun in the other, Jud Collins went downstairs. When he opened the door he saw Lonny Kesh.

'Come in, Lonny,' Jud Collins ordered. 'Come in. What in the world happened to you?'

There was blood on Lonny's face, blood on his leg where the trousers were cut away and a bandage showed. He bore every mark of having taken a beating.

'I give myself up to you,' Lonny said, and his eyes were wild. 'To you an' nobody else, Mr. Collins. You get the reward. I got Tobe an' Dock Lapman in the wagon.'

'Are you crazy?' Jud Collins demanded. 'Give yourself up? What are you talkin' about? You've got Tobe and Dock Lapman?'

'I rode with 'em,' Lonny said. 'There's a reward out for me. Them too. I want the bank to have it. I don't want the bank to go broke.'

'The bank ain't goin' broke,' Jud Collins said sternly. 'Sarah,' to his wife who stood behind him, 'put on your shoes and run over to Branch's. Tell Carl I want him. We'll see what you got in the wagon, Lonny.'

Tobe and Dock Lapman were in the wagon bed. While the mules stood wearily, while Lonny leaned weakly against the wagon box, Jud Collins held the lamp high so that he and Carl Branch could see. Tobe Lapman was bound with many turns of rope, his eyes were rolled back and he breathed stertorously through his mouth. There were two wounds on Tobe's head, half cuts, half burns.

Dock was not bound. Dock lay as inert as a sack of corn.

'He's dead,' Carl Branch said. 'You killed him, Lonny.'

'I had to.' Lonny's voice was sodden. 'They killed Frank Banner. They—'

He lost his hold on the edge of the box and slid down to the street. He was not made of iron; Lonny Kesh was through.

'You'd better get Mike Groome, Carl,' Jud Collins said, 'and bring the doctor. An' listen, Carl, before you go—'

Mike Groome did not get to see Lonny until nearly noon. What with jailing his prisoner and getting Dock laid out and sending telegrams, Mike was busy, and anyhow the doctor said that Lonny was in no shape to answer questions. But just before noon Mike climbed puffing up the stairs to Jud Collins' bedroom.

Lonny was in bed, his eyes open and his head bandaged. Lonny had taken a lot of punishment. Jud sat beside the bed and Carl Branch, Cal Rutherford and Dolf Tawson occupied other chairs.

'They're the Lapman boys, all right,' the sheriff announced. 'The one that ain't dead finally come to an' admitted it. He's Tobe, an' the dead one's Dock. An' you know what? Tobe Lapman claims that Lonny was one of their bunch. He says that Lonny was with 'em at Plainfield.'

Lonny stirred and tried to sit up, but Jud Collins' broad hand restrained him. Jud's voice was calm. 'Now ain't that just like them fellows?' Jud asked. 'Tryin' to drag somebody into their meannesses? Tobe Lapman is tryin' to get even with Lonny. You can see that, can't you, Mike?'

Carl Branch and Dolf Tawson and Cal Rutherford nodded solemnly. Cal had come by Lonny's place early, and when he saw the wreck of the kitchen, and the blood, and found the mules and wagon gone, he struck out for Dolf's. They had come hotfoot to town to learn what had happened to Lonny, and wound up at Jud Collins' house.

'Maybe that's it,' Mike said dubiously, 'but I got to question Lonny.'

Lonny opened his mouth to speak and tried to sit up again, but once more Jud Collins restrained him. Jud's deep voice spoke smooth interruption.

'The doctor don't want Lonny excited,' Jud said. 'You can't question him right now, Mike. But that business about Lonny bein' with the Lapmans at Plainfield is just a plain damn lie. He couldn't have been there.'

Astonishment struck Lonny Kesh and he ceased to push against Jud's hand. His eyes widened as far as the bruises would allow and he slumped back against the pillows.

'I'll tell you why,' the banker continued. 'Me and Carl an' Dolf knew where Lonny was all the time. We'd wrote him that his folks was dead an' he was on the way home when that Plainfield business happened. Ain't that so, boys?'

Again the trio nodded solemnly.

'You certainly ain't goin' to take an outlaw's word against ours, are you, Mike?' Jud Collins concluded.

'No,' Mike said slowly, 'of course not, Jud.' Mike was still puzzled. There was a thing here that Mike Groome did not understand. 'Just the same,' Mike said, 'I'd like to talk to Lonny. I got to know what happened. An' I've got to get things straight on account of the rewards an' all.'

'Sure,' Jud Collins said. 'You want to get things straight, an' there are those rewards to think about. I'll tell you what happened, Mike. You got word that the Lapmans were around, so you set a trap for 'em. You got Lonny to help you because you could trust him and because he's handy with a gun an' so on. That's what happened. Dock Lapman got killed in the fracas an' you arrested Tobe, so of course you get the rewards, you bein' an officer an' Lonny just a private citizen. The way I look at it, Double Rivers is lucky to have a smart an' efficient deputy sheriff, an' real proud of him. That two thousand dollars is goin' to come in mighty handy, ain't it, Mike?' Jud's face was a mask, his expression that of a poker player holding a pat hand.

Halfway through Jud's recital, Mike Groome had picked up his hat and begun to fan himself. It was coming just a little fast for Mike, but Mike was not dumb. He could see as far down a rat hole as the next man, and two thousand dollars sheds a powerful light.

'But,' Mike said, 'I didn't—'

'Of course you did,' Jud interrupted. 'Just think back an' you'll remember.'

Mike got up. He put on his hat carefully, then took it off again.

He scratched his head, buzzing with ideas. He looked at Jud and Cal and Carl and Dolf, four of the big men of Double Rivers, prosperous, substantial citizens. Mike scratched his head again.

'Seems to me you're right,' Mike agreed. 'I did stop by an' talk to Lonny about the Lapmans that time I was lookin' for John Hance. That's right. I did.'

'Now you're getting it,' Jud Collins praised, and his cohorts grunted approbation. 'Sure you did, Mike. Just take it from there.'

A sudden grin broke all across Mike Groome's face, a two-thousand-dollar grin, and he started for the door. He placed his hand on the doorknob, then turned back to the room. 'There'll be some talk,' he said, dubious once more. 'There's bound to be.'

'Talk?' Jud Collins waved a contemptuous hand. 'There's always talk. Folks talk about everything. Why, there was even talk about the bank, just because the examiner come, an' everybody knows the bank is sound as salt. We all got money in it.'

THE FIRE KILLER

By Steve Frazee

YOUNG Bill Orahood, the Sky Hook owner, was waiting for Ken Baylor where the trail forked near the fall-dry bed of Little Teton Creek. Orahood was mostly arms and legs and a long neck. Without a word he swung his chunky sorrel in beside Baylor and they rode toward Crowheart.

They went a quarter of a mile before Orahood blurted out the question that everyone in the Crowheart country was asking: 'What do you suppose got Paxton?'

Baylor shook his head. Maybe Doc Raven knew by now. Raven had not been in town late yesterday afternoon when a drifting rider brought Bill Paxton's body out of Big Ghost Basin.

'You saw Paxton?' Orahood asked. 'After–'

'Yeah.' It was something to forget, if a man could.

A mile from town they caught up with big Arn Kullhem. A wide chunk of a man, his flat jaw bristling with sandy stubble, Kullhem looked at them from deep-set eyes and did not even grunt when they spoke. His Double K lay right on the break into Big Ghost. More than any rancher, he had suffered from what was happening down in the basin.

Bridle bits and saddle leather and hooves against the autumn-crisp grass made the only sounds around them until they came to the top of the last rolling hill above Crowheart. Then Kullhem said, 'Doc Raven didn't give us no help on them first two.'

Bill Paxton was the third man to die in Big Ghost. First, an unknown rider, and then Perry Franks, Kullhem's foreman. Both Franks and Paxton, one of the twins of Crow Tracks, had staked out in the basin to get a line on the shadowy men who were wrecking the Crowheart ranchers. If they had died from bullets, Baylor thought, the situation would be clear enough.

'Who's going to stay down in the basin now?' Kullhem growled.

Orahood and Baylor looked at each other. Strain had been building higher on Orahood's blistered face the closer they rode to town. He and Baylor glanced over their shoulders at the hazed ridges that marked the break above the gloomy forests of Big Ghost.

Up here the grass was good, but when the creeks ran low cattle went over the break to the timber and the swamps in the basin—and then they disappeared. Big Ghost was an Indian reservation, without an Indian on it. Fearful spirits, the ghosts of mutilated dead from an ancient battle with Teton Sioux, walked the dark forests of the basin, the Shoshones said. Even bronco Indians stayed clear of Big Ghost.

The cowmen had no rights in the basin; they had been warned repeatedly about trespassing on Indian land, but their cattle were unimpressed by governmental orders. That made the basin a wealthy raiding ground for rustlers from the west prairies, who came through the Wall in perfectly timed swoops.

For a time the Crowheart ranchers had checked the raids by leaving a man in Big Ghost as lookout. Franks, then Bill Paxton. Baylor knew there was not a man left up here who would volunteer to be the third lookout in Big Ghost—not unless Doc Raven could say what it was a man had to face down there.

They crossed Miller Creek, just west of town. A man on a long-legged blue roan was riding out to meet them. Baylor looked up the street at a small group of men in front of Raven's office, and then across the street at a larger group on the shaded porch of the Shoshone Saloon.

Kullhem spat. 'You still say, Baylor, that Baldray ain't behind all this hell?'

'I do.' Jim Baldray, the Englishman, owned the I.O.T. His range was fenced all along the break, with permanent camps where the wire winged out. Baldray had the money to keep his wire in place. I.O.T. stuff did not drift down into Big Ghost. There was nothing against the Englishman, Baylor thought, except a sort of jealous resentment that edged toward suspicion.

'You and your brother-in-law don't agree, then,' Kullhem said harshly.

Pierce Paxton, the twin brother of the man now lying on

Raven's table, was not Baylor's brother-in-law yet, but he would be in another month.

Hap Crosby met them at the lower end of the street. He was the oldest rancher in the country. Sweat was streaking down from his thick, grey sideburns. He looked at Baylor. 'Baldray's here. Pierce wants to question him—if Raven don't have the answer.'

All the Paxtons had been savagely impatient when anger was on them. Pierce, the last one, would ask questions, answer them himself, then go for his pistol. Baldray would be forced to kill him. Pistol work was the first custom of the country the Englishman had learned; and he had mastered it.

'All right, Hap.' Baylor looked up the street again. He saw it now. He should have seen it before: the tension there on the Shoshone porch was as tangible as the feel of the hot sun.

'Did Doc—has he—' Orahood asked.

'No, not yet,' Crosby said curtly. 'Baldray's drinking with that drifter who brought Bill Paxton in.'

'Does that mean anything?' Baylor asked evenly.

'I didn't say so, did I?' Crosby answered.

Four other ranchers were waiting with Pierce Paxton at the hitch rail in front of Raven's office. Paxton did not look around. Sharp-featured, tense, his black hat pushed back on thick brown curly hair, he kept staring at the doorway of the Shoshone. He was wound up, dangerous. He was fixing to get himself buried with his brother that afternoon, Baylor thought.

Slowly, sullenly, Arn Kullhem said, 'By God, I think he's right.'

'How far would you go to back that?' Baylor asked. 'Across the street?'

Kullhem's deep-set eyes did not waver. 'I wonder sometimes just where you stand in this thing, Baylor.'

Old Crosby's features turned fighting-bleak and his voice ran hard with authority when he said, 'Shut up, the both of you! We got trouble enough.'

It was the slamming of Doc Raven's back door, and then the whining of his well sheave that broke the scene and gave both Baylor and Kullhem a chance to look away from each other.

The ranchers stood there in the hot strike of the sun, listening to the doctor washing his hands. Orahood's spittle clung to his lips, and a greyness began to underlay his blisters. A few of the loafers from the Shoshone porch started across the street.

Doc Raven came around the corner of his building, wiping his hands on his shirt. He was a brisk, little, grey-haired man who had come to the country to retire from medicine and study geology.

'Well?' Kullhem rumbled, even before Raven reached the group.

Raven shook his head. His eyes were quick, sharp; his skin thinly laid and pink, as if it never required shaving. 'He was smashed by at least a dozen blows, any one of which would have caused death. His clothing was literally knocked from him, not ripped off. I can't even guess what did it.'

The sweat on Crosby's cheeks had coursed down through dust and was hanging in little drops on the side of his jaw. 'Maybe a grizzly, Doc?'

Raven took a corncob pipe from his pocket. He nodded. 'A silver bear would have the power, yes. But there isn't so much as a puncture or a claw mark on Paxton.'

'No bear then,' Orahood muttered.

Raven scratched a match on the hitch rail. 'It's like those other two cases. I don't know what killed any of them.'

With one eye on Pierce Paxton, Baylor asked, 'Could it be he was thrown from a cliff first, then–'

'No,' Raven said. 'Those granite cliffs would have left rock particles ground into the clothes and flesh.'

Pierce Paxton had turned his head to watch the doctor. Now he started across the street. Baylor caught his arm and stopped him.

'No, Pierce. You're off on the wrong foot.'

Paxton's face was like a wedge. 'The hell! How much of *your* stuff was in Baldray's holding corral that time?'

Baylor said, 'You know his men had pushed that stuff out of the wire angle. There was a man on his way to Crow Tracks to tell you when you and Bill happened by the I.O.T.'

'That's right, Pierce,' Crosby said.

'Say it was, then.' Paxton's lips were thin against his teeth.
'I want to ask Baldray how it happens he can ride Big Ghost,
camp out there whenever he pleases, and ride out again, but
Franks and my brother–'

'I ride it, too,' Raven said.

Paxton backed a step away from Baylor. 'They know damned
well, Doc, that you're just looking for rocks!'

'Who are *they*?' Kullhem asked.

'That's what I'm going to ask Baldray.' Paxton knocked Baylor's
hand away and started across the street. One of the loafers had
already scurried inside. Baylor walked beside Paxton, talking in
a low voice. The words did no good, and then Baldray was
standing in the doorway, squinting.

The I.O.T. owner was a long, lean man, without much chin.
He wore no hat. His squint bunched little ridges of tanned flesh
around his eyes and made him appear nearsighted, almost simple.
The last two to make an error about that expression had been
drifting toughs, who jeered Baldray as a foreigner until they
finally got a fight out of him. It had lasted two shots, both
Baldray's.

Baldray blinked rapidly. 'Not you also, Baylor?'

Paxton stopped, set himself. The Englishman stepped clear of
the doorway.

'Baldray–' Paxton said.

Baylor's rope-scarred right hand hit Paxton under the ear. The
blow landed him on his side in the dust. Crosby and Doc Raven
came running.

'Give a hand here!' Raven said crisply. Two of them stepped
out to help carry Paxton away.

'The hotel,' Crosby said. He looked back at Baylor. 'I can
handle him now.'

Baldray smiled uncertainly. 'Come have a drink, men!'

Across the street, the little knot of ranchers stared silently. Then
Kullhem swung up, and said something to the others in a low
voice. Orahood was the last. Baylor went into the Shoshone.

The gloom of the big room reminded him of the silent, waiting
forests of Big Ghost. He stood at the bar beside Baldray, who
was half a head taller. Kreider, who had found Bill Paxton at

the edge of the timber in Battleground Park, took his drink with him toward a table. A man in his middle twenties, Baylor guessed. The rough black beard made him appear older. Just a drifting rider?

Baldray poured the drinks. 'Hard business, Baylor, a moment ago. I would have been forced to shoot him.'

'Yeah.' Baylor took his drink.

'Raven found nothing?'

'Nothing—just like the two others. What do you make of it, Baldray?'

The Englishman's horsy face was thoughtful. He smoothed the silky strands of his pale hair. 'A beast. It *must* be an animal of some kind. As a young man in Africa I saw things you would not believe, Baylor; but I still contend there must have been credible explanations. . . . And yet there are strange things that are never explained, and they leave you wondering forever.'

There was a hollow chord in Baldray's voice, and it left a chill on Baylor's spine when he thought of Big Ghost and of the way Bill Paxton had been smashed.

'The rustlers always did steal in and out of the basin, of course,' Baldray said. 'They nearly ruined me before I fenced the break and hired a big crew. You fellows made it nip-and-tuck by keeping a scout down there, but now with this thing getting your men . . .' Baldray poured another drink.

The 'thing' rammed hard at Baylor's mind.

'Isn't it sort of strange that this animal gets just our men, Baldray? After this last deal we won't be able to find a rider with guts enough to stay overnight in the basin. That means we'll be cleaned out properly.'

Baldray nodded. 'It does appear that this thing is working for the rustlers—or being used by them, perhaps. The solution, of course, is to have Big Ghost declared public domain.'

'Fifty years from now.'

'It's possible sooner, perhaps.' Baldray's face took on a deeper colour. 'Fence. I'll lend what's needed for thirty miles. Damn it, Baylor, we're all neighbours!'

He had made the offer before and Kullhem had growled it down in rancher's meeting. Fencing was not all the answer for the little owners. It was all right for I.O.T. because Baldray could afford a big crew, and because the cattle of other ranchers were drifting into the basin. Shut all the drifting over the breakoff, and then the rustlers would be cutting wire by night. The smaller ranchers could not hire men enough to stop that practice.

Baylor looked glumly at his glass. The immediate answer to the problem was to go into Big Ghost and find out what was making it impossible to keep a lookout there. He walked across to Kreider.

'Would you ride down with me to where you found Bill Paxton?'

No man could simulate the unease that stirred on Kreider's dark face. 'You figure to come out before dark?'

'Why?'

'You could tell that this Paxton had been in his blankets when he got it. He shot his pistol empty before...' Kreider took his drink quickly. 'No, I don't guess I want to go down into the basin, even in daylight—not for a while.' He looked at Baldray. 'You don't run stuff down there, do you, Mr. Baldray?'

Baldray shook his head.

So the Englishman had hired this man, Baylor thought. There was nothing unusual about that, but yet it left an uneasy movement in Baylor's mind. 'You're afraid to go down there, huh?' he asked.

Kreider was staring into space. 'Uh-huh,' he said. 'Right now I am.' He was still looking at something in his own mind when Baylor went out.

She was young, with red-gold hair and an eye-catching fullness in the right places. She could ride like a demon and sometimes she cursed like one. Ken Baylor looked at his sister across the supper table at Hitchrack, and then he slammed his fist hard against the wood.

'Sherry!' he said, 'I'll paddle your pants like Pop used to if you ever even think about riding down there again!'

'Can it. Your face might freeze like that.'

Baylor leaned back in his chair, glowering. After a few moments he asked, 'Where was this moccasin track?'

'By a rotted log, just south of where Bill Paxton had camped.'

No Indian. Raven sometimes wore moccasins.

'There was a mound of earth where Bill's fire had been. Smoothed out.'

Kreider had mentioned the mound, but not the smoothness. 'At least that puts a man into it,' Baylor said.

Sherry gave him a quick, narrow look. 'You felt it?'

'Felt what?'

'A feeling that something is waiting down there, that maybe those Shoshone yarns are not so silly after all.' She hurried on. 'Sure, I know whatever it is must be related in some way to the rustling, but just the same . . .'

After a long silence she spoke again. 'No one would go with you, huh?'

'Orahood. Just to prove that he wasn't scared.'

After he left Crowheart that morning Baylor had found the ranchers meeting at Kullhem's. If it had not been for Crosby, they would not have invited him to get down; and even then, desperate, on the edge of ruin, they had been suspicious, both of Baylor and each other.

'Old Hap Crosby wasn't afraid, was he?' Sherry asked.

'No. But he wasn't sure that getting this thing would cure the rustling. He favoured more pressure on the Territorial representatives to have Big Ghost thrown out as reservation land. Then we could camp down there in force.'

The others had ideas of their own, but threaded through all the talk had been the green rot of distrust—and fear of Big Ghost Basin. Baylor told Sherry about it.

'Damned idiots!' she said. 'In their hearts they know that Baldray—or no other rancher up here—is mixed in with the rustlers!'

Baylor hoped it was that way. He got up to help with the dishes, stalling to the last. They heard Gary Owen, one of Hitchrack's three hands, come in from riding the break.

'Take *him*,' Sherry said. 'He's not afraid of the devil himself.'

Baylor nodded.

'I'm going to Crowheart,' Sherry said. 'If Pierce still wants trouble with Baldray, it will start in town—except that I'll see it doesn't start.' She rode away a little later, calling back, 'So long, Bat-Ears. Be careful down there.'

Owen's brown face tightened when he heard the 'down there.' He was standing at the corral with Baylor. 'You headed into the Ghost?' he asked.

'Tonight.'

'Saw two men on the Snake Hip Trail today, a long ways off.'

Owen removed his dun Scotch cap, replaced it. He lit a short-stemmed pipe. 'Want me to go along?' He forced it out.

Baylor tried to be casual. 'One man will do better, Gary.'

'Say so, and I'll go!'

Baylor shook his head. They could not smooth it out with talk.

Three times the ranchers had gone over the escarpment in daylight, ready for full-scale battle. On the second try they had found horse tracks leading away from cattle bunched for a drive through the West Wall. Crosby claimed the rustlers had a man in the basin at all times, watching the break. Baylor thought so, too. But the idea had been lost in the general distrust of each other after the third failure.

Baylor was not thinking of men as the neck of the dun sloped away from him on this night descent in the huge puddle of waiting blackness. The night and Big Ghost were working on him long before he reached the first stream in the basin.

He stopped, listening. The tiny fingers of elementary fear began to test for climbing holds along the crevices of Baylor's brain. He swung in the saddle, and when he put his pistol away he told himself that he was a fool.

Shroud moss hanging across the trail touched his face. He tore at it savagely in the instant before he gained control. He came from the trees into the first park. War Dance Creek was running on his right, sullenly, without splash or leap.

All the streams down here were like that. Imagination, Baylor argued. He had come over the break unseen. The moss proved he was the first one down the trail in some time. *The first rider, maybe. What is behind you now?* Before he could stop himself, he whirled so quickly he startled the dun.

Back there was blackness, utter quiet. He strained to see, and his imagination prodded him. There was cold sweat on his face. He cursed himself for cowardice.

Where the trail crossed the creek, he would turn into dense timber and stake out for the night. He was here, safe. There was nothing he could do tonight. In the morning . . .

It was night when the Thing got Paxton. . . .

The dun's right forefoot make a sucking sound. The animal stumbled. There was no quick jar of the saddle under Baylor, and he knew, even as he kicked free and jumped, that the stumble had been nothing, that the horse had bent its knee to recover balance before he was clear of leather.

Baylor stood in the wet grass, shaken by the realization of how deeply wound with fear he was. The dun nosed him questioningly. He patted the trim, warm neck and mounted again. If there were anything behind him, the dun would be uneasy.

'. . . *there are strange things that will never be explained, Baylor* . . .' Baldray had said that in the Shoshone, and now Baylor was sure he had not been mocking him or trying to plant an idea.

Baylor spent the night sitting against a tree, with his blankets draped around him. The dun was tied on the other side of the tree. Baylor's carbine was close at hand, lying on the sheepskin of the saddle skirts. The carbine was too small of calibre, Baylor thought, too small for what he was looking for. What *was* he looking for?

Out of the dead silence, from the ancient, waiting forest, came another chilling question. *What is looking for you, Baylor?*

of the saddle ckirts. The carbine was too small of calibre, Baylor rose stiffly. He ate roast beef from his sack, and finished with a cold boiled potato. Raven was the only other man he knew who liked a cold spud. Raven had come to the Crowheart country just about the time cattle rustling began in earnest, after a long period of inactivity.

The nameless fears that had passed were now replaced with the suspicions of the conscious mind.

Early sunlight was killing dew when Baylor rode into Battle-ground Park. He picked up the tracks of Sherry's little mare, coming into the park from the Snake Hip Trail. Owen had seen two riders on the Snake Hip the day before, but there was no sign that they had come this far. He followed Sherry's trail straight to where Paxton had been killed.

Baylor studied the earth mound over the fire site. It was too smooth, and so was the torn ground around it; and yet, the earth scars still spoke of power and fury and compulsion. An ant hill made a bare spot in the grass not fifteen feet away. Paxton would have used that. Because of the nature of his business here he would have had it figured in advance.

Baylor picked up a tip cluster of pine needles. He stared at the spruces. Their lower branches were withered, but here was broken freshness from high above. He went slowly among the trees close to the fire site. Here and there Paxton had broken dead limbs for his fire, but there was no evidence that anything had come down from the high branches.

He tossed the tip cluster away and went south of the camp to the rich, brown mark of a rotted log. There were Sherry's tracks again, but no moccasin print.

Out in the grass the dun whirled up-trail. Baylor drew his pistol and stepped behind a tree. A little later Baldray, wearing a fringed buckskin shirt, rode into the park with Doc Raven.

'We knew your horse,' Raven said. He was wearing Shoshone moccasins, Baylor observed.

Baldray's face turned bone-bleak when he saw a jumper fragment on a bush. 'Oh! This is the place, eh?' He swung down easily. 'Let's have a look, Raven.'

The doctor moved briskly. 'The devil!' he muttered. 'See how the fire has been covered.' His smooth, pink face was puzzled. He picked up the piece of jumper. 'Good Lord!'

Baldray's heel struck the tip cluster of pine needles and punched them into the soft earth. 'Did you discover anything, Baylor?'

'Nothing.' Baylor shook his head. Raven's saddlebags appeared to be already filled with rocks. Gary Owen said the doctor started at the escarpment and tried to haul half the country with him every time he went out. 'You fellows came down the Snake Hip?'

Raven was studying tree burls. 'We started in yesterday,' he said, 'but I had forgotten a manual I needed, so we rode out last evening.' He looked at Baldray. 'You know, James, in the big burn along the cliffs I've seen jackpine seeds completely embedded in the trunks. I have a theory—'

'Rocks, this time,' Baldray said. 'If you want to look at that quartz on the West Wall before night you'd better forget the tree seeds.' He blinked. 'Tree seeds? Now isn't that odd?'

When the two men rode west Baylor stared at their backs, not knowing just what he thought.

Baylor spent the day working the edges of the swamps along lower War Dance. Cattle were wallowing everywhere. He was nagged by not knowing what he was looking for; he had expected to find some sign where Paxton had been killed, at least the moccasin track.

At sunset he came out in the big burn. Several years before, Indians had thrown firebrands from the cliffs to start a fire to drive game from the basin. The wind had veered, and the fire, instead of crowning across the basin, had roared along the cliffs in a mile-wide swath. That cured the Indians. Evil spirits, they said, had blown a mighty breath to change the wind.

With the bare cliffs at his back, Baylor looked across the spear points of the trees. The parks were green islands, the largest being Battleground Park, where Paxton had died. The Wall was far to his right, a red granite barrier that appeared impassable; but there were breaks in it, he knew, the holes where Crowheart cattle seeped away.

About a half-mile air-line a grey horse came to the edge of one of the emerald parks. Bill Paxton had ridden a grey into Big Ghost. Kreider had brought out only the rig.

Once down in the timber, it took an hour of steady searching before Baylor found the right park. The limping grey knee-high in grass was Paxton's horse, all right. It saw Baylor when he led the dun from the timber. It snorted and broke like a wild animal for cover. There was never a chance to catch it.

Baylor recoiled his rope, listening to the grey crashing away like a frightened elk. The horse had not been here long enough to go mustang. The terror of the night the Thing had got Bill Paxton was riding on the grey.

Night was coming now. Gloom was crouched among the trees. The little golden sounds of day were dead. *You are afraid, Big Ghost said. You will be like Paxton's horse if you stay here.*

Baylor went through a neck of timber between parks. In the dying light on lower War Dance he cut his own trail of the morning. Beside the dun's tracks, in the middle of a mud bar, he saw a round imprint. He hung low in the saddle to look. A man wearing moccasins had been on his trail. Here the man had leaped halfway across the mud bar, putting down only the toes and the ball of one foot to gain purchase for another jump to where the grass left no mark. The foot had slid a trifle forward when it struck, and so there was no way to estimate how large—or small—it had been.

Baylor was relieved. He could deal with a man, even one who used Indian tricks like that. If this fellow wanted to play hide-and-seek, Baylor would take him on—and catch him in the end, and find out why the man had erased the track that Sherry had seen.

Dog-tired, he made a cold camp far enough from War Dance so that the muttering water would not cover close sounds. He freed the dun to graze, ate a cold meal, and rolled up in his blankets. A wind ran through the timber.

Baylor rolled a smoke, and then he crumpled it. The scent of tobacco smoke would drift a long way to guide a man creeping in.

No man killed Paxton or the others.

Baylor lay wide awake, straining at the darkness, for a long time, until finally he slept from sheer exhaustion.

The morning sun was a wondrous friend. Baylor slopped the icy water of the stream against his face. The dun came from the wet grass and greeted him.

He rode south, then swung toward the Wall, crossing parks he had never seen before. He took it slowly, not watching his backrail. In the middle of the day, after crossing a park just like a dozen others, he dismounted in the timber and crept back to make a test.

For an hour he waited behind a windfall. The first sound came, the breaking of a stick on the other side of the tiny green spot. Baylor had been half dozing by then. Too easy, he thought; something was wrong. He heard hooves on the needle mat.

He had expected a man on foot. He crawled away and ran back to the dun, placing one hand on its nose, ready for the gentle pressure that would prevent a whinny. A little later he heard sounds off to his left. The man was going around, sticking to the timber. Slowly Baylor led his horse to intercept the sounds. The other man came slowly also, and then Baylor caught the movement of a sorrel, saw an outline of its rider.

He dropped the reins then and went in as quickly as he could. He made noise. The dun whinnied. The other rider hit the ground. A carbine blasted, funnelling pulp from a tree ahead of Baylor. He shot toward the sound with his pistol. The sorrel reared, then bolted straight ahead.

It flashed across a relatively open spot. It was Pierce Paxton's stallion. 'Oh, God!' Baylor muttered. 'Pierce.'

'Pierce!' he yelled.

There was silence before the answer came. 'Baylor?' It was Pierce Paxton. He was unshaven, red-eyed.

He said. 'Who the hell did you think you were trying to take!'

Baylor put his pistol away. 'Moccasin Joe. Who were you shooting at?'

'Anybody that tried to close in on me like that!' Tenseness was still laid flat on Paxton's thin features. 'Who's Moccasin Joe?'

Baylor told everything he knew about the man.

Paxton shook his head, staring around him at the trees. 'It's not Raven. I've been watching him and Baldray from the time they went across Agate Park.'

'Why?'

Paxton stared. 'You know why.' He rubbed his hand across his eyes. 'I think maybe I was wrong. We lost two men down here, Baylor, but Baldray and Raven never had any trouble. Now I know why. They got a cabin hidden in the rocks near the wall. They don't stay out in the open.' Paxton saw the quick suspicion on Baylor's face.

'Uh-huh, I thought so too, at first, Ken. I thought they knew what's loose down here, that they were hooked up with the rustlers. I watched them for a day and a half. All they did was pound quartz rock and laugh like two kids. They may be quite. crazy Baylor, but I don't think they're hooked up with the rustlers.'

Paxton rubbed his eyes again. 'Made a fool of myself the other day, didn't I? What did Sherry say?'

'Nothing much. We both made fools of ourselves a minute ago, Pierce. . . . Let's catch your horse.'

The stallion had stopped in the next park west. Paxton went in and towed the horse back on the run. It saw the dun and tried to break over to start trouble. Paxton sawed down brutally on the bit before he got the horse quieted. That was not like Paxton. The nights down here had worked on his nerves, too.

They went back in the timber and sprawled out. Paxton lay with his hands over his face.

'How you fixed for grub?' Baylor asked.

'Ran out yesterday.' Paxton heard Baylor rustling in his gunny sack. 'I'm not hungry.' But he finally ate, and he kept looking sidewise at Baylor until he asked, 'You've been here two nights?'

'Yeah.'

'Any trouble?'

'Scared myself some,' Baylor said. 'Did you?'

'I didn't have to. Since the first night I spent here I've been jumping three feet every time a squirrel cut loose. I had a little fire on Hellion Creek that night, with a couple of hatfuls of wet sand, just in case.'

Paxton had started with a defensive edge to his voice, but now it was gone and his bloodshot eyes were tight. 'The stallion just naturally raised hell. He got snarled up on his picket rope and almost paunched himself on a snag. I got him out of that and then I doused the fire.

'From the way the horse moved and pointed, I knew something was prowling. It went all around the camp, and once I heard it brush a tree.'

The hackles on Baylor's neck were up.

'You know how a lion will do that,' Paxton said. He shook his head. 'No lion. The next morning, in some fresh dirt where a squirrel had been digging under a tree, I saw a track'–Paxton put his hands side by side–'like that, Ken. No pads–just a big mess!' Paxton's hands were shaking.

'What was it, Baylor? The Thing that got Bill?'

The Thing. What else could a man call it? Baylor thought. He said, 'There's an explanation to everything.'

'Explain it then!'

'Take it easy, Pierce. We'll get it.'

The thought of action always helped steady Paxton. 'How?' he asked.

'First, we get this Moccasin Joe.' Baylor thought of something so clear he wondered how he had missed it. 'Did you stop in Battleground Park?'

'I didn't come down the Snake Hip.'

'Old Moccasin Joe has trailed me once, and now I think I know why.' The thought carried a chill. 'Here's what we'll do, Paxton. . . .'

Later, Baylor divided the food. It would be parched corn now, and jerky, about enough for two days, if a man did not care how hungry he got. 'Day after tomorrow,' Baylor said.

They rode away in different directions, Baylor going back to Battleground Park. He found the tip cluster that Baldray had stepped on, and dug it out of the earth and held it only a moment before dropping it again. Pine needles. Everything here was spruce. The fact had not registered the first time.

That tip cluster had come from a branch that Moccasin Joe had used to brush out sign. Probably he had carried the branch from across the creek. Moccasin Joe knew what the Thing was. He was covering up for it.

The dun whinnied. Baldray was riding into the lower end of the park. He veered over when he saw Baylor's horse.

'You haven't moved!' Baldray grinned to show he was joking. He was clean-shaven. He appeared rested, calm. That came easier when a man slept in a cabin and ate his fill, Baylor thought.

'You look done in,' Baldray said.

'I'm all right.'

Baldray squinted at the fringes of his beaded shirt. His face began to redden. 'It's no good sleeping out. Bumps and things, you know. I have a cabin near the Wall. Built it four years ago. Raven's there now. I wish you'd use it, Baylor. I'll tell you how to find it.'

Paxton had taken care of that.

'I know,' Baylor said.

Baldray blinked. 'Oh!' He raised pale brows. 'Well, yes, I've been a little selfish. Reservation land, so-called. If the fact got around that someone had built here—'

Baylor picked up the tip cluster. 'What kind of tree is that from?'

Baldray squinted. 'Evergreen.'

'Spruce or pine?'

The Englishman laughed. 'You and Raven! I know evergreen from canoe birch, but that's about all.'

Baldray was one Englishman who had not run for home after the big die-ups of the no-chinook years. He should know pine needles from spruce; but maybe he did not.

Baldray's face was stone-serious when he asked, 'Any luck?'

Baylor shook his head.

'There are harsh thoughts about me.' Baldray's voice was crisp. 'Fifteen years here and I'm still not quite a resident, except with you and Crosby.' Baldray looked around the park. 'This won't be reservation always. Room for I.O.T. down here, as well as the rest—once the rustlers are dealt with, and the government sees the light.'

Baldray slouched in the saddle, rolling a cigarette. 'I have watched the breaks in the Wall from the rocks near my cabin. There is a sort of pattern to the way the scoundrels come and go. I would say, Baylor—it is a guess, but I would say—the next raid might be due to go out through Windy Trail.'

His smoke rolled and lit, Baldray started away. 'Windy Trail. I'm going to tell Crosby, some of the others. Good name, Crosby. English, you know.'

He rode away.

.   .   .   .

It was not entirely hunger that made Baylor's stomach tighten as he rode across the burn the next afternoon. Like the others, the night before had been a bad one, with his mind and the deep, still forests speaking to him. He did not know now whether or not he was being trailed, but he had played the game all the way, and if Paxton had done his part, things might come off as planned.

Paxton was there, crouched in the rocks near the east side of the burn. They exchanged clothes behind the jumble of fire-chipped stone.

'I went out,' Paxton said. 'Sherry wants to see you tomorrow morning in Battleground Park.'

'Why didn't you talk her out of it?'

'You know better.' Paxton was stuffing paper under the sweatband of Baylor's hat.

'What does she want?'

'I don't know. She told me to go to hell when I ordered her not to come down here. Then she rode over to I.O.T. to see Baldray. I left a note in the bunkhouse for Gary Owen to come here with her.'

They were dressed.

'Keep in plain sight on the burn.' Baylor said. 'And keep going.'

'All right.' Paxton took the reins. 'Kullhem found out that Kreider was riding with the rustlers on the west prairie two weeks ago.'

'Fine. Just right. Get going.'

He watched Paxton ride away, past the black snags and leaning trees. The dun had gone into the rocks and the dun had gone out a few minutes later, and the rider was dressed exactly as he had been when going in. It might work, if Moccasin Joe was still trailing with his little pine-branch broom. The dirty bastard.

The sun died behind the red Wall. A wind came down across the rocks and stirred the tiny jackpines in the burn. Murk crept into the basin.

The man came from sparse timber at the east edge of the burn. Buckskins. Probably moccasins. Long yellow hair under a slouch hat. He paused and looked up where the dun had disappeared two hours before.

Baylor watched from a crack between the rocks. The man came clear, lifting his body easily over fallen trees. He walked straight at the rocks, then swung a little to the uphill side. Baylor drew his pistol and took a position behind a rock where the man would likely pass.

The steps were close, just around the rock. They stopped. With his stomach sucked in, breathing through a wide-open mouth, Baylor waited to fit the next soft scrape to the man's position. Silence pinched at nerve ends before the fellow moved again.

In two driving steps Baylor went around the rock. He was just a fraction late, almost on top of a beard-matted face, two startled eyes and that tangle of yellow hair. He swung the pistol.

Moccasin Joe went back like a cat, clutching a knife in his belt. Baylor's blow missed. The pistol rang on rock, and by then the knife was coming clear. Baylor drove in with his shoulder turned. The knife was coming down when the shoulder caught the man at the throat lacing of his shirt.

Baylor was on top when they went down. He got the knife arm then, and suddenly threw all his power into a side push. The man's hand went against the rock. Baylor began to grind it along the granite.

The rock was running red before Moccasin Joe dropped the knife. With the explosive strength of a deer he arched his body, throwing Baylor sidewise against the rock. One of the man's knees doubled back like a trap spring, then the foot lashed out and knocked Baylor away.

Moccasin Joe leaped up. He did not run. He dived in. Baylor caught him with a heeled hand under the chin. The man's head snapped back but his weight came on. A knee struck Baylor in the groin.

Sick with the searing agony of it, Baylor grabbed the long hair with both hands. He kept swinging Moccasin Joe's head into the rock until there was no resistance but limp weight.

For several moments Baylor lay under the weight, grinding

his teeth in pain; and then he pushed free, straightening up by degrees, stabbing his feet against the ground. The front sight of his pistol was smeared, the muzzle burred, and maybe the barrel was bent a little.

But he had the man who was going to tell him what was killing ranch scouts in Big Ghost Basin. Except for the knife, Moccasin Joe had carried no other weapon. Baylor cut the fellow's belt and tied his hands behind him. Blood was smeared in the tangled yellow hair.

Baylor had never seen him before.

Going down the burn, the prisoner was wobbly, but he was walking steadily enough before they reached the park, where Paxton was to come soon after dark. It was almost dark now. Just inside the timber Baylor made Joe lie down, then tied his ankles with Paxton's belt.

Firelight was a blessed relief after black, cold nights. 'The first man killed here was one of yours, Joe,' Baylor said. 'You boys got on to something that makes it impossible for us to keep a man here. What is it?'

After a long silence Baylor removed one of his prisoner's moccasins. The man's eyes rolled as he stared at the fire. Baylor squatted by the flames, turning the knife slowly in the heat until the thin edge of the blade was showing dull red.

Where the hell was Pierce Paxton?

'Put out the fire,' Moccasin Joe said.

'Talk some more.' Baylor kept turning the blade. 'That first man was one of yours, wasn't he?'

'Yeah.' Moccasin Joe was beginning to sweat. The skin above his beard was turning dirty yellow.

Baylor lifted the knife to let him see it.

'Your Thing has got us stopped,' Baylor said. 'What is it?'

The firelight ran on a growing fear in the captive's eyes. He started to speak, and then he lay back.

'First, the flat of the blade against the bottom of your arch, then the point between the hock and the tendon. I'll reheat each time, of course.' Even to Baylor his own words seemed to carry conviction.

'Put the fire out!'

Baylor lifted the knife again. The blade was bright red. 'I saw Teton Sioux do this once,' he lied calmly.

Moccasin Joe's breath was coming hard.

'You covered up something where Paxton was killed, didn't you? And then you checked back and wiped out a track of your own that you had overlooked.'

'Yeah.'

'Keep talking.'

'I want a smoke. I won't tell you anything until I get one!'

Baylor stared at the tangled face, at the terror in the man's eyes. For a customer as tough as this one had proved up in the rocks, he was softening pretty fast under a torture bluff.

Baylor laid the knife where the blade would stay hot. He rolled two smokes and lit them. He put one in Moccasin Joe's mouth.

'You got to untie my hands.'

'You can smoke without that.'

The cigarette stuck to the captive's lips. He tried to roll it free and it fell into his beard. He jerked his head back and the smoke fell on the ground. Baylor put it back in the man's mouth. He untied the fellow's hands.

Moccasin Joe sat up and puffed his cigarette, rolling his shoulders.

'Let's have it,' Baylor said.

'The bunch that's been raiding here ain't the one from the west prairie, like you think. We been hanging out on the regular reservation. The agent is getting his cut.'

It sounded like a quickly made-up lie. 'Is Kreider one of the bunch?'

The captive hesitated. 'Sure.'

'Describe him.'

Moccasin Joe did that well enough.

'What killed Paxton?'

'Which one was he?'

'The last one—in Battleground Park.'

'I'll tell you.' Moccasin Joe made sucking sounds, trying to get smoke from a dead cigarette.

Baylor took a twig from the fire. He leaned down. The captive's hands came up from his lap like springs. They clamped behind Baylor's neck and jerked. At the same time Moccasin Joe ducked his own head. Baylor came within an ace of getting his face smashed against hard bone.

He spread his hands between his face and the battering block just in time. Even so, he felt his nose crunch, and it seemed that every tooth in his mouth was loosened. He was in a crouch then, and Moccasin Joe's thumbs were digging at his throat. Baylor drove his right knee straight ahead.

Moccasin Joe's hands loosened. He fell back without a sound. Baylor stood there rubbing his knee. He could not stand on the leg for a while. The sensitive ligaments above the cap had struck squarely on the point of Moccasin Joe's jaw.

Once more Baylor cinched the man's arms tight behind his back. Let him die for want of a smoke. Blood dripped into the fire as Baylor put on more wood. He stared at the red-hot knife, wishing for just an instant that he was callous enough to use it.

Where in hell is Paxton? he thought.

Blood began to stream down his lips. He felt his way to the creek and washed his face and dipped cold water down the back of his neck. After a while the bleeding stopped. Both sides of his nose were swollen so tight he could not breathe through them. His lips were cut.

I'm lucky, he told himself, getting out with only a busted nose after falling for an old gag like that.

You're not out of it yet, Baylor. It's night again.

Once more the old voices of Big Ghost were running in his mind.

Baylor dipped Paxton's hat full of water and went back to the fire and Moccasin Joe.

'Sit up if you want a drink.'

It was a struggle for Moccasin Joe but he made it. His eyes were still a little hazy, but clear enough to look at Baylor with hatred.

Baylor took the knife from the fire and stood over his

captive, tapping his boot against the man's bare foot. Moccasin Joe looked at the glowing steel, and then at Baylor. His eyes showed no fear.

'You ain't got the guts.'

The bluff was no good. Baylor drove the knife into the ground near the fire. 'I've got guts enough to help hang you,' he said. 'We know you're one of the rustlers, and we know you've been doing chores for the Thing in the basin that's killed our men. Better loosen up, Joe.'

'My name ain't Joe.'

'That won't make any difference when you swing.'

'Talk away, cowboy.'

He's not afraid of me, Baylor thought, but it's up in his neck because of what he knows is out there.

It's out there, the night said.

Paxton should be coming. He should have been here an hour ago.

He went to the edge of the park, listening for the hoof sounds of the dun. There was nothing on the park but ancient night and aching quiet. Grunting sounds and the cracking of twigs sent Baylor running back to the fire. Moccasin Joe was trying to get away, pushing himself by digging his heels into the ground. He had gone almost twenty feet.

Baylor hauled him back to the fire. The man's muscles were jerking. 'They'll kill me,' he said, 'but that'll be the best way. Put out the fire. I'll tell you!'

'You've pulled a couple of fast ones already.'

'Put it out!'

Brutal fear came like a bad odour from the man. Baylor's back was crawling. He turned toward the creek to get another hatful of water.

Twigs popped. Something thudded softly out in the forest.

'It's coming! Turn me loose!' Moccasin Joe's voice rose in a hoarse, quavering scream. 'O Jesus ...' And then he was silent.

.   .   .   .

Standing at the edge of firelight, with his bent-barrelled pistol in his hand, Baylor was in a cold sweat.

Paxton's voice came from the forest. 'Baylor!'

'Here!' Baylor made two efforts before he got the pistol back in leather. By the time Paxton came in, leading the dun, Baylor's fear had turned to anger.

'Did you make another trip out to visit and have a shave?'

Paxton was in no light mood, either. His face was swelling from mosquito bites. He had clawed at them and smeared mud from his hairline to his throat. 'I got bogged down in a stinking swamp! Lost your carbine there, too.' He looked at Moccasin Joe. 'I see you got– What ails him?'

Moccasin Joe's eyes were set, unseeing. His jaw was jerking and little strings of saliva were spilling into his beard.

Mice feet tracked on Baylor's spine. 'Umm!' he said in a long breath. 'He thought you were the Thing!'

'The Thing! Good God!' Paxton's eyes rolled white in his mud-smeared face. His voice dropped. 'Your horse raised hell back there a minute ago.'

The dun was shuddering now, its ears set toward the creek. It was ready to bolt. Paxton drew his pistol.

'Put that popgun away!' Baylor cried. 'Help me get him on the horse!' He grabbed the knife and slashed the belt around Joe's ankles. 'Stand up!'

The man rose obediently, numbly, his jaw still working. Paxton leaped to grab the dun's reins when the horse tried to bolt toward the park.

Baylor threw Moccasin Joe across the saddle of the plunging horse.

'Lead the horse out of here!'

They crashed toward the park, with the horse fighting to get away, with Baylor fighting to keep Moccasin Joe across the saddle. The dun tried to bolt until they were in timber at the lower end of the park, and then it quieted.

'How far to the cabin where Raven is?' Baylor asked.

'Maybe four miles,' Paxton answered. 'I won't try no short cuts through a swamp this time.' He laughed shakily.

They spoke but little as they moved through the deep night of Big Ghost Basin. Baylor walked behind now. Paxton broke off a limb and used it as a feeler overhead when they were in timber. Each time he said 'Limb!' they heard Moccasin Joe grunt a little as he ducked against the horn.

Baylor guessed it was well after midnight when Paxton stopped in the rocks and said, 'It's close to here—some place. I'll go ahead and see.'

Baylor was alone. He heard Paxton's footsteps fade into the rocks. The dun was droop-headed now. Moccasin Joe was a dark lump in the saddle.

Relief ran through Baylor when he heard the mumble of voices somewhere ahead, and presently Paxton came back. 'The cabin is about a hundred yards from here. Raven's there.'

Paxton took care of the dun. Raven and Baylor led the captive inside. Moccasin Joe was like a robot. Light from a brass Rivers lamp showed a four-bunk layout, with a large fireplace at one end. There was a shelf of books near the fireplace, and rock specimens scattered everywhere else.

Raven's hair was rumpled. He was in his undershirt and boots. His pink face was shining and his eyes were sharp. He looked at Moccasin Joe and said, 'I thought *I* brought in specimens.'

Moccasin Joe was staring.

Raven took the man's right hand and looked at the grated knuckles. He stood on tiptoe to peer at the marks where Baylor had banged Moccasin Joe's head against the rock.

'I roughed him up,' Baylor said.

'You didn't hurt him.' Raven passed his hand before the man's face. 'Oregon! Oregon!' he said.

'Huh?' the man said dully.

'You know him?' Baylor asked.

'I saw him out on the west prairie a month ago, camped with a group of men. They called him that.'

'Rustlers, huh?'

'Probably. I ride where I like. Nobody bothers me. I've doctored a man or two out that way, without asking his business.'

'What's wrong with this one?' Baylor asked.

'Shock. His mind, roughly, is locked on something. Did you try to scare him to death?'

'Not me. Something scared the hell out of me, and Paxton, too. Maybe if we'd known what it was, we'd be like Mocc–Oregon.'

Paxton came in. Raven glanced at his face. 'Wash it off, and quit scratching the lumps, Paxton. Get some grease out of that jar there by the books.' Raven motioned Oregon toward a chair. 'Sit down there.'

Doc Raven went to work. He cleansed and dressed Oregon's hand, and took care of the cuts on his head, shearing into the long hair with evident satisfaction. 'Retire!' he muttered. 'I've got so I don't go to an out-building without taking a medical kit along.'

Raven was completely happy, Baylor thought.

'Help yourselves to the grub, boys,' the doctor said.

Oregon ate mechanically, staring at Raven most of the time. When Raven was briskly directing him into a bunk afterward, the doctor asked casually, 'Did Martin get over that dislocated shoulder all right?'

'Yeah,' Oregon said. 'Yeah, he's all right,' and then his eyes slipped back to dullness once more.

Raven looked at Paxton and Baylor. 'I think he'll be coming out of it after a night's rest. Go to bed. I'll just sit here and read.'

'I don't want that man to get away,' Baylor said. 'He's going to tell me something in the morning.'

Raven shook his head. 'You won't get anything out of this one, Baylor. I probed two bullets out of his chest once, and he never made a peep.'

Raven smiled at the suspicious stares of the two ranchers. 'I'm a doctor,' he said. 'Retired.' He laughed. 'Now go to bed, both of you.'

Raven was cooking when Baylor woke up. Paxton was still sound asleep. Oregon was lying in his bunk awake. There was complete awareness in his eyes when he looked at Baylor. Baylor said, 'Ready to talk?'

'To hell with you,' Oregon said.

Paxton woke up while Baylor was dressing. He took his pistol from under his blankets and walked across the room to Oregon. 'That was my brother that was killed by your pet a few days ago.'

Paxton turned toward Baylor. 'Let's stake this bastard out by a fire tonight—and leave him!'

'That's enough!' Raven's voice cut sharply. 'Oregon is yours, but let's have no more of that kind of talk.'

'What'll we do?' Paxton asked. 'I want to go with you to meet Sherry this morning, and—' He glanced at Raven.

'You stay here,' Baylor said. 'I'll see Sherry. What the hell does she want?'

The first hot meal in several days was like water in a desert. After breakfast Baylor brought the dun from a barred enclosure where a spring made a green spot in the rocks.

Paxton grumped about being left to watch the prisoner. Sherry would take some of that out of him soon enough, after they were married, Baylor thought.

Baylor went inside for one last word with Oregon. 'I know you lied about your bunch hanging out on the reservation, Oregon. How about Kreider?'

'You find out,' Oregon said.

Baylor looked at Paxton.

'Don't fret,' Paxton said. 'I'll watch him, all right.'

Raven walked outside with him. 'I know how you boys feel, Baylor. Out here you try to make things all black or all white. There's shades between the two, Baylor. I don't defend Oregon. I don't condemn him. You understand?'

'I'm trying to.'

'That helps. You want my rifle?'

'Carbine.' Baylor shook his head. 'Thanks, no.'

Sherry and Gary Owen were waiting in Battleground Park when he reached there. It was close to where Bill Paxton had been killed.

'What happened to your nose?' Sherry asked.

'Froze it in the creek. Nice place you picked to meet me.'

'Yeah.' Owen looked toward the little mound that covered the fire site. 'She picked it.'

Sherry said, 'Did you see anyone last night?'

'Pierce and me met a man, not socially, though. Who do you mean?'

'Any of the ranchers, tight-mouth. They came in last night, the crews from every outfit. Crosby and Baldray got them together. They're going to filter around and trap the rustlers tomorrow or the next day near the Wall.'

'Baldray's idea?' Baylor asked.

Owen nodded. 'Him and Kreider.'

'Kreider!'

'He's a special agent of the Indian Department,' Owen said. 'He was sent here to investigate a rumour that the rustlers were operating from reservation land. For a while he was in solid with them. From what we gathered, he's got a chum still with the bunch on the west prairie, and that fellow tipped Kreider off about the next raid.'

The rustlers must have caught on to Kreider, Baylor thought. That was why Oregon had been so willing to identify him as one of the gang. Tomorrow or the next day . . . Plenty of time for what Baylor had to do. He looked at a 45-50 Winchester in Owen's saddle boot.

'I'd like to borrow your rifle, Gary.'

'I brought one for you,' Sherry said. She walked into the grass and returned with a double-barrelled weapon.

Baylor hefted the piece. 'One of Baldray's.'

'Elephant gun,' Sherry said. 'A .577, whatever that is. She gave her brother, one by one, a half-dozen cartridges. 'Pierce told me he saw the track of something down here that scared him. Where is Pierce?'

His sister was quite a woman, Baylor thought. He told her and Owen about capturing Oregon. 'I figure it will be easier to get a line on this Thing, now that Oregon is out of the way.'

Owen stared at the timber edges of the park. 'Thing,' he muttered. 'I'll stay with you, Ken.'

'Take Sherry back to the benches—'

'I know the way,' Sherry said. 'You know something? Kreider says there's a bill going into the next Congress to make Big Ghost public land again.'

'Owen's taking you back to the benches,' Baylor said.

'You know who got action started on that bill?' Sherry asked. 'Jim Baldray.'

'Yeah,' Owen said. 'Even Kullhem admits now that he must have had the wrong idea about Baldray. I'll stay down here with you, Ken.'

'The two of you work well together,' Baylor said, 'changing the subject, throwing me off. All right, get out of here, Sherry, and be sure you're good and out before night.'

The girl got on her horse. Her face was pale under its tan. 'Don't depend entirely on that elephant gun, Ken. Get up in a tree, or something.'

'I figured on that,' Baylor said. 'So long, Red.'

The two men watched until she disappeared into the timber at the upper end of Battleground Park.

'Fighting rustlers don't scare me no more than a man's got a right to be scared,' Owen said abruptly. He dug out his short-stemmed pipe and lit it. 'But after I saw Paxton—and them other two, I'll admit I didn't have the guts to come down here at night. Now I'm here, I'll stay.'

Baylor was glad to have him—with that big-bored Winchester.

'I don't know what we're after,' Baylor said. 'But maybe in a couple of hours we'll know. Come on.'

They went back in the timber, and stayed out of sight until they came to the park below the burn, the place where Baylor had built his fire the night before. The memory of the night began to work on Baylor.

He felt a chill when he saw that the fire he and Paxton had left burning in their quick retreat had been covered with a great heap of dirt and needles. There were long marks in the torn ground, but no sharp imprints. The story was there. The fire had kept on smouldering under the first weight of dirt and dry forest mat, and the Thing had continued to throw dirt in a savage frenzy until the smoke had ceased. Fire. That was the magnet.

Owen sucked nervously on his pipe, staring.

'What done it?'

Baylor shook his head. 'Let's try the soft ground by the creek.'

They stood on the east bank. Baylor stared at the choke of willows and trees on the other side. Last night he had dipped water from this very spot, and over there somewhere the Thing had been pacing, circling, working up to coming in. It must have been quite close when he threw Oregon at the dun and ran in terror.

Night will come again, the voices said.

Baylor and Owen stayed close together while they searched. Farther up the stream they found where the Thing had leaped the creek in one bound. Four imprints in the muddy bank.

'I'll be dipped in what!' There was a little fracture in Owen's voice. 'That ain't no track of nothing I ever seen!'

The outlines were mushy. The mud was firm, but still there was no clear definition of form. The whole thing was a patchwork of bumps and ridges that would not fit any living creature Baylor had ever seen or heard of.

'That's no bear,' he said.

'Back in Ireland my grandmother used to scare us . . .' Owen shook his head.

On a limb snag across the creek they found a small patch of short, brittle hair with a scab scale clinging to it.

'There ain't nothing in the world with hair like that!' Owen cried.

Here with the shroud moss motionless on grey limbs, in the ancient stillness of Big Ghost, Baylor was again prey to fear of the Unknown, and for a moment there was no civilization because nothing fitted previous experience.

'The rustlers have seen it,' he said. 'Oregon said it got one of their men. They wouldn't have covered up for it if they hadn't been afraid we might recognize the sign.' He stared at Owen. 'Fire, Gary. Fire is what brings it!'

'I been here at night—with fire.' Owen hunched his shoulders.

'It's a big hole. A man might be lucky here for a long time, and then one night . . . Where are the ranchers going to meet?'

'They'll camp out in little bunches on those timbered hogbacks that point toward the West Wall. When they see Crosby's smoke signal from the Wall—'

'We've got to warn them, Gary. Orahood never spent a night

out in his life without building a fire. Get down there and pass the word—no fires!'

'That leaves you alone.'

'I've been several nights alone. Take the dun with you. I don't want him hurt.'

'Holy God, Ken! You don't want the dun hurt, but you—'

'Stick to the timber, Gary, so you won't mess up their trap.'

Baylor took both ropes from the saddles. Ready to leave, Owen said:

'Take my rifle. That elephant business only shoots twice.'

'I'll do better than that, from where I'll be. Tonight you'll like the feel of that big barrel across your knees, Gary,'

'Don't scare me. I already know I'm a damned coward. I *want* to leave here. I'll admit it.' Owen rode away.

Baylor did not like to admit how alone he felt.

Big Ghost nights always seemed to settle as if they had special purpose in making the basin a black hole. From his platform of laced rope between two limbs of a spruce tree, Baylor peered down to where his pile of wood was ready for a match. He had pulled in other fuel close to the site, enough to keep a fairly large fire all night.

It was about time to light it. The sooner the better. The smoke would make a long trail through the forest, the flames a little bright spot in the murk, and this Thing that must kill fire might be attracted. It would be a cinch from here.

A cinch? Maybe the Thing climbs trees.

Baylor climbed down and lit the fire. He waited just long enough to know that it would burn, and then he climbed again to his rope perch.

The blackness laughed at his haste.

Smoke came up between the ropes and began to choke him. That was a point he had not thought of at all; but presently the fire took hold in earnest, light reached out to touch the grey boles of waiting trees, and a small wind began to drift the smoke at a lower level.

Baylor tried to settle comfortably against the ropes. The sling of the heavy double-barrel was over a limb above him, so the weapon could not fall. The four spare cartridges were buttoned in the breast pocket of his jumper. He felt the cold, big roundness of them when he took out the makings of a cigarette.

It was as dark as a pocket up in the tree. For a while the oddness of being where he was intrigued Baylor, and then he thought of a dozen flaws in his plan. But if it did not work tonight, he would stay with it until it did. He reached over to touch the .577. The four spare cartridges did not count. He had two shots coming. They should be enough.

Bill Paxton's forty-five was empty when Kreider found him.

The night lagged. Big Ghost gathered all its secrets to it, and the darkness whispered. Three times Baylor went down to put wood on the fire. Each time he took the heavy rifle, and each time his flesh crawled until he was back on the rope net once more.

He smoked all his tobacco. Thirst started. He listened to the creek. It was not very far.

Go get yourself a drink, Baylor.

He tried not to listen. His thirst grew out of all proportions, and he knew it was not real. He could not be thirsty; he had drunk just before dark.

Get yourself a drink. Don't be a fool.

He waited till the fire needed wood. After building it up, he stood a moment by the tree, with one hand on the rope that led to safety.

Go on, Baylor. Are you afraid to get a drink?

The water was icy cold against the sweat on his face. He drank from cupped hands, then wiped them on his jumper, staring at the blackness across the creek. Last night the Thing had been somewhere out there. It might be there now.

He took two steps toward the fire. Something splashed in the water behind him. He was cocking the gun and swinging around all the time he knew the splash had come from a muskrat.

For a few moments he stood drying his hands over the heat, a little gesture of striking back at the Unknown. But when he started up the tree he went all the way with a rush.

In the cold hours long after midnight he was on the ground to tend the fire when he heard a soft sound beyond the limits of the light. He unslung the rifle and felt the thumping of his heart.

It's there. It's watching you.

He turned toward the tree. He heard the crush of dry pine needles. He cocked the gun and backed toward the tree, feeling behind him for the rope. Something moved on the edge of firelight. An enormous, shadowy form emerged from blackness. It rocked from side to side. A hoarse roar enveloped Baylor.

He fired the right barrel, and then the left. The Thing came in, bellowing.

Straight across the dying fire it charged, scattering embers. Baylor had another cartridge out, but he dropped it and clubbed the rifle. He was completely stripped now of all the thinking of evolved and civilized man.

The bellowing became a strangled grunt. The Thing was down, its hind legs in the flames. It tried to crawl toward Baylor, and then it was still. Baylor rammed another cartridge in and fired a third shot. The great bulk took the fearful impact without stirring.

Cordite rankness was in Baylor's nostrils as he kicked embers back toward the fire and put on fuel with shaking hands. The stench of burning hair sickened him. He pulled the flames away from the hind legs of the beast.

He had known what he was up against from the moment the animal had stood higher than a horse there on the edge of firelight, then dropped to the ground to charge. He had killed a grizzly bear.

When the flames were high he examined it. The feet were huge, misshapen, lacking the divisions of pads. All four were tortured, scrambled flesh that had fused grotesquely after being cruelly burned. Along the back and on one side of the bear were scabby patches where the hair had come back crisp and short. Around the mouth the flesh was lumpy, hideous from scar tissue. The jaws had been seared so terribly that the fangs and front teeth had dropped out.

He lifted one of the forelegs with both hands. There were traces of claws, some ingrown, the others, brittle, undeveloped fragments.

The forest fire several years before! The bear had been a cub then, or perhaps half grown. The poor devil, caught by the flames, probably against the rocks, since only one side was scarred. He pictured it whimpering as it covered its face with its forepaws. And then, when it could no longer stand the pain and fear, it must have gone loping wildly across the burning forest mat.

Before it recovered it must have been a skinny, tortured brute. No wonder it had gone crazy afterward at the smell and sight of flames.

He found one of his bullet holes in the throat. That had to be the first shot, when the grizzly had been erect. The other must be in the shoulder that was underneath, and it would take a horse and rope to make sure. He cut into a lump on the shoulder that was up. Just a few inches below the tough hide, under the fat, he found a .45 bullet. One of Bill Paxton's, probably.

That was enough examination. The poor, damned thing.

He was asleep by a dead fire when the savage crackling of gunfire roused him shortly after dawn. He sat up quickly. The firing ran furiously, somewhere near the Wall. Then the sounds dwindled to single cracks, at intervals. A little later Big Ghost was quiet.

Baylor hoped there was truth in what Owen had said about the basin going back to range. For the first time in days he heard the wakening sounds of birds. Before, he had been listening for something else.

He was asleep in the sun out in the park when the clatter roused him. The ranchers were coming out. Kullhem, his left arm in a sling, was riding with Baldray in the lead. Farther back, a man was tarpaulin-draped across his saddle.

Owen and Paxton spurred ahead to Baylor, who pointed toward the tarpaulin.

'Orahood,' Owen said. 'The only man we lost.'

Baylor was stabbed by the thought of Orahood's wife alone at Sky Hook, with a baby coming on.

Paxton said, 'We caught 'em foul on Windy Trail! We broke their backs!'

'Oregon?' Baylor asked.

'He tried one of his little tricks.'

Owen kept looking toward the forest.

264

'It's there,' Baylor said wearily.

Men gathered around the grizzly.

'Good Lord!' Crosby kept saying. 'Would you look at the size of that!'

'That must have been a spot of fun, eh, Baylor?' Baldray frowned, not satisfied with his words. 'You know I mean a narrow place—a tight one.'

Raven was all around the bear, like a fly. 'Unusually fine condition,' he mused. 'How did he get food while he was recovering from those burns?'

'He healed himself in a swamp,' Kullhem growled. 'There's always cows and calves bogged down in the swamps.'

'A remarkable specimen, nonetheless.' Raven drew a sheath knife. 'I'll have a look at that stomach and a few other organs.' He hesitated. 'Your bear, of course, Baylor. You don't mind?'

'Yeah.' Baylor shook his head slowly. 'Leave him be, Raven. The poor devil suffered enough when he was alive.'

Raven stood up reluctantly. He put his knife away. 'I guess I understand.'

Baldray's bony face showed that he understood. 'Fire killer,' he said. 'The poor damned beast.'

HANGING FIRE

By Richard Deming

E L LOBO was half drunk when rumour of the intended lynching first seeped into the Royal Pastime Café. Had he not been, he probably would have sat the affair out with cautious disinterest, for he was not prone to borrow the troubles of others. But alcohol spurred his natural mischievousness.

There was a lot of mischief in El Lobo to be spurred, though you would not have guessed it by cursory examination of his bland face. For that matter, you would hardly understand how such a mild-appearing youngster had earned the title El Lobo, for there was nothing wolf-like in his appearance.

Small, slight of build and tow-headed, he had a wide friendly mouth with slightly protruding but beautifully regular teeth, a span of freckles across his button nose and brilliant blue eyes which stared at the world with what seemed to be childlike curiosity. Worn levis, scarred boots run down at the heels and an ancient Stetson somehow fitted the rest of his appearance, marking him a drifting range hand. The tied-down forty-fours he wore low on either hip could have been ascribed to the affectation of a boy trying to pass as a man.

He was forty dollars down in the poker game and was incautiously considering reaching inside his shirt for the money belt next to his skin when news of the intended lynching temporarily broke up the game. It started with a mutter running along the bar, moved restlessly through the room and reached the preoccupied gamblers last. El Lobo grew conscious of it when fat Tim Harris, the dealer, stopped in the middle of a shuffle, looked up at a kibitzing cowhand and said sharply, 'Johnny Carson? Why he's only a kid!'

'Old enough to steal cattle, seems like,' the cowhand said laconically. 'They caught him red-handed with the money on him and riding the same horse he used to steal the steers.'

Tim Harris lay down the cards, slapped both hands on the table and pushed his fat body erect. He was an enormous man, well over six feet and encased in nearly three hundred pounds of fat. His normally cheerful face was set with determination.

'Anybody says old Henty Carson's kid is a rustler has got to prove it to me before they string him up,' he announced. 'You boys just leave your chips lay and we'll resume after I break up a lynching.'

When the cowhand who had delivered the news emitted a mocking laugh, the fat gambler glared at him.

Sobering, the cowhand said in explanation, 'Gregg Stanton, with the whole Circle K behind him, has got the kid. Think you can back down Gregg?'

'I can try!' the fat man snapped.

Lumbering to the bar, he disappeared behind it and when he reappeared he was buckling a gun belt beneath his long black frock coat. Like a charging buffalo his huge body crashed aside the batwings as he left the café.

'This I gotta see,' one of the poker players remarked, rising to follow the fat man.

When the remaining players joined the general exodus from the Grand Pastime, El Lobo rose languidly and trailed in their wake. He was not really interested, for the name Johnny Carson meant nothing to him, and during his hectic twenty-two years he had too often been the elusive quarry of lynching parties to generate much curiosity about one whose attention was centred on someone other than himself. Had he been a substantial winner in the poker game, he might have appointed himself Tim Harris' bodyguard simply to insure the gambler stayed alive to cash in chips, but since at the time the game was suspended El Lobo had before him only a single white chip worth twenty-five cents, he had no stake to protect. He trailed along simply because otherwise he would have been left sitting alone in the café.

The lynching party was gathered beneath the crossbeam at the entrance to Nelson's Corral. It consisted of some twenty lean, range-hard hands of the Circle K, led by their foreman, Gregg Stanton.

The victim, a lank gangling youngster of about nineteen, was backed against the corral fence, his hands tied behind his back. He was making a determined effort to appear unfrightened, but his long, horse-like face was a dirty grey and he constantly licked his lips as he watched his captors from enormous eyes.

Gregg Stanton, a noosed rope trailing from one hand, seemed to be arguing with another man when El Lobo pressed through the crowd to within earshot. Stanton was a powerfully built man with hunched shoulders and arms nearly as thick as his bull neck. His square face, scarred and battered from countless barroom fights, was not unkindly, but it was the stubborn face of a man who rules by force and understands no other form of leadership.

The man Gregg Stanton addressed was a thin, middle-aged man dressed in store clothes of impeccable cut. He had an intelligent but somewhat weak-chinned face, its weakness at the moment enhanced by its proximity to the large jaw of Gregg Stanton, which was thrust within inches of it. Apparently the thin man had ridden up to the lynching party and then dismounted, for his left hand clasped the reins of a magnificent black stallion bearing the Circle K brand.

'It seems to me the least we could do is check the boy's story,' he was saying in a mildly protesting tone.

'It's the same pony, ain't it?' Gregg Stanton growled. 'Indian Charlie says it leaves the same track as the rustler's, and Indian Charlie never made a tracking mistake in his life.'

'But the lad says he won the pony at Juarez,' the thin man objected. 'Why can't we send one of the men down there to check his story?'

'And wait two days till he gets back? What's the matter with you, Mr. Galt? Anybody'd think they weren't your cattle, the way you're trying to discourage us from convincing rustlers it ain't safe to steal from the Circle K.'

El Lobo asked the man next to him, 'Who's the thin fellow in the glad rags?'

'Emil Galt,' the man said from the side of his mouth. 'Owns the bank and a lot of other things, including the Circle K. Stanton runs the Circle K for him, but the way he acts, you'd think Gregg owned it. A dollar'll get you two Stanton gets his way.'

El Lobo shook his head. 'No bet.'

Tim Harris managed to force his fat frame through the encircling crowd to where the Circle K owner and his tophand argued. Panting from the exertion of shouldering passage through the human wall, he paused to wipe his perspiring face with a bandanna. Then he tucked it away, hitched up his gun belt and glared belligerently at Emil Galt.

'You thinking of taking the law in your own hands, Mr. Galt?'

The thin man glanced at him with distaste, and in the face of this flank attack unexpectedly switched sides.

In a cold tone he said, 'I don't see any other law around here, Harris.'

'They's a sheriff's office at the county seat,' the gambler said tartly. 'And we'd have a town marshal if certain influential citizens wasn't too niggardly to kick in with enough to pay a salary.' He swung his eyes to the youth against the fence, then back to Galt. In a flat tone he said, 'You ain't hanging Henty Carson's son without a fair trial.'

'He had a fair trial,' Gregg Stanton snapped. 'He was riding the rustler's horse and we caught him coming back across the Rio Grande with six hundred dollars in his jeans. That bandit El Diablo pays twenty dollars a head for prime beef, and thirty head comes to six hundred dollars. Where else would a kid like Johnny Carson get six hundred dollars? He never had more than ten dollars at once in his life before.'

Momentarily Tim Harris looked shaken. Then his eyes hardened again. 'You just let me talk to the boy a minute, Stanton.'

He took a step toward the silent youngster, but Gregg Stanton placed one huge hand against his chest and pushed him back.

'I'm through arguing,' he growled. 'We're hanging this cow-thief right now!' He tossed the rope he had been holding toward the group of Circle K hands ringing Johnny Carson. 'String him up boys!'

Tim Harris brushed back his coat tail to fumble for his gun. His clumsiness was almost ludicrous, and the Circle K foreman watched mockingly until the gambler's pudgy hand grasped the stock. Then with deft suddenness Gregg's gun jumped into his hand and centred on the fat man's stomach. Tim hurriedly raised both hands palm outward and backed a step.

'Guess that settles that argument,' Gregg said contemptuously, slamming his pistol back in its sheath.

At that point the whiskey in El Lobo got the best of his natural caution. There was not enough in him to affect his muscular co-ordination, for he was too often dependent on that co-ordination ever to let alcohol imperil his life, but there was sufficient to bring out his latent desire to throw monkey wrenches in machinery.

Opening a lane through the remainder of the crowd jammed between himself and the lynch mob by the simple expedient of drawing one of his .44's and firing a bullet in the ground, he resheathed the weapon and casually strolled to the rope Stanton had tossed down.

In a conversational tone he announced, 'First man to touch this rope gets a bullet through his head.'

As though the air behind El Lobo were suddenly contaminated, the crowd immediately disappeared from the general area Circle K bullets might go if they missed the slim youth confronting them.

The Circle K riders at first stared at him in astonishment, hardly believing such a mild-looking youngster had dared to defy them. But when they noted the indolence of his stance and the alert glitter of his brilliantly blue eyes, they shifted uneasily. For there was something about this young man which spelled danger, an aura of recklessness which suggested a false move would start both the big guns at his thighs spitting death.

After a long silence Gregg Stanton said truculently. 'Who the hell are you?'

El Lobo's eyes rested on the foreman steadily until the big man flushed.

Then he said in a mild tone, 'Just a guy interested in justice. Let's hear your evidence against this kid. If it's good enough, I might let you hang him.'

'You might *let* us!' Gregg roared, and his hand dived for his gun.

His fingers were still inches from it when both El Lobo's .44's boomed so closely together it sounded like one drawnout explosion.

The heels disappeared from Gregg Stanton's boots, knocking him off balance so that he sat heavily in the dust. Open-mouthed he stared up at the smiling youth.

Without sheathing his smoking weapons, but without pointing them at anything in particular either, El Lobo waited until the big man had scrambled to his feet.

Then he said in the same mild tone, 'Like I said, I may let you hang the kid if you got good enough evidence. So start talking.'

Teetering on his heelless boots, Gregg Stanton scowled at him. His eyes momentarily rested on the heavy .44's, then moved to examine an empty space on the ground nearby.

'Five days ago a rustler run off thirty head of Circle K steers,' he said in a sulky voice. 'We got an Apache tracker named Indian Charlie to cut sign, and he tracked him across the Rio Grande into El Diablo territory. The rustler was riding a cow pony with a cracked front shoe. We didn't have enough men to tangle with El Diablo, so we turned back. But we left an outpost at the river, and this morning Johnny Carson rode across from the Mexican side on a pony Indian Charlie says is the same one he tracked. The kid had six-hundred dollars on him, which is just about what El Diablo would have paid for thirty head of stolen cattle.'

Thoughtfully El Lobo looked at the bound youngster. 'Where'd you get the money, kid?'

Johnny Carson licked his lips and made two attempts before he was able to speak. Then he said in a cracked voice, 'I was lucky in a poker game over to Juarez. Won the horse in the same game.'

'You think maybe you won it from the rustler?'

Johnny shook his head. 'From a horse trader named Midget Mike. Everybody over that way knows him. He ain't above sharp dealing in a swap, but he's no cow-thief. He said he bought the pony from El Diablo himself.'

El Lobo glanced back at Gregg Stanton. 'That makes sense, Stanton. A smart cow-thief would make a horse trade with El Diablo as part of the deal, so he wouldn't be tracked. And El Diablo would unload it on a trader the first chance he got.'

'Too much coincidence,' Gregg objected. 'What with the money being the exact amount and everything.'

'What kind of money was it?'

Stanton looked at him blankly for a moment. Then he said, 'All kinds. Some currency, some gold, a little silver. Mostly American dollars, with a few Mexican gold pieces.'

El Lobo chuckled. 'Just about what a man might win in a poker game, huh? You don't know much about El Diablo, do you?'

'I know he's a murdering bandit, and we'd all be better off if the U.S. Cavalry would go down in those hills and wipe him out!'

'But you don't know how he operates,' El Lobo insisted. 'Anybody along the border could tell you he hangs on to every bit of American money he gets in his hands. He's supposed to be building up a stake so he can move north and live respectable some day. El Diablo pays off in Mexican gold. Always. The kid here couldn't possibly have gotten American money for your steers.'

A sound like the expelling of held breath moved over the listening crowd.

The dapper Emil Galt managed to find his voice. 'I told you we were being too hasty, Gregg. Not that I'm entirely convinced Carson is innocent. But I suggest we lock him up a day or two and send one of the boys over to Juarez to track down Midget Mike. If he verifies Carson's story, we'll turn the kid loose.'

Murmurs of assent rose from the crowd, and even from the ring of Circle K riders around the prisoner.

When the crowd began drifting back into the Royal Pastime a few minutes later, El Lobo was standing at the bar reviving the fine whiskey edge the excitement of gunplay had deadened. Tim Harris entered and self-consciously inquired if he wanted back in the game.

El Lobo thoughtfully considered the money belt under his shirt, and in his more sober state decided not to risk it. 'I'll cash in,' he said.

The gambler handed him a quarter, then, before returning to his table, laid a silver dollar on the bar.

'Pour this young man whiskey until the dollar's gone,' he told the bartender.

At twenty cents each there were five drinks in the silver dollar. Buying for himself, El Lobo probably would have stopped at three, but he was not inclined to look a gift horse in the mouth. He was on his fifth drink when Emil Galt and Gregg Stanton came in. Both men made straight for him.

'That was a fine thing you did out there, young man,' the ranch owner said. 'And I want you to know neither my foreman nor I harbour any resentment because you had to shoot his heels off.'

The big man smiled a strained smile.

'I was way out of line, kid,' he said gruffly. 'Can I buy you a drink?'

'It's my buy,' El Lobo said magnanimously. 'Only fair after ruining your boots.' Rattling his glass on the bar, he called, 'Hey bartender! Two more glasses here, and a better brand of whiskey!'

As the barkeep complied, he felt in his pocket for money and produced the lone quarter Tim Harris had given him. Shrugging, he unbuttoned his shirt, fumbled inside and drew out his heavily laden money belt. With fingers whose deftness was unimpaired by the alcohol numbing his brain, he untied the draw strings and unfolded the chamois belt on the bar. He opened it wide, disclosing a sizeable quantity of Mexican gold.

Then something in the strained attitude of the men either side of him suddenly cleared his brain. Casually he separated a single coin from the pile, refolded and retied the belt and thrust it back under his shirt. With a movement so fast it caught both his companions unaware, he thrust back from the bar and stood facing them with his hands indolently at his sides, his wide lips smiling and his blue eyes glittering.

'That's a lot of Mexican gold you got there, Kid,' Gregg Stanton said in a tense voice. 'I'd guess about six hundred dollars.'

'Exactly six hundred,' El Lobo said.

He backed away, his eyes holding the two men motionless with the certainty their slightest move would be their last, and his retreat toward the door was so easy, none of the other customers even glanced at him. Eight feet away from them his back touched the batwings and he paused.

'Drink up that gold piece I left,' he said in a friendly voice.

The batwings opened and closed again. For an instant Stanton and Galt stood frozen, then both jerked guns and raced toward the door.

But before they even reached it they heard hoofs clattering away in the direction of the border.

THE UNBELIEVER

★ THE UNBELIEVER ★

By D. M. Johnson

MAHLON MITCHELL lived with the Crows for five years when he was a young man, left them without farewell and returned to them when he was old and defeated. Whatever you think about Mahlon Mitchell, you must say he was a brave man. He was afraid to go back to the Crows, but he went anyway–and it does not matter that he went because he was desperate. He was never more afraid in his life.

There were six in the party that went looking for Yellow Calf's village. Lieutenant Bradford had with him Sergeant O'Hara and three troopers; that made five. The sixth man was red-haired Mahlon Mitchell, wearing buckskin while the others wore Cavalry blue. He was the scout who would find the Crows for them. He was the white man who knew Indians because he had been one. He was important for the first time in thirty years.

There was no man anywhere better fitted for his job as scout and interpreter, but he had to beg to get it.

'I got influence with the Crows,' Mitchell had boasted to the major back at the fort. 'I was a headman among 'em.'

The major had frowned with a frozen look about his mouth that was as insulting as spoken doubt. Mitchell was not then a scout; he was only a rheumatic old civilian woodcutter for the fort, too stiffened with age and old wounds to do a good day's work. And he was desperate, because he knew he would be sent back to the States with the next wagon train, back to oblivion.

He volunteered for the mission to the Crows.

'I doubt if you could stand the trip,' the major said coolly. 'You might play out.'

Mitchell forgot that he was a petitioner. 'Play out?' he shouted. 'I rode ninety miles and crawled ten with a broken leg one time. I didn't play out!'

'You're an old man now,' the major reminded him.

This was no time for anger. It was a time for pride. With his head back, staring scornfully, he said, 'I'm still Mahlon Mitchell. I'm the man they called Iron Head, for my red hair. I've counted coup with the best of 'em. And the Crows ain't forgot me!'

The major would not admit that white men, too, remembered Mahlon Mitchell. 'Very well,' he said at last. 'Lieutenant Bradford is to find Yellow Calf's band and give them presents, promising more presents if they will stop trading ammunition to the Sioux.'

Crows and Sioux were enemies, but they did business together when it was worth while–and ammunition the Crows got from white men was blasting at other white men out of Sioux guns.

'You will have an escort of twenty men as far as Green Springs,' the major said. 'That'll get you through Sioux country.'

They had got through, and the escort had gone back, and the scout was Mahlon Mitchell, but that was all he had to cling to. The journey to the Crows was a new path to danger, and what end would there be if he lived through it? Only the perilous return to the fort, the banishment back to the States, the slow withering in a poorhouse.

But he would have this to remember: that he had once more courted danger.

The Crows had found them. Mitchell had been keeping the news to himself for a quarter of an hour, silently superior to the vigilant troopers who looked without seeing.

'Lieutenant,' he remarked, 'here's where we better wait. There's a couple of injuns up over that hill, and right here is a good place to talk.'

They waited, the soldiers as patient as their horses.

Mitchell remembered the way he had taken leave of the Crows thirty years before–on impulse, because the opportunity came, but the idea had been a long time growing.

It started with a sneer on the face of a fur trader's clerk when Mitchell rode in to a trading post with a party of Crows and saw to it they drove a hard bargain. The clerk's attitude had said without words: Squaw man. Injun lover. Living with a bunch of savages. And you were a white man once!

When the time came, Mitchell went back to be a white man again.

He had been one of a party that went afoot to steal horses from the Cheyenne. They were discovered, and, with a Crow named Drives His Horses, he had got separated in the resulting fight. Drives His Horses was wounded, and they had one horse for the two of them. When they reached a stream ten miles from the Cheyenne camp, Mitchell knew the wounded man could not live.

Mitchell stayed with him until dawn. Then he finished him off with a knife and rode away on the captured pony.

After a while he convinced himself that killing Drives His Horses had been necessary and even merciful; he had put the suffering man out of his misery. He had scalped him, too, to make it look like Cheyenne work, but he preferred to forget that.

If the Crows, to whom he was now returning, guessed the truth about his departure, his own finish would not be quick or merciful.

When the two Indian scouts came down over the hill, Mitchell expelled his breath. Nobody could have said he sighed. With a sweeping gesture, he took off his ragged hat, so the Crows could see what remained of the bushy red hair that had been his pride. The thin, curling remnants hung to his shoulders.

Watching the two Indians sidle their horses down the hill, he realized: They're too young to remember me.

They were seasoned warriors, from the looks of them, but not old enough to have been his comrades on horse raids against the Cheyenne or war parties seeking vengeance from the Sioux.

The two Crows pulled up their horses, staring. One of them asked a question; Mitchell could not catch the words. He knew cold terror: Have I forgot the Crow tongue, or am I getting deaf?

The Indian spoke again–and Mitchell no longer doubted anything. What the Crow said, in a tone of awe, was 'Iron Head! Iron Head has come back!'

'I am Iron Head,' he answered. 'I have come back to my brothers.'

The man who had spoken dismounted and walked forward. There was pride in his movements and honour in the ornaments he wore. He was a warrior with standing in the only profession fit for a man. But he came without arrogance. He came as one asking equality.

He stared into Mitchell's face and said, 'I am Bull Shoulders. I am the son of Iron Head.'

Mitchell squinted. 'Well, by God,' he muttered, 'it could be you are!'

And what about the Quiet One, your mother? he wanted to ask. Is she living and old? Or did she die young, long ago?

He did not speak her name. There could be no good news about the Quiet One. He did not want to know that she was dead. He did not want to know that she was old.

He could feel the lieutenant's growing irritation, but he let Bradford wait for a translation of what they were saying.

To Bull Shoulders he said, 'My son is a warrior. He has counted coup?'

'Many times,' Bull Shoulders answered with proper pride.

Mitchell held out his hand, and the warrior took it.

Mitchell grinned at the lieutenant. 'I told you I had influence with 'em. They ain't forgot Iron Head. This young fellow says he's my son, and I never knew I had one.'

Mitchell and Bradford rode side by side when they entered the Crow village.

They never caught on about Drives His Horses, Mitchell told himself with relief. They remember only the good things –and that's how it ought to be. Well, I brought 'em luck all the time; they always said so. I was good medicine–until that last fight.

.   .   .   .

Their hunts were successful in those old days, and their war parties came home singing, with scalps and captured horses and tales of valour.

They were always lucky—until that last raid, when the warriors were surprised and scattered, and Iron Head killed his friend to become Mahlon Mitchell again.

'They think well of you,' the lieutenant commented.

Mitchell could afford to be modest. 'They said I was good medicine.'

But I wasn't good medicine for myself after I left them, he admitted, remembering the dreary years of failure at farming and trading, as blacksmith and deck hand and bullwhacker.

He had drifted back at last to the frontier country of his youth to work for the Army, cutting wood. Life had no savour any more. Before the years of dull disaster there had been the years of danger when his blood ran hot in his veins. Youth could not be revived, but its companion, peril, could still be found by a man who took the trouble to look.

When he volunteered as a scout on the mission to the Crows, he knew he might be setting forth to his last adventure.

'You know Yellow Calf, you said,' Bradford reminded him.

'Well enough. I knowed his older brother.' (And I left him dead beside a creek.) 'Yellow Calf is maybe ten years younger'n me. He was just a boy, getting ready to pray for his medicine, when I first met the Crows. When I left, he was a brave. I remember the first war party he ever went on.'

There was a stern, fierce orderliness about life for a Crow Indian. He grew up longing for glory; he starved and prayed for magic, for medicine; when he thought he had it, he went seeking danger. And after a while, he died. The life of a white man was infinitely more complicated. There were too many things a man could want, and too many ways to fail in trying to get them.

We were young a long time ago, Michell realized with a shock when the chief came toward them. Time had dug furrows in the dark cheeks.

Yellow Calf did not extend his hand. He stood staring into

Mitchell's face. He asked with respect, almost with humility, 'Is it Iron Head himself who has come back to his brothers?'

It ain't because he don't recognize me, Mitchell understood. It's because he's scared. Thinks maybe I'm a spirit.

'It is Iron Head himself, who once lived with spirits,' he answered. 'The story is for Yellow Calf alone.'

The warriors who sat and smoked with the lieutenant on that first night in the village were distinguished men of whose company no man need be ashamed. But they were only sub-chiefs.

In another lodge, Yellow Calf himself sat with Mahlon Mitchell, who was in no hurry to spin his tale.

'Yellow Calf is a great warrior and a leader of his people,' Mitchell said. 'When we were young men, I knew it would be so.'

'I did not know it,' Yellow Calf answered thoughtfully. 'Iron Head's medicine must have told him. His medicine was always strong.' He added, after a pause, 'I hope my brother Iron Head still has his medicine.'

Mitchell could not admit failure. Boasting was in his very blood. 'I have better medicine now,' he lied. 'Because for a time—I do not know how long it was—I lived with spirit people.'

He smoked silently, letting the chief's anxiety increase, before he told the story. He made it up as he went, borrowing from all the magic tales he had ever heard in the Crow lodges. He told of fighting side by side with Drives His Horses against a warrior who grew taller and taller and finally turned into a white wolf that took Mitchell far away on a cloud to a place where all people were wolves, and kept him there.

Yellow Calf covered his mouth, indicating wonder, and shook his head in sympathy for his friend.

Mitchell ended, 'I did not see Drives His Horses any more. I did not see him today. Nor Hump Bull nor Whirlwind, who were with us that day.'

Yellow Calf shook his head. 'They are dead, and many others. Whirlwind lies not very far from here. Long after that fight,

I went back to that place and hunted until I found my brother, Drives His Horses. I knew his bones by the things that were with them. I brought them back wrapped in a blanket. I thought the Cheyenne had killed him. Now I know it was the white wolf spirit.'

Mitchell said sadly, 'Even after the white wolf put me down by a river in the darkness with a crash of thunder, I did not come back to the Crows. I thought I might be unlucky for them, because the spirits took away my medicine bag. So I went back to the white men to find out. But it was not so. Everywhere I went, the white men were lucky. I think I have even better medicine now than before.'

'It is true they get stronger and richer,' Yellow Calf agreed. 'I am glad Iron Head has come again to the Crows.'

As if, Mitchell thought, he figured I was going to stay. The Crows ain't so well off as they used to be. Not so many good horses, and the lodges are ragged. Hunger is just over the ridge.

'Iron Head planted a seed among the Crows,' Yellow Calf remarked. 'It has grown to a strong tree. I have sons, too, and so I do not fight any more in battle. In the lodge prepared for Iron Head, there is a woman waiting. She is old. Maybe Iron Head would rather have a young woman there.'

'Iron Head is not young any more,' Mitchell answered, grinning.

Walking toward the lodge, he recalled: She was never a beauty, and she'll be an old, sagging squaw now. But she never talked my head off, the way most of them do. By God, it's like coming home!

Contentment warmed him. Here, he thought, they treat a man right. When he's old, he don't have to fight any more.

She was waiting by the entrance, where old women were allowed to sit, with her blanket over her face. Without seeing, he knew how she looked. Shapeless and seamed with wrinkles, without joy—but with a silent pride that no one could take away unless she lost her son as she had lost his father.

Mitchell sat down in the master's place. Without greeting, he said, 'Iron Head wants his woman to brush his hair.'

She came without a word. In peaceful silence, she brushed his hair with the furry tail of an animal. She might have said his hair was thin or that he had deserted her. She might have railed in bitterness. But the only thing she said was after a time, 'It is good that Iron Head has come back to his people.'

My people, he thought. More than the whites ever were. And what if I was to stay with 'em? 'I had two white women for my wives,' he told her. 'The Quiet One is a better wife than either.'

That much he could give her to remember and to tell her friends. . . .

Lieutenant Bradford's mission was accomplished with astonishing ease, though the talk about it took half a day of eloquence. Yes, the Crows would stop trading ammunition to the Sioux. The Sioux were enemies; the only reason for trading was to get things the Crows did not have. The Crows would be glad to accept these things as gifts from their white father.

Yellow Calf spoke. 'Once our brother, Iron Head, lived with us. His medicine was good. We were a rich people with many strong fighting men and many good horses. We were not often hungry.'

He went on in detail, with proofs of his people's greatness and the bravery of Iron Head and the good luck Iron Head had brought them.

'Then Iron Head went away and we did not know why. Now he has come back to tell us what happened.'

Mitchell told them the same story Yellow Calf had heard, without deviation in a single detail, as stories were supposed to be told. Then he sat down again, and when Lieutenant Bradford frowned because he had not interpreted the long speech, he paid no attention. His medicine was good again.

One after another, the stern warriors spoke, offering him paradise. Iron Head had come back; Iron Head should stay and the Crows would be strong again.

For Mahlon Mitchell there could be no better life than this, among the Crows. Age had put aches in his bones, stiffness in his joints, but he was no longer required to compete with the young men for glory. He could count his coups among his equals, and his deeds were as splendid now as when he had performed them. As long as he lived, his deeds would be examples for the chattering women to pass on to little boys. His woman would look after his comfort.

True, the Indians were never far ahead of starvation, never safe from swift attack. But here was honour and as much security as a man could get anywhere—if the man was Mitchell. But he must not let them think he was easy to woo.

'Iron Head has come back to his brothers,' he replied gravely. 'He would like to stay with them. But his medicine told him only to come back. He does not know whether he was meant to stay. He must ask his medicine. Tomorrow he will go to find out what to do.'

Ah, my brothers, you are easier to fool than the white men! I can wind you around my little finger. I will never let you guess that only with you is my medicine strong!

When he set out for the hill where he would speak to his medicine, he took a roundabout way. Yellow Calf had told him where the body of Whirlwind had been placed after that warrior had died of wounds nine winters before. There had been great mourning. His women had cut their hair and gashed their legs.

On a platform of branches in a spreading tree, what was left of Whirlwind lay under the sky. Tatters of a blanket that had wrapped the body shredded down from the sagging platform. No birds were there; crows and buzzards had finished long ago. Under the tree were tumbled the time-whitened bones of a sacrificed horse.

Mitchell dismounted, grunting with stiffness and pain. He stood with his fist on his hips, looking up, feeling dull anger because the years were gone.

Whirlwind had been born in a Crow lodge and had died on the prairie. He had lived with valour and without doubts, fitting the environment to which he was destined and never needing to search for a better one.

'Does that horse they killed for you come when you whistle?'

Mitchell asked aloud. 'Does that rotten blanket keep you warm in winter?'

Superstitious fools, the lot of them, he told himself. They were all afraid of everything—except death. Any animal might be a spirit, any bird song might be a message. The messages were mystery, the spirits were almost always bad. The Crows were savages, shivering with terror of all that was around them, yearning for good medicine to save them from perils they did not understand.

But Mitchell burned with envy for a man whose life had been perfect, unquestioning, without deviation; for a man who was honourably dead and beyond all torment.

He hobbled his horse at the foot of a medicine hill, wanting to open his heart to the magic that would be there if he were an Indian, but scorning it as nonsense because he was a white man.

He had been through this before, the hunger and thirst alone on a mountain, and had gone back to tell the details of the medicine dream he had not had at all. But he had convinced the elders and he had got his medicine bag.

This time the misery was greater, because he was no longer young and had no hope of experiencing the awe and wonder that an Indian would find there because he expected it. He went through the motions of praying. Officially, he would not eat or drink until he had a message from a spirit. But who could see, after dark, if he chewed pemmican filched from a parfleche of the Quiet One or crept down to drink from a spring? In daylight he danced and chanted.

Aching with rheumatism, he danced stiffly before the unseen, unnamed spirits, but he got no message from them, because he knew they did not exist.

The third day, he rested from pain, waiting for time to pass. Mahlon Mitchell, who would soon be Iron Head again and forever, held up his face to the sun's warmth and smiled.

Lieutenant Bradford was with the Indians who came to meet him. He told Bradford his decision. 'I'm going to live with the Crows,' he said.

'Really, Mr. Mitchell? The choice is up to you, of course.'

'It sure is. Nobody can make me go back to the fort, can they?'

Of course the white men wanted him to go back, to make sure they'd get there, maybe to back up the lieutenant when he reported to the major. But nobody was going to push Iron Head around. Mahlon Mitchell, that white man, he could be pushed; he could be licked—and had been, for too long. But Iron Head was a Crow warrior.

'I wouldn't even try to make you go back,' Bradford said. 'But of course if you don't choose to go, you'll never collect your pay. It seems to me that in your place I would want to come back to them with presents. I wouldn't want to come empty-handed. Poor.'

'What I've got is worth more than presents,' Mitchell said. 'What I can give them is good luck.'

They rode in silence thereafter, but Mitchell was thinking hard. Come to them poor and they'd take him in, sure, with their arms outspread in friendship. But they might remember if the good luck ran out. Come to them rich, with trade goods to hand out like a lord, and they wouldn't forget that, either.

He was still thinking about that after the sweat bath, when the Quiet One was, with humble pride, helping him to dress for the council at which he would relate what his medicine had told him to do. She brought him paint and a precious scrap of mirror. She brought him bead ornaments and a necklace made of claws. She had a feather for his hair—the single eagle feather that only a proved warrior could wear.

He was wrapped in contentment. He was going back to the good life he remembered, and this time he would stay. Oh, there would be hungry times, and winter cold was bitter when you lived in a lodge made of hides. A toothache could be sure hell, and a blacksmith with a pair of tongs could handle it better than any medicine man with all his charms. There were always stinks around an Indian camp, and their heathen religion was a nuisance, and there was always too much racket. But respect and honour and being wanted—these balanced all the rest.

The Quiet One stood away, murmuring, and he turned to see Bradford at the lodge entrance.

The lieutenant asked courteously, 'Will they object if I am present at the council?'

'They might,' Mitchell said. 'But I can talk 'em into it.'

He was suddenly ashamed at being seen in this getup of nakedness and paint and beads and bits of fur and claws. When he was young, there had been nothing extraordinary about a white man wearing Indian trimmings. But in those days there had been no uniformed Cavalry officers to observe in silence that might hide scorn.

He wanted to put the lieutenant in his place. He said, 'Reckon you boys can find your way back to the fort and keep your hair besides?'

'I think so.' Bradford answered. He added thoughtfully, 'If it weren't for your reputation for valour, I might think you were staying here because you don't want to go back through Sioux country.'

Rage flooded through Mitchell, but caution tempered it. He spoke evenly. 'I'll let that pass, Lieutenant. You came to the Crows as a friend. We'll let you go that way.'

When his son and several other warriors came to take him to the council lodge, Mitchell knew exactly what he was going to say.

Sitting in the council with the dark, stern-faced warriors ringing the fire, he sighed softly, letting himself sink into the warmth of old friendship, of being so much wanted. But before they could be sure of him, he would make them want him still more—and show the lieutenant something besides.

After the long smoking and the slow ceremonial oratory, he stood. 'Iron Head will live with his brothers, the Crows,' he said gravely. 'He is coming back, and the Crows will be his people forever. His medicine told him this.'

He said it again, in English, for Bradford, while the Indians waited.

The feathered heads moved, and firelight flashed on the fierce faces.

Yellow Calf said, 'It is good that Iron Head comes back

to his people. Now they will be strong again, because Iron Head is good medicine. But he says he is coming back. I would like to know what this means. He is here already.'

'Iron Head goes first to the fort where the white soldiers are,' Mitchell explained. 'He has made a vow to go to the fort and tell the white chiefs that the Crows are their friends. Then he will come back with gifts.'

That, too, he repeated in English for the lieutenant.

The response was more than he had hoped. The Indians pleaded. One after another, they gave their reasons why Iron Head should stay with them now and not go back to the fort at all.

Maybe he had not understood what his medicine said, one man suggested, and the rest agreed, murmuring, that this might indeed be true. They were deeply disturbed, Mitchell saw.

Sadly, he assured them there could be no mistake. He must go first to the fort. Then he would stay with the Crows for ever.

It seemed to him that he saw grief in the dark faces. I've got them in the palm of my hand! he told himself.

One thing they demanded: that he remain another day. There would be a feast for him. . . .

The white men started back early in the morning after the feast was over. The procession that went with them honoured Iron Head, the good medicine.

Mitchell wished his insides felt better, so he could better enjoy this triumph. Yellow Calf went with them, and Bull Shoulders, and a dozen other men and even a few women to look after the baggage. His own woman, the Quiet One, was among them. She rode a spotted pony and led another that dragged a travois.

By noon he was feeling too sick to care what the rest of them were doing. The lieutenant commented. 'Too much dog at the feast, perhaps? It turned my stomach at the time.'

'I've eat dog before,' Mitchell grunted. 'Dog meat's all right.'

He almost collapsed when he dismounted. When he tried to sleep, the Quiet One sat beside him. He woke up, moaning, to feel her hand comforting his wet forehead.

In the morning he was no better.

'We'll hurry up to the fort,' Bradford said.

Mitchell did not want to hurry anywhere. He was racked with stomach cramps. He could not remember how many days' travel they must be from the fort.

'I'll send a man on ahead for the doctor,' Bradford promised, 'when we get through Sioux country.'

Mitchell, writhing, did not answer.

That day he did not ride. They tied him on a travois, to be pulled behind the spotted pony.

He revived enough to tell the lieutenant, 'This is how—they brought me in—after a fight with Blackfeet.'

I lived through that, he remembered, as he swayed into black sickness.

But he remembered something else: I never was as sick as this before. I could die this time!

Sometimes the blackness divided like a curtain, and behind it was Mitchel drowning in a flood of pain. He had glimpses of faces when the curtain parted: Bradford leaning over him, looking distressed, asking some question he could not answer; Sergeant O'Hara, bringing water he could not drink; the Quiet One, laying her hand on his forehead. That shocked him to consciousness. She had so far forgotten her place that, before them all, she showed her possession of Iron Head.

He began to know a kind of fear he had never felt before. He fought against panic. But he was too sick to push the Quiet One away.

He saw the face of his Indian son, Bull Shoulders, stern and watchful.

The lieutenant again, grim with worry.

'Stop the horse!' Mitchell gasped.

He had to wait for something. There was no use trying to keep ahead of it. Let it come now and end the agony.

He saw the dark face of his friend, Yellow Calf. The chief

looked down at him with an expression he had never before seen on that dark, seamed face.

In a sweep of horror, Iron Head understood that he did not hold the Crows in the palm of his hand. For what he saw in that savage face was—compassion.

The feast—that's when they poisoned me! he realized. He cried out in English, 'Why? Why?'

Yellow Calf answered in the Crow tongue, 'We are sorry to do this thing. But Iron Head is good medicine for my people. Now he will never go away from his brothers who need him.' . . .

The white soldiers rode on fast, without their escort, after crossing a river.

On the bank, the Quiet One, with bleeding gashes on her arms, was at work with another squaw, making a platform in a tree to receive the body of Iron Head, so that the good medicine could be kept safely forever in the country of the Crows.

MAN-TAMING WOMAN

By *Michael Fessier*

T HE small town of Buffalo Bend was asleep in the dust and
the only signs of life were a dog ambling aimlessly down
the centre of the otherwise deserted street and a fat man
sitting on a bench in front of the general store reading the
label on a bottle of chilli sauce. Suddenly the stagnant silence
was shattered by shouts and a shot from the interior of the
Chinaman's Chance saloon, and a small pale man wearing city
clothes darted through the swinging doors and scuttled across
the street, coming to a stop before the fat man.

'Oh, golly!' he gasped. 'It's terrible! It's frightful! That big
man's going to kill everybody in town! Where's the sheriff?'

'Fishing,' said the fat man, holding the bottle of sauce closer
to his eyes, so as not to miss any details of the fine print.

'But isn't anybody going to do anything about it?' demanded
the small pale man. 'He's stark, staring mad! I just escaped by
the skin of my teeth!'

The fat man extracted the last bit of suspense from the
only literature available to him, then regretfully tossed the bottle
aside.

'If I were you, I wouldn't worry none, stranger,' he said.
'That's only Dolph Dorcas letting off steam. He ain't going
to kill anybody important. All he aims to do is wreck that
there saloon.' There was the sound of breaking glass, as if
someone were throwing bottles at a bar mirror. Then there
was again silence. 'He probably saved one for himself,' observed
the fat man. 'He'll drink peaceful-like now for a while, until
somebody comes along drunk or foolhardy enough to give him
a fight.'

'You speak as if this thing were an ordinary occurrence,' said the
pale little man.

'It ain't exactly ordinary,' said the fat man, but it does happen at predictable intervals. That's why almost everybody in town's down to the river with the sheriff fishing.'

'You mean that that one big man has this whole town buffaloed?' inquired the small pale man, sitting on the bench and keeping an apprehensive eye on the saloon across the street.

'He ain't exactly got us buffaloed,' stated the fat man, 'but he is of a size and stature such as to make fishing a highly feasible occupation when he's in one of his more exuberant moods. Besides, Buffalo Bend is kind of proud of him—in a left-handed sort of way. He's sort of a local landmark. Whereas other communities have Niagara Falls, or the Grand Canyon, or spouting geysers, we got Dolph Dorcas, which we point out to out-of-town strangers. You're one of the lucky few who happened to catch him while he's erupting.'

'I wouldn't call it luck,' said the little pale man, shivering a little. 'What makes Dolph Dorcas behave like that?'

'Well, it's a long story,' said the fat man, looking at his watch, 'and I've just about got time enough to tell it to you before Dolph works up another head of steam. Would you care to hear it?'

The little man nodded, not for an instant taking his eye off the entrance to the Chinaman's Chance.

It was well along toward the calf-roping season [the fat man said] and about an hour before falling-down-drunk time, when the citizens of Buffalo Bend first set eyes on Dolph Dorcas. He was as big a man then, of course, as he is now, only that shaggy mane of hair was all black, and not touched with grey around the temples as it is at the present moment. He came abusting into the Chinaman's Chance as turbulent and tempestuous as a tornado, and when he shoved his huge shoulders up against the bar he occupied the space usually taken up by two big men and a medium-sized sheep-herder. He grabbed the half-full bottle out of the barkeep's hand, drained it in two gulps, then threw the bottle at the barkeep's head, which the barkeep withdrew just in time to escape being brained.

Then Dolph turned and looked at the assembled barflies and card players with an uncongenial expression in the dark eyes, which were shaded from sun and glare by bushy eyebrows the size and shape of a couple of buzzards' nests.

'My name,' he announced in a voice that caused a whole tier of beer steins to collapse and crash to the floor, 'is Dolph Dorcas and I am the greatest single catastrophe which hit humankind since the destruction of Nineveh and Tyre.' He let that sink in before he imparted further biographical information. 'I,' he went on finally, 'have a deleterious effect which is worse than the Black Death on people which I don't like. Furthermore,' he added, 'I don't like nobody.'

'Which, outside of the foreword to the Constitution,' said Judge Gorman, 'is the most impressive preamble I've ever heard, and I'm scared considerable. Just out of curiosity, are we to construe your remarks as a statement of intention or are you merely blowing out hot air to ventilate your whiskers?'

'Why, goodness me!' said Dolph, peering down at the judge. 'If you ain't a manly little feller, all fat and shiny and pink, like a yearling shoat, which, if I was in the habit of carrying a knife, I'd slice up and eat for sandwiches. Your remarks to me, sir, show considerable promise of eventualities. Do you aim to pursue them to the point where I can in all conscience turn you over my knee and spank you or do you think you've sufficiently impressed your lily-livered comrades with your audacity?'

'I,' said Judge Gorman, 'am of a judicial turn of mind and I know where bravado ends and downright foolhardiness begins. I know when I'm outdrawed and outgunned. For the sake of the record, I'll rise to remark that I consider you to have all the lovable qualities and endearing personality of a poisoned polecat, and nothing would please me more than to see you carted away from here in a defunct condition. Unless, however, I am goaded beyond endurance, I have no intention whatsoever of putting our difference of opinion on any physical basis. I ain't built for it and, besides, I'm a justice of the peace, sworn to uphold law and order—such as it is and what there is of it—around these diggings.'

'You are a well-spoken little feller, at that,' said Dolph approvingly. 'I can see you've been well brought up and gently reared.' Then he gazed contemptuously about him. 'And that goes for the rest of you galoots,' he remarked, spitting across the bar and knocking a bottle of fine old Kentucky red-eye off the shelf.

'Which, speaking of lily livers,' said Bart McCutcheon, who was almost as big and mean as Dolph, 'I'd sure admire to see the colour of yourn.'

With that he pulled a knife and leaped at Dolph, all spraddled out and with intentions that weren't conducive to Dolph's longevity any whatsoever. We all backed away to give Bart elbowroom and to gain vantage points from which to watch what we expected to be the battle of the age. We were sure disappointed. Dolph swung his great big fist and, all of a sudden, Bart wasn't there any more. Dolph looked about him and shook his head in considerable bewilderment.

'I misses him,' he complained. 'What happens to him? Where does he go to?'

'You ain't missed him none at all,' says Pott Manders, pointing. 'He's over there.'

Bart had sailed clean across the room, and he was now resting in a nest of broken chairs, a peaceful, dreamy look on his face.

'Are you gonna take this laying down?' demanded Pott, running over to Bart. 'Ain't you gonna get up'n' fight?'

'I sure ain't,' said Bart, carefully opening one eye and looking at him. 'Why, if I was to get up, that big, ugly guy over there'd just knock me down again, and I don't want to put him to any more trouble than he's already been to.' With that he closed his eye and went back to sleep.

'Well,' said Dolph in a disappointed voice, 'I came here looking for a little recreation, but I don't suppose it'll hurt me to spend one quiet evening. . . . Bartender, set up a keg of whisky.'

The poke he threw down on the bar was about the size of a sofa cushion and it was filled with gold dust.

Dolph was chewing away on his fifth beer stein of whisky when Panamint Polly and Lance Warring, her sweetheart, came into the Chinaman's Chance. Lance was a good-looking young man, but when he was with Polly nobody noticed him. Polly was one of nature's masterpieces, a great, big, strapping girl with raven hair and flashing eyes and skin the colour of rose-tinted ivory. There was a whole heaping plenty of her, but not an ounce could be considered excess baggage. Polly dealt cards in the Chinaman's Chance, and, although every male within miles had tried in one way or another, nobody, including Lance, had ever succeeded in getting any action out of Polly excepting in a game of draw poker with cards on the table. Polly and Lance stood beside Dolph, who, not noticing them, was telling how he'd singlehandedly wiped out a tribe of Mescalero Indians in a quarrel over a water hole.

'. . . I outmanoeuvres 'em,' he was saying. 'First I infiltrates 'em and then I surrounds 'em on all sides, after which I executes a flanking movement and drives in for the kill. There is only eight hundred of 'em, but they puts up a right smart scrap for a while, but eventually I take all their scalps and sell 'em to an itinerant fur trader, which starts quite a fad among ladies in the East—'

At this juncture Lance made the gravest error of his life. He laughed at Dolph—a sneering laugh that was filled with disbelief and derision. Dolph turned, hit him in the face with a backhanded blow. Lance came to rest under a table, and he was about as unfunctional as you can get this side of being dead.

'I sure hates to disarrange your escort that-a-way,' Dolph told Polly, 'but I'm plumb allergic to having my word doubted and disparaged even when I'm telling a lie—especially by a gent which wears a little bitty moustache and looks like he's got three eyebrows.'

Polly was looking at the poke of gold dust with a soft, shining, yearning expression most women display when they gaze at a little green cottage with a white picket fence and children romping on the lawn. Then she tore her glance from the poke, and when she looked at Dolph it was obvious to all of us that her commercial instinct had just lost a nip-and-tuck battle with an even more overpowering passion. Her eyes were crackling with the righteous and justifiable anger of a woman who has just recently seen her sweetheart slapped under a table with one blow from the back of a bigger man's hand.

'You—you dog's funeral!' she choked.

'Madame,' said Dolph, considerably stunned and flabbergasted, 'I been everywhere and had all sorts of things done to me. I been called everything the human brain can imagine or the human tongue lay words to, but never in my born days has I ever been called a dog's funeral. That is an epithet which nonplusses me a whole heap and leaves me no opportunity for rebuttal or repartee. I takes my hat off to you. . . . Bartender, a drink for the lady.'

The barkeep placed a glass of whisky in front of Polly, and without hesitation she picked it up and sloshed it in Dolph's face. We all drew back, anticipating considerable of an eruption, but Dolph remained calm and unruffled in the face of Polly's unladylike conduct. He took a bandanna from his pocket, carefully wiped his features, tucked the bandanna back in his pocket, then wrapped his big arms around Polly and kissed her on the mouth. For a moment Polly's eyes protruded from their sockets and spun around like pinwheels, then she closed them and struggled with all her might to break Dolph's grip. None of us had ever seen such a kiss before. It went on and on, as if Dolph were out to set some kind of endurance record.

'My gosh!' Billy Feeney said in a shocked voice. 'No man should kiss a woman that-a-way until three weeks after he's been married to her in a great big church in front of a hundred witnesses by at least a bishop.'

'In addition to which, if he don't let her up for air pretty soon, she's liable to suffocate,' observed Pott Manders.

'I think,' said Judge Gorman, 'that this here strange gent has gone a whole heap too far. When he came in here bellowing like the Bull of Bashan, I put it down to an overdose of selfconfidence. When he fractured Bart McCutcheon and Lance Warring, I considered it merely youthful high spirits. But when he rides roughshod over a range none of the rest of us has ever been allowed to set a foot on, I think it's time some of you men uphold the honour of Buffalo Bend.'

With that he ducked to safety behing the bar and, after a brief discussion of tactics and strategy, the rest of us deployed our forces and began the attack. We soon found out that Dolph's opening statement in our midst was the result of sheer modesty and understatement. He was twice as rough and unmanageable as he had claimed to be. He fought us with fists, feet, teeth, beer bottles and whisky kegs, which he used as bowling balls to mow us down like ninepins. Judge Gorman scuttled out for reinforcements and came back with the sheriff and four deputies, but that merely served to equalize the odds of battle. Finally, after the Chinaman's Chance had been reduced to a whisky-soaked rubble, it was Panamint Polly suffering from outraged virtue and other assorted feminine peeves, who put an end to the ruckus. She got behind Dolph, swatted him over the head with a timber that'd been torn from the rafters and laid him out cold.

When Dolph came to, he was trussed up with a dozen lariats and about seven yards of barbed wire which somebody had thoughtfully removed from the corral fence. He looked about him, spat out a tooth and grinned amiably at us.

'I'm much obliged,' he said. 'I never have so much fun in years.' Then he studied us closely, noting the various degrees of our disability. 'And I must admit that you puts up a right good fight,' he declared, 'considering that I has you outnumbered.'

'About them Indians,' said Bart. 'Are you sure there were only eight hundred of 'em?'

'More or less,' grins Dolph. 'Now if you gents will only untie me, I'll be on my way, thanking you all for a very pleasant time.'

'That would be all very well and good ordinarily,' said Judge Gorman, 'but, considering the circumstances, I'm afraid that we're going to have to put you under arrest, Dolph.'

'Arrest?' said Dolph uncomprehendingly. 'Did I break a law or something?'

'Well,' said Judge Gorman, 'our sheriff is dead and, in most law-abiding localities, killing a peace officer is considered plumb illegal.'

He pointed to the centre of the floor, where the sheriff was lying on his face with a knife sticking out of his back. Dolph shook his head in a dazed fashion.

'Don't look at me, gents,' he said. 'I admits that if I gets a chance to kill your sheriff, I sure enough does it, but in fair combat—not with a knife. Knives are carried by effeminate people which pares their fingernails and, where I come from, we don't eat no meat we can't cut with a spoon.'

'He could of very easy snatched a knife from somebody else and done the deed,' declared Billy Feeney.

'Yeah, but nobody seen him do it,' declared Bart McCutcheon, who admired anybody that could knock him across a room with one blow, 'and that's a sure enough proof of innocence and nonresponsibility.'

'You got something there,' admitted Judge Gorman. Then he looked around the room. 'Didn't anybody see this here tarantula pull a knife on our late lamented sheriff?' he inquired.

For a moment there was silence, and then Panamint Polly stepped forward and looked straight at Dolph.

'I saw it,' she declared. 'I don't know where he got the knife, but I saw him stab the sheriff with it.'

Dolph stared at her, and it seemed he was trying to clear his brain from the dizzying effects of the fight and all the whisky he'd consumed.

'Well, I'll be blowed!' he said.

'In that case,' said Judge Gorman rubbing hands together with satisfaction, 'I guess we'll be having a little necktie party around here sometime tomorrow afternoon.'

'You mean,' asked Bart, outraged, 'that we're gonna hang this man just because he killed our sheriff?'

'I'd sure consider it mighty inhospitable of you,' said Dolph glumly.

'So far this year,' said Billy Feeney, looking at the ceiling, 'they've had four hangings in O'Leary's Lapse.' Then he looked at his fingernails. 'We,' he declared, 'ain't had none.'

'O'Leary's Lapse,' said Judge Gorman, 'has always been more civic-minded than we are. If people're allowed to come in here and kill off our sheriffs with impunity, then what's going to happen to our real-estate values?'

'In addition to which,' said Billy Feeney, 'O'Leary's Lapse has already stole the annual rodeo right out from under us and we ain't figured out a counter-attraction.'

'Well, they'd better not try to steal our hanging,' said Pott Manders, with an excess of patriotism. 'We gotta draw the line somewhere.'

'Just a minute,' said Bart. 'We ain't gonna hang nobody without he has a fair and square trial. I hereby constitute myself the guilty party's defence attorney.'

'I ain't,' said Dolph apathetically, 'been found guilty as yet.'

'You will be, don't worry,' said Billy Feeney. 'I hereby constitute myself the prosecuting attorney.'

'And I, being judge,' said Judge Gorman, 'will see that you get every legal right coming to you before we take you out and hang you.'

A dozen men lifted Dolph and started to drag him unprotestingly toward the door. On the way he spotted Panamint Polly and he gazed into her eyes and gave her a puzzled look.

'I just plumb don't understand it, miss,' he said. 'I sure enough must of been drunker'n I suspected. How could I kill your sheriff without remembering a thing about it?'

Polly met his glance for a moment, then flushed scarlet and walked away. Dolph allowed himself to be led off, still shaking his head in puzzlement.

Almost everybody in town was jammed into what was left of the Chinaman's Chance the next day when the deputies led Dolph Dorcas, looking subdued and introspective, into the place.

Walking alongside Dolph was Bart McCutcheon, and behind him was Panamint Polly, wearing an inscrutable expression on her handsome face. Judge Gorman, who sat on a high stool behind the bar, pounded with a bung starter.

'The prisoner being present,' he said, 'I hereby declare court in session.' Then he turned to Billy Feeney. 'What are the charges, Mr. Prosecuting Attorney?' he asked. 'As if we didn't know.'

'I charge,' said Billy, 'that that there mangy coyote, Dolph Dorcas, by name, did wilfully and maliciously, and with intent to do the deceased no good whatsoever, stab our sheriff to death on these very premises. I move that, after we find him guilty, we take him out and hang him on a scaffold which has already been festively decorated with bunting for the purpose, after which there will be a barbecue and foot races.'

The judge rapped on the bar again with the bung starter and turned to Bart.

'And what has the defence got to offer by way of mitigating or ameliorating this hideous crime? As if it'd do you any good.'

'I,' said Bart, 'consider the remarks of the prosecuting attorney highly libellous and defamatory to the sterling character and spotless reputation of my client, who has never been proved to kill no sheriff with no knife at no time. By way of defence, I charge that the sheriff was guilty of contributory negligence for messing into the fight, in the first place. In the second place, I maintain that my client was drunk and didn't know what he was doing. In the third place, I assert that nobody seen him do it when he done it.'

'What do you mean, nobody seen him do it?' howled Billy Feeney. 'Panamint Polly seen him do it.'

'Panamint Polly,' said Bart, 'ain't no longer eligible as a witness.'

'Why isn't Panamint Polly eligible as a witness?' demanded Judge Gorman. 'Just you tell me that, Bart McCutcheon.'

'Because,' said Bart, 'according to the laws, regulations, protocols and ordinances of this here great commonwealth, a wife can't be forced to testify against her lawfully wedded husband.' Then he gave Billy Feeney a gloating look. 'How do you like them persimmons?' he asked.

At this, pandemonium busted loose. There was a lot of shouting and hollering and pushing and shoving, during which Panamint Polly blushed modestly and toyed with a wedding ring on her finger. Everybody was of the opinion that we had been made the victims of a dirty underhanded trick, and many were in favour of hanging not only Dolph Dorcas but Bart McCutcheon as well. Judge Gorman pounded on the bar with the bung starter until he had restored some semblance of order.

'Just when,' he demanded, 'was this foul miscarriage of justice perpetrated?'

'Last night at the jail,' responded Bart. 'These two children was joined in holy wedlock through the bars of the cell by a preacher which I brought over from O'Leary's Lapse.'

At the mention of O'Leary's Lapse pandemonium set in again, and the sentiment in favour of hanging both Dolph and Bart became stronger by the minute. At last Judge Gorman succeeded in pounding the angry shouts down to a sullen murmur.

'Although I deeply sympathize with you in your sense of loss and frustration,' he said, 'I've got to admit that this low skunk of a defence attorney has outdrawed us and he holds all the cards. Inasmuch as an illegal hanging is worse than no hanging at all would be, I see nothing to do but to dismiss the charges.'

'I objects!' yelled Dolph.

'You object?' said Judge Gorman, some surprised. 'It seems to me that you're the beneficiary of this skulduggery. On what grounds do you object, Dolph?'

'On the grounds that my constitutional rights are invaded,' said Dolph. 'I don't realize what I'm doing at the time. The defence attorney talks me into this here matrimonial deal while I'm incompetent, irrelevant and immaterial, and I demands that the whole thing be nol-prossed by reason of habeas corpus and caveat emptor.'

'I've always said,' declared Polly with an air of righteousness as phony as a Chinese faro deck, 'that men are the most ungrateful animals there are. How can he say such things about me, judge, when I sacrificed my all to save his ugly neck from the noose?'

'Seeing's how Dolph was locked up at the time,' commented Judge Gorman, 'I don't think you've sacrificed anything to speak of. Just what did you get out of this little deal, Polly?'

'Well,' said Polly, glancing down at a bulge in her waistline that could only have been made by a money belt filled with gold dust, 'he did with all his wordly goods me endow.'

'I cheerfully allows her to keep the worldly goods,' said Dolph, 'but rather than remain married to this here hellcat of a card sharp of yours, I willingly pleads guilty to erasing your sheriff and I requests that you takes me out and hangs me pronto. I desires to die with my boots on.'

'Motion denied,' declared Judge Gorman. 'I hereby condemn the culprit to serve out the sentence inflicted on him by the sky pilot from O'Leary's Lapse. I forthwith adjourn court and suggest that we go over to our rival metropolis and witness the rodeo.'

Their spirits dampened by having a hanging blow up in their faces, the citizens of Buffalo Bend sadly filed out of the Chinaman's Chance, leaving Polly, Dolph and Bart alone in the wreckage.

'How come you're acting so surly and petulant?' Bart asked

300

Dolph in a disgusted voice. 'I saved your life, didn't I? And, besides, you didn't demonstrate any great antipathy toward Polly last night. I never seen a man so determined to get on intimate terms with a gal in all my born days.'

'I know,' admitted Dolph, 'but at the time I was merely riffling the deck. I don't have any chips on the table, and I don't intend to play out any such hand as you two deals me while I'm not in my right mind.'

'What makes you think that I aim to play out the hand?' demanded Polly. 'Didn't you ever hear of an annulment?'

'I tried to explain that to you last night,' said Bart, as Dolph gave him a questioning look. 'As things now stand, you 'n' Polly are man and wife in name only, and it ain't what they call a marriage of fact as yet. If you keep it that way, all you have to do it go to O'Leary's Lapse and get the marriage dissolved by the presiding judge.'

'You're sure enough a ringtailed wonder, Bart,' said Dolph joyfully, 'and if I ever kills another sheriff I gives you my business.' Then he stared doubtfully at Polly. 'But it seems to me,' he added, 'that you kind of cold-decks the bride. . . . I hope, lady,' he said to Polly, 'that the gold dust is enough to compensate you in part of your bereavement.'

'What bereavement?' demanded Polly with flashing eyes. 'Why, I wouldn't stay married to you if you were the next to the last man on earth. I'm a virtuous woman and I consider that even being your lawfully wedded wife is a fate worse than death. I can hardly wait to get the annulment over with and, for that purpose, I have a buckboard waiting outside.'

The fat man paused in his narrative and watched as three burly cowboys, all staggering a little, entered the Chinaman's Chance.

'In just a few minutes,' observed the fat man, 'there's going to be high old hell popping over there.'

'I'm afraid so,' said the small pale man. 'But why? Why has Dolph got a grudge against this town? It seems to me he's a very lucky man. He wasn't hanged and his marriage was annulled and—'

'Well, as for that annulment,' said the fat man, 'it never did

come off quite as planned. It seems that, on the way to O'Leary's
Lapse with Dolph, Polly ran across a ranch that was for sale
at such a bargain price that she just couldn't resist buying it with
some of that gold dust she wore around her waist. After that,
one thing and another happened, and the first thing you know,
Polly started having babies as regularly as calf-roping season came
along.'

'Now,' said the pale little man, 'I understand why Dolph hates
Buffalo Bend.'

'It ain't that at all,' said the fat man. 'Dolph's one of the most
prosperous men in our community and, for a married man, he's
reasonably happy, even if Polly does sort of rule the roost and
keep him under a tight checkrein.'

From across the street there was a wild shouting and crashing
and banging, and then the three burly cowboys came rolling out
beneath the swinging doors of the Chinaman's Chance saloon like
so many tumbleweeds. They picked themselves up and legged
it down the dusty street, leaving their horses still hitched to the
rack.

'Dolph,' commented the pale little man, 'doesn't behave as if
anyone were keeping a tight checkrein on him.'

'Polly,' said the fat man, 'is a sensible woman, and she knows
that she has to let Dolph blow off steam once in a while, even
if they do have to pay for the rebuilding of the Chinaman's
Chance at least once a year. Besides, she feels she owes him
an occasional spree on account of that cold-decking she gave
him the night of the murder.'

'Cold-decking?' inquired the small pale man.

'Yeah,' said the fat man. 'You see, it later turned out that
Dolph didn't kill our sheriff none whatsoever. It was Lance
Warring, who, at the time, had some sort of personal grudge
against him. Not,' he explained, 'that Polly intended to let us
hang Dolph. She just wanted to give Lance a chance to get out
of town, which was a waste of good intentions, inasmuch as
Lance headed straight for O'Leary's Lapse, where he killed
another man and was hanged as the *pièce de résistance* of rodeo
day.'

There was a defiant bellowing, and then the sound of breaking glass from across the street. A buckboard drew up before the saloon and a tall handsome woman, her dark hair only slightly touched by grey, descended with majestic calm and marched regally into the Chinaman's Chance. A moment later a huge shaggy man came docilely out, followed by the handsome woman. He helped her into the buckboard, got into the driver's seat, gathering up the reins, gazed about him with the expression of a man well content with his lot in life, and then drove off.

'It must have,' said the small pale man, 'been that kiss that did it.'

But the fat man didn't answer. He had retrieved the bottle of chilli sauce and was reading the label with the absorbed attention of a man who has decided that one cannot get too much of good literature.

DUEL IN CAPTIVE VALLEY

By Will C. Brown

★　DUEL IN CAPTIVE VALLEY　★

WEST and north of 'Dobe Walls was the endless waste. First there was Lost Basin, and beyond that the thin blue vapour that was the unpromising ridges of Capitan Hills, and beyond the Capitans was nothing a rational white man would want to ride far enough to look at. The Basin itself was like the unsavoury dry sediment left in a pan bottom where a giant had washed dirty hands, and at its westward rim the Capitans' barren cliffs were crooked tusks in a monstrous skull long scalped and bleached. Some said a few Tonkawa outcasts existed beyond the Capitans, exiled from their tribe for one cause or another, and some said nothing alive was back there, that it was a place the Maker had not finished yet.

The fact remained, all trails led east from 'Dobe Walls. If you rode west, the tracks of your horse were yours alone in the Basin, and within a matter of miles it was as if a gigantic curtain had billowed down behind and shut off everything living, leaving one little germ of a man cast outside to plod eternal space.

The man 'Dobe Walls knew briefly as Dennis Blair chose to ride into the Basin at night. One day he was there, visible but scarcely known, without a past; and the next he was gone and there were only traces of hoofprints, already being filled as the dry wind fingered Basin sands back into place.

And like the sands, talk about him drifted loosely in the settlement for a day or two until the subject was covered and forgotten. It was said that his led horse was weighted with water canteens from the settlement's gypsum-smelling well, that he had stocked sparingly with food and ammunition at Spinner's store, and those who saw said that every knot and rope about his pack and gear were neat with military detail.

By the time 'Dobe had forgotten him, Dennis Blair had forgotten 'Dobe too, for it took no more than two days westward for the sand, the heat, the heavy desolation to blot out any recollection that other time or place existed. Life then was reduced to land wastes and sun, a universe of enemies. It was as if they raged to know what could furnish the impelling desperation to lure a man to dare them, which of the devil's choice duo of ancient enticement—gold or woman?

On the night of the third day, Blair shot his led horse. The animal had done its chore, for its water load was lightened now, with but one canteen remaining, and that Blair transferred to his saddle horse. The shot that killed the pack animal was fired from his heavy revolver and the explosion sound was swallowed quickly in the vastness. But it gave rise to a possibility—too soon, though, he thought—and he walked a little way off and emptied the rest of the loads into the night.

The first sound he heard that was not of the wastes came at midnight as he slept fitfully, drawn tightly within his blanket from the cold. The sound was the crunching whisper of feet breaking the thin crust of surface sand. Blair sat erect and peered into the greyness.

'Young-Knife?'

The answer was slow in coming. When it did, it sounded quite near, but still from beyond his vision.

'Lieutenant Blair?' Then, 'Are you alone, sir?'

'Over here, Young-Knife.'

Blair was standing, gun hanging loosely in hand. As if his shots had reached far to lure it at last out of reluctant distance, a form with dark granite face took shape in shadowy outline.

For the white man there was grim magic in the moment. Here in this vast God-forgotten nowhere, two pinpoints had met, almost as if by orderly appointment on a village street. His first feeling of accomplishment, the partial satisfaction of a player who has won the first small and tentative bet of a game destined for higher stakes, was oddly laced with incongruous memories.

Crazily, other parts of an old scene played across his mind. *Scout Juarez Young-Knife, it is my duty to inform you that the order of the court-martial is that you shall die at dawn before a battalion firing squad as a traitor to the Army of the Confederacy.*

There was one thing he had to know, ahead of everything else. It gnawed so deeply that he could not maintain the dignity to wait, knowing that another second of waiting would make his voice tremble when he asked it.

'Is she—alive?'

The graven stone hesitated. Then it spoke slowly. 'She is alive.'

Blair struggled to hold his voice steady. 'You can take me to her, Young-Knife?'

The silence across the shadowy space lasted so long that Blair found himself straining against it, gun shaking in impatient hand.

'Damn it, man! What about it? There's six years of this back of me! Can you get me there and get both of us out again?'

The answering voice was aloof with a half-breed's conscious inferiority but the words were planed to English grain by long association with white soldiers.

'Is the lieutenant so sure that she wants to leave my people?'

'Why wouldn't she be!' Blair demanded, too sharply, he realized, and tried to control his voice. It was the old and haunting anxieties rising up. 'Why, that's all she'd be thinking about, Young-Knife. Every hour and day since the raid. Waiting and waiting, wondering why somebody—'

Young-Knife moved closer. 'The Tonkawas were wrong to raid and kill in the settlements, Lieutenant, while the white men were away fighting in the South. But I know that Ilene Markham was one captive they treated well.'

'She is all right, then?'

'The lieutenant may judge for himself when he sees her.'

Blair sank to a seat on his bed tarp and fingered for tobacco.

'Why don't you drop that "lieutenant" business, and that "sir," too? That's all past. I wasn't the one who claimed you worked for both sides.'

'In the Tonkawa memory, years are only like minutes, Blair.'

'Look, you're not holding anything against me on account of that trouble? You saved my life at that outpost. That's why I arranged for your escape the night after your trial, which you well know. They could have shot me for it.'

'When I heard from the girl your name, I sent word everywhere east of the Capitans,' Young-Knife retorted.

'I'm grateful. I'll never know how you did it.'

'Word flutters along like a crippled crow on one wing.'

'Well, it got back. I've combed the settlements, everywhere! Everyone had given up—they called this just another damn wild-goose chase. Even her kin. They think she's dead.'

'She is not dead.'

'It was on the Pecos that I heard your name. Beyond the Basin, beyond the Capitans, rumours said. A white girl. A Tonkawa settlement. It began to add up. 'Dobe Walls was the place to take off.'

'And it came to us,' Young-Knife said, 'that a white man would head across the Basin from 'Dobe Walls.'

'Tell me about Ilene Markham—tell me about her, Young-Knife. You know we were just betrothed, and she was sixteen, when I went off to war. And the raid happened soon after that. Tell me—'

The scout said shortly, 'We should travel now while the night is cool. When the sun is on top tomorrow, we will come to a water hole in the first roughs.'

'That's good. Water is what I want to see.'

'When the Indian finds the water he wants, there is always a white man who is thirsty, too,' Young-Knife said.

Now that he had broken the final barrier of his quest, and was at last to grips with the fate that had shrouded Ilene Markham since the Tonkawa raid, Blair realized that his hopes were being attacked by some new and unaccountable sense of dread. They worked their horses through jagged cuts in the foothills. The single-file travel, with Young-Knife well ahead, made easy talk almost impossible, even if the half-breed had been disposed to talk.

Blair spent his time trying to conjure up in his mind how she might look. How much had she changed? Memory had left him only the haunting picture of her blonde loveliness, the graceful settlement girl of sixteen, and of their troth exchanged.

And now, he thought, a half-breed Army scout to whom he had once read a traitor's death sentence, and then aided to escape, had come to be his final link to her. Young-Knife had saved his life once in a Union ambush, as he had saved Young-Knife's in full settlement of the debt. He had to trust the silent, dark-skinned man now, as he had never trusted a man before. Yet, as they followed the twisting canyons, he knew with growing certainty that it was an uneasy trust.

As for Ilene, in those dragging years it had been his not knowing that hurt. That was torture to twist a man's soul. The sleepless nights at first, the later toilsome search, sometimes patient, sometimes frenzied. All that came back to fever his mind.

There came a moment on their second day into the Capitans when Young-Knife halted his horse and raised a long arm, pointing.

'There is where my people live,' he said, motioning to the valley haze, without looking at the white man.

The terrain below was surprisingly green, seeming studded with vegetation, Blair saw, and mentioned that.

'But it is not their home,' Young-Knife said tightly.

'That's true,' Blair commented. 'Yet, it looks like a country they could be happy in.'

Young-Knife turned to him and words came out in bitter intensity. 'The white man has taken their old country. Someday the white man will take this, too. And after that, there is no place for the Indian to go. The dawn of their firing squad is surely coming.'

'Firing squad?'

'Already, they are doomed, as I was doomed. But there is no escape for them.'

'You haven't forgotten that trouble, have you?'

The set mask was back over the dark face. 'It has always been the Indian's life to give up to the white man what the white man wanted to take.'

So now he had one part of it. This man still harboured vin-dictive resentment for the strain and humiliation of the treason conviction. But that was not all. There was that, and something more. It put hard knots in his jaws.

The lean and weathered white man raked the Indian's face with eyes turned cold and cutting. The truth was trying to speak to him out of the strained silence and he thought that he heard it. And he knew, all at once, in his bones, that Juarez Young-Knife was not his friend.

He forced his voice to casual tones. 'You will have no trouble, you think, in getting us out of here?'

'Trouble?' Young-Knife shrugged.

'About Ilene, I mean—will the tribe give her up without a council, or what? I can imagine this woman might be almost like a goddess to them by now. She might even have a lover among the bucks.'

For the first time, Young-Knife turned and looked directly at Blair. For a moment, Blair saw the thin-slit mouth tighten to a smile. It was gone and Young-Knife said:

'The white man is torturing himself. He should leave that to those who have always done it better.'

Eyes were on him from somewhere. Blair, with the soldier's sixth sense of hidden danger, could feel them, and both horses lifted their noses.

Slowly, the Indians came out of the scrub brush and trailside boulders.

The bulb-nosed paunchy one in the lead, with massive head topped by stiff, black sombrero, held up a hand. Young-Knife returned the sign.

Six men and six rifles. Ragged, nondescript pieces of white men's clothing, from what settlement victims no one would ever know. Blair's own saddle carbine was in its boot, his Army Colt in the holster on his leg. He did not move.

For each of the six here there would be another over in the roughs, with rifle sights fastened upon him. Grimly, his mind racing ahead of the moment, he knew that much of the rest of it depended upon decisions made here and now. Yet, he noted that the interest of the Indians seemed drawn to Young-Knife. Blair thought he caught a vague uncertainty in them, that he did not understand.

Bluntly, he pulled their attention away from the half-breed and to himself, using the sharp Army voice, the old tone of authority and finality.

'If you are Quevilito, you understand white man's talk.'

The old one with the spread nose blinked up at him, the

thousand dried ridges of his ancient face unrelieved by expression.

'Then listen to what I say. Your grandson has brought his friend across the Capitans, here to Quevilito's tribe. I have come to get the white woman and take her back to her people. When that is done, all the white settlements will rejoice and praise the name of the great Quevilito and his grandson, Juarez Young-Knife.'

The old one folded his arms and held his eye slits no higher than Blair's saddle horn. The wrinkled mouth worked.

'The white man has talked strange words,' he said, very slowly. 'The white man has been brought across the Capitans by his friend of the wars. That is so the white man and Young-Knife can stand like brothers of the blood when my grandson takes a wife.'

Blair's tongue felt dried out. 'When Young-Knife takes a wife?'

'My grandson and the white woman will be married.'

'The chief of the Tonkawas is telling me what I did not know.'

'That is why Young-Knife went to guide you here. It is the woman's wish that you come to the ceremony, that it may be done in white man's way.'

His hands gripped the saddle horn so tightly the knuckles stretched white, and his jaw knots went set like rounded stones.

'The white man's way will be to wait until he hears *her* say this thing, with his own ears.'

Young-Knife laughed harshly. 'That you will soon hear. Tonight you will see the ceremony dance begin.'

Blair turned, eyes clashed and locked. There was mocking wariness in the gaze of the half-breed, changing into sullen evasion.

He knew, now, that he was openly being shown the unsavoury fruit of this man's patient purpose. Young-Knife had lured him out of the east, with crafty word that he could guide Blair to Ilene Markham. Here was the full shape of Young-Knife's scheming, a way to hit back at all the past. It rang through his mind again, the words of Young-Knife's that the Indian's way of torture was better.

But behind it all lurked the dread that it might be true, that the captive girl he loved actually had promised herself to Juarez

Young-Knife. Even as he refused to consider this, the taunting whisper kept coming that *it could be so.* Six years of her Indian life were undeniably there, rising up to threaten and bewilder every rational hope.

Quevilito made a quick motion with his head. The Indian nearest Blair's horse glided forward and quickly withdrew the saddle rifle from its boot. Blair forced himself to sit unmoving, eyes on the chief. Then he felt the heavy tug, and his hip gun slid away. The Indian stepped back, holding carbine and revolver, and Blair felt the nakedness of a fighting man deprived of his arms in hostile circumstances.

Quevilito spoke a short word to Young-Knife, who pulled his black mustang into a walk. Blair followed him down the trail, not looking back, his eyes ahead to the cluster of pole houses and weathered tepees taking form in the tree-dotted valley below.

The western peaks were throwing smoky shadows across the village. It was not quite dusk and the sight of the white man, trailing Young-Knife into the settlement, brought chattering squaws crowding after them. These Young-Knife dispersed with a fling of harsh words, and the Tonkawas dropped back, watching. Blair heard the receding mumble of talk among them like distant growls of a disturbed wolf den as he rode a twisting course among haphazardly placed shacks and buffalo tents.

His eyes searched out each doorway, each shadowy form peering from within. But he did not find the face he sought. He found himself in doubt of what he expected to see. The tension inside him seemed to be blurring his eyes. How would she look, how would she be changed? Would he, perhaps, not be able to recognize her at first, in this darkening strangeness, and what word must he carefully use in that first moment of meeting?

In spite of soldier nerves long steeled to uncertainties, he knew a sensation of fingers clutching his lungs. Then Young-Knife halted and dismounted before a long structure of crudely laid logs and low sod roof.

Blair swung out of the saddle. He moved in quick strides until he stood almost touching Young-Knife, confronting him and forcing the half-breed to meet his eyes.

'Tell it with your own tongue, Young-Knife. Does the grandson of Quevilito have only an old squaw's courage, to be so ashamed of his plot that he must let his chief talk for him? Tell me your fine lie with a man's voice, my friend.'

He saw angered twitching in the muscles of the dark face.

'The white woman made the condition. She would marry Young-Knife only if I brought you here.'

'That was her price?'

Young-Knife whirled back to face him, mouth twisted with hate and old inferiority revealed in his eyes. His fingers moved up to feel the hide-wrapped handle of the long knife at his belt.

'There are no white soldiers to imprison me now!' he said savagely. 'I will marry the woman who was Ilene Markham. Whatever it took, I would do it, and this is what she demanded.'

'That you were to bring me here for the wedding?'

'What her reason was I do not know. But she has promised. She will keep her word.'

Blair knew. Suddenly he knew, as if it magically appeared in bold writing across the scrawny log front of the dark building. He understood, all at once, the uncertainty of the Indians back on the trail. He knew, because the white man's logic was greater than the red man's mind, his reasoning whetted to keener edges beyond the limits of Young-Knife's reasoning.

'You have paid an expensive price, Young-Knife!' His voice almost dropped to a whisper. 'Once again, you will find it costly—this thing the soldiers called a spy who double-crossed!'

Young-Knife snarled an angry word, but Blair did not stop. 'Get her. Bring her here!'

With deliberate scorn, he turned his back and stalked into the wide opening of the house.

Quevilito was there. Blair reasoned that the chief and his men must have had their horses in the hills, that they had ridden back by short cut. Quevilito motioned to the others, who moved away and sat on the bare earthen floor. A gathering of other figures were dim forms back in the gloom of the building. The white man, towering over the squat bulk of the inscrutable chief, waited.

Quevilito's halting words came in deep-chested dignity to break the silence.

'The white man was brave to come back of the Capitans alone. The word of a woman reaches far like the light of many fires. You are welcome here, among the people of him whose life you spared to us.'

Blair nodded. 'I am honoured to be among the people of the chief's grandson, who was my friend.'

'These are the last of my people,' Quevilito said in his low, careful monotone. 'Some of us live in the late sun of our years. But our young ones will see the white men come nearer, and nearer, until the last of my people are driven to join the big tribe in the Indian Nation. Then all the days of our freedom will be gone like dead ashes in the wind. The chief must always think of his people. There will be white men who will want pain and punishment for the Tonkawas. When the last days come, it will help my people with the white rulers if they are found to be led by Quevilito's grandson—and his white wife!'

He waited, and Blair chose his words carefully.

'I am not deaf to the wisdom of what the great chief is saying. But I ask now to see the girl who was Ilene Markham. There has been a promise made, to Juarez Young-Knife. But there was a promise made before that. It was the promise the white girl made to me, Dennis Blair, before the big war of the white men—before she was captured and taken away from her people by Quevilito's warriors. Now I would hear her speak—and your council men will hear her say which promise she will keep.'

Quevilito slowly nodded. He raised his hand, and there was a stir in the group at the distant end of the building. One form separated itself from the others, and Blair saw it move out of the gloom in slow approach toward him.

Suddenly, fire flared up, and torches held in the hands of three men gave off smoky illumination, casting jumpy yellow light over the room.

She walked toward him, slowly and alone.

And all the doubts he had fought dropped away, one by one. The soft white face, the gleaming braids of light flaxen hair, took on detail in the light. He knew she had not changed.

This was the Ilene Markham of his settlement boyhood. The

half-parted lips, the blue eyes raised to him and unafraid, were the eyes and lips that had spoken her promise to him. There was age added, of course, and the years and hardships had made their sign on her, as she must be seeing they had on him. But it was not important. The years fell away. He heard only the faint rustling sound of soft antelope skirts and the light step of small moccasined feet.

Then they were face to face. Her eyes spoke to him first, and he saw the assurance in them, assurance for him alone to see, and then, a change, a signal that he took to mean caution. He heard her voice, calm and distinct.

'Dennis.'

She touched his arm. She whispered. 'Always, I kept living just for this moment.'

He might have touched her. He struggled to separate the words that crowded his throat. But the moment suddenly was shadowed by the brush of another presence, the knowledge that the hard breathing he heard was not his own. He cut his glance to see Young-Knife planted beside him, glinting eyes on Ilene and face fixed with the hard smile of knowledge. She turned her head away.

It was Quevilito who moved to her and gently placed a gnarled hand upon her shoulder.

'This is my daughter in place of my daughter long dead. In the eyes of the Tonkawas, she is one of us. As the wife of my grandson Young-Knife she will live out her days with the last of my people. This is the word of Quevilito.'

Young-Knife folded strong arms across his chest, his expression flashing challenge to all. But Blair was hearing the tone in the chief's voice—sound from a hollow log. And he had the taut knowledge that Young-Knife's brittle moment would be shattered, that the man did not know the full resentment against him here. It had shown in the men who had met them on the trail, and it showed here again in the tone of Quevilito. For they were words spoken without heart. The steady glance he got from Ilene confirmed that.

Blair moved a pace. His shoulder pushed in front of Young-Knife, and with slow purpose he reached to take Quevilito's arm and firmly lift the hand from Ilene's shoulder. The gesture and its decisive meaning caused a ripple over the room.

'The white woman will say it with her own words.'

Ilene turned to Quevilito. 'I will go away with the white man, back to my own. My promise to Young-Knife was the talk of two tongues, like the Tonkawa promise of peace before they raided my home and killed my people.'

She lightly touched her fingers to the arm of the wrinkled chief. 'This you have known—Quevilito has been my father in place of my father long dead—Quevilito himself, with the sun-down of his years upon him, *knew my plan in his own great wisdom.*'

Blair saw the chief's chin sag to his chest, but now that it was out, the old one's mouth seemed set with foxlike satisfaction.

Shifting his glance to Young-Knife, frozen beside him, Blair saw the flare of chagrin and hatred.

Quevilito mumbled, 'I have said what a chief should say. The morning will now speak its own decision.'

He made a sign and the people began to melt from the room.

Blair heard her quick whispered words: 'You are safe here tonight. Then—at daylight!' and she, too, was gone. He was alone. They were leaving the final settlement to the process of their ancient way. They knew, and it was ominously plain—*the morning would bring its own decision.*

An old man came, after a while, leaving him food and water, and indicated a crude corner bunk of buffalo robes.

At daylight, he found his rifle and Colt on the floor at his feet. Stepping quickly to the doorway, he saw with satisfaction his horse was there, and another, and two saddles were on the ground, with canteens and trail packs. He looked to the loads of his guns.

She came alone, down the silent settlement street in the grey light of dawn. No words were spoken, except those spoken to him from her eyes. Then she pushed into his arms and for a moment he held her tightly.

There was no sound, no movement from the scattering of darkened hovels as they rode away.

In the first jagged cuts of the hills they looked back and down into the settlement. Up here the sun sent glints of pink against boulders and cliff sides, but in the valley the Tonkawa houses were vague forms still murky in the thin haze.

She murmured, 'I prayed that this would come someday, Dennis. Now I pray that it will be you when this day ends.'

'He will be waiting ahead?' Blair asked.

'It is their way. They know that I used him to bring you here. It was my only chance. They are strange people. They will not interfere.'

'They are not for him, nor against him, I think.'

'His blood and his arrogance are against him here, as they must have been among white men. The man of two bloods is forever at war within himself. He must bring me back. He must save face. That is how he must prove himself to Quevilito and his people. That—or he will always be the outcast.'

He looked ahead at the unwelcome shadows up the trail. 'Will it be soon, you think?'

'There is no way to know. This, I will have to leave with you. All I can do is hope.'

He nodded. 'I will ride ahead, now. When it is over, I will wait for you. Do not think of it as being any other way.'

Without looking back, he pushed his horse along the canyon trail, a soldier's eye moving restlessly to search each shadow for any tiny alien thing. When the light of the morning was strong, he dismounted and led the horse by bridle, trying to keep alongside the animal on the side of the trail, because Young-Knife would be to the right, not facing against the sun.

It could be here, happening swiftly as a lightning burst, he thought. Or it could be in the distance, at any point in the gauntlet of miles. That was the devilish advantage for Young-Knife. Blair sifted it out with methodical coldness, applying a soldier's hard reasoning, and returned to his first conclusion. *It would be soon.*

The cunning and patience in half-breed veins would be outweighed by Young-Knife's violent urge for quick triumph, by damaged dignity, the burning vanity to hurry back to the waiting tribe with the white man's woman and the white man's scalp. And having made his best calculation, Blair pushed all chips on it, for the other elements of the gamble were scattered and many and he could not cover them all.

The first hour dragged by. With each step, he searched out the terrain, watching the boulders ahead and across the neck of his mount, getting what little cover he could from the animal's body, and whirling back constantly to search behind him.

Then his mount faltered. For just one stride there was an almost imperceptible off-rhythm in replacing a lifted forefoot to earth. To Blair's straining senses, the break in the steady plod of hoofs telegraphed its warning. He caught the movement of the horse's head, slightly raised, bit shaken in mouth, ears stiffly forward. The animal's nose veered to the left and even as Blair spotted the cracked black boulder he was hit by knowledge of Young-Knife's cunning. The half-breed had anticipated that the white man's concentration would be for the east side. Together, they had worked dangerous trails before. And so he had chosen to watch against the sun.

It was too late, now. Blair made himself keep unbroken stride, for already the rifle bead would be on him. Young-Knife could squeeze the trigger at any time, now. Blair's hand carried his six-gun but he had to continue the pace, walking on the exposed side of his horse. He would have to outguess, by a split second, when Young-Knife was satisfied with the closing range. Five steps, he counted, and five more.

He forced his head to face the east side, to the pretence of watching there, holding the black boulder with the tail of his eye. And when he caught the almost invisible movement of rifle barrel, like a dead stick in the crack of the rock, he unleashed coiled muscles and violently plunged aside.

The dead stick moved. Young-Knife had changed aim too quickly. The bullet whined above the man rolling on the ground, and Blair flipped to his feet in continuation of the roll, running now in a zig-zag crouch. The new angle he made altered the rifle rest in the split boulder. Young-Knife had to raise his head to fix his target, and Blair was ready.

The big six-gun blasted hoarsely. One shot, triggered with care. One shot held for the one fraction of certainty that counted. One chance was all that he would have. The rifle whipped back its retort in the same instant and fire pricked his neck like the sting of passing blade. Rifle barrel waved skyward, then collapsed from sight.

Blair ran, still crouched, his breath churning, desperation still in his legs. He rounded the boulder.

The figure that sprawled there, with rifle flung a little way aside, was unmoving.

'Young-Knife!'

He saw the lips twitch and stooped to hear blood-choked whispers.

'Lieutenant—it is dark—in this prison—'

The sun beat down on lips drawn tight. Young-Knife's eyes fluttered once and were still. Blair wiped sweat from his own eyes and blood from his jaw.

He took Young-Knife's faded campaign hat, the old hat of a soldier, up from the dirt and turned it over in his hands. He brushed the dust from it, and placed it over Young-Knife's face. He holstered his gun and turned to search for his horse. He walked away, stepping quietly over the rocks.

Far down the canyon to the west he saw the dot of movement coming—Ilene Markham emerging from her captivity. Somewhere to the east was the last water hole, and then the ordeal of the Basin, and beyond, the advancing world of white men. The two of them would bridge that, too, as they both had bridged the bad years.

He waited for her on the trail.

SHADOW OF THE BUTTE

★   ★

By *Thomas Thompson*

TWO women joined the little group around Ellen Tremaine there in front of Jake Paxton's store, and as Hamp Donnelly passed them he heard Ellen talking with that peculiar rush of words which marks a woman starved for conversation. He glanced at her and saw that she could still smile, and he was glad. He went inside the store, and the storekeeper turned his head and spit at a coffee can he always kept near by. 'Some looker, ain't she?'

'Miss Ellen?' Hamp said.

'Kinda picky, though. She'll have to get used to the fact that Bigforks ain't Philadelphia. Asked fer stuff I never even heerd of.'

'Start totin' it out,' Hamp said. 'I gotta get loaded.'

The storekeeper wiggled his body as if he were trying to dig his elbows into the counter. 'What you gonna do, Hamp, the hay crew quittin' on Miss Ellen that way? How you gonna get your hay cut?'

'I'll bite it off with my teeth,' Hamp said. He picked up a bolt of material that Ellen Tremaine had chosen for curtains. 'Wrap something around this.'

The storekeeper's faded eyes were sharp behind his glasses. 'You reckon the hay crew quit because they figgered there'd be trouble?'

'Are you asking questions, Jake, or running a store?'

'Now, Hamp,' the storekeeper said, 'no call for you to get sore at me.'

He was talking to empty space. Hamp Donnelly had picked up a box of groceries and now he was outside, loading it into the wagon. He glanced down the street to where a trail-sweaty horse was tied in front of the town's only saloon and he knew Tuna Stinson, the owner of that horse, was inside. He was inside getting drunk, making his brag, waiting for Hamp to start it. Hamp turned back to enter the store, and Ned Crockett, the town marshal, was here, blocking his way. 'You stay away from Tuna, Hamp,' the marshal said.

'Tell him the same, then, Ned,' Hamp said. He went back into the store, leaving the marshal standing there, a young man, lean and weathered and tough.

The storekeeper kept twisting and digging his elbows into the counter. He had a tic in his left eye. 'Hamp, what kinda feller's Miss Ellen's brother?' he asked. 'I only seen him that first day when they come in on the stage. Is the brother anything like their uncle was? I hear tell the brother and Dallas Rombeck is thick as fleas.'

'You hear a lot, don't you, Jake?' Hamp said. He picked up a hundred-pound sack of sugar and tossed it across his shoulder. 'Make sure you got a spud stuck on the spout of that coal-oil can,' he said. 'I don't want it leaking all over this sugar.'

Hamp finished loading the wagon, and from time to time he glanced down toward the saloon, the feeling of suppressed anger strong in him. Tuna Stinson's horse was still there. That was like Tuna. He would spend his first day in town getting drunk, building up his anger and whetting his hatred. Hamp wished he could start it now, get it over. He passed a rope around a hook on the wagon bed and secured it over the top of the tarp. He was a tall man in his middle twenties, his skin saddle-brown from wind and weather, his eyes blue, crowfooted with looking at distance. He was freshly shaved, and his skin seemed tight for his face. His hands were heavy and square from work and they were bulky and big against the rope, but they were not clumsy.

The marshal came out of the two-story hotel and walked back up the street toward the wagon. He walked as if he were tired. 'I just talked to Boyd Novis,' the marshal said.

'Did you expect Novis to admit he sent for Tuna?' Hamp said.

'Well, Hamp,' the marshal said, 'I can only do so much.'

Hamp's expression softened as he looked at the younger man.

'Sure, Ned,' he said. 'Forget it.' He walked around the wagon and stood there, his hat pushed back on his unruly blond hair. 'All loaded, Miss Ellen.'

She glanced at him, impatiently, he thought, but she said good-bye to the women and then she came to the wagon. He helped her up, a tall girl with red hair and grey-green eyes and too much worry about her. His hands were strong around her waist and he lifted her easily until her foot was on the hub. She climbed into the seat hurriedly, wanting to be free of the touch of his hands.

'Thank you,' she said. She didn't look directly at him. She never did.

Hamp thought, 'Do you think I enjoyed killing a man any more than you enjoy thinking about it?'

His hands gripped the lines with an angry strength. He kicked off the brake and tooled the Anchor-branded team of matched bays away from the store porch. 'I want to stop by the school a minute and say hello to my sister,' he said.

'Of course.' She was staring straight ahead, her lips tight, sitting far over on her side of the seat, as she always did when she was with him.

Do you want to see my hands? he thought. Do you want to see the blood on them?

They drove down the single street of the town, past the law office of Dallas Rombeck, and he noticed the office was closed. Dallas was spending most of his time with Paul Tremaine these days. Hamp slapped the lines against the backs of the bays. He wanted to forget Dallas.

The town was old and weathered before its time, a collection of false-front buildings and tired cottages badly in need of paint. Behind them the low brown hills ran up to the stunted sage and juniper of the Bake Oven Plateau, and ahead of them, across the little valley, the hills lifted again, marked by the single twisting road that led into the broken country toward Anchor Ranch and the lush valleys of the John Day River.

Gradually the anger ran out of Hamp, and he began trying

to visualize what it would be like if all this were as strange to him as it was to her. It annoyed him at times that she and her brother Paul hadn't been better prepared for it. They had always known that some day they would inherit the Anchor. They were Dusty Tremaine's only relatives, and Hamp himself had read a dozen letters in which Dusty had told his niece and nephew that he wanted to leave Anchor to them.

The anger was gone and he felt an affection for Ellen, not because she was a woman but because she was Dusty's niece. She was doing all right and he wanted to tell her so. The way she had handled that hay crew. A small grin crinkled the corners of his eyes. 'That hay crew will have red ears for a week,' he said.

He saw her chin come up, her lips tighten, and it pleased him. 'Quit, will they?' she said. 'Of all the worthless, no-good trash!' Her chin was trembling a bit and she didn't try to say more. But she knew how to take trouble, he decided. She'd do. He turned the team and his elbow brushed her shoulder. He felt her wince away from him as if his elbow had been a hot iron.

The schoolhouse was in a field by the road, a small, one-room building. It was recess time and a dozen children were playing noisily. Two boys were wrestling, rolling around in the dirt of a hard-packed yard, while a young woman stood near them, trying to stop them. Three pigtailed girls clung to the woman's skirts and moved when she moved, like chicks around a mother hen.

Hamp Donnelly put his foot against the brake and spoke to the team as he twisted his hands against the lines. 'I'll just be a minute.'

'Your sister is very pretty,' Ellen Tremaine said. She waved at the two little boys who had run out toward the road at breakneck speed and then stopped dead-still to stand and stare.

'She takes after me,' Hamp said. It didn't sound very funny. He got down from the wagon and walked across the yard, tousling the head of a ten-year-old boy who came out to meet him. The teacher shooed the girls away before coming over to join her brother. She turned and walked with him toward the pump that stood in back of the school building.

Hamp pushed back his hat, placed his hand under the spout of the pump, worked the handle, and drank the dammed-up water.

'How's it going, Sue?' he said.

She stood there, a small, beautifully formed girl, just out of her teens. Her eyes were a deep blue, her hair black, and he always had trouble remembering that she had grown up. 'All right,' she said. 'How's the Queen?'

'Miss Ellen?' He grinned. 'She's all right.' It was more than an answer to the question. 'She really gave that hay crew a piece of her mind.'

Sue still stood there, watching him. 'Well, why don't you say what you came here to say?'

Hamp shrugged. 'Dallas Rombeck ain't the only man left in the world.'

'Suppose I tell you he is for me?' There was an amazing amount of determination in that small body.

He crooked his finger under her chin and tried to grin. 'I've never tried to make up your mind for you, Sue, but I won't lie and say Dallas Rombeck is the one I'd pick for a brother-in-law. He's a little highfalutin' for my taste.'

'But not for the Queen's taste?'

'She's just lonesome, that's all. Dallas knew some people back East she knew. I reckon they talk the same language.'

Sue folded her arms defiantly across her breast. 'Don't tell me she's got you seeing stars, too?'

Hamp ignored the remark. 'Come on out to the wagon and say hello to her, at least.'

'Do I have to?' she asked sulkily.

'Yes.'

They walked together, back around the school building. The children clamoured at Hamp, calling him by his first name. There was a wild babble of voices, a dozen conversations, none of them making sense, and then one voice, young and strident, was louder than the rest: 'Hamp could lick Tuna Stinson with one hand tied behind him!'

'Yeah?' another jeered. 'Did you see Tuna when he come ridin' down the road a while ago? Did you talk to him like I did?'

'You're a liar! You didn't talk to Tuna.'

Sue's face had drained of colour. 'When did he come back, Hamp?'

'About an hour ago.'

'Why didn't you tell me?'

'For what?' Hamp said. 'He's here, so he's here. It's a free country.'

Her voice was trembling with emotion: 'Don't fight with him, Hamp. Go away some place for a while.'

'That's crazy talk,' he said flatly.

Sue's voice was bitter. 'How long are you going to keep this up? Are you going to get yourself killed just so she can go on being the grand lady?'

'I guess it don't seem very grand to her,' he said. He took his sister's arm. 'Look, Sue. You've lived here all your life and you can understand things like this. You knew I had to kill Orvie Stinson; you knew Tuna would come back sometime. Miss Ellen's different, Sue. I don't want her to know about Tuna being here. Not just yet.'

She pulled away from him and stood there. 'You're a fool, Hamp.'

'Maybe,' he said. 'You be nice to her.' He put his hand under Sue's elbow and they walked on toward the wagon.

Ellen had climbed down from the wagon and she was half kneeling, her full skirt spread around her, her arm around a dingy child who stood embarrassed, thumb in mouth. A nine-year-old boy strutted in front of her and spit across the centre of his lip. Ellen put her free arm around the boy and squeezed him close, and the boy dug his bare toe in the dirt and ducked his head. Ellen looked up and saw Hamp and Sue watching her, and she stood up, smoothing her skirt. There was a wistful half-smile in her eyes as she watched the children run back toward the schoolhouse. 'Kids are all alike, aren't they?' she said.

'Very much so,' Sue Donnelly said. 'I'm afraid Easterners think our children out here run around naked with feathers in their hair. Actually–'

Hamp coughed against the back of his hand. 'I reckon we better be moseyin' along before it gets too late.'

'I wish you'd come out and see me, Sue,' Ellen said. 'I bought some curtain material and several things for the house. I'm dying to have you see them. It's really pretty difficult, though, shopping in Bigforks–'

'I've shopped there all my life without any trouble,' Sue said. The girl who was monitor started dinging the teacher's desk bell and children ran from every direction. 'If you'll excuse me–' Sue turned quickly and walked over to the school steps and stood there clapping her hands together, calling to the children. Hamp Donnelly saw the smile fade slowly from Ellen Tremaine's face.

The wagon lifted immediately into the barren hills, winding and dipping and always climbing. The red dust clung to the rims of the wheels and fell loose and left a pale pink cloud behind them. Hamp Donnelly drove silently, his eyes squinted against the bright light that reflected from the blue sky and burned back from the brown grass. Streamers of dust trailed from the stunted sage and drifted into the scattered juniper. The land was alive with the brittle dryness of early fall, spiced with tarweed and cured grass.

Hamp pulled up at the summit and turned in the seat. 'There's a good look at Bigforks,' he said, jerking his head toward the town, back and below them. 'I guess it ain't as big as Philadelphia, is it?'

The town was a block of green in the centre of the small valley. Over-enthusiastic promoters had planted Lombardy poplars twenty years back, and now they leaned in the wind, dropping their speckled shade on streets that had never existed. They could see the school and the roof of Jake Paxton's store and here and there a few weathered shingles. A man walked down the centre of the road between the school and the town. He was like an ant crawling along a shimmering pink ribbon.

'It's pretty small,' she said.

'The big country is this way,' he said.

He looked across the distance to the canyon of the John Day River, twisting and green, and beyond that to more brown hills, lonely and never ending in their sameness, dismally alike to one who didn't know them, comforting in their permanence and sameness to one who did. He glanced at her hands gripped in her lap, her eyes straight ahead.

'This was your uncle's favourite spot,' he said quietly. 'His grave is yonder on that flat butte.'

Perhaps it was mention of her uncle, or maybe it was only that emotions could be held just so long. She turned toward him, and her eyes were bright, her lips set in a hard line. She wasn't really beautiful, he realized. She was just close to beauty. So close that a man watched her constantly, expecting each change of expression to bring perfection. She was angry now. Angry and hurt.

'Why do they hate me?' she said. 'What have I done to any of them?'

'Miss Ellen, they don't hate you—'

'Even your sister. What have I ever done to her? That haying crew. Why did they walk out just when we needed them most?'

'You can't depend on a crew like that,' he said patiently. 'Next month they'll be up in the Umatilla country workin' the wheat. Maybe later they'll be down at the mouth of the Columbia, canning salmon. They're just drifters.'

'They were hired away from us, just like the crew before them. Boyd Novis hired them. He paid them twice what we could pay them.'

'We'll get by, Miss Ellen,' he said.

The entire distance between the deep canyon of the Deschutes and the winding green valleys of the John Day was there below them, a high land of gently rolling hills, sharp canyons, flats and valleys, grey with sage, brown with grass, musty green with scattered juniper. East, the significance of Mt. Hood reared unbroken snow fields above the darkness of fir forests, and to the South Mt. Jefferson stood in isolated splendour, and beyond that were blue mountains and snow peaks.

A faint odour of sage and cured grass spiced the thin, clean air with an illusive fragrance, and the reds and the golds retreated from the purple hills.

For a moment he was close to her. She was not afraid of him and he could say things he had been wanting to say, let her know that she wasn't alone, that he himself cared very much what happened to her and her brother, and that old 'Judge' Norton, who had a small ranch next to Anchor, cared just as much.

'You've done good for the short time you've been here, Miss Ellen,' he said quietly. 'You and your brother, both. If Dusty's watching you from up there he's mighty proud of you.'

She turned and looked at him. He was gazing off into space and the hard lines of his face softened and there was a dream in his eyes. For the first time she thought of him as a man instead of as a fixture she had inherited with the ranch. The thought surprised her, but it passed quickly, and again she was remembering that this man had killed—that he was as hard and ruthless as the land itself.

He glanced at her and saw the change in her expression. There was a lot he wanted to tell her but he couldn't just yet. He couldn't tell her until she was ready to understand. He looked away. 'Me and the Judge worried about you and your brother coming out here, everything new to you.' He hadn't realized he would have so much trouble saying the simple thing he wanted to say. 'We know now you'll make out all right, Miss Ellen. When you turned down the cash offer Boyd Novis made you, we knew you liked Anchor well enough to want to keep it.'

She sat there staring at him, listening to this man who until today had spoken in monosyllables, and she felt the land around them, barren and vast and unfriendly. A land that could kill, peopled with men who killed. A terrifying wave of loneliness swept over her and grew into a homesickness that was physical pain. She thought of her brother Paul and of how he fit this even less than she did. She spoke without even meaning to say the words aloud: 'Like it?' She was looking straight at him now and all the bitterness was in her eyes. 'I hate it! I hate every stone and every blade of grass and every cow and every piece of dust and every breath of air I breathe!'

The humour ran out of Hamp Donnelly's eyes. He felt as if someone had hit him in the pit of the stomach. He took his foot off the brake and drove down the hill toward the ranch in the valley, and he kept thinking, over and over, 'Do you know this, Dallas Rombeck? Do you know how she feels?' . . .

The buildings of Anchor, surrounded by the inevitable wind-break poplars, lay on a bench overlooking the river valley. It was not a vast holding, but over the years Dusty Tremaine had been able to pick up a parcel here and another there, until now the land that comprised Anchor was owned land rather than leased, as so many larger operations were. Anchor had always run cattle, a good grade of Shorthorn and Durham, descendants of cattle brought across the plains with the first settlers. To the north was the Columbia river-port town of The Dalles, and down the river at its junction with the Willamette was the fast-growing city of Portland. There was a market for beef, and Anchor was a good living for anyone.

It was home to Hamp Donnelly, practically the only home he had ever known, and he felt the strong tug of it as he tooled the wagon into the hardpacked yard between the ranch house and the barn and pulled the now sweaty team to a stop. Paul Tremaine and Dallas Rombeck, talking in the house, had heard the creak of the wagon and the grind of the wheels a half-hour before the outfit came in sight. They were out in the yard waiting.

Ellen didn't wait for Hamp to help her down. She ran to Paul and kissed him on the cheek and gave her hand to Rombeck, and the touch of his fingers was as if, reaching out, she had found something familiar in a dark room. Dallas had gone to school in the East and he had spent a summer in Philadelphia. He knew people by name whom she knew by name, and they talked about them often, until those people who were only names became close mutual friends when contrasted against her loneliness here.

Things that were amusing to her were amusing to Dallas, and for this moment, at least, she could pretend. 'Dallas! Paul! Wait until you see what I bought. Three kinds of curtain material and a new reflector lamp for the kitchen wall and—you'll love this, Paul—some stove blacking for Iron Dragon.' Dallas had named the kitchen stove that. She felt if she didn't keep talking she would cry.

'It must have been very gay,' Paul Tremaine said. 'Did you get out before they rolled the streets up?'

'Street, singular, my friend,' Dallas Rombeck said. 'Don't try to foist growth upon our fair city. Anything but that.'

'The place gives me the creeps,' Paul said. He was a handsome man, a little too heavy, a streak of premature grey in his dark hair. His eyes were brown and moody and his rather doughy face was fixed in a constant scowl.

'Oh, come, Paul,' Rombeck said, slapping his friend on the back. 'We're not all savages here, in spite of what you think.'

'Dallas, what would we do without you?' Ellen said. She took both men by the arm and led them toward the substantial frame house that sat close to the ground in the barren yard. 'Come along, you two, if you want any dinner.'

'A banquet,' Dallas said. 'I brought you some select wine.' He kissed his finger tips.

Hamp stood there and watched them go toward the house, three people totally different and yet much alike. He saw the neat cut of Dallas Rombeck's coat, the tailored shoulders and fitted waist. The brown trousers were a perfect fit, tight at the ankles, snug above the polished black boots that looked as if they had never seen dust. Successful or not, Dallas Rombeck always looked the part of the prosperous young attorney. There was a studied carelessness about Paul's dress, and Hamp sensed that it was something that could be achieved only by a man who knew exactly how to dress. Hamp started unhitching the team, his hands moving swiftly.

The screen door of the bunkhouse opened and slammed closed, and 'Judge' Norton stood there on the step a moment, the coal in his stubby pipe reflecting against the lower half of his seamed face. He was an old man who enjoyed the sun and the rest that retirement had brought him. A bachelor, he had been a successful lawyer in The Dalles. Then, twenty years ago, he had counted his money and quit, coming back to be with people he knew and liked. He owned a few acres of land on which he let meadow hay raise itself. He had been around when Hamp's widowed father came to Anchor with a broken-down rig and two kids six months before his death. The Judge had had a hand in raising Hamp and Sue, and he loved them both.

Knocking the coal from his pipe, he crossed over to the corral, walking carefully, mindful of his joints. His voice was as dry and as seamed as his skin: 'Did she pay 'em off?'

'She paid 'em off and told 'em off,' Hamp said. 'She's got plenty spunk.'

'That makes eight men in all Boyd Novis has hired away from her.'

'He's getting pretty anxious. Too anxious, maybe.'

There was quick concern in the Judge's pin-bright eyes. 'What do you mean by that?'

'Tuna Stinson's in town.'

The Judge removed the pipe from his mouth. He held it in his hand, gripping it until the bowl burned his thin flesh. 'Does she know?'

'About Tuna?' Hamp shrugged. He pulled the harness free and hung it on the fence. 'She will. Somebody will see to that.'

A lighted lamp flared up in the living-room of the ranch house. Hamp and the Judge could hear Ellen and Dallas Rombeck laughing together. The two men stood there, one old, one young, their features growing dim in the gathering dusk. 'You couldn't keep it away from her forever,' the Judge said.

'I didn't expect to.'

There was a long silence between them and Hamp thought of the grave on the butte. He tried to think the way Dusty Tremaine would have thought. He led the horses to the trough and let them drink, hearing them swallow noisily in the gathering darkness, and then he turned them into the corral. For a moment he stood there, watching them circle and paw before lying down to roll the sweat out of their hides. He could hear the Judge breathing heavily with a dry, rasping sound, as if trying to control what he wanted to say, weighing and testing each word before he said it.

'Maybe it's no good, Hamp,' he said finally. 'Maybe it's not worth it.'

'Dusty wanted them to stay, didn't he?' Hamp said.

From inside the house he could hear Ellen's laughter. He stood there a moment, listening, and he remembered a time when he and Sue were small and Sue had refused to go to a birthday party because she didn't like some of the little girls who were going to be there. Sue's and Hamp's father had told her if she didn't go and have a good time she'd get a darn good licking. Sue went; she had a good time; she laughed and played harder than anyone; and all the time she was thinking about getting that licking. Ellen Tremaine's laughter made Hamp think of that.

'We better get washed up for supper,' he said.

'She didn't ask me for supper,' the Judge said. 'Maybe I'd better not come.'

'Since when do you have to be asked to eat at Dusty Tremaine's table?' Hamp said.

They went over to the kitchen door, where a bucket and tin basin sat on a water-and-soap-soaked bench. Inside, busy in the kitchen, Ellen could hear them washing and she could hear that peculiar burbling sound the Judge always made when he washed his face. She was slightly annoyed that the Judge was going to stay. She wished just she, Paul and Dallas could have eaten alone.

She could hear Dallas and Paul talking in the dining-room, and she went to the door and looked in, giving Dallas her quick smile. Paul was pacing back and forth across the room, his hands thrust deep into his trousers pockets, the eternal scowl on his face. The crystal wine decanter which she had brought with her from Philadelphia was there on the table, two-thirds empty now.

Dallas looked up and saw her and returned her smile. 'Isn't there something I can do to help you?' He was a handsome man, always pleasant, always completely at ease. It was comforting to have him around.

'You can set the table,' she said, and she held the door open for him. His shoulder brushed hers as he came into the kitchen. She pushed a strand of hair off her forehead with her wrist and pointed to the cupboard with a spatula. 'If you can find five plates to match,' she said, 'we'll make this dinner formal.'

'Five?'

'Judge Norton is staying.'

'He practically lives here, doesn't he?'

She didn't answer. Hamp and the Judge came in through the back door. There was fifty years difference in their age, a foot difference in their height, and yet they looked alike, somehow, just as she found most men did in this country. Their faces were scrubbed, their hair combed in that peculiar fashion which made it look as if it would stay in place exactly for the duration of the meal, no longer. They passed through the kitchen, hats in hand, and they hung their hats on the elk antlers in the dining-room where Dusty Tremaine's old single action .45 hung in its holster, loaded, just as he had left it. Ellen had intended a dozen times to put that gun away, but she didn't like the thought of handling it.

Rombeck nodded to Hamp and the Judge and gave his attention to Ellen. 'The silver candelabra, perhaps, Madame? And the crystal service?'

'The cups with handles,' she said, 'and be thankful.'

Hamp and the Judge pulled out their chairs and sat down, and now they were sitting there, wondering what to do with their hands. Hamp never seemed to be entirely at ease unless he was outside.

'How about a glass of wine?' she heard Paul say. She thought Paul's voice was a little loud and she hurried with the meal.

The food was good; the candles she had placed on the table gave a small festive glow she liked, though she had the feeling Hamp and the Judge were searching for their food in the semi-darkness. Rombeck's conversation was pleasant, and even the Judge seemed to be trying hard tonight, but the meal was spoiled because of Paul.

He had had too much wine, and instead of cheering him it had driven him farther into his morose shell. His dark eyes were bright, his lips too red against the pallor of his skin. He put his knife and fork down too hard. 'Gravy,' he said. 'Fried meat. Fried potatoes. What I'd give for a dozen oysters on the half shell.'

'First time you get over to Portland there's a restaurant there famous for oysters,' Hamp said. 'Never tried 'em myself.'

'Speaking of oysters,' Dallas Rombeck said, 'remember that little place just off Market in Philadelphia? You went downstairs.' He touched his lips with his napkin. 'I remember one night several of us—James Pitkin was along. Ellen, you remember James Pitkin?'

She was really interested in what Dallas had to say. It made her homesick in the comforting way a visitor from home makes one homesick. She wanted to listen, but she couldn't. She was watching Paul, worried now. He had taken the stopper from the wine decanter and dropped it. He poured his glass full.

Ellen got up quickly, some of the colour going from her face. She was smiling gaily, too gaily, Hamp thought. 'Of course I remember James Pitkin,' she said as she passed Dallas's chair. 'Didn't he marry that Lawford girl? What was her name?' She took the wine decanter from the table and set it on the oak sideboard at the far side of the room. For just a second Paul Tremaine was looking at his sister and his mouth was ugly.

'What do you hear about the election, Dallas?' Hamp said. This was a safe subject and Ellen was grateful for it, but she was glad when Hamp and the Judge had finished and gone back outside. Paul found a chair in the big, bare living-room and promptly went to sleep.

Dallas stayed and helped with the dishes, and later he and Ellen had a second cup of coffee together. He acted as if the dinner had been a perfect success, but he was only being kind, Ellen knew. It bothered her that he should have to be kind to her. She had never before been in that position with an eligible male. She looked at Dallas quickly, the thought troubling her. A girl would have to be careful in this country. Homesickness and worry and a handsome man could be a bad combination. She knew that, but when he suggested that perhaps he should be going she insisted he stay a little longer. She didn't want him to leave.

Out on the bunkhouse step Hamp smoked his fourth cigarette

and watched the front door of the ranch house. 'Is he going to stay all night?' he said finally, throwing down his cigarette.

'Wouldn't know,' Judge Norton said.

'Dusty would turn over in his grave.'

'You ought to be glad,' the Judge said. 'Sue's rid of Dallas.' The Judge was watching Hamp closely and there was a little twinkle of devilment in his eyes.

'Women.'

'That's why I never married,' the Judge said.

'Why?'

'Women.'

Hamp rolled another cigarette and stood up, tall and lean, his jeans skintight, his feet small for the width of his shoulders. He wanted to talk to Ellen a moment. He wanted to reassure her about getting another haying crew. At least, that's what he thought he wanted to talk to her about. The ranch house door opened and Dallas and Ellen were silhouetted there for a moment. Hamp let the cigarette slip from his fingers.

They stood there together, saying good night, and then Ellen came out onto the porch, closing the door behind her, and now Hamp could see only their shapes, outlined by the light from the window. He knew Dallas was holding her hands and he could hear the faint murmur of voices, and then the two forms were moving closer together and Rombeck's head was bending down and Ellen's arms were reaching up. Hamp's throat was constricted and tight.

'I reckon he's leaving now,' Judge Norton said.

Dallas Rombeck came out toward the barn. He saw Hamp start for the house, and he walked over to intercept him. 'I wouldn't try to talk to her now, Hamp,' he said. 'She is upset.'

The idea of Rombeck advising him angered him and there was another anger, swifter, more deadly. He reached out and gripped Rombeck's arm. 'You just have to talk so much, don't you, shyster?'

Rombeck jerked his arm free. 'Don't you think she has a right to know?'

'Maybe she's got a right to know it was Boyd Novis who sent for him.'

'All right,' Dallas said. 'She knows it. I've told you a dozen times I have no more regard for Boyd Novis personally than you have. In my business a man doesn't pick his clients because of their sterling character.'

'It must be a fine business,' Hamp said. He walked swiftly toward the house.

Ellen heard him on the porch and opened the door before he had a chance to knock. For a moment she stood there, looking at him as if he were a stranger, a feeling that was almost revulsion touching her. He pulled the door closed and stood there, his hat in his hands, the light throwing shadows across his face.

If he would only say something she thought. How could he be so calm? . . . 'I suppose you'll want to be leaving,' she said to him. 'It's all right.'

'Leaving where, Miss Ellen?'

Paul Tremaine stirred in his chair and leaned forward, his hands gripped before his knees. 'Tell you what, Dallas old man,' he said. 'Don't tell old moneybags we won't sell. Leave the door open. Try to get him to raise the ante another thousand.'

She ignored her brother. 'Dallas told me about it,' she said to Hamp. 'I'm glad he did.' She couldn't bring herself to put it into words—to say that Dallas had told her that the brother of the man Hamp had killed was back.

'Get him to raise it a thousand dollars, Dallas,' Paul said. He sat up suddenly. 'Oh. Hamp. Thought it was Dallas.' He ran both hands through his hair and sat there, his head down.

'Don't just stand there!' she said, and now her voice was near the breaking point. She tried to picture in her mind what Tuna Stinson would be like—a man who had come with a gun to kill another man—and then she looked at Hamp, making herself realize that this man, too, had killed, and perhaps would kill again or be killed. She couldn't control her horror and revulsion any longer. The tears came and the taste of them was in her throat.

'Can't you say something?' she said. 'What will you do?'

'I figgered I'd ride over and see those two squatter outfits just south of us tomorrow morning,' he said. 'I think I can get them to work in the hay for us.'

She didn't want him to see her cry. She couldn't stand that. 'Get out,' she said. 'Please go.' She turned swiftly, so that her back was to him as she opened the door and held it.

He went through the door, still holding his hat. Then he paused for a second and looked at her, and she had to meet his eyes. Killer's eyes, she thought. She closed the door and stood there, knowing she couldn't bear any more.

Paul's voice was thick with wine. 'That's right,' he said. 'Turn on the tears. Little brother drank too much.'

The sob caught in her throat and she looked at her brother. She thought of the hundred times she had gone through this, each time thinking she could never face it again, but now it was something tangible, something she could understand. It was easier than trying to understand men who killed. 'Paul, you promised,' she said. 'Everyone noticed it.'

'And do you think I care what any of these yokels notice or think?' He lurched out of the chair and faced her belligerently. 'How much longer are you going to stay in this dreary hole? Do you know Boyd Novis has been after this place—heaven knows why—for a dozen years? Dallas will get us a good price for it.'

Now she was angry, and the anger was a relief. 'You'd like selling out, wouldn't you? You'd like it, because then you'd never have to face the fact that you had failed.'

His eyes cleared and they were hard with defensive anger. 'That was a pleasant, sisterly thing to say.'

'Perhaps it was, Paul,' she said. 'You made me say it.'

He walked swiftly across the room toward her. 'All right,' he said, thrusting his face close. 'Go ahead and tell me I'm no good. I've never amounted to anything and I never will.'

'I didn't say that, Paul. But you did promise that this time you would try.'

'Try what? Try to spit out of the middle of my mouth like Hamp Donnelly? I told you what I'd do with this place, didn't I? Sell it. Get some money out of it. Let's get back to civilization.'

'And then what? The same people? The same drinking? The same gambling and losing it all and living off our friends?'

'Maybe you'd like to have me go out and shoot myself.' These arguments always ended the same way. Always in any argument, anything that called for decision, Paul would back down under a remark as childish as that one.

She bit her lip. 'Go on to bed, Paul. We'll talk about it tomorrow.'

She watched him go down the hall and heard him slam the bedroom door. When he was gone she sat down in a chair by the cold fireplace and started to cry. She cried for a long time. When she looked up, the chimney of the lamp was smoky and the room with its oak and leather furniture was gloomy and cold. She looked at the elk horns in the dining-room where the men hung their hats and she saw the loaded pistol there. She wanted to put it away, yet she was afraid to touch it. Then she looked at the black square of window and thought of two men with guns like that, stalking each other like animals. . . .

In the bunkhouse Hamp Donnelly carefully cleaned a .45, a twin to the one Dusty Tremaine had owned. He wiped off oil with a soft cloth and tried the gun twice in its plain leather holster. The light of the lantern was blood-red against his face.

'Getting late, Judge,' he said.

'She doesn't belong here, Hamp,' the Judge said quietly. 'She doesn't belong here any more than Paul does.'

'I promised Dusty I'd try, didn't I?' Hamp Donnelly said. 'You coming over tomorrow?'

'I'm not going home,' the Judge said. 'I'm staying here.'

Hamp looked at his old friend. 'It's between Tuna and me, Judge. You don't have to get mixed up in that part of it.'

'I didn't say I did,' the Judge said. There was a double-barrel shotgun in the corner of the room. The Judge picked it up, broke it, and squinted down the 12-gauge barrels. He went to a wooden box nailed on the wall, and from the bottom shelf he took two shells, and after weighing them once in his hand he shoved them into the gun and snapped the weapon closed. After that the set the gun by one of the bunks and kicked off his boots. He stretched his scrawny frame out on the bed. 'I'm tired tonight,' he said. . . .

Dallas Rombeck drove his rented red-wheeled buggy towards

Bigforks with growing impatience. He had wasted nearly three weeks and just tonight realized it for sure. When it came right down to signing the papers for the sale of Anchor, Paul wasn't going to have a thing to say about it. He was sure of that now.

Money. How it ground into a man and pushed and squeezed. It seemed to him at this moment that there had never been a time in his life when he wasn't short of money. And just when a man got a little breathing space something always happened. Three times, previous to his coming to Bigforks, he had made a start in the right direction, and always something had happened. There was that time in The Dalles when he and his law partner had really built up a clientele. They were beginning to get a lot of legal business from the River Transportation Company. But his partner had a young wife, and the young wife felt she was neglected. He had been a fool, Dallas knew, but there was no use crying about it now. A scandal like that, even in a town the size of The Dalles, could ruin a man.

Perhaps he should have stayed in Portland. He was doing well there, but again it was a case of money. The people with whom he wanted to be identified—the people on the hill—never had to think about money, and the more he became involved with them the deeper he went into debt. There were still a lot of unpaid bills in Portland. He thought of Jeanette Apperson. Jeanette, with the blond hair and the soft eyes and the softer lips and half a million dollars. He sighed deeply. He guessed he had been in love with Jeanette. He had wanted to marry her. There was just the small matter of half a million dollars and forty hardheaded Yankee relatives standing in the way of it.

And now tonight he was going to have to face Boyd Novis again. 'These things take time, Mr. Novis,' he would say. 'Perhaps if you increased the offer—say, a thousand dollars.' It wouldn't work and he knew it, and here was a fat commission slipping through his fingers, just as Sue Donnelly had said it would.

He took out his handkerchief and wiped his lips. He was going to have trouble with Sue Donnelly, too. He should never have gotten mixed up with her. She was too young, too emotional. She didn't understand that a man could have a future by keeping on the good side of someone like Boyd Novis. And if he could manage the sale of Anchor he'd be in solid with Novis, he knew. Why couldn't women ever be reasonable? He thought of Ellen Tremaine and he knew that now he was on the right track. If Boyd Novis wouldn't get too impatient.

As he drove down the poplar-lined street of the darkened town he saw the girl move away from the white picket fence and stand there. His first thought was that he would ignore her, but he couldn't do that. She would call out, call his name. He pulled the mare to a stop, and the girl ran out and stood by the off-wheel, looking up at him. 'Sue! What on earth are you doing out here?'

'I had to talk to you. I've been waiting for two hours.'

'Sue, this is silly.'

'I had to know about Hamp. Is he all right? Is Tuna–?'

He felt a quick relief. 'Hamp's all right. He can take care of himself, Sue. You mustn't worry about it.'

'I saw Tuna leave town this evening. He took the short-cut trail over across the river.'

'Maybe he's going over to Condon. Maybe he's decided to forget it.'

'Dallas, how much longer is this going on?'

'Sue, I can't tell. No one tells Hamp how to run his affairs. You know that.'

'I don't mean that, Dallas. I mean us.'

'Please, Sue. Let's don't start that. Not now.'

'You're falling in love with her, aren't you?'

'Sue, be reasonable.'

'But you are.'

'It's just business, I tell you. Boyd Novis wants to buy Anchor and if I can get Ellen to sell I'd be crazy not to. There's a good commission in it. I told you, Sue, I need money.'

'Don't you ever get sick of kissing Boyd Novis's feet? I know what you want, Dallas. You think Novis is going to run this country. You think you'll get a big job out of it.'

'Sue, you're being impossible.'

'Am I? I used to know you pretty well before she came here. You were in love with me once, remember?'

'Nothing's changed. As soon as I close this deal—'

'You're not going to close it, Dallas. I told you that, right from the first. Anchor's not for sale, regardless of what you think. It's just going to wind up in another big fight.' She stopped suddenly as if she had already said too much.

'I have to go, Sue.' He clicked his tongue at the mare and the buggy rolled forward. He knew Sue was walking along beside the rig, her pace increasing with the speed of the buggy. He jerked the lines savagely. 'Sue, please—'

'Let's go away like we planned, Dallas. Take me with you and we'll go some place and start over.'

'I can't do that.'

'Because you're in love with her?'

'I've told you—'

'Get down and stand by me and tell me.'

He sat there a moment, his teeth tightly clenched, glad that she couldn't see his face. This could go on all night. He wrapped the lines around the whipstock and got down. She came into his arms, moving out of the darkness, clinging to him. 'Dallas—'

He brushed his lips close to her ear and turned her so he could look down the street toward the saloon. The lights made a bright path across the street. He wondered if Boyd Novis would be at the hotel. 'Don't worry so much, darling,' he whispered. 'Do you think I could ever forget you?' He tilted her head so that while he kissed her he could still watch the street. He felt her lips, eager and young, and he felt her fingers digging into his back. He wondered if he should go to the saloon or to the hotel first. The pressure of Sue's fingers relaxed and she pushed away from him. 'There, darling,' he said. 'You see?'

She was standing close to him, her hands at her sides, her face tilted upward, a pale blot in the darkness. 'Someday I'm going to learn to hate you, Dallas,' she said quietly. 'When I do it will be the happiest day of my life.' She turned and walked into the darkness, and he heard a gate latch rise and fall.

He drove on to the stable and turned in the rig, paying for it with the last money he had. The stableman blinked sleep from his eyes and pocketed the money. 'Boyd Novis was lookin' for you,' he said. 'Said to tell you to come on up to the hotel.'

'All right,' Dallas said. He whipped the dust from his coat and trousers with the back of his hand and re-creased his beaver hat. He was a little tired of being at Novis's beck and call twenty-four hours a day, but a man had to sacrifice something for opportunity.

He crossed over to the hotel, and the clerk, a thin-faced man with a green eye-shade, looked up and saw him. 'Mr. Novis wants to see you, Mr. Rombeck.'

Dallas didn't answer. He crossed the sparsely furnished lobby and went up the stairs to the second floor. There was a light coming from under a door halfway down the hall. He went there, and before he knocked he took a deep breath. The voice that asked him to come in was thin and dry.

It was a drab room, dingy and cluttered, and it went well with the small, almost dwarfed man who sat at a table playing solitaire. Boyd Novis glanced up, his eyes red-rimmed behind his silver-rimmed glasses. His face was thin, his chin and jaws blue-black with close-cropped beard. 'Well?' he said.

There was a knock on the door, and Dallas was grateful for the interruption. He needed time to think. The door opened and the night clerk was there. He kept opening and closing his hands with the uncertainty of a man afraid of his job. 'Mr. Novis?'

'I'm listening.'

'Mr. Novis, Joe over at the saloon says he run out of Meadowcreek rye and he wonders–'

Boyd Novis had risen to his feet. His lack of height was accented by the thick lifts he wore on his shoes. The lapels of his black broadcloth coat were stained and he wore a collarband shirt without the collar. 'I told you what to get, didn't I?'

The night clerk swallowed hard. 'It wasn't my fault, Mr. Novis.'

'Then find out whose fault it was,' Boyd Novis said. 'And get me a quart of Meadowcreek rye, some water, and a glass.'

'I'll sure try, Mr. Novis.'

'You do that, Herman,' Novis said. The clerk closed the door carefully and backed out into the hall. Boyd Novis shook his head. 'Just a drink, that's all I wanted.' He looked at Dallas and smiled. 'Now, what were you saying?'

'I think they're about ready to sell, Mr. Novis.'

'You think?' Boyd Novis said.

'Look, Mr. Novis – these things take time. I told you right from the first–'

'You got it wrong, Rombeck,' Boyd Novis said. 'You didn't tell me. I told you. I told you to buy Anchor.'

'Well, if you'll just be patient.'

'You tell that to my sheep, will you, Rombeck?' Novis said. 'I'm overstocked and overgrazed, and I just bought another band from the Hogan brothers in Prineville. That band will be here in a few days and I want graze for them when they get here.'

'You should have held off a while, Mr. Novis.'

'You're telling me how to run my business?' Novis said. 'I've made a half a million dollars, Rombeck. How much have you made?'

'If you'll just listen to me–'

'You listen to me, Rombeck,' Novis said. He had placed his hands against the edge of the table. His fingers were bony and long, his nails dirty. He leaned forward, his eyes boring into Rombeck. 'Do you know why I use you at all, Rombeck? Because it makes me feel good, that's why. I like to see you strutting around in those fine clothes–which my money bought. I like to think about you having that fine education and talking so pretty and all, and then I think about how I didn't have nothing, how I started out as a sheep herder. That makes me feel good, Rombeck, but any time you don't jump when I holler I can find something else to feel good about. Just remember, Rombeck, you need me but I don't need you. I was doing fine before you ever showed up.'

There was a timid knock on the door. 'Come in, Herman,' Novis said.

The night clerk sidled into the room. He had a bottle and a pitcher of water and one glass. 'I found some, Mr. Novis,' he said eagerly. 'Got it from that drummer in 27. It's got a couple of drinks gone, but it's Meadowcreek.'

'You're a good boy, Herman,' Novis said. Herman backed out, smiling gratefully. 'There's a good boy, Rombeck,' Novis said. 'He gets what I send him after.'

'If you'll let me explain—'

'There's nothing to explain, Rombeck,' Novis said. He poured a meagre amount of whiskey into the glass and filled the glass with water. He stood there, sloshing the thin, brown mixture. 'I want Anchor. I get what I want.' He took a small drink. 'Did you know Tuna Stinson is going to herd sheep for me?' he said. 'Tuna is a good sheep herder.'

'Mr. Novis, as your attorney I think that was a mistake.'

'And what you think doesn't impress me,' Novis said. He sipped his drink and his eyes were bright. 'I hired Tuna to herd sheep, that's all. What he does outside of that is entirely his business.'

'You can't afford to be connected with Tuna, Mr. Novis. You know what will happen between him and Hamp Donnelly.'

'And would it be so tragic if something happened to Donnelly?' Novis said. 'Who does he think he is?' He peered through his glasses. 'Maybe without Hamp Donnelly around there, the Tremaines would be more anxious to sell.'

'Donnelly's tough, Mr. Novis. You've got no guarantee Tuna can whip him.' Rombeck was sweating.

'I thought of that,' Novis said. He tilted his glass and drained it slowly, and he set it down on the table. 'I told Tuna to be careful.' He smiled. 'Money is a wonderful thing, Rombeck. You can even hire a man to be careful.' He walked over and opened the door and held it, and as Dallas reached the hall and turned, frightened now, wanting to argue further, Novis smiled. 'Oh, by the way, Rombeck. I nearly forgot.'

'Yes sir?'

'Unless you get some immediate action I don't see that there's any sense of me keeping you on a retainer, do you?' . . .

Hamp Donnelly was fully awake. By the feel of the night and the quiet he knew it was nearly midnight. Like Judge Norton he hadn't bothered to undress, but had removed his boots and stretched out on the bunk, covering himself with a blanket. He lay there now, listening, knowing that some unusual sound had awakened him, unable to tell what it was.

He could hear the familiar noise of the horses moving around in the corral and he knew that that alone wouldn't have disturbed him. Some place far off a coyote yammered at a rising moon. Across the room Judge Norton's blankets moved and the old man's voice was a thin, phlegm-cracked whisper: 'You awake, Hamp?'

'Yeah.'

'Out by the barn,' the Judge said.

'I'll take a look,' Hamp said. He threw back the blankets, pulled on his boots, and his hand reached out and touched the familiar cedar butt of his gun. He thumbed back the hammer, and the click of it was loud in the silent room. With his forefinger he rolled the cylinder around to a loaded chamber and let the hammer down carefully. Then he thrust the weapon into the waistband of his trousers. The Judge moved from under his blankets, reaching for his shotgun.

Hamp opened the door carefully and stood there a minute, listening. A horse nickered in low complaint, as a horse does when reluctant to leave the home corral, and then there were hoofbeats, the sound of a horse walking, not in the dust of the corral but across the hard-packed yard. Hamp moved swiftly into the darkness, keeping close to the corral fence. He reached the side of the barn, edging his way along cautiously. He could see the rider, riding slowly out toward the main gate. He ran on around to the front of the barn. 'Paul! Is that you, Paul?'

The rider turned in his saddle, looking back, and then the horse gave a grunt of protest as if he had been kicked hard or slapped with a quirt. There was a quick pound of hoofs and the horse was in a full gallop, heading up toward the short-cut trail that led to Bigforks.

A light flared in the ranch house. The front door opened, and Ellen's voice high, charged with worry, called, 'What is it?'

'It's nothing,' Hamp said. 'It's all right.' He hurried back toward the bunkhouse, careless in his haste, and when he reached the edge of the corral he saw the quick blur of movement by the bunkhouse window.

Judge Norton's thin voice stung him like a whip: 'Hamp! Watch it!'

There was a spurt of yellow flame, the crack of a six-shooter, and lead splintered the post a foot from Hamp's head. He heard Ellen Tremaine scream, and he tugged the gun from his waistband, but now he was afraid to shoot, unable to see in the darkness, not knowing where Judge Norton was.

The Judge's voice came again, floating across the space between the bunkhouse and the corral: 'Drop it, Tuna, or I'll pull both these triggers at once!' There was a low curse, the sound of a heavy object hitting the ground. 'I got him, Hamp,' the Judge said.

Hamp started toward the bunkhouse, and he heard Ellen running across the yard. 'Get back in the house and stay there,' he told her, his voice brusque.

He went on. The sky was thinning with the rising moon and now he could see Tuna Stinson standing there, his hands shoulder-high, a huge hulking man, his features hidden in the darkness, a man who looked much like the brother Hamp Donnelly had killed. Hamp remembered those colourless eyes, the long, sandy hair that hung in ropelike strands from under the battered hat, the big mouth, slack and wide.

'He was by the window,' Judge Norton said. 'Figured he'd get you while you were asleep. He was playing it safe.'

'Take that gun out of my back, old man,' Tuna Stinson said. His voice was low in his throat. 'Take that gun out of my back and I'll kill him. I'll kill him with my hands.'

'You're through killing anybody, Tuna,' Judge Norton said.

'I'll kill him.'

It was only a rush of movement in the darkness, a swift sweep of sound as his hands came down, and that tremendous shape was hurtling forward. Hamp felt the crushing impact, felt the breath go from his lungs. His fist lashed out and landed solidly. There was a grunt of pain, and Tuna was rushing in, clubbing down with both fists, and Ellen was there, screaming at them to stop. The horses in the corral, bunched from the shock of the gunshot, snorted and shied and crowded against the fence. Tuna's shoulder caught Hamp in the chest and they were down, their arms locked, rolling in the dust.

The world exploded in a red mist when Tuna's fist landed against Hamp's temple. Hamp groped with his hands, trying to find Tuna's throat, and again that fist smashed down. There was blood in Hamp's mouth. He felt as if every tooth in his head had been jarred loose.

He kicked with his feet, and felt savage joy at Tuna's curse of pain. Hamp was on top now, slugging with his fists. He had taken the best Tuna had to offer, he knew that now, and the knowledge of it gave him a second wind, a second strength.

Tuna was twisting and turning, his thumb gouging for Hamp's eye. His thumb slipped, the nail ripping across Hamp's cheek, the thumb catching the corner of Hamp's mouth. There was no sound except their breathing, a strangled, choking, coughing sound.

They lay there that way, straining against each other, until Hamp got his right hand free and he drove it down into the hollow of Tuna's throat. He hit again and again, the jar of his blows tearing with a white-hot pain through the bones of his arm, until finally he knew there was no resistance. Tuna was lying there, his head rolling from side to side with the blows.

Hamp pushed himself free and stood up, his legs trembling with fatigue. Blood was running down his face and dripping on his chest. He had lost his gun. He stood there, breathing through his mouth, sucking in great gulps of air, completely oblivious of his surroundings. The light was grey and eerie and the dust cloud settled around his feet. Judge Norton, his face as thin as the blade of a hatchet, stood there holding a double-barrel shotgun. And Ellen was there, a dressing gown drawn tightly around her. Hamp could see her face. He lowered his eyes, not wanting to see what he had seen there before, and he saw Tuna lying there on the ground.

He heard Tuna moan and saw him roll over. Almost too late he saw Tuna's left hand reach out. There was a glint of metal. Hamp's boot rose and crushed down against Tuna's left hand. He felt the flesh tear, felt the fingers open. He tromped down again, and now he reached down and gripped Tuna by the shirt collar and jerked him to his feet. Then Ellen was pushing between them, saying only: 'Don't!' Her arms were holding Hamp's arms to his side and Tuna Stinson was staggering away.

Hamp watched Tuna stumble into the night, disappearing into the darkness of the windbreak poplars around the house. In a moment a horse and rider came out. Tuna was leaning across the saddle horn, hunched over like a sick man, his head dobbing crazily on his short, thick neck.

'Don't let him go, Hamp,' Judge Norton said softly. 'You're crazy if you let him go.'

The girl held Hamp's arms tightly. 'Please.'

He shook his head, and his brain cleared. Ellen was standing close to him, her arms holding his arms against his side. She was looking up at him and he could see her face but he couldn't see her eyes. He remembered how she had looked at him last night. 'All right,' he said. He pushed away from her and went to the back of the house, where the water bucket and basin stood on the bench. He poured the basin full and doused his head and his face until the water turned red with his own blood.

He could hear Ellen moving around inside the house and he heard her calling Paul's name, softly at first, then frantically. The back door opened and she stood there. 'Paul's gone!'

'I know, Miss Ellen,' he said. 'I was fixing to go after him.'

She looked at him and saw his battered mouth and the wicked gash that ran from his temple to his chin. Judge Norton was there, too, appearing out of nowhere as he often did. She stared at the two men and she heard Hamp's quiet voice: 'I know, Miss Ellen. I was fixing to go after him.' *Know what?* She knew then that Hamp knew everything there was to know about Paul. Hamp knew everything she knew, but he wasn't criticizing, any more than she would criticize. He knew Paul, and he wanted to help.

She looked at Hamp Donnelly, remembering that this man had killed, remembering the brutality of the fight, remembering the revulsion and horror she had felt. She still felt it, but it was a detached feeling, and her concern for Paul was real. She couldn't wait this out alone. Not this time, because this time had to be the last time. She had promised herself that. Always before, some mutual friend stayed to bring Paul home; someone they had known for years bailed him out of jail and failed to mention it again. But this was different. This was a new place. These men were strangers, and perhaps it was better that way. She shook her head. 'No, Hamp. Don't go after him. He's a grown man. He can work things out for himself.'

She saw Hamp's face, battered and torn, and she tried to think of it as a killer's face, but for this moment it wasn't that. 'I guess that's best, Miss Ellen,' Hamp said. 'A man needs to make up his own mind.'

The grey light of morning was everywhere, a harsh, cold light with no softness about it. She looked at Hamp and the Judge and forced herself to realize that they wanted to be friends. 'Here,' she said, 'let me help you.' She dampened a towel and wiped the blood from the cuts on Hamp's face. And once, when her face was close to his, she saw his eyes and for a second was held by what she saw. She lowered her gaze and worked swiftly. 'I'll bandage your hand,' she said. 'It's badly hurt.'

Paul Tremaine had awakened with a brutal headache and a dry, cottony taste in his mouth. He raised up on his elbows, and the bed moved sickeningly. After a while he got his feet on the floor and he sat there on the edge of the bed.

Just one drink, he thought, that was all, and then he could sleep. No, he decided. Not this time. This time he wouldn't take that first drink. He'd battle it out. For a half-hour then he paced up and down the room. He was cold and he dressed, putting on his coat. He had to have a drink of water. He opened the door into the hall carefully and walked on tiptoe to the kitchen and drank greedily, directly from the bucket. After a moment he felt a pleasant giddiness.

Maybe a breath of fresh air would help. Moving stealthily, he let himself out the back door.

He walked toward the barn, the cool, night air pleasant against his skin. He stood by the barn door a long time, and the longer he stood there the more he felt alone. If there were only someone to talk to. It was the silence of this place.

He thought of the little town of Bigforks and tried to remember just how far away it was, and he thought of it in measures of time and not of miles. He wondered what time it was. Eleven, maybe. He wanted a cigarette but he didn't have any. He'd go into the house and get some. He took two steps and knew that he couldn't go back there and be alone in that house.

In the corral a horse nickered softly. Paul made up his mind. He ran to the corral and opened the gate and went inside. He tried to catch one of the horses but they shied away from him. He went to the barn and found a thick, hair rope, and he ran back and managed to get one of the horses in a corner. He slipped the rope around the animal's neck.

There were four saddles in the barn. He took the first one. He worked furiously, his thirst growing with his exertion, and he pulled himself into the saddle. He started riding, slowly, holding in on the horse's reins. He was halfway to the gate when he heard Hamp Donnelly calling his name. Paul glanced back. He slapped the horse on the shoulder with the long ends of the reins. The animal lurched forward and Paul gripped the saddle horn, and then the horse was in a long, smooth gallop, heading for the short-cut trail to Bigforks. Behind him there was a shot, and Paul felt a sudden terror. He kicked the horse with all his strength.

He came into town on a full run, the horse streaked with foam, its breathing loud in the night. A dozen dogs started barking and someplace a baby cried and a light flared on in a window. At the far end of the street the windows of the hotel laid a yellow pattern on the dust, and across from that two horses were tied at a hitch rail. He rode there and he saw the faded sign of the Elkhorn Saloon.

He dismounted carefully and forced himself to walk across the board porch into the saloon. The bartender gave him a brief, uninterested glance. Two men playing cards at a table looked up. There was no one else there. Paul moved over to the bar and laid down a silver dollar, the only one he had. 'Can a man buy a drink here?' he said.

The bartender said nothing. He knew this was Paul Tremaine, but that didn't surprise him. Nothing surprised the bartender any more. He got a bottle and shot glass and shoved them out on the bar, tiredly. Three drinks, usually, then they started to tell all about themselves. The bartender yawned. After that they wanted to borrow money. Just until tomorrow. The bartender stretched and yawned again. It would be all right, he supposed. Hamp would make it good. He watched Paul take his third drink. Here it comes, he thought.

At the table two of Boyd Novi's sheep herders shuffled the cards. They had been waiting for Tuna Stinson. He was supposed to come in and have a game with them. The bartender glanced at the clock on the wall. Pretty late. Three more hours and he'd close this firetrap and get some sleep. Paul Tremaine was talking now and the bartender was answering, but he wasn't hearing anything. They all said the same thing; they all wanted the same answers. 'Sure,' he said finally. 'I knew your uncle well. Fine man.' He tossed a pad and a pencil on the bar. 'Just give me an IOU. I don't own the place. I got to have something to put in the till.'

A half-hour later Paul Tremaine was playing poker with Boyd Novis's two sheep herders. It was good to have someone to talk to. Even sheep herders. He had another drink and laughed at a poor joke. Sheep herders weren't so bad. The cards made a whispering sound against the green top of the table....

The sunlight was red in the kitchen windows. Ellen had dressed and brushed her hair. She put more wood in the stove and started a second pot of coffee. The thin fragrance of cigarette smoke came from the dining-room, where Hamp and Judge Norton were finishing their breakfast.

She was waiting again, just as she had waited so many times, but this time it was different. This time she was not waiting alone. For years now she had tried to cover up for Paul, feeling she could never stand the humiliation of anyone knowing. But Hamp knew and Judge Norton knew, and they had known all along, even before Ellen and Paul had come here. There was no sense of humiliation about it at all. Rather it was a sense of security, a sense of having someone to share her worry and help her with it.

She glanced through the door and saw Hamp sitting there, his chair directly beneath the elk horns, and she saw her uncle's gun in its holster. Yesterday when she had looked at that gun she had thought of Hamp and of how he had killed a man. She had wondered if she could face him again, knowing that about him. Now even that feeling was gone. It didn't seem to matter in the same way.

Last night seemed like an age ago, a different world. The fact that Paul had been troublesome did not set the night aside and give it shape. It was just one more night in a hundred nights.

She thought of Dallas Rombeck, and her pulse quickened. In a way, she felt cheap about that. She had been at an emotional breaking point, he sympathetic, understanding. She had no real feeling for Dallas except that he had tried to be a friend to Paul, she told herself. It was only appreciation. But there was a small excitement in her. Making excuses like that was the first danger signal, and she knew it.

Through the window she could see the rolling hills and the winding silver of the river. Yesterday she had hated it; today she didn't. There was no way to explain it. Unless it could be that she had found two things she had never known, two things she had needed. She could have Dallas Rombeck's love—she felt sure of that. And with Hamp and the Judge to help her she had a security that had been lacking all her life. She could even forgive Hamp for his fight. A man had a right to fight for his life.

She could understand that now. She couldn't understand how a man could kill but she could understand how a man could fight. In a way, she was making Paul fight for his life. It couldn't be accomplished all at once. He was in town now, undoubtedly. But she had decided to let him fight this one out himself, and when he came home, repentant, contrite, as he always was, she would say as little as possible. But she wouldn't back down. Not this time, She would stay, and Paul would make a go of Anchor and she would help him. When he had succeeded—then would be time enough to think of Dallas Rombeck. . . .

Hamp brought the dishes in from the dining-room and set them on the sink. The bandage on his left hand was working loose, and she took his hand and retied it, saying nothing until she was finished. He turned his hand and looked at the bandage. 'You said last night you thought you could get those farmers south of us to work in the hay,' she said.

'I think so,' he said.

'All right,' she said. 'See what you can do. We have to get the hay in.'

She met his eyes and she realized that without telling him anything she had told him what she had decided. She tried to read what she saw in his eyes and decided it was pride. It made her feel humble and strong at the same time. She wished she could tell him that Dallas had had a part in this decision.

Hamp's lips were battered and swollen but he was smiling. 'All right, boss,' he said. He took his hat from the elk horns and crossed the yard toward the barn, walking with a long, determined stride.

Judge Norton's voice didn't seem so cracked and dry as usual. It was fuller, rounder. 'Your uncle would have been proud of you, Ellen.' She didn't answer. She walked across the living-room and stared out the west window, and from here she could see the road lifting up to the summit and she could see the butte with the flat top. She thought of the grave that was there, and she thought of the town beyond and of Paul. She came back to the dining-room table and sat down and waited.

She was grateful for the company of Judge Norton. The old man talked with an old man's balance, the present playing against the past, Bigforks and Anchor and the surrounding country becoming a world. He told her things about her uncle that she had never known, until finally she could understand him, a man with dreams and ideals. The Judge was drawing a picture of Hamp, too, and she wanted to know more.

'Tell me about Orvie Stinson,' she said, no longer afraid to hear it.

'The Stinson brothers used to own the strip across the river. They ran sheep. They tried to cross over one night, and Dusty stopped them. Orvie tried to shoot your uncle in the back. It took a jury seven minutes to turn Hamp loose. Tuna left town and Boyd Novis bought the place.'

'So it isn't over for Hamp, is it?' she said. 'Whipping a man like Tuna Stinson with fists isn't enough. It isn't enough for Hamp; it isn't enough for Tuna.'

'That's right,' the Judge said. 'It isn't enough.'

'I'll be glad when we get the hay in,' she said. She went out to the kitchen and stirred up the fire and made more coffee, and for a long time she stood there, looking out the window, looking at Anchor. Here it has to be the big fight, she thought. Here it has to be all the way.

'There's some other things I want to tell you,' the Judge said. An hour had gone and she was sitting across from him, sitting so that she could look out the window and see the road that led up the hill and by the butte. 'Even after I retired I took care of your uncle's legal work, you know.'

'I know.' She put her finger against the handle of the cup and turned the cup around in its saucer. 'My uncle thought a lot of Hamp, didn't he?'

'He loved him like a son,' the Judge said.

'I'm surprised he didn't leave Anchor to him.'

'I guess he did,' the Judge said. He was watching her closely. 'Depends on how you look at it. He told you to keep him on as foreman, didn't he?'

'In a dozen letters.'

'A man like Hamp doesn't need to own land or cattle,' the Judge said. 'He's here and things are going the way Dusty wanted them to go. For Hamp that's enough.'

'Yes,' she said quietly. I suppose it is.' She was surprised that the thought distressed her. Hamp Donnelly would never need anything more than this. Nor would he ever need anyone.

'He's proved that,' the Judge said. 'He could have had Anchor if he had wanted it. He could have discouraged you, made you want to give up.'

Ellen only half heard at first, and then suddenly the words reached her. She looked at the Judge, realizing he was trying to tell her something he had wanted to tell her for a long time. 'I don't understand.'

'Didn't you ever think it was odd a man like your uncle didn't have a formal will?'

'I had all his letters. He always said he wanted Paul and me to have the place. No one ever contested it.'

'He did leave a will, Ellen. I have it.'

She couldn't decide what he was trying to tell her. 'But if that's so—'

'Hamp wouldn't let me probate it.' The Judge reached out and touched her hand. 'You see, Ellen, Dusty wanted the ranch to belong to you and Paul. He wanted that more than anything else, because you are Tremaines. But there was always the chance you wouldn't like it or Paul wouldn't straighten out.' He shrugged. 'Dusty didn't want Anchor sold, Ellen. It meant too much to him. He made sure it would always belong to someone who wanted it.'

She stood up, the colour draining from her face. 'What are you trying to say?'

'Hamp wouldn't let me probate the will because he thought it wouldn't be fair to Paul. He was afraid it would make Paul feel he was on trial.' The Judge stood beside her, a thin little man, trying to be kind. 'Dusty knew all about Paul, Ellen. He knew it the first time he came back to Philadelphia to see you; he knew it from your letters. He left it up to Hamp to work it out, and if it didn't work out he wanted Anchor to go to Hamp.'

'He wouldn't do that. He couldn't trust a man that much. Any man.'

'He could trust Hamp Donnelly that much, Ellen.'

Ellen sat down. Now so many things made sense. The dogged persistence of Hamp; the way he had tried to make her see beauty in this land. His thinly masked dislike for Dallas. 'Yes,' she said, 'I suppose he could.' She looked through the window toward the road. A buggy topped the summit and started down the hill, the dust of its wheels rising and forming a thin curtain of pink transparency across the front of the butte where Dusty Tremaine was buried. She knew it was Dallas Rombeck and she knew he would be bringing Paul home.

She felt the dead weight of disappointment. It was like being back in Philadelphia, trying to hide Paul's escapades from people, having friends be kind and considerate, wounding with their very consideration.

'I wouldn't have told you, Ellen,' the Judge said, 'but this morning I knew it would be all right. I knew you would stay, regardless of what happened.'

Yes, she thought. Regardless of what happened. She went outside and waited there in the yard. 'Don't be kind, Dallas,' she thought. If you really care for me, don't be kind. She wished that anyone but Dallas could have been the one to see Paul like this, and then she didn't care. If Dallas loved her it wouldn't make any difference.

Dallas didn't offer sympathy, and she was glad for that. Paul was slumped in the seat. She stood aside while Dallas and the Judge got him out of the buggy and led him into the house.

'A full house,' Paul mumbled, as they sat him in the living-room. 'How could he beat a full house?'

'Ellen, I don't like to tell you this.' Dallas was cracking the knuckles of his hands.

'Gambling?'

'That's right.'

'How much?'

'Two thousand, Ellen.'

'To you?'

'Of course not, Ellen,' Dallas said; and she was sorry she had said that. 'A couple of sheep herders.'

'Pretty big game for sheep herders, isn't it?' Judge Norton said.

'I suppose it was,' Dallas said, 'but it won't keep them from collecting. If they had lost they would have paid off. I made sure of that.'

'You mean Boyd Novis would have paid off for them?' the Judge said.

'Novis backs his men up, Judge. You know that.'

'Where it will do him some good.'

'Ellen, I hate this.' Dallas took a handkerchief from his pocket and mopped his face.

'We'll pay,' she said. 'Somehow we'll pay. Maybe Paul will have to herd sheep, but we'll pay.'

'You don't have to pay, Ellen,' the Judge said quietly. 'A man drunk, not knowing what he's doing.'

'He signed an IOU,' Dallas said.

'Suppose he did? You can't collect it.' There was anger in the Judge's voice.

'Judge, don't be a complete fool,' Dallas said bluntly. 'They'll take it out of his skin and you know it. They're friends of Tuna Stinson's.'

Ellen thought of that hulking shape she had seen in the darkness and she thought of him riding away into the night like a wounded animal.

'I said we'd pay.'

'Ellen, why don't you get out of this?' Dallas said. 'This is no place for you, or Paul, either.' He came close to her and put his arm around her. 'Go ahead and sell out, and let Boyd Novis worry about whether or not he'll pay this IOU. I talked to him this morning and he's willing to settle with the two men.'

'If Ellen sells Anchor to him, is that it?' the Judge said.

'I'm only trying to do what's best for Ellen and Paul.'

'And make a commission for yourself.'

The colour flooded into Rombeck's face, but he didn't lose his poise. 'I could take care of the sale of Anchor for you, Ellen. You could take a stage out of his place tomorrow.'

'I'm afraid not, Dallas.'

'But don't you realize what you're doing to Paul? Those men won't wait for their money. This isn't Philadelphia, Ellen. Men have been killed over gambling debts.' Dallas had hoped he wouldn't have to go this far. He had hated the assignment right from the first, hated it when Boyd Novis had called him to his room and shown him the IOU, hated the smugness and certainty he had seen in Boyd Novis's face. He had felt like a fool, hauling Paul out of the saloon where he had slept all night, signing a release for Ned Crockett, the marshal. And he had hated most having Sue Donnelly see him, for he hadn't fooled Sue. She had known he was crawling for Boyd Novis again. 'You've got to for Paul's sake, Ellen.'

'I can't, Dallas,' Ellen said quietly. 'Anchor isn't mine to sell.'

'Well, Paul, then—'

'It isn't Paul's either. It belongs to Hamp Donnelly.'

It took a moment for that to sink in, and even then it meant
nothing. Dallas looked at Ellen and then at the Judge, and he
saw satisfaction in the Judge's eyes. Dallas beat down a rising
panic. This was his last chance and he knew it. Boyd Novis had
made that plain. He thought of the year he had spent licking
Boyd Novis's boots, confident that it would pay off, sure that
Boyd Novis would grow and continue to grow, and a man who
kept close to him would grow with him. 'I don't know what
you're talking about.' He had trouble with his voice.

'About Anchor, Dallas,' the Judge said. 'It's not for sale to
anyone except Hamp. I've got Dusty's will to back it up.'

'There wasn't any will,' Dallas said, his voice rising. He looked
at Paul, slumped in the chair, and he thought of how he had
hauled Paul out of the saloon with everyone watching, humbling,
even degrading himself. He remembered the way Boyd Novis
had shoved him around. 'I saw the letters, Ellen. I helped you
with them.'

'There was a will, Dallas.'

'Then it's no good,' he said. He knew he was shouting but he
couldn't stop it. 'It hasn't been probated. It won't hold!'

'It would hold with me, Dallas, whether it was legally valid
or not,' Ellen said.

His panic was complete. Everything that he had worked for
was going to smash. And there was Sue. He would have to face
Sue.

The Judge said, 'Tell Novis it didn't work, Dallas.'

'But Paul,' Dallas said. 'Ellen, can't you see Paul's in danger?'

'Paul will have to decide about that, Dallas,' Ellen said.

Dallas felt the perspiration running down his back. They
couldn't do this to him. It meant too much. It meant everything.
Only last night he had been so close. He had kissed Ellen and
held her in his arms. He knew she trusted him. He forced
himself to smile. 'All right, Elllen,' he said. 'I only want to help
you, and I thought this was the best way. If you want to stay and
fight it out, I want you to know I'll be with you. Whatever you
do, I want to help you.'

'I appreciate that, Dallas. More than you know.'

'It hasn't been easy for me, trying to keep this on a business basis, knowing if I did sell Anchor for you you'd be leaving here. It was the only way I knew to do what I thought was best for you and Paul.' He took both her hands in his and stood there looking down at her.

'You've been kind, Dallas.' He saw the curve of her lips and the pulse in her throat. The pressure of his fingers tightened around her hands.

'Surely you know why, Ellen. After last night you must know.' He pulled her toward him and he saw the surprise in her eyes. He knew he would have to be careful.

Ellen was tired of being alone. So tired of it. She would have let him take her into his arms, but the Judge was standing there, listening to them, and she saw Paul, slumped in his chair, watching with bloodshot eyes as Dallas put his arms around her. It was suddenly cheap and tawdry. She twisted aside. 'Don't, Dallas.'

'I have to, Ellen. I can't keep quiet any longer. I want to marry you, Ellen.'

She hesitated, knowing she had wanted to hear those words, but everything was wrong. 'Please, Dallas.'

'We can work this out together, Ellen. For Paul's sake. I know these people. I know Boyd Novis. Please, Ellen. I love you. I can work everything out.'

'I suppose you could,' Judge Norton said quietly. 'You could sell off the cattle and lease the land to Boyd Novis, maybe.'

Dallas whirled, his mouth hard. 'Get out, will you? Haven't you any decency at all?'

'You'd double-cross your own mother, wouldn't you, Rombeck? You've kissed Novis's feet hoping he'd get you a political job, and now that you can't produce you figure you'll marry Anchor and hold him up for it.'

'Judge, I'll handle this,' Ellen said, frightened. The men's voices were almost shouts.

'Get out of here.' Dallas was suddenly calm. He started moving toward the Judge, his fists clenched at his sides.

'Have you told Sue Donnelly about your plans?' the Judge asked. 'Or did you just think of this when you found out Anchor wasn't for sale?'

'Shut your lying mouth!' Dallas Rombeck's arm drew back and lashed out, sending the old man crashing back against the wall.

The Judge raised a thin, shaking hand and touched the blood that had started from his nose. 'You dirty, rotten rat,' he said softly. 'The only decent thing you ever did in your life was to throw Sue over.'

Dallas lunged forward. He had the Judge by the throat and he was holding him up as his fist drove in. Paul stumbled to his feet, his eyes furious.

Ellen didn't cry out. The disgust she felt was too great for that. She saw Dallas turn and throw the Judge halfway across the room, and she saw him crumple there, a little old man.

'Ellen, listen to me.' Dallas was coming toward her.

She started to back away. She saw Paul try to stop Dallas, saw Dallas push him aside and Paul fall back into the chair. She backed across the dining-room, pushing a chair in front of herself, and then she was against the wall, directly under the elk horns.

'Ellen, you don't understand!'

'I understand,' she said. Her hand reached up and back, and the holstered .45 that had belonged to her uncle was there. She gripped it and pulled it free of the holster. It was heavy. She held it with both hands and she pulled back the hammer. 'Get out, Dallas.'

'Ellen, don't be a fool.'

'Get out,' she said. 'Get out before I kill you!'

It was all a blind haze. She knew he had gone and she heard the buggy, the wheels grating and rattling as the horse broke into a run. Now she knew how it was that a man could kill. Dust came in through the open door and she was on her knees by the Judge, the gun forgotten on the table. The Judge was unconscious, a cut on his head where he had hit the floor. She looked up, and Paul was standing there. He seemed sober and older and his eyes were clear. He reached down and pulled her to her feet.

He stood there a second holding her, and then he kissed her. 'I'll take care of this, Ellen,' he said. He started toward the door.

'Paul, don't leave!'

'You said once I never finished anything I started, Ellen. You were right. I'll finish this. I am going to straighten this out with Novis myself.'

There was something in Paul's voice that frightened her and at the same time reassured her—a new strength, almost as if he, too, had made his decision. The Judge moaned and she turned toward him, and when she looked again Paul was gone. She ran to the door and called to him, but he didn't answer. She knew he was in the barn, saddling a horse.

She ran back to the Judge, afraid to leave him now, afraid he might die. The basin and the towel were there and she bathed the Judge's face. She lifted his head and it was like lifting the head of a child. She saw Paul ride through the gate and take the short-cut trail toward town. It wasn't until he was gone that she realized her uncle's gun was missing. . . .

Hamp Donnelly hired two men and two sixteen-year-old boys to work in the hay. It wasn't much of a crew, but it would do all right. There was a singing inside him that wouldn't go away even when he thought of Tuna Stinson. He hadn't ended anything last night, he knew. He would have to face Tuna again. Nothing was changed. And yet it was. The most important thing of all. Even when it did happen with Tuna he felt now he could face Ellen and explain. Perhaps then he wouldn't see the one thing he feared in her eyes. Last night, he knew, had made a difference.

He was in love with Ellen. He knew that. He wondered how he would tell her, or if he ever would. He knew that from now on just being on Anchor, working things out the way Dusty had wanted them, wouldn't be enough. He rode into Anchor headquarters about three in the afternoon.

He sensed something wrong even before he dismounted. Then he saw Ellen running toward him, calling his name. He threw himself out of the saddle and started toward her, and she came into his arms, sobbing against his chest, saying his name over and over. He let his hand caress her hair. 'It's all right,' he said softly. 'Whatever it is, it's all right.'

He led her toward the house, his arm around her, and bit by bit she told him everything. He felt his anger mounting, higher and higher. He went into the house, and the Judge was there, stretched out on the divan, a cold cloth pressed against his face. 'Take care of him, Ellen,' Hamp said. He went outside and he knew she was following him.

'I'm going with you.'

'You better not, Ellen.'

'I'm going with you.' She met his eyes, and he saw she was no longer afraid of him.

He fought to control his excitement. She understood now. Understood how it was that a man might have to kill. He would never have to explain. Last night she had looked at him as if he were an outcast; now, for the first time, she was accepting him as he was. She wanted to go with him, and she had a right to go. 'I'll hitch up the buckboard, then,' he said.

Hamp coaxed all the speed there was out of the team, running them where the road dipped on a downgrade, walking them on the steeper pulls. At the summit he stopped to let them rest. He hadn't spoken a word since leaving the ranch. Ellen sat beside him, her right hand gripping the iron handrail, her left hand clenched against the edge of the seat board. Over his shoulder Hamp saw the butte, dancing with afternoon sun now, the shadow a pool of blue directly under its own bluffs. The horses stood with muscles quivering, sweat dripping from their bellies. He walked them slowly for half a mile and then whipped them into a run down the slope toward Bigforks.

They passed the schoolhouse, and he slowed the team. He knew there was trouble here. It was in the vacant schoolyard and it lay on the dust of the street and lurked in the death-still leaves of the poplars. There was a crowd in the street, down near Paxton's store. Hamp pulled the team into the shade and wrapped the lines around the brake. 'You wait,' he said, and he climbed down and walked down the centre of the street. The holstered gun slapped against his thigh.

A woman was standing to one side, crying, and Sue was there, trying to keep the children back. He met Sue's eyes and saw the warning, and then he was pushing through the crowd, elbowing them aside. He heard a soft curse. Ned Crockett, the marshal, stood inside the circle trying to push the people back. A body lay in the street and blood was black on the dust. It was Paul.

Hamp felt the sickness turn in his stomach, and then the crowd was pushing, surging against him, and Ellen was there. He tried to stop her. He tried to hide her face against his chest. She pulled away from him, and she was down in the dust. He heard her voice, crying out as if to an injured child: 'Paul! Paul!' Hamp's anger rose to a white heat, and when he moved back through the crowd they parted and made an aisle to let him through. He saw Jake Paxton and a dozen men he knew but their faces were blurs.

'He come ridin' into town like a mad man.' It was Jake Paxton talking to him, talking with a hushed voice, his words rushing. 'He wanted to see Boyd Novis. Hamp, it was like Dusty himself, the way he walked up the street. He met Novis right there where he's layin'. Tuna was with Novis. Tremaine said something and reached into his pocket, and Tuna drew on him. Tremaine had a gun all right, but, Hamp, he didn't have a chance against Tuna.'

The marshal came out of the crowd. He put his hand on Hamp's arm. 'Take it easy, Hamp.'

'Where's Tuna?'

'He's in the hotel. I've got it covered, Hamp. He can't get out. . . . Hamp! Wait a minute!' The marshal gripped Hamp's arm and spun him around. 'You can't go in there, Hamp.'

'It's my fight, ain't it?'

'You try to go in that hotel, Hamp, I'll have to stop you.'

'I wouldn't try it if I was you, Ned,' Hamp Donnelly said softly. 'You and me have been friends a long time.' He jerked away from Ned Crockett and started walking up the street toward the hotel. Everyone was talking.

'Boyd Novis hired Tuna Stinson as a gun guard.'

'Tremaine got drunk last night and lost a lot of money.'

'The game was crooked.'

'We ought to hang Stinson and run Novis out of town.'

'Hamp!' Ellen's voice was clear and strong, close to his elbow. She reached out and tried to stop him. 'Hamp,' Ellen said, 'I can't stand any more of it.' He kept walking. 'Hamp!' She was crying now. 'It doesn't matter, Hamp. Nothing matters. Let Novis have Anchor. Let them have what they want. It isn't worth your life.' Her voice faded behind him, a broken sob that stayed with him and was with him when he entered the deserted lobby of the hotel.

He drew his gun and crossed the lobby to the foot of the stairs, keeping to one side. 'Tuna?' His voice echoed through the empty building.

'Up here, Donnelly.' Tuna's voice was heavy, taunting. 'Come on up and have a drink.'

'Stay away from here, Donnelly!' Boyd Novis was with Tuna. The sheepman's voice was charged with fear.

There was a potted fern on the newel post. Hamp reached out and pushed it over. It hit the floor with a crash and the pot broke. The balled plant rolled back and forth on the floor. Two shots cracked out in rapid succession and splinters jumped from the floor at the foot of the stairs. There was a long silence. 'How about that, Donnelly?' Tuna called.

'High and to the left,' Hamp yelled. 'You'll have to do better than that.' He picked up a bentwood chair and threw it against the lobby desk. Tuna didn't fall for the trap.

Carefully, then, Hamp edged his way along the wall, into the dining-room, and out into the kitchen. He thought of the outside covered stairway that led to the second floor. Ned Crockett would have guards posted there. Hamp decided he would have to risk it. Snatching up a dish towel, he opened the back door and waved the towel and then dashed out. He heard a voice say, 'There he goes!' A rifle bullet tore into the wooden wall, but he was around the corner and into the protection of the covered stairway.

He stood there, panting, and then he started up, a step at a time, testing each board with his feet. He opened the door of the second floor, his gun in his hand, and he was in the far end of the dark hallway. Boyd Novis's room was down toward the front window.

It seemed like an hour that he waited. Then the door of Novis's room inched open. It opened out and it was between Hamp and the man who was opening it. Tuna's voice was loud: 'You still down there, Donnelly?'

'Right here, Tuna.'

There was a burst of gunfire and the panel of the door splintered outward. Tuna was firing through the door, hiding behind it. Hamp threw himself across the hall, and now he could see Tuna, behind the door. He fired once, saw Tuna turn. He could see the battered face, the stringy hair hanging from under the black hat. He remembered Orvie Stinson and the look on his face when he–Hamp–had come up behind Orvie that night just as the latter was drawing a bead on Dusty Tremaine's back.

A bullet tore a furrow in the wall at the side of his head, and now he was firing back, the gun bucking against the palm of his hand. He saw Tuna crash back against the doorjamb, saw him try to raise the gun. Tuna's hand opened. The gun dropped and Tuna slid down the doorjamb. He sat there on the floor a full second before he fell to one side.

Hamp Donnelly walked down the hall, the gun still in his hand. He turned in at the door, and Boyd Novis was crouched behind his desk. 'Don't come in here, Donnelly, I warn you–'

Hamp holstered his gun and walked into the room.

'I didn't have anything to do with this, Donnelly. This was a fight between you and Tuna Stinson. Everybody knows that.'

'You've got an IOU against Paul Tremaine?'

'And I'll collect it, too! It had nothing to do with this. Tremaine was a crazy drunk. He tried to kill me.'

'Let me have that IOU.'

'You stay away from me! You haven't any right to do that!' Novis was standing now, a withered little man, too small for his clothes, a man who had hated his size all his life. Paul Tremaine's IOU was there on the desk. Hamp picked up the piece of paper, and Novis screamed at him, 'I'll have the law on you! That IOU is perfectly legal.'

Hamp moved around the desk and Novis backed away, his eyes wide. He kept watching the piece of paper in Hamp's hand, saw Hamp work it into a ball. 'I'll collect it, I tell you,' he said weakly.

Hamp thrust the balled paper in front of Novis's face. 'Eat it,' he said. His left hand shot up and he gripped Novis's cheeks between thumb and forefinger and squeezed the way he might have opened the mouth of a stubborn horse. 'Eat it and swallow it,' Hamp said.

Boyd Novis stood there, panting and choking, gagging on the mangled paper. 'I'll get you, Donnelly,' he raved. 'I'll drive you out of the country. I'll buy Anchor and every other piece of property around here and I'll drive you out of the country.'

'You're whipped, Novis,' Hamp said quietly. 'You're whipped all the way.' He stood looking at Novis and gradually his anger died, leaving only disgust. 'You might as well get used to it, Novis,' he said softly. 'If you owned every acre of land in Oregon it wouldn't make you two inches taller.'

He turned and walked out into the hall and down the stairs and out on to the street. There was a silent crowd around the entrance to the hotel.

He saw the marshal and he nodded, indicating that it was over.

'Sorry I had to cross you, Ned,' he said.

The marshal looked at him; his eyes were hard but there was understanding in them. 'I could have stopped you if I had wanted to, Hamp,' the marshal said.

Hamp Donnelly looked at the man he had known a long time, a young man, good-looking, capable. 'I believe you could have, Ned,' he said. He walked on through the crowd until he reached Sue and Ellen. Sue had her arm around Ellen's waist. He stood by them but they didn't see him.

'I didn't know about you and Dallas, Sue,' Ellen said. 'I didn't know anything about it.'

'It's all right, Ellen,' Sue Donnelly said. 'I've been trying to learn to hate him for a long time. Now that it's happened I'm surprised how very easy it is.'

Hamp walked over and put his arm around Ellen's shoulder. 'I'll take you home,' he said. 'Your friends will take care of things here.'

Dallas Rombeck watched them drive out of town. He knew it was over here for him, just as it had been over in The Dalles and in Portland. And what had, until this moment, been terror, turned to a consuming rage against Hamp Donnelly. He saw Ned Crockett, and he ran up to him and gripped the lapels of Ned's coat. 'Are you going to let him drive off like that? Don't you know anything about the law you are supposed to enforce? He killed a man, didn't he?'

Ned Crockett reached up and unpinned the badge from his shirt and dropped it into his pocket. He unbuckled his gun belt then and let it drop to the ground. He looked at Sue Donnelly. He had always liked her. 'Sure, Dallas,' he said. 'I'm gonna do something.' His fist travelled six inches, and Dallas went over backward, his hand shoulder-high. Ned Crockett reached down and got his gun belt and fastened it around his middle. He took the star from his pocket and pinned it back on his shirt. 'I'm sorry, Sue,' he said. 'It's just that I been wantin' to do that for a long time.' . . .

The shadows were blue across the rolling hills above Bigforks and there was sun only on top of the butte. There were a thousand things Hamp Donnelly wanted to say and he couldn't say any of them. Most of all he wanted to tell Ellen that he wanted her to stay, wanted it more than anything else in the world. Ahead of them, on the road toward Anchor, three buggies left a trail of dust.

'I wonder who that is?' she said, her voice dead and empty.

'Neighbours,' he said. 'Folks from town. They'll be coming out to stay with you and help any way they can.' He heard her quick sob.

They stopped at the summit, and the wind was fresh off the sage and it flattened the dry grass in silver patches. The butte seemed near in the gathering evening. He put his arm around her shoulder and turned her so that she could see it, but he didn't look at her face. He was looking off across the land, a land he understood, a land that perhaps she would never know.

'I think Dusty would like it if Paul were buried up there, beside him,' he said quietly.

She clutched his shirt and hid her face against his chest. 'Paul—'

'He acted like a man, Ellen,' Hamp said. His lips were against her hair, so lightly that she didn't know. 'No one can do more than that.'

The evening gathered into dusk and the purples and golds came down out of the hills and faded into the blue of the canyons. It was over now. She had to realize that. All the nights she had waited up for Paul, all the love and understanding she had tried to give him. It had all led to this day.

She turned and looked once at the butte, and then she was gazing out into the gathering shadows. The hills were soft and blue and permanent, and they would be there forever. Yes, she decided, this was Paul's place. And it was her place, too, for once Paul was buried here he would be a part of this and she would be a part of it. A part of herself would be buried with Paul.

'I hired a hay crew,' Hamp said. 'I'll have them hold off a week or so.'

She thought of Anchor and of what it had meant to her uncle and to Hamp, and she wondered if some day it would mean the same to her. She hoped it would, because now she knew she would stay. 'No,' she said. 'Don't hold them up. We'll have to get the hay in before it rains.'

He looked at her, and she thought of how much he was like the land, a strong land, even cruel at times, but a permanent land, a thing to cling to. Yes, she thought, he was like the land. And a woman could learn to love the land. She knew that was so.

DUST STORM

By Max Brand

FOR seven days the wind came out of the northeast over the Powder Mountains and blew the skirts of a dust storm between Digger Hill and Bender Hill into the hollow where Lindsay was living in his shack. During that week Lindsay waked and slept with a piece of black coat-lining worn across his mouth and nostrils, but the dust penetrated like cosmic rays through the chinks in the walls of the cabin, through the mask and to the bottom of his lungs, so that every night he roused from sleep gasping for breath with a nightmare of being buried alive. Even lamplight could not drive that bad dream farther away than the misty corners of the room.

The blow began on a Tuesday morning and by twilight of that day he knew what he was in for, so he went out through the whistling murk and led Jenny and Lind, his two mules, and Mustard, his old cream-coloured mustang, from the pasture into the barn. There he had in the mow a good heap of the volunteer hay which he had cut last May on the southeast forty, but the thin silt of the storm soon whitened the hay to such a degree that he had to shake it thoroughly before he fed the stock. Every two hours during that week he roused himself by an alarm-clock instinct and went out to wash the nostrils and mouths of the stock, prying their teeth open and reaching right in to swab the black off their tongues. On Wednesday, Jenny, like the fool and villainess that she was, closed on his right forearm and raked off eight inches of skin.

Monotony of diet was more terrible to Lindsay than the storm. He had been on the point of riding to town and borrowing money from the bank on his growing crop so as to lay in a stock of provisions, but now he was confined with a bushel of potatoes and the heel of a side of bacon.

.   .   .   .

Only labour like that of the harvest field could make such food palatable and, in confinement as he was, never thoroughly stretching his muscles once a day, Lindsay began to revolt in belly and then in spirit. He even lacked coffee to give savour to the menu; he could not force himself more than once a day to eat potatoes, boiled or fried in bacon fat, with the dust gritting continually between his teeth.

He had no comfort whatever except for Caesar, his mongrel dog, and half a bottle of whisky, from which he gave himself a nip once a day. Then in the night of the seventh day there came to Lindsay a dream of a country where rolling waves of grass washed from horizon to horizon and all the winds of the earth could not blow a single breath of dust into the blue of the sky. He wakened with the dawn visible through the cracks in the shanty walls and a strange expectancy in his mind.

That singular expectation remained in him when he threw the door open and looked across the black of the hills toward the green light that was opening like a fan in the east; then he realized that it was the silence after the storm that seemed more enormous than all the stretch of landscape between him and the Powder Mountains. Caesar ran out past his legs to leap and bark and sneeze until something over-awed him, in turn, and sent him skulking here and there with his nose to the ground as though he were following invisible bird trails. It was true that the face of the land was changed.

As the light grew, Lindsay saw that the water hole in the hollow was a black wallow of mud and against the woodshed leaned a sloping mass of dust like a drift of snow. The sight of this started him on the run for his eighty acres of winter-sown summer fallow. From a distance he saw the disaster but could not believe it until his feet were wading deep in the dust. Except for a few marginal strips, the whole swale of the ploughed land was covered with wind-filtered soil, a yard thick in the deepest places.

Two-thirds of his farm was wiped out, two-thirds of it was erased into permanent sterility; and the work of nearly ten years was entombed. He glanced down at the palms of his hands, for he was thinking of the burning, pulpy blisters that had covered them day after day when he was digging holes with the blunt post auger.

He looked up, then, at the distant ridges of the Powder Mountains. Ten years before in the morning light he had been able almost to count the great pines which walked up the slopes and stood on the mountains' crests, but the whole range had been cut over in the interim and the thick coat of forest which bound with its roots the accumulated soil of a million years had been mowed down. That was why the teeth of the wind had found substance they could eat into.

The entire burden of precious loam that dressed the mountains had been blown adrift in recent years and now the worthless underclay, made friable by a dry season, was laid in a stifling coat of silt across the farmlands of the lower valleys and the upper pastures of the range.

Lindsay did not think about anything for a time. His feet, and an automatic impulse that made him turn always to the stock first, took him to the barn, where he turned loose the confined animals. Even the mules were glad enough to kick up their heels a few times, and fifteen years of hard living could not keep Mustard from exploding like a bomb all over the pasture, bucking as though a ghost were on his back and knocking up a puff of dust every time he hit the ground.

Lindsay, standing with feet spread and folded arms, a huge figure in the door of the barn, watched the antics of his old horse with a vacant smile, for he was trying to rouse himself and failing wretchedly. Instead, he could see himself standing in line with signed application slips in his hand, and then in front of a desk where some hired clerk with an insolent face put sharp questions to him. A month hence, when people asked him how things went, he would have to say: 'I'm on the county.'

When he had gone that far in his thinking, his soul at last rose in him but to such a cold, swift altitude that he was filled with fear, and he found his lips repeating words, stiffly, whispering them aloud: 'I'll be damned and dead first!' The fear of what he would do with his own hands grew stronger and stronger, for he felt that he had made a promise which would be heard recorded by that living, inmost god of all honest men, his higher self.

Once more, automatically, his feet took him on to the next step in the day: breakfast. Back in the shanty, his lips twitched with disgust as he started frying potatoes; the rank smell of the bacon grease mounted to his brain and gathered in clouds there, but his unthinking hands finished the cookery and dumped the fried potatoes into a tin plate.

A faint chorus came down to him then out of the windless sky. He snatched the loaded pistol from the holster that hung against the wall and ran outside, for sometimes the wild geese, flying north, came very low over the hill as they rose from the marsh south of it, but now he found himself agape like a schoolboy, staring up.

He should have known by the dimness of the honking and by the melancholy harmony which distance added to it that the geese were half a mile up in the sky. Thousands of them were streaming north in a great wedge that kept shuffling and reshuffling at the open ends; ten tons of meat on the wing.

A tin pan crashed inside the shack and Caesar came out on wings with his tail between his legs; Lindsay went inside and found the plate of potatoes overturned on the floor. He called: 'Come in here, Caesar, you damned old thief. Come in here and get it, if you want the stuff. I'm better without.'

The dog came back skulking. From the doorway, he prospected the face of his master for a moment, slavering with greed, then he sneaked to the food on the floor and began to eat, guiltily, but Lindsay already had forgotten him. All through the hollow which a week before had been a shining tremor of yellow-green wheat stalks, the rising wind of the morning was now stirring little airy whirlpools and walking ghosts of dust that made a step or two and vanished.

It seemed to Lindsay that he had endured long enough. He was thirty-five. He had twenty years of hard work behind him. And he would not–by God, he would not be a government pensioner! The wild geese had called the gun into his hand; he felt, suddenly, that it must be used for one last shot anyway. As for life, there was a stinking savour of bacon that clung inevitably to it. He looked with fearless eyes into the big muzzle of the gun.

Then Mustard whinnied not far from the house and Lindsay lifted his head with a faint smile, for there was a stallion's trumpet sound in the neigh of the old gelding, always, just as there was always an active devil in his heels and his teeth. He combined the savage instincts of a wildcat with the intellectual, patient malevolence of a mule, but Lindsay loved the brute because no winter cold was sharp enough to freeze the big heart in him and no dry summer march was long enough to wither it. At fifteen, the old fellow still could put fifty miles of hard country behind him between dawn and dark. For years Lindsay had felt that those long, mulish ears must eventually point the way to some great destiny.

He stepped into the doorway now and saw that Mustard was whinnying a challenge to a horseman who jogged up the Gavvigan Trail with a tell-tale dust cloud boiling up behind. Mechanical instinct, again, made Lindsay drop the gun into the old leather holster that hung on the wall.

Then he stepped outside to wait.

Half a mile off, the approaching rider put his horse into a lope and Lindsay recognized, by his slant in the saddle, that inveterate range tramp and worthless roustabout, Gypsy Renner. He reined in at the door of the shack, lifted his bandanna from nose and mouth, and spat black.

'Got a drink, Bob?' he asked without other greeting.

'I've got a drink for you,' said Lindsay.

'I'll get off a minute, then,' replied Renner, and swung out of the saddle.

Lindsay poured some whisky into a tin cup and Renner received it without thanks. Dust was still rising like thick smoke from his shoulders.

'You been far?' asked Lindsay.

'From Boulder,' said Renner.

'Much of the range like out yonder?'

'Mostly,' said Renner.

He finished the whisky and held out the cup. Lindsay poured the rest of the bottle.

'If much of the range is like this,' said Lindsay, 'it's gonna be hell.'

'It's gonna be and it is,' said Renner. 'It's hell already over on the Oliver Range.'

'Wait a minute. That's where Andy Barnes and John Street run their cows. What you mean it's hell up there?'

'That's where I'm bound,' said Renner. 'They're hiring men and guns on both sides. Most of the water holes and tanks on Andy Barnes' place are filled up with mud, right to the ridge of the Oliver Hills, and his cows are choking. And John Street, his land is clean because the wind kind of funnelled the dust up over the hills and it landed beyond him. Andy has to water those cows and Street wants to charge ten cents a head. Andy says he'll be damned if he pays money for the water that God put free on earth. So there's gonna be a fight.'

Lindsay looked through the door at that lumpheaded mustang of his and saw, between his mind and the world, a moonlit night with five thousand head of cattle, market-fat and full of beans, stampeding into the northeast with a thunder and rattle of split hoofs and a swordlike clashing of horns. He saw riders galloping ahead, vainly shooting into the face of the herd in the vain hope of turning it, until two of those cowpunchers, going it blind, clapped together and went down, head over heels.

'They used to be friends,' said Lindsay. 'They come so close to dying together, one night, that they been living side by side ever since; and they used to be friends.'

'They got too damn rich,' suggested Renner. 'A rich man ain't nobody's friend. . . . It was you that saved the two hides of them one night in a stampede, ten, twelve years ago, wasn't it?'

Lindsay pointed to Mustard.

'Now, I'm gonna tell you something about that,' he said. 'The fact is that those cows would've washed right over the whole three of us, but I was riding that Mustard horse, and when I turned him back and pointed him at the herd, he just went off like a Roman candle and scattered sparks right up to the Milky Way. He pitched so damn' hard that he pretty near snapped my head off and he made himself look so big that those steers doggone near fainted and pushed aside from that spot.'

Renner looked at the mustang with his natural sneer. Then he said: 'Anyway, there's gonna be a fight up there, and it's gonna be paid for.'

'There oughtn't be no fight,' answered big Bob Lindsay, frowning.

'They're mean enough to fight,' said Renner. 'Didn't you save their scalps? And ain't they left you to starve here on a hundred and twenty acres of blowsand that can't raise enough to keep a dog fat?'

'Yeah?' said Lindsay. 'Maybe you better be vamoosing along.'

Renner looked at him, left the shack, and swung into the saddle. When he was safely there he muttered: 'Ah, to hell with you?' and jogged away.

Lindsay, with a troubled mind, watched him out of sight. An hour later he saddled Mustard and took the way toward the Oliver Hills.

The Oliver Hills lie west of the Powder Mountains, their sides fat with grasslands all the way to the ridge, and right over the crest walked the posts of the fence that separated the holdings of Andy Barnes from those of John Street. Lindsay, as he came up the old Mexican Trail, stopped on a hilltop and took a careful view of the picture.

He had to strain his eyes a little because dust was blowing like battlesmoke off the whitened acres of Andy Barnes and over the ridge, and that dust was stirred up by thousands of cattle which milled close to the fence line, drawn by the smell of water. Down the eastern hollows some of the beeves were wallowing in the holes where water once had been and where there was only mud now. But west of the ridge the lands of John Street were clean as green velvet under the noonday sun.

Scattered down the Street side of the fence, a score of riders wandered up and down with significant lines of light balancing across the pommels of the saddles. Those were the rifles. As many more cowpunchers headed the milling cattle of Andy Barnes with difficulty, for in clear view of the cows, but on Street's side of the fence, ran a knee-deep stream of silver water that spread out into a quiet blue lake, halfway down the slope.

He found a gate on to the Street land and went through it. Two or three of the line-riders hailed him with waving hats. One of them sang out: 'Where's your rifle, brother? Men ain't worth a damn here without they got rifles.'

He found John Street sitting on a spectacular black horse just west of a hilltop, where the rise of land gave him shelter from ambitious sharpshooters. When he saw Lindsay he grabbed him by the shoulders and bellowed like a bull in spring: 'I knew you'd be over and I knew you'd be on the right side. By God, it's been eleven years since I was as glad to see you as I am today. . . . Boys, I wanta tell you what Bob Lindsay here done for me when I got caught in–'

'Shut up, will you?' said Lindsay. 'Looks like Andy has got some pretty dry cows, over yonder.'

'I hope they dry up till there's nothing but wind in their bellies,' said John Street.

'I thought you and Andy been pretty good friends,' said Lindsay.

'If he was my brother–if he was two brothers–if he was my son and daughter and my pa and ma, he's so damn' mean that I'd see him in hell-fire before I'd give him a cup of water to wash the hell-fire cinders out of his throat,' said John Street, in part.

So Lindsay rode back to the gate and around to the party of Andy Barnes, passing steers with caked, dry mud of the choked water holes layered around their muzzles. They were red-eyed with thirst and their bellowing seemed to rise like an unnatural thunder out of the ground instead of booming from the skies. Yearlings, already knock-kneed with weakness, were shouldered to the ground by the heavier stock and lay there, surrendering.

Andy Barnes sat cross-legged on the ground inside the rock circle of an old Indian camp on a hilltop, picking the grass, chewing it, spitting it out. He had grown much fatter and redder of face and the fat had got into his eyes, leaving them a little dull and staring.

Lindsay sat down beside him.

'You know something, Bob?' said Andy.

'Know what?' asked Lindsay.

'My wife's kid sister is over to the house,' said Andy. 'She's just turned twenty-three and she's got enough sense to cook a man a steak and onions. As tall as your shoulder and the bluest damn' pair of eyes you ever seen outside a blind horse. Never had bridle or saddle on her and I dunno how she'd go in harness but you got a pair of hands. What you say? She's heard about Bob Lindsay for ten years and she don't believe that there's that much man outside of a fairy story.'

'Shut up, will you?' said Lindsay. 'Seems like ten cents ain't much to pay for the difference between two thousand dead steers and two thousand dogies, all picking grass and fat and happy.'

'Look up at that sky,' said Andy.

'I'm looking,' said Lindsay.

'Look blue?'

'Yeah. Kind of.'

'Who put the blue in it?'

'God, maybe.'

'Anybody ever pay him for it? And who put the water in the ground and made it leak out again? And why should I pay for *that?*'

'There's a lot of difference,' said Lindsay, 'between a dead steer on the range and a live steer in Chicago.'

'Maybe,' dreamed Andy, 'but I guess they won't all be dead. You see that yearling over yonder, standing kind of spray-legged, with its nose pretty near on the ground?'

'I see it,' said Lindsay.

'When that yearling kneels down,' said Andy, 'there's gonna be something happen. Ain't that old Mustard?'

'Yeah, that's Mustard,' said Lindsay, rising.

'If you ever get through with him,' said Andy, 'I got a lot of pasture land nothing ain't using where he could just range around and laugh himself to death. I ain't forgot when he was bucking the saddle off his back and knocking splinters out of the stars, that night. He must've looked like a mountain to them steers, eh?'

Lindsay got on Mustard and rode over the hill. He went

straight up to the fence which divided the two estates and dismounted before it with a wire pincers in his hand. He felt scorn and uttermost detestation for the thing he was about to do. Men who cut fences are dirty rustlers and horse thieves and every man jack of them ought to be strung up as high as the top of the Powder Mountains; but the thirsty uproar of the cattle drove him on to what he felt was both a crime and a sin.

It had been a far easier thing, eleven years ago, to save Barnes and Street from the stampeding herd than it was to save them now from the petty hatred that had grown up between them without cause, without reason. The posts stood at such distance apart that the wires were strung with an extra heavy tension. When the steel edges cut through the topmost strand it parted with a twang and leaped back to either side, coiling and tangling like thin, bright metallic snakes around the posts.

Yelling voices of protest came shouting through the dusty wind. Lindsay could see men dropping off their horses and lying prone to level their rifles at him; and all at once it seemed to him that the odour of frying bacon grease was thickening in his nostrils again and that this was the true savour of existence.

He saw the Powder Mountains lifting their sides from brown to blue in the distant sky with a promise of better lands beyond that horizon; but the promise was a lie, he knew. No matter what he did, he felt assured that ten years hence he would be as now, a poor unrespected squatter on the range, slaving endlessly not even for a monthly pay check but merely to fill his larder with— bacon and Irish potatoes! Hope, as vital to the soul as breath to the nostrils, had been subtracted from him, and therefore what he did with his life was of no importance whatever. He leaned a little and snapped the pincers through the second wire of the fence.

He did not hear the sharp twanging sound of the parting strand, for a louder noise struck at his ear, a ringing rifle report full of resonance, like two heavy sledge-hammers struck face to face. At his feet a riffle of dust lifted; he heard the bullet hiss like a snake through the grass. Then a whole volley crashed. Bullets went by him on rising notes of inquiry; and just behind him a slug spatted into the flesh of Mustard. Sometimes an axe makes a sound like that when it sinks into green wood.

He turned and saw Mustard sitting down like a dog, with his long, mulish ears pointing straight ahead and a look of pleased expectancy in his eyes. Out of a hole in his breast blood was pumping in long, thin jets.

Lindsay leaned and cut the third and last wire.

When he straightened again he heard the body of Mustard slump down against the ground with a squeaking, jouncing noise of liquids inside his belly. He did not lie on his side but with his head outstretched and his legs doubled under him as though he were playing a game and would spring up again in a moment.

Lindsay looked toward the guns. They never should have missed him the first time except that something like buckfever must have shaken the marksmen. He walked right through the open gap in the fence to meet the fire with a feeling that the wire clipper in his hand was marking him down like a cattle thief for the lowest sort of a death.

Then someone began to scream in a shrill falsetto. He recognized the voice of Big John Street, transformed by hysterical emotion. Street himself broke over the top of the hill with the black horse at a full gallop, yelling for his men to stop firing.

The wind of the gallop furled up the wide brim of his sombrero and he made a noble picture, considering the rifles of Andy Barnes which must be sighting curiously at him by this time; then a hammer-stroke clipped Lindsay on the side of the head. The Powder Mountains whirled into a mist of brown and blue; the grass spun before him like running water; he dropped to his knees, and down his face ran a soft, warm stream.

Into his dizzy view came the legs and the sliding hoofs of the black horse, cutting shallow furrows in the grass as it slid to a halt, and he heard the voice of John Street, dismounted beside him, yelling terrible oaths. He was grabbed beneath the armpits and lifted.

'Are you dead, Bob?' yelled Street.

'I'm gonna be all right,' said Lindsay. He ran a finger tip through the bullet furrow in his scalp and felt the hard bone of the skull all the way. 'I'm gonna be fine,' he stated, and turned toward the uproar that was pouring through the gap he had cut in the fence.

For the outburst of rifle-fire had taken the attention of Barnes' men from their herding and the cattle had surged past them toward water. Nothing now could stop that hungry stampede as they crowded through the gap with rattling hoofs and the steady clashing of horns. Inside the fence, the stream divided right and left and rushed on toward water, some to the noisy white cataract, some to the wide blue pool.

'I'm sorry, John,' said Lindsay, 'but those cows looked kind of dry to me.'

Then a nausea of body and a whirling dimness of mind overtook him and did not clear away again until he found himself lying with a bandaged head on the broad top of a hill. John Street was one side of him and Andy Barnes on the other. They were holding hands like children and peering down at him anxiously.

'How are you, Bob, old son?' asked Andy.

'Fine,' said Lindsay, sitting up. 'Fine as a fiddle,' he added, rising to his feet.

Street supported him hastily by one arm and Barnes by the other. Below him he could see the Barnes cattle thronging into the shallow water of the creek.

'About that ten cents a head,' said Andy, 'it's all right with me.'

'Damn the money,' said Street. 'I wouldn't take money from you if you were made of gold. ... I guess Bob has paid for the water like he paid for our two hides eleven years ago. Bob, don't you give a hang about nothing? Don't you care nothing about your life?'

'The cows seemed kind of dry to me,' said Lindsay, helplessly.

'You're comin' home with me,' said Street.

'I got *two* females in my place to look after him,' pointed out Andy Barnes.

'I got a cook that's a doggone sight better than a doctor,' said Street.

'I don't need any doctor,' said Lindsay. 'You two just shut up and say goodbye to me, will you? I'm going home. I got work to do, tomorrow.'

This remark produced a silence out of which Lindsay heard, from the surrounding circle of cowmen, a voice that murmured: 'He's gonna go home!' And another said: 'He's got the chores to do, I guess.'

Andy looked at John Street.

'He's gonna go, John,' he said.

'There ain't any changing him,' said John Street, sadly. 'Hey, Bob, take this here horse of mine, will you?'

'Don'cha do it!' shouted Barnes. 'Hey, Mickie, bring up that grey, will you? ... Look at that piece of grey sky and wind, Bob, will you?'

'They're a mighty slick pair,' said Lindsay. 'I never seen a more upstanding pair of hellcats in my life. It would take a lot of barley and oats to keep them sleeked up so's they shine like this.... But if you wanta wish a horse on to me, how about that down-headed, wise-lookin' cayuse over there? He's got some bottom to him and the hellfire is kind of worked out of his eyes.'

He pointed to a brown gelding which seemed to have fallen half asleep.

Another silence was spread by this remark. Then someone said: 'He's picked out Slim's cuttin' horse.... He's gone and picked out old Dick.'

'Give them reins to Bob, Slim!' commanded Andy Barnes, 'and leave the horse tied right on to the reins, too.'

Lindsay said: 'Am I parting you from something, Slim?'

Slim screwed up his face and looked at the sky.

'Why, I've heard about you, Lindsay,' he said, 'and today I've seen you. I guess when a horse goes to you, he's just going home; and this Dick horse of mine, I had the making of him and he sure rates a home.... If you just ease him along the first half hour, that horse'll be ready to die for you all the rest of the day.'

'Thanks,' said Lindsay, shaking hands. 'I'm gonna value him, brother.'

He swung into the saddle and waved his adieu. John Street followed him a few steps, and so did Andy Barnes.

'Are you gonna be comin' over? Are you gonna be comin' back, Bob?' they asked him.

'Are you two gonna stop being damn' fools?' he replied.

They laughed and waved a cheerful agreement and they were still waving as he jogged Dick down the hill. The pain in his head burned him to the brain with every pulse of his blood but a strange feeling of triumph rose in his heart. He felt he never would be impatient again, for he could see that he was enriched forever.

The twilight found him close to home and planning the work of the next days. If he put a drag behind the two mules he could sweep back the dust where it thinned out at the margin and so redeem from total loss a few more acres. With any luck, he would get seed for the next year; and as for food, he could do what he had scorned all his days—he could make a kitchen garden and irrigate it from the windmill.

It was dark when he came up the last slope and the stars rose like fireflies over the edge of the hill. Against them he made out Jenny and Lind waiting for him beside the door of the shack. He paused to stare at the vague silhouettes and remembered poor Mustard with a great stroke in his heart.

Caesar came with a shrill howl of delight to leap about his master and bark at the new horse but Dick merely pricked his ears with patient understanding as though he knew he had come home indeed.

Inside the shanty, the hand of Lindsay found the lantern. Lighting it brought a suffocating odour of kerosene fumes but even through this Lindsay could detect the smell of fried bacon and potatoes in the air. He took a deep breath of it, for it seemed to him the most delicious savour in the world.

SQUAW FEVER

By Bill Gulick

CHARLEY SMITH, the best white scout west of the Mississippi, had once tackled a grizzly bear with a hunting knife and come out winner, but when it came to women he was as skittery of the creatures as a wild mustang colt is of a hair rope. Charley was a small shy man with a pink skin that the sun somehow never tanned, and innocent-looking wide blue eyes that made one think here was a tenderfoot ripe to be skinned—which feat a few men had attempted, much to their sorrow. Charley wasn't afraid of anything that walked, crawled or flew, except women. He learned about them the year he caught squaw fever.

Trapping had been good in the Rockies that winter. When spring came, Charley and his Cayuse Indian partner, Bear Claw, sold their furs in Fort Laramie, went on a week-long spree to celebrate, and then fell to discussing what they would do next.

'I'd kind of like to drift east to the buffalo country,' Charley said.

Bear Claw sat and pondered for a while, as was his habit. At last he shook his head. 'Been gone from Cayuse country six months. Go there. See if new squaw Bear Claw got last year has any papooses yet.'

Charley looked at his friend in some surprise. 'New squaw? What did you do with the old one?'

'Took her back to her family.' Bear Claw's eyes glittered darkly and he muttered, 'Woman all talk, no work. Not worth the five ponies she cost me. But good squaw now—cost ten ponies. Lots of work, not much talk.'

'Did you get back the ponies you gave for the first one?'

Bear Claw, whom contact with Charley had civilized to the extent that he could swear in English, swore fluently, then added an expressive Cayuse word which meant that the girl's father was a cheap skate who would not stand behind his merchandise.

'But no matter,' the Indian said philosophically. 'Got lots of money to buy ponies now. You come home with me and we live good all summer. Lots of eat. Lots of sleep.'

'I think,' Charley said, 'that I'd rather go buffalo hunting.'

'Do that too. We go to Cayuse country and see squaw for one moon, then we cross Bitter Root Mountains and hunt buffalo. Good?'

To Charley, a buffalo was a buffalo, and it didn't matter to him whether he encountered it on the plains of Kansas or in the Bitter Root Valley.

'Suits me,' he said. 'When do we start?'

It was a bright June morning a week later when they headed out of Fort Laramie over the long trail to the Cayuse country, which lay in a region of green mountains and winding rivers along the eastern border of that vast country called Oregon. The smell of the greening sod was sweet in Charley's nostrils, but inside him was a feeling of melancholy, a loneliness that Bear Claw's presence beside him intensified rather than soothed away. The Cayuse was riding home to see his wife and family, Charley brooded, but whom was he riding home to? Nobody; nobody at all.

They topped a swell in the prairie and saw a wagon train camped in the valley below, sunlight glittering off the white canvas tops.

'Tents that roll on wheels!' Bear Claw snorted scornfully. 'Why don't white man stay at home?'

Because he was so lonely, Charley let sentiment get the better of him for the moment. 'That's why they're goin' to Oregon,' he said wistfully. 'They're lookin' for homes.'

As they trotted down the slope and swung off to go around the wagon train, a bearded, buckskin-clad man rode toward them, waving a hand in a gesture for them to stop. Recognizing Sam West, a professional scout and guide who made Fort Laramie his headquarters, Charley reined up and waited.

West glanced at the two well-laden pack horses trailing behind them and said, 'Headed up Oregon way?'

Charley admitted they were.

'How'd you like to take a wagon train through?'

'No like,' Bear Claw said with a scowl.

'We're travellin' light an' fast,' Charley explained. 'Bear Claw's in a hurry to see his squaw.'

West laughed. 'She can wait. This bunch of greenhorns really needs help. Got lost three times 'tween here and Council Bluffs, an' gosh knows anybody that can't find their way across the plains will never git through the mountains 'tween here and Oregon. I'd take 'em myself, but I'm tied up. Come an' talk to 'em anyhow.'

Bear Claw lapsed into a sullen silence.

Charley said reluctantly, 'All right, but it won't do 'em no good.'

The wagons were drawn up in a large circle, inside of which breakfast fires still smouldered. Children scampered in and out, playing hide-and-seek under the wagon beds, and gingham-clad women bustled about, doing their morning chores. A group of lean, gaunt-looking men turned away from an animated discussion as Charley and Bear Claw followed Sam West into the enclosure. Charley and West dismounted, but Bear Claw stayed atop his horse, gazing haughtily off into the distance.

'Mr. Reynolds,' West said to the tall, hawk-faced man who seemed to be the leader of the group, 'shake hands with Charley Smith, the best guide in the West.'

'We don't need no guide,' Reynolds said crustily, glaring at Charley. 'I kin find the way myself. Got us here all the way from Arkansas.'

'In that case,' Charley said gratefully, 'we'll be ridin'.'

'Wait a minute!' A square, solid-looking woman with the most determined chin Charley had ever seen pushed her way into the centre of the group. 'You shut yore mouth, Zeke. Who was it got us lost before we got to Fort Kearny? Who made us take the wrong turn at the forks of the Platte? Who'd 'a' had us in Santa Fé 'stead of Oregon, if we'd 'a' listened to him?'

' 'T weren't my fault,' Reynolds said uncomfortably. 'There weren't ary sign tellin' us which way to go.'

'An' there won't be ary signs from here on,' the woman said triumphantly. She turned and looked searchingly at Charley. 'Do you know the trail, young man?'

Charley took off his hat and crushed it in his hands, his pink face growing pinker. 'I reckon I do, ma'am. But me an' Bear Claw—'

'How long will it take to get to Walla Walla?'

'Three, four months; according to how fast you travel. But Bear Claw says—'

'How much will you charge to guide us through?'

Before Charley could answer, Bear Claw grunted, 'Twenty dollar a day.'

The emigrants looked at one another in dismay.

Charley said hastily, 'It ain't a matter of money. We just happen to be in a hurry an' a wagon train moves powerful slow—'

'We're in a hurry too,' said a sweet feminine voice at Charley's elbow.

Charley turned. A slim, dark-eyed girl stood smiling up at him. She wore a yellow dress that fitted her trim waist and full bosom like no dress Charley had ever seen on any woman. Shiny black hair cascaded down from under her sunbonnet, framing a creamy golden face the likes of which Charley had never known existed. The beautiful vision was so unexpected that he even forgot to blush.

'Hello,' the girl said. 'I'm Susan Reynolds.'

'Pleased to meet you.'

'Your Indian friend was just joking when he said you'd charge us twenty dollars a day to guide us through, wasn't he?'

'I—I reckon so,' Charley faltered. 'Bear Claw's got quite a sense of humour.'

'How much would you do it for?'

'Well, guides usually get about four dollars. Only, Bear Claw an' me—'

'Then you will take us?' Susan turned to the square-jawed woman and exclaimed, 'Oh, ma, he says he'll take us!'

Charley didn't recall having said anything of the kind, but now that she mentioned it, it seemed like a mighty fine idea. Bear Claw gave a disgusted snort. Charley, lost in the smiling depths of the prettiest pair of black eyes he had ever seen, didn't even hear it.

'Ma'am,' he said gallantly, 'it would be a pleasure to guide you anywheres.'

The wagon train, despite its late start, made twelve miles up the valley of the North Platte that day. As evening came, the wagons were formed in the customary circle, oxen were unyoked and turned out to pasture, and supper fires began to crackle in the growing dusk. Charley and Bear Claw ate in silence, then Charley lay back with his hands crossed behind his head and stared dreamily up at the darkening sky. Around him he could hear the laughter of children, the voices of women calling to their men, and he was no longer lonely.

'Nice night, ain't it?'

'Squaw camp no good,' Bear Claw grunted. 'Too much talk. Why you let squaw make you take job of guiding tents that roll on wheels?'

Charley sat up. 'Nobody made me do nothin'.'

'Huh! You got bad case of squaw fever.'

'What's squaw fever?'

Bear Claw sat cross-legged in front of the fire, drawing designs absently on the ground with a stick. He said solemnly, 'Squaw fever like smallpox—a sickness. Men catch it from women, makes them feel funny in their belly and think foolish in their head.'

'I do feel kind of funny,' Charley admitted, 'but I figured it was the red-eye we drunk last week.' He looked at Bear Claw. 'What do you do for squaw fever?'

'Get a squaw. She cure fever plenty quick—make you sorry you had it.'

Charley grew thoughtful. 'Maybe I should get married,' he mused.

'Good!' Bear Claw exclaimed. 'We leave wagon train tomorrow and ride plenty damn fast to Cayuse country. For ten ponies Bear Claw find you good fat squaw. For five ponies find you pretty good skinny squaw. For two ponies—'

'I don't want an Indian squaw,' Charley interrupted. 'I want a white one.'

'White squaw no good,' Bear Claw said with a vehement shake of his head. 'Make man chop wood, plough fields, skin buffalo. Indian woman do all that while man sleep.'

'I still want a white one,' Charley said plaintively.

'Big fool. What does white man do when white squaw talk

all the time? Got to sit and listen. Indian just walk off and go hunting.' He looked hopefully at Charley. 'Maybe we start to Cayuse country tomorrow?'

Charley lay down again. 'I'm stayin' with the wagon train. You can ride on alone if you want to.'

Bear Claw got up, stood staring down at Charley for a moment, then muttered, 'Bear Claw don't leave good friend when he is sick. You plenty sick.'

Charley smiled wistfully. 'Did you notice how purty her eyes were, Bear Claw?'

Bear Claw turned on his heel and stalked off into the darkness.

It took Charley a couple of weeks to get the fifty-odd wagons in the train out of the aimless habits of disorder that Zeke Reynolds had got them into. Reynolds proved to be a crusty, hard-headed, opinionated man, who, Charley guessed, had been elected wagon captain only because he had the loudest voice with which to cuss out the oxen. But his bluster was mostly wind, and it didn't take Charley long to discover that it was Mrs. Reynolds who wore the breeches in that family. Once she made up her mind to something, stopping her was like trying to stop a yoke of oxen short of the river when they had smelled water after a long, hot day. Charley often marvelled that anything as sweet and gentle as Susan could come out of a union between people like Zeke and Mrs. Reynolds.

The weather stayed clear and sunny as the wagons lumbered their way up the Platte. At the mouth of Poison Spider Creek, the train clambered laboriously out of the river valley, crossed to the Sweetwater and moved on westward, through country which grew more rugged with each passing mile. At last the wide high valley which led across the Continental Divide through South Pass came in view. Just before time to halt the train for the night, Charley rode alongside the Reynolds' wagon and pointed ahead.

'See that ridge, Miss Reynolds? When we cross it, the streams will all be flowin' to the Pacific.'

'Oh!' Susan's voice held an appreciative awe. She turned her lovely head and looked at him with respect in her eyes. 'How did you ever learn so much about such a big country?'

Charley blushed and picked an imaginary cocklebur out of his horse's mane. 'Reckon I just picked it up here an' there. I drift around a good bit.'

'Doesn't your wife miss you when you're away from home so long?'

'I ain't–uh–married.'

'You're teasing! Imagine, a good-looking man like you not being married at your age!'

'Honest to Gawd–gosh, I mean–I ain't, Miss Susan.'

Bear Claw came riding up at that moment with word that one of the lead wagons had broken a wheel.

As Charley spurred his horse to ride away, Susan called, 'Oh, Charley!'

He stopped. 'Yes, ma'am?'

'Ma says I should invite you to eat supper with us tonight. Will you?'

'Ma'am, it would be a pleasure,' Charley said.

As they galloped along the line of wagons, Bear Claw muttered, 'Too bad. Charley plenty sick.'

Charley smiled vacantly; he had reached the point where he didn't care how sick he got.

It was the best supper Charley had ever eaten. After living on his own and Bear Claw's indifferent cooking for so long, the tender buffalo steak, baked potatoes and delicately browned white-flour biscuits tasted like food for the gods.

'More honey?' Susan asked, passing Charley the jar again.

'Sure is good honey,' Charley said as he liberally smeared another biscuit.

'Back home we kept our own bees. Are there bees in Oregon?'

Charley said he guessed there were. Some of the honey dripped off the biscuit on to his finger, and he was just starting to put the finger in his mouth to lick it clean when he caught Susan looking at him. He turned red. 'Reckon my manners ain't so good,' he apologized. 'It's been a long time since I ate in civilized company.'

Susan smiled forgivingly.

Mrs. Reynolds said, 'Manners ain't everything. Fine feathers may make fine birds, but fine birds don't keep the larder full.'

Charley allowed that that was true.

'Out here,' Mrs. Reynolds continued, warming up to the subject, 'the thing that counts in a man is how good a shot he is and how well he can swing an axe. A man's got to be a good provider. If I was a young girl lookin' for a husband—'

'You ain't, ma,' Zeke Reynolds interrupted. 'You got me.'

'I know.' Mrs. Reynolds sighed. 'But if I was looking for a husband, I'd make sure he was a good provider.'

'I'm a purty good shot,' Charley said innocently. 'I always kept Bear Claw and me in meat.'

When supper was over, Susan started to help her mother with the dishes, but Mrs. Reynolds shooed her away. 'You entertain Charley. We got to be polite to our company.'

'Huh!' Zeke grunted.

Susan looked shyly at Charley. 'We could go for a walk.'

Charley swallowed hard and said he guessed they could.

A blue, cool twilight was gathering over the uplands as they walked slowly across the enclosure around which the wagons were parked. Charley couldn't remember when he had seen a prettier night. Susan looked out past the circle of wagons toward a hill whose rounded top showed faintly against the starlit sky.

'Would it be safe to walk up there?'

'Don't see why not. There ain't an Indian in a hundred miles.'

A shadow moved out from one of the near-by wagons, and Bear Claw grunted, 'No go. Saw trail of thousand Pawnees on hilltop today.'

'Go away,' Charley snapped, 'an' quit followin' Miss Susan an' me.'

As they left the enclosure, Susan put her hand in Charley's. 'I'd be afraid with anybody but you,' she murmured.

Charley was doing his best to swallow the rock that had lodged in his throat, when he heard the clatter of hoofs. Shadows topped the hill and came galloping down toward the wagon train.

Susan squeezed Charley's hand and said in a terrified voice, 'Indians!'

'Cavalry,' Charley said quickly. 'Indians don't ride in formation.'

The wagon guard called out a challenge. A command was given and the riders reined in. The guard shouted, 'Who is it?'

'Captain Vardon and a company of United States cavalry!' called a bold voice. 'Where are you bound?'

'Oregon!'

'Where's your wagon captain? I want to talk to him!'

Before Charley could answer, Zeke Reynolds ambled over and said, 'That's me. What can I do for you?'

The officer dismounted, handed his horse's reins to an orderly and strode into the circle of firelight. He was a tall, erect man whose chest filled every square inch of the blue cavalry blouse. The lines of his face were strong and handsome, and, when he smiled, even white teeth flashed against tanned, healthy skin.

'Do you mind if we make camp next to you? This is the only good water in miles.'

'Help yoreself; it's all free. Say, you headed for Oregon too?'

Captain Vardon nodded. 'We're going to Fort Walla Walla.'

'If that ain't luck! So are we! We'd be mighty obliged to have you travel with us, jest in case Injuns jump us.'

'No danger of that. All the tribes are pretty well under control. Besides, we're in a hurry.'

As Charley and Susan approached, Captain Vardon turned and looked at them.

Susan smiled and said, 'Hello.'

The officer bowed from the waist. When he straightened, his eyes caught Susan's and lingered there. Charley didn't like the gleam that came to them. 'Good evening, ma'am.'

'Are you sure there's no danger from Indians?' Susan asked anxiously.

The officer's handsome brow wrinkled thoughtfully. 'At the moment the savages are peaceful enough, but it's difficult to say how long they will stay that way. You may be attacked farther up the trail.'

'There ain't an Indian on the warpath west of the Rockies.' Charley snapped.

'That,' Captain Vardon said, giving Charley a haughty look, 'may be your opinion. The Army has more accurate sources of information. Fighting Indians is its business.'

'The Army,' Charley muttered, 'couldn't fight its way out of a paper barn with a boatload of howitzers.'

'Charley!' Susan said reprovingly. She looked up at Captain Vardon and smiled. 'What were you saying about Indians?'

The frown on the captain's face deepened as he looked at Susan. He removed his gauntlets and stood absently slapping them against the palm of his left hand. Suddenly he exclaimed, 'It's my duty to see that emigrant trains get through safely.' He turned to Zeke Reynolds. 'Sir, we will accept your invitation and accompany you.'

'You're shore welcome!' Zeke exclaimed.

'I'm so glad,' Susan said demurely. 'I'll feel so much safer with the Army guarding our wagon train.'

'Huh!' Charley snorted. 'More likely it'll be the wagon train guardin' the Army!'

Captain Vardon, being occupied with gazing into a pair of black, enchanting eyes, did not bother to answer.

The wagon train lumbered its slow way over the divide, across the long miles of dry, barren plateau on the other side, then swung north along Bear River and headed into the mountains again. It was wild, beautiful country, but Charley had no eye for its beauty; everywhere he looked, he saw Captain Vardon's handsome, arrogant face smiling down at Susan Reynolds.

'What in tarnation does she see in that tin soldier?' he demanded of Bear Claw one day.

'All squaws crazy,' Bear Claw grunted, 'specially white ones.'

'But she seemed to like me 'fore he came along. Now she looks at me like I was somethin' that had been dead a week an' hadn't been skinned yet.'

'White squaws different from Indians. Indian squaw glad to get any man that will feed her and not beat her too much. White squaw pick husband like a fool pick a horse—just look to see how pretty he is, not how fast he run.'

'Maybe I ain't as purty as Captain Vardon. But I'd feed her good an' I wouldn't beat her at all.'

Bear Claw looked hopefully at Charley. 'Now Charley ready to leave wagon train and ride to Cayuse country?'

'When I start something,' Charley said, with a stubborn shake of his head, 'I aim to finish it. I'll show her who's the best man yet. We're stayin'.'

They struck the tumbling, rapids-filled Snake River at Fort Hall two weeks later and turned down it, moving now into country bare of vegetation, where steep mountains crowded the river into deep, twisting canyons. Grass for the oxen and horses grew scarce. The canyon rim along which the trail led held no water, and the torture of thirst was doubly severe because of the cool, tumbling, inaccessible river below. The animals suffered so much that one evening Charley could stand their plaintive lowing no longer.

'Bring me some barrels,' he told Zeke Reynolds. 'I'm goin' down an' git some water.'

Captain Vardon frowned at the sheer two-hundred-foot drop to the narrow river bed, then snapped scornfully, 'When did you sprout wings?'

Charley did not bother to answer; he simply tied several lengths of rope together, lashed one end around the hub of a wagon and the other about his waist, and went over the edge. For two hours he stood knee-deep in the bitingly cold shallows at the river's edge, filling barrels and sending them up. When darkness fell, he tied the rope around his waist again, and the men above hauled him up as unceremoniously as they had the barrels. He was tired, bruised and sore from his labours, but as he scrambled over the edge of the cliff there was a feeling of grim satisfaction in him. He looked around for Susan, and found her standing beside Captain Vardon, gazing off to the west, where the sun was sinking behind distant purple mountains.

'Look at that display of colour,' the captain said reverently, taking another sip of water out of the dipper in his hand. 'It's as if the sun were blushing and had set the sky on fire.'

'Oh, Edward!' Susan exclaimed. 'You express yourself so well! I think that's such an admirable quality in a man.'

Charley snorted and limped off to see if Bear Claw had left any sowbelly and beans in the pot he'd put on the fire.

.   .   .   .

The canyon of the Snake grew deeper and more tortuous twisting back and forth upon itself in curves so sharp that frequently after a hard day's journey the wagon train found itself camped only a mile or two, as an eagle might fly, from the spot where it had camped the night before. The emigrants, weary from the long months of travel, began to grumble.

' 'Pears to me,' Zeke complained to Charley, 'that we're takin' the long way round. There ought to be an easier trail to Oregon than this.'

'There ain't,' Charley answered.

'Are you sure you know where we are?' Captain Vardon asked.

'We're five miles from where we were yesterday, an', if we're lucky, we'll be ten miles down the river come dark.'

The captain shaded his eyes as he stared off to the northwest, where a faint jagged line sawed at the clear Sky. 'Aren't those the Blue Mountains?'

'Yeah.'

'Walla Walla lies just beyond them. Why can't we cut straight across here and save all this winding back and forth?'

'Because the trail don't go that away. We got to stick to the Snake for another week 'fore we can cross the Blues.'

The wagon train moved on, but, as Captain Vardon and Zeke Reynolds turned away, Charley could hear them grumbling to each other.

He had ridden several miles ahead and was returning to the train shortly before noon the next day when he saw that the wagons had halted and a knot of men were gathered around Zeke Reynolds and Captain Vardon. The officer was intently studying a map spread out on the ground.

'What's the trouble?' Charley demanded.

'If we swing west here,' Captain Vardon said, 'we can go through the Blues and save ourselves a week. Look, it shows a trail on the map.'

'The map,' Charley grunted, 'is wrong.'

Captain Vardon gave him a sharp look. 'This map was drawn up by the Army.'

'Then the Army's wrong too. We can't get through that way.'

Captain Vardon angrily thrust the map in Charley's face. 'It says in plain English: "Passable all year round." '

Charley gave the map a quick look, flushed and then raised his eyes. 'Don't care what it says.'

Captain Vardon stared at him, then exclaimed triumphantly, 'You can't even read!'

Charley looked down at the tips of his worn boots. 'Never had no chance to learn,' he admitted.

He could feel Susan's eyes upon him, contempt growing in them. Captain Vardon whirled and spoke to the crowd of men around. 'Are you going to take the word of an illiterate guide or do you want to put your trust in this map?'

An angry discussion broke out. Zeke Reynolds glared at Charley. 'You're tryin' to take us the long way jest so you'll get more pay.'

'We got to stick to the river,' Charley muttered stubbornly.

'The devil we do! You're fired!' Zeke wheeled to Captain Vardon. 'Can you lead us through?'

'Certainly.'

'Then lead away! Oregon, here we come!'

Charley stood beside his horse, watching them go. Bear Claw came up.

'Now we ride to Cayuse country?'

Charley shook his head. 'They ain't through the mountains yet—not by a jugful. I'm stickin' with 'em.'

'Plenty big fool to help them now.'

'I ain't goin' along to help,' Charley said grimly; 'I'm going along just to wach 'em sweat when they hit Needle Canyon.'

For the first few days, the wagon train made good time across flat, gently lifting land. The spirits of the emigrants rose with each mile that fell behind. Nearer and nearer loomed the Blue Mountains, the last barrier between them and the sweet green land of Oregon.

'We'll be in Walla Walla in another week!' the Arkansawyers told one another jubilantly.

'This shore beats followin' the Snake!'

Charley, riding along with Bear Claw off to one side of the train, out of the dust, stared patiently ahead at the towering Blues and said nothing.

Grass dwindled away and then disappeared altogether as the character of the land underwent a change. Eroded, grey-brown buttes lifted their scowling faces at a brassy sky. Deep gullies, invariably dry, cut across the plateau. A family milk cow, worn with heat, thirst and hunger, dropped after two hours travelling one morning and did not rise again, her thin sides weakly heaving in exhaustion until a pistol bullet ended her misery.

'We'll be sure to find water this evening,' Captain Vardon promised them.

Just before noon, the wagon train met a hunting party of half a dozen friendly Nez Percés, who told them where they would find a water hole. Bear Claw rode out and talked to one of the Indians, seeking news of his own tribe, then returned to Charley with eyes glittering proudly.

'Bear Claw got new papoose now. Big fat boy.'

'Why don't you go on home, then? It ain't far.'

Bear Claw shook his head. 'Where Charley go, I go. Sent word for squaw to come to Walla Walla.'

That night the wagon train camped at the water hole, a circular, shallow sink half filled with brackish alkaline water. By the time the emigrants had drunk themselves and filled their water barrels, there was nothing left for the oxen but sticky mud. Charley and Bear Claw made their camp a short distance apart from that of the wagon train, as they had done since leaving the Snake, but as Charley was walking away from the water hole after filling his canteen, Susan appeared in the dusk before him. She started to pass without speaking, then stopped.

'Hello, Charley.'

'Evenin', ma'am.'

'It's pretty bad, isn't it?'

'It'll git worse 'fore it gits better,' Charley said walking on.

The camp the next night was a dry one. So was the camp the night after that. The wagon train was in the heart of the mountains now, but the Blues were not the cool, forest-covered, abundantly watered slopes that the Rockies had been. Here were only harsh, upended rock strata, long miles of black lava beds which slashed the animals' hoofs like glass, and steep grey peaks on which no living thing grew.

After supper the emigrants held a meeting. Charley squatted on his heels beside a wagon, took out his knife and whittled, taking no part. The discussion went on for some time, growing more and more heated, but getting nowhere.

Finally Zeke Reynolds demanded of Captain Vardon, 'Are you sure we're headed right?'

Charley looked up. The dusty faces of the men were grim in the firelight. Captain Vardon didn't look as handsome now as he had the first night he had joined the train, for there had been no water with which to shave or wash for more than a week, and the quarter inch of black beard stubble on his chin did not improve his appearance.

'Certainly we're headed right,' the officer snapped. 'Don't you think I can follow a map?'

'I don't care a hang about the map,' an emigrant broke in. 'My oxen are dyin.' I give 'em the last bit of grain I had yesterday, an' there ain't a blade of grass in a hundred miles.'

'My horses are in the same shape,' the captain said wearily. 'Why jump me about it?'

' 'Cause you was the fella that told us he could lead us through the short way,' Zeke cut in pointedly.

'I'll get you through all right. We're past the worst of it now.' The officer's eyes went to Charley, and he demanded hopefully, 'Aren't we, Charley?'

Charley spat indifferently upon the ground. 'I can't read. What does your map say?'

He closed his pocketknife with a snap, got up and walked slowly away from the group around the fire. A slim form moved toward him and a hand touched his arm.

'Charley,' Susan pleaded, 'tell me the truth. Are we lost?'

'You an' the captain may be, but I damned sure ain't,' Charley grunted, and shrugged the hand off.

The next day the trail wound up a twisting canyon which grew narrower and steeper with each mile, threading up toward a pass between two towering bare peaks. When the wagon train crossed that pass, it would be on the other side of the Blues, Captain Vardon claimed, and from there on the going would be easy.

'It's all downhill,' he promised, 'and there's plenty of grass and water.'

All morning the wagons laboured upward. At noon the crest of the pass was reached, the exhausted oxen given an hour to rest, then the wagon train moved in single file down a steep, sheer-walled canyon which grew deeper and deeper until its sides rose far above, nearly closing together at the top, like the eye of a needle. Far off in the distance to the northwest, a green, wide valley could be seen through the open space at the lower end of the canyon.

'A river!' one of the emigrants cried.

'And it flows north! All we got to do is follow it and it'll take us right into Walla Walla!'

That, Charley mused as he squinted off into the distance, was exactly right. Only trouble was, you had to get to the river before you could follow it anywhere.

The wagon alongside of which he rode suddenly came to a stop, its progress halted by the wagons ahead.

The ox driver shouted impatiently, 'What's holdin' things up?'

Charley spurred his horse forward past the long line of halted wagons, until he reached the head of the train. There he found the emigrants gathered around Captain Vardon and Zeke Reynolds, who stood with bleak dismay on their faces as they stared down at an abrupt three-hundred-foot drop.

Charley got off his horse and inquired mildly, 'What are we waitin' on?'

'There ain't no more trail,' Zeke said in a grim voice.

'Sure there is.' Charley pointed down at a narrow ledge which led diagonally across the face of the precipice. 'See, there it goes yonder.'

'That goat path? You can't call that a trail.'

Charley jerked his head at Captain Vardon, who sat frowning down at the map in his hand. 'His map called it a trail. The Army ain't never wrong. 'Cept it forgot to mention that it's a trail for horses, not for wagons. But I reckon that's a small matter. All you got to do is put wings on your wagons an' fly 'em down into the valley. . . . Ain't that right, captain?'

The officer's face was pale. Angrily he crumpled the map and tossed it aside. 'We'll have to turn around and go back,' he snapped.

Charley grinned. He was really beginning to enjoy himself. 'You'll never make it. It'll take you a week to get back to water, two weeks to grass. Your stock, I figure, is good for about two days.'

'He's right as rain, captain,' Zeke said miserably.

'Then we'll go on without the wagons,' Captain Vardon said in desperation. 'We can make it down the trail on horseback.'

A silence fell on the emigrants. The women had got out of the wagons to see why the train had stopped; now one of them started sobbing hysterically. For once, Charley noted with satisfaction, neither Mrs. Reynolds nor Susan had a word to say.

Zeke Reynolds said huskily, 'Everything we own is in them wagons.'

'I'll have to leave my company's supply wagons behind,' Captain Vardon reminded him. 'We're all in the same boat.'

'Except that the Army can stand to lose a few wagons,' Susan cut in, her black eyes blazing, 'and we can't.'

The captain whirled on her and snapped, 'What do you expect me to do, sit down and cry about it?'

'I expect you to act like a man and figure out some way to get the wagons through.'

'The age of miracles is past,' the captain said sarcastically.

Charley took out his pocketknife and started whistling. Bear Claw rode up, the two pack horses trailing behind him. 'We go now?'

'Pretty quick,' Charley said.

'Go?' Susan demanded. 'Go where?'

'Why, to Walla Walla,' Charley said calmly. 'That's where we're all headed, ain't it?'

'You wouldn't go off and leave us stranded here!'

'I beg your pardon, ma'am, but you ain't stranded. You got two good feet and there's the trail yonder. All you got to do is start walkin'.'

'But what will we do with the wagons?'

'I don't reckon you'll have to do anything. The Injuns will find 'em soon enough an' take care of 'em for you. Injuns sure do like to see things burn.' Charley put the knife in his pocket and turned to his horse. 'Reckon Bear Claw an' me will be ridin'. See you in Walla Walla.'

Susan looked at him with stricken eyes for a long moment, then dropped her gaze to the ground. She made an obvious effort to hold back the tears, failed, and her long black eyelashes glistened with moisture.

'I didn't know you hated me so much, Charley,' she murmured brokenly.

'We go quick!' Bear Claw said in alarm.

Charley began to feel uncomfortable 'Aw, I don't hate you, Miss Susan.'

'You do, else you wouldn't run off and leave me!'

'Aw, Miss Susan–'

'Not that I blame you for going. After the way we've treated you, it would serve us right if you just left us here to die.'

'It ain't that bad, Miss Susan. You ain't going to die.'

She looked up quickly, her eyes sparkling. 'Then you can get us through?'

'I didn't say I could. I ain't your guide no more.'

'But if you were, Charley, what would you do?'

She was close to him now, smiling up at him. Bear Claw tugged at his arm, but Charley waved him away. He could take care of himself ... even though his head did feel kind of funny.

'If I'd been your guide, we wouldn't have come this away,' he said gruffly. 'We'd a stayed on the main trail.'

'But suppose–just suppose, Charley–that we had come this way? I'll bet a man as clever as you are wouldn't let a little thing like this stop him.'

'Little thing!' Captain Vardon snorted. 'She calls a three-hundred-foot canyon a little thing!'

Charley looked belligerently up at the officer. 'It ain't polite to make fun of a lady like that. Specially when she's right. That canyon ain't nothin' to work yourself into a stew about. Anybody with sense enough to pound sand in a rat hole could figger out a way to git the wagons down, if he'd jest sit an' think a bit.'

'How?' the captain exploded.

'Tie ropes to 'em an' lower 'em.'

'A wonderful idea, except that I had already thought of it and it won't work. We've got just enough rope to let a wagon down halfway. Where do we go from there?'

'Git more rope, captain,' Charley said calmly. He walked over and laid a hand on the dusty back of an ox. 'We got plenty of it. Trouble is, you just don't recognize it when it's alive an' walkin' around. Ever see a braided-leather lariat?'

Three nights later, the wagon train camped on the south side of the river just across from Walla Walla. Bear Claw was impatient to cross at once, but Charley said, 'You go on without me. I promised the Reynoldses I'd eat supper with 'em.'

'Bear Claw wait until the moon rise,' the Cayuse said. 'If Charley not ready then, never be ready.'

It was an excellent supper. Mrs. Reynolds beamed at Charley all through the meal, never letting his plate get empty. Susan sat and smiled shyly at him, her sparkling black eyes saying things that made him get that dizzy feeling again. Zeke slapped his back so many times and showered him with so many verbal compliments that it was a question whether Charley's back or ears burned most.

'Yes sir, it's jest like I told ma,' Zeke exclaimed, 'the thing that counts in this country ain't manners or education or money, but how much horse sense a man's got. Trouble with Captain Vardon was he'd been so busy gettin' educated, he'd never learned how to skin a cow.'

Darkness had fallen by the time the meal was over. Charley got up. 'Sure was a good supper, Mrs. Reynolds.'

'Do you have to go?' Susan pouted.

'I told Bear Claw I'd meet him in half an hour. We're crossin' the river.'

'I'll walk with you to the edge of camp.'

They walked slowly across the enclosure around which the wagons were parked. Susan seemed very subdued, as if she were expecting Charley to say something, but he kept silent. They passed beyond the circle of firelight and stopped near a grove of willows which fringed the river.

'Charley,' Susan murmured at last, 'why are you going away?'

'Bear Claw an' me are goin' buffalo huntin'.'

'Is that all you ever think about—hunting?'

' 'Course not. I think about lots of things.'

'Like settling down someplace and having a home and—a family?'

Charley flushed, glad of the darkness that hid his face. 'I reckon every man does . . . once in a while.'

'You used to like me, Charley.'

'I still do, Miss Susan.'

'But not enough to—' She broke off, then said sharply, 'Charley, I don't think you've told me the truth about yourself.'

He frowned. 'What do you mean?'

'About your not being married. 'I'll bet a woman's waiting for you in Walla Walla—that's why you're so anxious to leave.'

'There ain't, Miss Susan. Honest to gosh, I ain't hitched up to nobody.'

'I don't mean married exactly. Ma said that men like you always have Indian squaws they live with—sometimes three or four of them.'

'That ain't so!' Charley said indignantly. 'I never looked at a woman in my life, till you came along.'

She moved close to him, and the smell of her hair was sweet. 'Oh, Charley, then you do care!'

' 'Course I do. I like you a powerful lot.'

'I love you, too, Charley.'

Charley didn't understand exactly how it happened, but suddenly she was in his arms and he was kissing her warm, upturned lips. He discovered, then, that the fever hadn't left him at all; it had just been playing possum, for now he began to tingle from head to toe, as if he'd been tied to a stake and a fire kindled under him.

'Oh, Charley,' Susan whispered, 'we'll be so happy.'

'I reckon we will,' he muttered dazedly.

'You won't leave me, ever?'

' 'Course not.'

'And you'll go tell Bear Claw that you're not going with him?'

'Sure,' Charley said.

'We'll be married in Walla Walla tomorrow. I'll run back and tell ma right now. She'll be so happy!'

She kissed him again, turned and ran back toward the camp. Charley stood staring after her, numbly wondering what had happened to him. Whatever it was, it sure felt good.

The moon lifted above the rim of the mountains to the east, orange and huge. A figure moved toward him, leading a pair of horses. Bear Claw said, 'We go now?'

Charley shook his head. 'I ain't goin'.'

'White squaw talk Charley into marrying her?'

'She didn't talk me into nothin',' Charley exclaimed. 'Leastwise, I don't think she did.'

'But you going to marry her?'

Charley nodded.

Bear Claw was silent for a long while. Then sadly he shook his head. 'Too bad. You were a good friend.'

'We'll still be friends,' Charley said fervently. 'Me an' Susan will settle down somewheres close, an' you an' me can come see each other whenever we take the notion.'

Bear Claw shook his head again. 'Charley will never come to my lodge. Be too busy chopping wood, ploughing fields, milking cows. White squaw make man work. Bear Claw live in a lodge he can take down and carry on pony's back and go where the grass is green. Charley's squaw make him build a big cage out of trees and stones to hold her and papooses. Cage hold Charley too. Can't move it—too big for horse to carry.'

'We can still go huntin' together.'

'Charley hunt no more. His gun gather rust. The mountains see Charley no more. Charley too busy digging holes in the ground with a hoe.'

The wind stirred the willows along the river, and from the

hills far away, Charley heard a coyote crying at the rising moon.

'Maybe you're right,' he muttered. 'But I'm a white man. That's the way white men live.'

Bear Claw's finger touched Charley's heart, tapping it three times. 'Charley not white man there; Charley Indian.'

Bear Claw turned, mounted his horse and rode away. Charley stood listening to the sound of splashing in the river until the Cayuse reached swimming depth, then he walked thoughtfully back toward the wagon train.

Charley said he'd just as soon fix his own breakfast, next morning, but Mrs. Reynolds insisted that he eat with them. 'It'll give us a chance to get better acquainted with our new son-in-law,' she said with a smile.

'Sure will be fine to have you in the family,' Zeke said between bites. 'Tell you what, we'll get us a piece of good bottom land an' build us a cabin where we can all live together. You purty good with an axe?'

'I kind of figgered Susan and me would have a place of our own,' Charley said uncertainly.

'What for?'

'We'll live with ma and pa,' Susan said, 'for the first year or two, anyhow. You won't mind, will you, Charley?'

Charley scowled down at his plate and said he guessed he wouldn't.

There was a great bustle of activity as the emigrants yoked the oxen and broke up camp in preparation to cross the river.

Charley started to go saddle his horse, but Susan said, 'Dear, would you climb up in the wagon and get me that big brown box?'

Charley did.

'Say, Charley,' Zeke called from the front of the wagon, 'will you give me a hand with this yoke?'

Charley did that too.

'Charley,' Mrs. Reynolds said, 'would you mind taking this bucket down to the river and getting me some water?'

Charley looked defiantly at the empty bucket. 'I was figurin' on saddlin' up,' he said. 'Can't Zeke get it for you?'

'Pa's got a bad back and can't carry things,' Susan said quickly. 'Now, run and do what ma asked you.'

Charley picked up the bucket and walked slowly down to the river. It was a beautiful morning, the sky so blue and clear that it looked as if somebody had taken a fleecy white cloud and scrubbed it clean, then polished it till it shone. Charley stared wistfully across the river, wondering what Bear Claw was doing. He sighed, filled the bucket and went back to the wagon.

'Here's your water,' he told Mrs. Reynolds, slowly putting the bucket down.

Mrs. Reynolds was not looking at the bucket or at him. She was staring at something behind him. 'Who's that?'

Charley blinked. 'Who's what?'

'That woman you brought back.'

'I didn't bring back no woman,' Charley said, but he turned and looked behind him.

A young Indian squaw stood looking at him. Her eyes were black and unblinking. She did not speak, but as Charley stared at her, she looked down at the ground and giggled.

Charley laughed and turned away. 'Don't pay no attention to her. Injuns are powerful curious about white folks. She just wants to watch us.'

'It appears to me,' Susan said sharply, 'that she's not watching us. She's watching you. Tell her to go away.'

'Git!' Charley said, with a wave of his hand. 'Make tracks! Vamoose!'

The squaw giggled again and stayed where she was.

'She doesn't understand English,' Charley said apologetically.

Susan gave the woman a piercing look, then said to Charley, 'I'm through with this box now. You can put it back in the wagon.'

Charley stopped to pick it up. Moccasined feet padded swiftly toward him. Before he realized what was happening, the Indian woman had snatched the box out of his hand, carried it over and placed it in the wagon. Then she came back and stood where she had before, her soft eyes returning to his face. Charley slowly turned crimson.

A stricken silence fell over the Reynolds family. Zeke's jaw dropped three inches. Mrs. Reynolds opened her mouth as if to speak, but no words came. Susan stared, horrified, at Charley, then at the Indian woman.

The squaw turned so that the black head of the baby on her back was visible, and said in broken English, 'See new papoose, Charley? Big, fat boy.'

'Charley!' Susan screamed.

'You ornery, low-down skunk!' Zeke choked. 'I oughta horsewhip you!'

'I told you, Susan! I told you!' Mrs. Reynolds cried.

Charley stood numb and dazed, unable to speak for a moment. He looked at Susan with the odd feeling of detachment that sometimes comes to a man in times of stress, and he noticed suddenly how much her chin line resembled that of her mother. A woman like her would drive a man with a mighty long whip, he reckoned. First thing he knew, she'd make him just what her ma had made Zeke; maybe he'd even get to the point where, like Zeke, the only thing he'd be able to do would be bluster and blow.

'I reckon,' he said meekly, 'that I am a skunk.'

'Then you admit she's your wife?' Susan demanded.

'Well, not exactly. You see, we never was married by no minister.'

Susan turned pale. 'I–I think I'm going to faint!'

Zeke's face was a deep shade of purple as he started for the wagon. 'I'm goin' to git my gun. If you ain't gone in ten seconds–'

'I can make it in five,' Charley said, and, motioning for the squaw to follow, headed at a dead run for the timber along the river, where he figured Bear Claw would be waiting with the horses.

As twilight fell, Charley lay propped up on one elbow, peacefully watching Bear Claw's squaw as she went about cooking the evening meal. Bear Claw sat cross-legged beside him, drawing a picture of a buffalo on the ground with a pointed stick.

'That's sure a fine squaw you got,' Charley observed. 'Never saw a woman work so hard.'

'Huh!' Bear Claw grunted. 'Women supposed to work.'

'How did you persuade her to come into camp and act like she was my squaw?'

'No persuade. Just tell her.'

Charley gazed thoughtfully at the Cayuse woman. For some time, he'd been wondering about a thing Bear Claw had told him, and now it got to bothering him again.

'Bear Claw, you claim squaw fever is a disease—that right?'

'Bad one,' the Indian said with a sharp nod.

'Once you catch it, do you get over it?'

'Not until you get squaw.'

Charley sighed. That was just what he had been afraid of. 'I reckon, then, I better take the cure 'fore I get talked into something I don't want at all. Say, has your wife got a sister?'

Bear Claw's eyes gleamed with anticipation that any married man feels when he sees an opportunity to launch a bachelor friend upon the same stormy seas on which he is buffeted. 'Got fine sister. Good cook, good chop wood, no talk at all.'

'How many ponies?'

Bear Claw was thoughtfully silent for some time, then grunted, 'Her father say fifteen. But for you, maybe make it ten.'

Charley said that sounded like a bargain.

THE AVENGING

By Jonathan Lord

THEY *came for McIntyre on a misty morning a couple of hours before sunup. It was a long, hard ride to his cabin in the mountains, but the four men were tough, experienced riders who made the trip without a murmur. Then, too, three of the men were eager and awake with vengeance-hunger and lynch-hunger, and the fourth was sustained by a secret hope. . . .*

It was Obey Peters who found Dave Corey, lying in a ditch past the edge of town, his dead eyes staring up at the stars. Peters looked at him for a long minute, and then he turned him over with his toe and saw the bullet-holes in his back. He cussed aloud when he saw the bullet-holes, and after a while he took off his mackinaw and covered the body with it.

He found Corey's brother, Artie, at his ranch about a mile down the road from the spot where he'd found Dave. 'It was McIntyre done it,' he told him. 'He said he was going to get him, and he done it. In the back, too, just like you'd figure.'

Artie Corey, a big, rawboned man with a broad, intelligent face and deep lines running from his nose to his mouth, didn't say anything for a long while after Peters brought him the news. Finally, he said, quietly, 'Hell of a thing to happen over a saloon gal.'

Peters stepped up close to him and put a rough hand on his shoulder. 'For God's sake, Artie, that's not the point,' he said. 'This is no fair fight over a woman, out in the open—this is murder. He got shot in the back. Four slugs in the back, Artie. . . .'

Then he added, as quietly as Artie had spoken, a grim, final pronouncement. 'We've got to find McIntyre and kill him.'

Artie Corey knew where to find McIntyre, no problem about that. McIntyre was a skinny, sneaky little runt, a twobit gambler and hangeron, and Corey knew he'd never have the guts to stay around town and face the relatives after a killing. He had a little cabin deep along the mountain pass above Rawson, and that was where he would scuttle and dig in.

Corey went down to the corral and got horses, and on the way down the road they picked up Mel Mitchell, who had been the dead man's best friend. Mitchell didn't need any prompting; he heard the story, and the area around his lips turned white, and he went into his house and strapped on his guns. Then they ran into Joe Wallace, watering his horse in a stream not far from the ditch in which Dave's body lay, and he listened silently and got up on his horse and joined them.

Corey was glad to have Wallace along. He was a strange, reticent man, a soft-spoken Southerner who was different from all the other people in Rawson, and who could not and would not join in the social and political activities of the town, but who was universally respected as a man of complete fairness and justice. And, also, he was an exceptional marksman, and he might come in handy. McIntyre couldn't be expected to give up without a fight.

There wasn't much conversation during the ride. Mostly, each man rode with his own thoughts, and once in a while Corey called a brief halt and took out his guns and checked and rechecked them, and started the ride up again. The night's darkness was beginning to fade just a little when they made the final turn on the trail and sighted McIntyre's cabin. Corey, the lead rider, threw up a hand and they halted.

The look of the cabin worried him. There was no light showing anywhere, and it had a deserted, long-unused appearance about it.

'Maybe the lousy son isn't here,' Corey said. And then a bullet screamed past his head and buried itself in a near-by tree.

A voice spoke from inside the cabin. 'Stand where you are.'

'McIntyre?' Artie asked. It came out automatically, but he knew McIntyre's voice well enough to recognize it.

'Stand where you are,' McIntyre said again.

Corey jumped off his horse, and walked in front of it. 'You admitting you killed my brother, McIntyre?'

There was a silence. Then McIntyre said, 'I'm not admitting a damn thing. You're on my property, and I'll kill the first man who comes a step closer.'

Wallace reined his horse up to the foreground. He said, in his deep, soft voice. 'You haven't got a chance, McIntyre. There are four of us here. Come on out and we'll see to it that you get a fair trial.'

Again McIntyre was silent, and then he laughed. 'Fair trial? You mean a rope around my neck when you get me to the nearest tree.'

Wallace shook his head. 'I said a fair trial, McIntyre.'

Near Wallace, Corey roared, suddenly, 'Forget that, McIntyre.' He looked at Wallace and said, evenly, 'The minute the sneaking back-shooter comes into the sights of my guns, he dies.'

There was another bitter laugh from McIntyre, hidden inside the cabin. 'Thanks for the truth, anyway, Corey.' His voice was icy, a killer's voice. 'You boys better turn around and go on home. I'll get the lot of you before you get me.'

Wallace stared back at Corey, then turned and looked toward the cabin. 'Listen, McIntyre,' he said. 'Listen to me. . . .'

Corey pulled his horse in front of Wallace's, cut him off from the view of the man in the cabin. 'Button it up, Wallace,' he said. 'We didn't come up here to pussyfoot McIntyre back to no high-falutin' courts. We came up here to kill him for killing my brother.' He looked at the others. 'We'll get him, all right. Get off your horses and let's fan out. He can't get away from all of us.'

The other men nodded, and after a moment Wallace got off his horse and joined them. The four men spread out all around the cabin and began to bellycrawl slowly down toward it.

'Hold your fire for a while,' Corey said. 'When we're real close to him, we'll fire together. We'll blast the little son out of his hole.'

It took long minutes, almost twenty minutes for them to crawl as close to the cabin as Corey wanted. They had to move slowly, imperceptibly, so that McIntyre, watching in the cabin, could not pick off four easy targets. As they crawled, he fired whenever he saw something move, and two or three times his bullets came close.

The night was brightening up even more, and Corey could see the cabin clearly now. McIntyre had been moving from one window to another, firing from different spots, so he couldn't tell exactly where he was—but a strong barrage stood a good chance of getting him. Corey said, 'Let's go!'

The blast of all the guns together was like a sound of cannon fire, and the flashes of powder lit up the night. It was quite a sight, and it made quite a noise, but it didn't do any good at all. The bullets buried themselves in the fore of the thick cabin logs.

As the sounds died away, McIntyre's voice mocked them. 'I built this cabin solid,' he said. 'You won't blast me out if you shoot them guns from here to Wednesday.' Then he added: 'But it's going to be daylight soon, boys and then I'll see you all nice and clear. You better start saying your prayers.'

It made sense to Corey, too damn much sense. He shouted, from his position, 'He's right, men. That cabin's built too solid. We better get together and talk this over. . . .'

It took another twenty minutes to crawl back to safety, and to join each other. The streaks in the sky were spreading out now, wider and wider. Soon the streaks wouldn't be streaks any more; they'd be one solid mass of light. Corey knew they had to work fast.

'We got to try another way to get him out,' he said. 'We can't blast him out, so we'll do it Injun style.' He turned to Mitchell. 'You're a smokin' man, Mel. Give me your box of matches.'

Mitchell handed him the box of matches, but he did it reluctantly. 'We ain't got no bow and arrows like Injuns, Artie,' he said. 'You'll have to go right down to the cabin if you're thinking of firing it. You're crazy, Artie—he'll pick you off before you're halfway started.'

Corey shook his head. 'Not if there are three other men covering me with gunfire while I'm doing it.' He spat, impatiently.

'Hell, he's one man against four. I'll get that cabin blazing while you cover me. But one thing first. . . .'

He turned on his heel and faced Wallace. 'I want three men covering me when I go down there, Wallace, not two. I was watching you when we were firing that barrage at McIntyre–and, funny, it didn't look to me like there was any flashes coming from your direction.'

'There weren't any, Corey,' Wallace said quietly. 'There weren't any because I wasn't firing.'

The gun leaped upward in Corey's hand, and he covered the tall Southerner. Guns moved in the hands of Peters and Mitchell, too, but Wallace kept his own gun level at his side.

'What the devil is this, Wallace?' Corey said. 'You a pal of McIntyre's, maybe?'

A faint smile moved across Wallace's lips. 'I haven't spoken three words to the man since I've been in this town. I've got a reason, though, Corey, a good reason. . . .'

'What reason, Wallace? We're all listening.'

Wallace smiled again, but the smile had no humour in it. 'I'm not sure you'd understand, Corey. Anyway, there just isn't the time to discuss it now, not with daylight due to come up full in maybe ten minutes. I'll back your play.'

Corey dropped his gun to his side. 'All right,' he said. 'We'll let it ride for now. But I want you covering me with the others when I go on down.'

'I'll cover you,' Wallace said.

They started down toward the cabin again, Corey all the way off to one side, the other three men together. He waited until they were close, and then he began to run zigzag down toward the cabin, scooping up dry foliage as he went. Alongside him, guns began to blast, so loud he couldn't hear McIntyre's guns returning the fire.

He made it without trouble. He got the matches set, touched them to the mass of dry foliage, and pushed it through an oil-clothed window. Almost instantly, the cabin began to burn.

Then he ran back, zigzagging again, up to the others above him.

He turned and waited, guns ready, waited for McIntyre to be forced out of the cabin.

McIntyre did not come out.

He watched with growing amazement as the cabin began to char, and big pieces fell to the ground. Behind him, Peters said, 'Maybe we got him when we were firing.'

'I don't think so,' Corey said. 'I don't think your bullets even broke through the wood. I saw some of 'em sticking half out when I fired the cabin. It's hard to figure. . . .'

Then there was only the bare framework left of the cabin, and the flames were almost subsided. Guns ready, Corey and the others walked down to the cabin and began to kick through the mess, looking for McIntyre's body. It wasn't there.

Corey's lined face was bitter as he looked around him. 'It's simple enough,' he said, after a while. 'I'll bet there was a back door to this place, and he guessed what we were doing and he beat it. Well, there ain't much woods around here. We'll find him.'

Obey Peters broke in. 'We're in trouble, Artie,' he said. 'I know this territory, and he won't go hiding in no woods. And if he's gone where I think he's gone, we'll never get him.'

Corey said, impatiently, 'Don't talk around it, Obey. Where's he gone?'

'There's a cave near here,' Obey said, 'a kind of hole in the mountain on top of a small hill. If he's gone there, we'll never get him. He can sit at the mouth of the cave and pick us off as we climb up toward him. You got to hold on to make that climb; he'd pick us off like sittin' ducks.'

Mel Mitchell swore softly. 'He's right,' he said. 'I know that spot and we'll never get him if he's gone there. And you can bet that's where he's gone, and he's probably taken plenty of supplies up with him.'

'Wait a minute, wait a minute,' Corey said. 'You say it's a small hill. He's bound to show himself firing back at us. Couldn't we pick him off from the bottom of the hill?'

'You ain't never seen this place,' Obey said. 'That kind of shootin's too much for us. Maybe Wyatt Earp could do it; maybe Hickok. Not us. . .' His voice faded away as he saw Corey staring at Wallace. '. . . I bet Wallace could do it, though, Artie,' he said. 'He's supposed to be one of the best shots in the country. I bet he could pick him off.'

'Well, Wallace?' Corey said.

Wallace looked back at Corey without wavering. 'If I could, I wouldn't. I'm not going to kill McIntyre.'

Corey reached forward, took hold of the Southerner's shirtfront. 'Daylight don't mean nothing with McIntyre up in that cave, Wallace,' he said. 'Now we got plenty of time to hear what's been eating you tonight.'

'I'm still not sure you'd understand,' Wallace said. 'Let's just say I don't believe in your kind of justice.'

'You'd believe in it if it was your brother killed tonight,' Corey said. He let go of Wallace's shirt, and brought his gun up in his other hand. 'So we'll put it on a more personal basis. You kill McIntyre for me, Wallace—or, so help me, I'll kill *you*.'

Wallace made an impatient gesture. 'Go ahead. Go ahead and kill me. Then where would you be, Corey. You'd have the law on your neck for murder. . . . There isn't another man in this state with the gun-skill you need here, Corey. By the time you get a man in from Texas, the law would have come for McIntyre, and the sheriff would simply keep a guard on him until he came out and surrendered, or stayed and rotted.'

The gun sagged in Corey's hand and frustration made his face look thin and old.

Wallace looked at him coldly. 'Put the gun away, Corey,' he said. 'Then I'll make *you* a proposition.'

'Proposition? What kind of proposition?'

'Put the gun away,' Wallace said.

Corey slowly put his gun into his holster. 'What kind of proposition?'

Wallace said. 'I'll go to that cave and get McIntyre for you —nick him and make him helpless. I'll do it on one condition: that you take him back to trial.'

Corey stared. 'You sound like you're loco on that subject.' He shrugged his shoulders wearily. 'What the hell good would a court trial do me? Half the time they free the man. They'd free McIntyre, too—nobody saw him kill my brother.'

'You're wrong,' Wallace said, quietly. 'I saw him.'

'*You* saw him–?'

'I saw him,' Wallace said again. 'I saw him from the top of a hill, and I didn't get down to the valley in time to stop him or grab him, but I saw him all right. And my testimony in court'll hang him.'

Corey's voice, when he spoke again, was shrill and incredulous. 'You *are* loco,' he said. 'You're as loco as a bedbug. You're the only one among us who knew for sure McIntyre killed Dave, and yet you're the only one who's been insisting we don't kill him here and now. What the hell do we need a court of law for if we know he's guilty?'

'That's the point,' Wallace said. 'You didn't know for sure until just now that he was guilty, Corey, but you were still ready to kill him. You were even ready to kill me because *I* wouldn't kill him for you. That's what's been eating at me tonight, Corey....'

'You're wrong about court trials, Corey. Nothing's perfect, but I think guilty men get declared guilty ninety-nine times out of a hundred, and the men who go free after court trials should go free because they're innocent. That's justice, but your kind of justice is different. Your kind of justice stinks.'

Corey wasn't fighting him now. He was staring at Wallace, completely silent.

'This time you happen to be right about a murderer, but that don't mean you'll always be right. Then one day there'll be another murder, and you'll pick another murderer and kill him–and another murder, and you'll pick another murderer. And some of those times, later on, Corey, you won't be right. But try to break the lynching habit once you get it, Corey, and you won't be able to stop it–it's too blamed easy to pick a guilty man and shoot him or string him up.' He turned away from them. 'I saw that very clearly back home. That's the way I lost *my* brother, Corey. It wasn't until two months later they found out they'd lynched the wrong man.'

He looked back at Corey. 'Well, what do you say, Corey?' he asked. 'Is it a deal?'

'You bet it's a deal,' Corey said....

Yes, they came for McIntyre on a misty morning a couple of hours before sunup. It was a long, hard ride to his cabin in the mountains, but the four men who came after him were tough, experienced riders who made the trip without a murmur. Then, too, three of the men had been eager and awake with vengeance-hunger and lynch-hunger, and the fourth had been sustained by a secret hope....

And the thought went through Wallace's mind as he looked at McIntyre, wounded but alive, riding in front of him: My hope has been realized. He was no fool, this man Wallace who was *different from all the others, and he realized, too, that he hadn't accomplished such an awful hell of a lot. No man can kill the habit of lynching—that, he knew would continue in his country long after he had died. But every bit helps, and every man educated is a step closer to the goal.*

He jerked his head suddenly away from the view of the others, and said, 'There's a little stream. Let's stop for a minute and wash up.' And without waiting for agreement, he got off his horse and went over to the stream, scooped up water in his big, capable black hands, and let the water mingle with the salt streaks on his ebony-black face.

By *Ernest Haycox*

T HE Colonel's cigar lay arrested between his fingers while
he talked to Lieutenant Parke Stobo, its lighted tip forming
a dull red eye in the blackness of night. Day's incredible
heat had begun to dissolve and a faint breeze slid down the
near-by shoulder of the Mesquites. Elsewhere, distance ran flatly
into the southern Arizona deeps. The sky had the powdery
brilliance of its millionfold stars, though none of that infinitely
distant glow touched the earth.

'You will take a detail of twenty-five men, with Charley Boren
for guide, into the Mesquites by way of Pete Kemmel's ranch.
Do not ride beyond the neck of Stagecoach Pass. Rations for
three days. It is a routine detail. Your purpose is to give Lieutenant Wells, who is thoroughly green, a taste of the country.'

'Yes sir,' said Parke Stobo and went down officers' row with
the fragrance of the colonel's cigar starting up the sharp saliva
in his jaw. Out in the centre of Fort Tonto's baked parade the
trumpeters were sounding tattoo, all those notes fading across
the desert in long, beautiful layers of sound.

In his quarters young Lieutenant Philip Wells sat up to the
packing case desk with the pale flame of a government issue
candle before him and brought his diary to date. As the post's
newest officer, he rated the last house on the row, this being
nothing more than a single dobe-walled room with a rammed
earth floor and a roof of wattles and baked mud. West Point was
a month behind him and its extreme orderliness still showed. The
soap box affixed to the wall held his personal effects in neat
arrangement. His dress uniform hung from an improvised rafter,
its creases sharply defined and the yellow lining of the cape
creating quite a glow against the light. Before him, on the packing
case table, stood the few books of his profession, properly erect.
A cot, a locker trunk, a washbowl and water pitcher on a cheap

stand, and the chair he sat on—these things made up his furniture. And he was rounding out his diary with this solemn statement to the Wells descendants who would one day read it:

So I am convinced that a rigorous display of force will subdue the Apaches. There has been much irresolution among our frontier commanders. The Indian understands only fear, but that he does understand and once we apply the due weight of our forces against him I rest certain he will wilt and give way. It is ridiculous to suppose the untutored savage can make any respectable fight against our cavalry arm, which, when properly led, is the most magnificent body of men in the universe. Tomorrow I go on my first scout.

The trumpeters on the parade again were breathing tentative sounds into their instruments. Philip Wells closed the book, put away the pen and rose to the doorway. He was tall and ruddy-cheeked and his quite black hair lay rather long on his head, which was properly cavalry style. His lips held a young man's resolution. When the trumpets began to roll taps across the parade he straightened and a chill ran down his back.

Beyond the parade, out along the silver shining desert, the great traditions of the service were being repeated. The cavalry arm was the proper arm and campaigning in the West was the life for a full-blooded man whose gods were the impetuous Sheridan and the gallant Custer. The last trumpet notes died, closing the army day with a soft sad impermanence, like a prayer fading, like the wild ululation of the coyotes distant in the Mesquite hills. Lights winked off around Fort Tonto's square. The guard relief stamped by officers' row. Philip Wells extinguished the candle and took to his cot, there to lie awake with the eagerness and the improbable dreams of a young man having way with him. . . .

At dawn he crossed the parade to find the detail waiting. Twenty-five rawboned troopers, turned to a uniform ebony of skin, sat morosely in their saddles and watched him with the oblique interest of the enlisted man. Parke Stobo said: 'This is Charley Boren, our guide. Lieutenant Wells, Charley. New to the command.' Charley accepted Philip Wells's hand with a brief and noncommittal grip. He was small and bleached out and thoroughly unimpressive, this civilian guide, with a ragged sandy moustache laying its semicircle over little lips that occasionally stirred a cud of chewing tobacco. His eyes were palest agate, and mostly concealed by the droop of his lids, and he wore an ordinary pair of blue pants, and a vest, and a derby hat cocked low on his forehead. It was an outlandish getup, scarcely in keeping with those conceptions of Western plainsmen which Philip Wells had chiefly gathered from current Currier and Ives lithographs.

Parke Stobo grumbled a command that swung the whole detail into their saddles. Young Wells put a leg over in the best of style, which was his mistake; the horse simply fell to pieces beneath him and presently he was flat on the ground, more shocked than hurt. Charley Boren had seized the horse's free reins, and handed them back to Wells when the latter rose. Stobo said: 'Not quite like the Point nags, Lieutenant. The trick is to climb on fast.'

The command remained silent while Wells, a beautifully crimson complexion covering his face from eyebrows to Adam's apple, took to his saddle again. His legs clapped the beast with a force that sent echoes all across the parade. There was a little difficulty for a moment but he really had a decent seat and when the horse understood this the performance was over. Parke Stobo murmured another command that held none of the resonance and authority young Wells deemed proper; the detail swung into a column of twos, filing out of Fort Tonto's southern side. The guard at Post Number One came to salute.

Riding at the head of the column with Stobo and Charley Boren, Philip Wells felt a certain lack in this departure. No band music, no colonel to stand by and take the salute, no ladies waving their cambric handkerchiefs. They were merely twenty-five shapes lumped taciturnly in the leather, riding through the evaporating coolness of early morning while an ever-present dust already was rising to cloy their nostrils. Beyond the scattered camp of Kaminzin's peaceful Indians on Santa Rita Creek, just outside the post, they swung straight at the brown, barren shoulders of the Mesquites. All in the south lay the endless desert, marked by cacti—particularly by the giant saguaro's gaunt arms—and bordered in the deep distance by a faint blue haze. The sun rushed up from the east and presently, rising through the lonesome ravines of the Mesquites, the earth began to glitter.

At eight o'clock the sun began to bite into the young lieutenant's Eastern skin, and they had reached the broken tableland of the Mesquites. There was no clear area for any distance; it was a choppy sea of rounded buttes and sudden flinty stringers flung before them, with a scatter of mesquite and thorny bushes here and there. Far off and much higher in the sky stood a peak shaped like a cowpuncher's hat, its sides darkened by pine.

'Indian Peak,' said Parke Stobo.

Fort Tonto gossip had already informed Philip Wells that every foot of this ground was dangerous. The watchword was: If you saw Indian sign, be careful; if you saw no sign, be more careful. He could detect, however, no particular vigilance in Stobo's continuing dismal silence, or from Charley Boren, who never turned his head and never appeared to open his shuttered eyes. What he did not observe was the constant travelling of Charley Boren's glance. It reached from the nearby earth forward to the limits of the trail; it lay on the massed mesquite and touched the rising barricades of flinty earth. Behind Wells the troopers rode with that perfect disposition of weight which comes only from long campaigning. Sergeant O'Mara's Irish face was the colour of weathered terra cotta and his black dragoon's moustaches swept hugely across an expression permanently melancholy. Von Lauff, the junior sergeant, was an ex-member of the German Imperial Guards. He had a Prussian neck and an old-soldier's stony, angular featuring. Trumpeter Martin was merely a boy, a tough lad from the Eastern pavements; the front brim of his hat creased upward and his cheeks were smooth. Behind these the column advanced stolidly, half enveloped in its own mica-shot dust.

Stobo said: 'What's news from Tucson, Charley?'

'Heard it said Geronimo's back in the Dragoons again. Bill Mantis shot Brady King last week, on account of something said concernin' that Mrs. Cameron. Ed Shafter thinks he's found a lode in the Superstitions. The whisky in that town ain't gettin' no better.'

'I was thinking of fresh strawberries,' said Parke Stobo. 'Fresh strawberries and clotted cream.' Stobo was a reserved, olive-skinned officer, thick of hip and leg but slender at the waist, and somewhat hard to know. He wasn't many years older than Wells, but he had been on the frontier three seasons and showed its weathering. Any man who fought Apaches that long looked old.

Charley Boren pointed a hand. 'Over there–base of that butte–is where the Parker outfit was killed.' His glance touched Philip Wells with a brief and indirect force and went away.

'Why are we out today?' asked Wells.

Stobo said: 'Routine detail. We make an appearance on this side of the Mesquites so that it may influence the Apaches to keep on the other side, which helps the troops at Bowie to find them. The game is played that way.'

'You mean the Apaches are observing us?'

'Very likely.'

'Now?'

'I imagine so,' said Parke Stobo in his dry, reserved voice. 'The game is played that way–by both sides. Apaches are clever. Very clever. We can teach them nothing–and learn a good deal.'

'A savage is a savage,' said Philip Wells. 'My attitude is that we have temporized. There is our mistake. We ought to smash them, once and for all.'

'It is an attitude,' commented Parke Stobo.

Charley Boren's glance again touched Philip Wells but when Wells looked at the scout, he saw only a motionless profile.

This air was thin and at once like the radiant heat from a fire. When Philip Wells touched his lips to the canteen its metal neck suddenly stung him. The smell of dust was constant; it lay like a talcum coating on his face and cracked the tender skin around his eyes. The land appeared to undulate up and down without end; the distance intervening between the column and Indian Peak seemed never to diminish. At noon, and without warning, the column broke over a rim and came upon a dobe ranch house sitting beneath the halfshade of high mesquite trees. Water from a spring played into a shallow pond. This was Pete Kemmel's ranch.

The detail stopped for noon meal, which was a cold bacon sandwich out of the troopers' saddlebags. A few men came from the shadowed interior of the dobe, one of them stopping by Charley Boren. He was high and lean and old, with a great hat seated down against a sail-like pair of ears; he walked in a loose and exhausted manner.

'How the hell are you, Charley?'

'Seen Indians, Pete?'

'Ain't looked.'

'Sign all around here. Fresh.'

' 'Bout time, I guess.'

A girl appeared, whereupon Philip Wells straightened himself and stared. She was perhaps eighteen with hair as yellow as he had ever seen in a woman. A thoroughly plain dress lay carelessly against a robust shape. Her shoulders were firm and her breasts full-moulded against the dress. She smiled at Parke Stobo and spoke to Charley Boren; and then Philip Wells noticed she was barefooted. Her eyes came around and Wells felt the force of her glance. It made him flush and remove his hat. Parke Stobo said: 'Lieutenant Wells, Pete. New to the command. And Kitty Kemmel, Wells,' Philip Wells bowed. Charley Boren and Parke Stobo talked a little while with the rancher; and around one o'clock the detail moved off. Just before this pocketed ranch was lost to sight Philip Wells looked behind him, strongly stirred, and saw the girl standing against the dobe's wall, a hand shading her eyes as she watched the detail go. She waved once.

'If this is risky country,' he said, 'why do they stay?'

'Pete figures he's got to live some place,' said Charley Boren. 'He's fought Apaches a hell of a lot of years.'

'Just the same, I should think he'd regard his daughter's safety.'

'She's a pretty good shot, too.'

But Charley Boren was more alert than he had been. He showed it in the way he occasionally bent from the saddle to study the earth; in the way his neck began to swing. 'They're over here, Parke,' he grumbled to Stobo. 'A lot of 'em. Whut's brought 'em across the Mesquites, I dunno. Maybe Tucson is right and Geronimo is in the Dragoons.' He said, an hour later, 'Left,' and the column moved into more rugged ground, breaking across another small rim. Mesquite half rimmed a clearing that showed marks of a fire and of recent habitation. Charley Boren grunted: 'Rancheria. Recent as yesterday.'

'Indians?' asked Wells.

'Thick enough to smell,' said Charley Boren.

'I smell nothing. And see nothing.'

'It is something you will acquire,' said Parke Stobo.

The earth's glitter increased and the smoky heat haze closed down and the shape of Indian Peak was a formless smear ahead. Trumpeter Martin, half down the column, was relating some of his more amorous adventures in Tucson with a broad relish. 'The Mexican girls,' he said, 'they'll do.'

Sergeant O'Mara growled: 'Eads, was it your health you joined this army for?'

Private Eads's voice was soft and cultivated and belonged elsewhere than in this column of troopers. 'Health of a sort, O'Mara. But not your kind of health.'

'Now it may be I'm nawt so blind a man as ye'd guess,' retorted O'Mara.

But presently even this desultory talk ceased and they were all dumbly bearing up under a heat that had an acid burn when it struck the skin. There was no body to the air; a man's lungs could not bite into it. Philip Wells rode for a distance with his mouth open, feeling himself starved for wind, and then the dust caked his throat and he pressed his lips together and understood why it was Charley Boren's eyes had the habit of being three-quarters closed. The column of troopers furnished the only life in a punishing day. Nothing else in this land stirred. Nothing else made sound. The water of his canteen was flat and lukewarm and could not quench a thirst. Everything he wore had a dragging weight and his heart slugged laboriously against his chest; at times dizziness swayed him slightly.

At four they stopped for water at a high pool and even Philip Wells saw the unshod hoofmarks around it. Charley Boren said: 'This mornin'. They're swarmin'. So I guess Geronimo's back all right.'

'We're a routine detail, Charley,' said Parke Stobo, with a touch of irony in his voice. 'Our only purpose is to display the panoplied majesty of the government's might before the untutored savage, and so throw the fear of God into his simple heart. The error of that conception, Wells, is that the Apache isn't much impressed by the sight of a cavalry detail lumbering along at three miles an hour.'

Charley Boren added: 'You can say it quicker. The Apaches don't scare easy.'

Parke Stobo murmured: 'All this day the damnable fragments of a poem have rattled around my head.' He lifted his voice slightly and at once melody came to it:

> For oft, when on my couch I lie
> In vacant or in pensive mood,
> They flash—

He said: 'You know the rest of that, Wells?'

'No.'

'Well, it is nothing but a silly distraction. But you will come to appreciate distractions if you campaign long on the border.' At six, with the shape of Indian Peak no nearer, apparently, than it had ever been, they went into camp among a scatter of boulders deep in the heart of the Mesquites. The horses were hobbled and put on picket near by, under heavy guard; and other outposts took station around the camp. The violently red sun sank, dusk whirled around them, grey and immediate, and the solid dark of a moonless Arizona night fell like weight upon them. Bacon and coffee smell crept fragrantly through the shadows. The troopers' little fires were ruby eyes on the earth.

Philip Wells made his meal and elbowed down on the earth, unutterably tired. He was quick-eyed enough to see that Charley Boren showed signs of restlessness. The guide's head kept swinging, as though he were scenting this stifling black. The heat held on. Somebody was singing and Trumpeter Martin broke into a short, youthful laugh. 'Von Lauff, you don't know Mexican women at all. That girl at Bowie dam' near carved you up. She told me, next night.' Sergeant O'Mara stood over the adjoining fire, gaunt-shaped, the blood glow touching up that permanent melancholy of an old soldier.

Parke Stobo said:

> In vacant or in pensive mood,
> They flash—

Charley Boren rose off his haunches and made a half turn, the derby pushed back on his head. He faced the south and he was stiffly listening. Out of the near shadows came the slow tone of Trooper Eads:

> They flash upon that inward eye
>   Which is the bliss of solitude;
> And then my heart with pleasure fills
> And dances with the daffodils.

Stobo said: 'Thank you, Eads.' Philip Wells looked around and saw Trooper Eads's face fade away from the firelight.

Boren slapped a hand sharply against his thigh. At once Parke Stobo was up and Philip Wells was up. O'Mara was saying, down the line: 'Easy, boys. 'Tis a bad smell somewhere.'

The whole line had risen and everybody was drawing away from the firelight. Motionless on his weary legs, Philip Wells strained for some sound to break the tremendous silence and heard nothing at all. The weight of the night pressed in, hot and wild; the blackness made him lonely. A feeling ruffled along his spine.

'One rider,' murmured Charley Boren. But it was a full five minutes afterwards before Philip Wells heard the rider break the profound stillness. Far off this messenger started calling: 'Hello, camp! Hello, camp!' Sergeant O'Mara wheeled and vanished. The messenger's hoofs pounded on the flinty flooring of the hills and even then, from the unbridled rush of that oncoming pony, Philip Wells knew there was trouble. Sergeant O'Mara's bronze voice set up a beautiful racket down by the horses. 'Come up— come up. We'll be ridin'. Cawprul Gibbs, where the hell are you?'

The messenger heaved into the dimming circle of firelight and stopped there. He was a long, red-haired cowpuncher leaning down from the saddle, the streaked pattern of sweat and dust on his face. 'Pete Kemmel's place. I knowed you'd be around here somewheres. Apaches got everybody but me, I guess.'

Stobo's calm call went out: 'O'Mara.' But even then the detail's horses were coming up and the column had formed. Philip Wells accepted his horse from Trumpeter Martin and presently they were at a trot, reaching through the scatter of rocks in a thoroughly sightless night. Charley Boren and the redheaded puncher led the way.

Stobo said to Wells: 'This is a routine detail, but you never know. Something has been in my craw all day, and this is it. You get a feeling about these things if you stay on the border long enough. Never trust an Apache. We have seen nothing since sunup, yet these hills have been swarming with the devils.'

They went alternately at a trot and a gallop, back down the undulations of the Mesquite hills, and somewhere in the night—Wells had long since lost sense of time—the smell of wood smoke began to taint the still heated air. Dropping over a stringer of land he saw the dying glow of a fire below him in the Kemmel yard. Stobo laid a gentle call behind him and the troopers fanned into a line of skirmishers, and so came down in front of the dobe.

There had been a fire inside the house and one outside. The outside fire still smouldered and shed a low, saturnine light on the scene. Wells dismounted with the others. Charley Boren wheeled to the doorway and dropped on a knee. Somebody called from another quarter of the yard, 'Pete's lyin' over here with Ben Vorhees.' But Stobo and Wells followed Charley Boren and then Wells saw the yellow-haired girl lying stripped and broken and dead there. Her hair was no longer full and yellow. Wells whipped himself around and went away, remembering how she had smiled at him that noon. His stomach muscles tightened; he felt sick physically. He stood with one arm against his horse, for support. Stobo's voice was slow, and extraordinarily even. 'Nobody left. How many were here?'

'Five,' said Charley Boren. 'Pete fought Apaches too long. He got careless.'

'Where's the best water now, Charley?'

'North side of Indian Peak.'

'So they'll be there. O'Mara, lay these people inside the dobe and block the doorway.'

The troopers moved around the dark, lugging up Pete Kemmel

and the others. The surviving cowpuncher said: 'I'm going to ride through to the Glory Mine and bring the boys up here tonight.'

The troopers were assembling again. Parke Stobo came up to Philip Wells. The firelight vaguely touched his face. His bright glance bit into Wells. 'The first detail usually is a little hard,' he said, and swung into the saddle. Philip Wells followed suit and the detail climbed out of Kemmel's meadow and was lost again in the consuming dark. He heard Charley Boren say: 'I recognize Tansan's style in this. Well, Tansan likes the rough rocks northwest of the Peak. The lower trail, Stobo.'

Wells eased his weight in the saddle and recalled the girl's smile again. Sickness still pulsed in his stomach and left him weak. Of a sudden there was no security in the night at all and his confidence wavered. These Indians were as evasive as the shadows about him; they had the substance of wind. Behind him the column moved up with its sluggish rhythm, the sound of saddle leather and metal gear making a minute racket. That was all; there was no talk. Day's heat began to leave the earth reluctantly, coming up about him like a rising draught. His horse was tired and his own bones were aching. Dust worked its way all through his clothes, gritting against his skin. It lay on the roof of his mouth and clogged his nostrils.

They travelled slowly into a world Philip Wells couldn't see. Now and then Charley Boren's shape faded away, not to reappear for a quarter or half hour. Long later they rested; and went on. The blackness got deeper as the night wore through and a more obstinate shadow stood before them. Stars scattered the sky like diamond dust. From somewhere a faint breeze arrived.

Long past midnight, after two or three extended stops, Stobo said: 'You are in charge of the command, Wells. Wait here.' And disappeared with Charley Boren.

Dismounted beside the horse, Wells felt loneliness bear him down. His senses grew violently alive, and tricky, and false shadows moved around him and his ears began to hear a thousand sounds. He made a complete turn. Sergeant O'Mara's voice came from an arm's distance. 'Did the lieutenant speak?'

'No,' said Wells, but relief instantly eased him.

'There are no darker nights than Arizona nights,' said O'Mara in his reassuring tone. 'Like maybe the good God got ashamed of the day and wanted to wipe it out.'

Stobo and Charley Boren materialized, long later. The column proceeded again. The ground began to lift beneath Wells and that ever-present shadow before them showed a blacker substance. Stobo murmured, 'Indian Peak.' It was then, Wells judged, around three o'clock. They passed between rocky shoulders, with a current of air striking their faces, and came out into what seemed level ground. The smell of pine was in the wind. Stobo said: 'O'Mara, we leave the horses here.'

Stumbling on afoot, Philip took a good deal of pains to plant his boots before him; he was that weary. The big muscles of his thighs were altogether like lead. The day's sunlight had turned his face raw; when he swung his head the collar of his shirt scraped on cooked skin. There was a first milky colour in the darkness, sign of day. Stobo murmured, 'Here.' The column faded against the earth. Somewhere in the distance a dog barked and Philip Wells sat down with his back to a rock.

Something struck his ribs and he opened his eyes and was ashamed to know he had fallen asleep. Parke Stobo murmured, 'You will stay by me in what follows.' A sharpslanting earth had risen out of the night and in the grey dawn Wells saw the detail flattened against a kind of rocky parapet. Behind them the loosely pine-studded ground went swiftly downgrade. Turning, he saw Charley Boren on his hands and knees, peering over the natural parapet. Wells caught the smell of wood smoke. Charley Boren drew back and fixed his derby more securely on his head. He looked at Stobo and nodded. O'Mara watched Stobo's face and caught a sign; and the sergeant lifted his hand in signal to the waiting line.

Blood raced through Wells and his mouth was extraordinarily dry. All this line breasted the parapet, kneeling as though in prayer. Trumpeter Martin, whose post was properly behind the detail's commander, crawled over on his stomach, his young lips showing a grin through a solid mask of alkali. Charley Boren adjusted his hat again and took a fresh chew. Private Eads, adjoining Wells, lowered his thin face and drew a hard breath.

It was not, Wells thought, the reaction of a man in any degree afraid, but rather was the gesture of one who went into a disagreeable chore without interest. Parke Stobo made another signal and rose and stepped across the rocky parapet. The whole line rose immediately.

In that moment, drawing his service revolver, Philip Wells saw the scene distinctly. Ahead of them a hundred yards the grey mists of morning curled over a clearing in the high pines. There was a fire burning and Indians were just rising off the earth; and he saw one squaw. At this instant the line of troopers let out a rattling yell and fell into the charge, their carbines already beginning to blast the stillness.

Keeping abreast of that rolling line, he saw the Apaches break and weave and wheel. Some of them raced for picketed ponies on the clearing's edge. The detail's guns were searching out that corner, dropping Indians and horses alike. All this was telescoped confusion, with the bronze yelling of the troopers rising and the sudden whoops of the Apaches coming back and gunfire rocketing the meadow and dust boiling all about. Wells found himself in front of the squaw, who drew a long knife out of her skirt and lunged at him. He parried it partially with his revolver and felt the tip slice the skin of his upper arm. Private Eads came across his vision, knocking the squaw down and going on. An Indian rolled like a cat on the earth and presented a gun at Wells, firing point-blank. The scorch of that powder was on Wells's face as he fired in turn and saw the savage sink.

He saw them rise and he saw them fall. It was all a grey and blue and brown mixture. Parke Stobo made a stand, his right arm kicking back from the discharged revolver, and crooking for another shot, and kicking back again. He was a cool shape in the mêlée, with Trumpeter Martin kneeling and firing beside him. The big carbines rolled up a heavy thunder. Apaches were rushing away and horses were sinking on their forelegs. Sergeant O'Mara appeared beside Wells and fired twice and Wells, half wheeling, saw a tawny, naked shape fall away. O'Mara yelled: 'Watch sharp, Lieutenant!'

But it was over then. The squaw knelt on the ground with her head bowed over; she was wailing up a sound that turned

Wells's blood cold. The remaining handful of the raiding party pushed away, barebacked, while the bullets of the troopers went booming after. And presently the firing died and silence came creeping into this powder-stenched clearing on the high flanks of Indian Peak. Wells saw horses and Apaches lying as a distorted scatter of colour on the earth. As for himself, he could not recall his actions, and was half surprised to find himself with his feet straddling a dead brave and his gun hanging full length in his fist.

Trumpeter Martin whipped his instrument to his lips and blew recall. Parke Stobo turned, the balls of his eyes white in the grey morning and his face quite strict. 'Nicely done, Wells.' The troopers came back in loose-kneed reluctance. Charley Boren stood over the squaw, talking her tongue brusquely. Wells saw Private Eads lying dead near the campfire.

'That will be all,' said Stobo.

He looked a long while at Private Eads on the ground. . . .

Late in the evening of one more blistering day, Parke Stobo's detail came by Post Number One at Fort Tonto with Private Eads lashed across a saddle. The brutal force of thirty-six hours' riding weighted them down. Wells dismounted with difficulty, turned over his horse and stood spraddle–legged, watching the colonel come across the parade. Parke Stobo said to the colonel:

'Reporting back from detail, sir. A band under Tansan raided Pete Kemmel's ranch and killed them. We made chase and had a brush with them on the Salduro Park, killing several and dispersing the rest. I regret to inform you of the loss of Private Eads.'

'Very well, Lieutenant.'

Charley Boren shook Parke Stobo's hand, and shook Philip Wells's hand–the grip as brief and lifeless as ever–and ambled over the parade with his derby hat well tilted. Philip Wells walked to his own quarters, stiffness increasing in his legs, not hearing Stobo's low-pitched remark to the colonel: 'He'll do, sir.'

He lighted a candle and immediately upended the water jar on the washstand and drank with an immoderate haste. Water spilled out of his lip corners, down the front of his shirt. He pushed his legs farther apart, oppressed by the trapped heat of this little room. The sap was completely out of him. He remained on his feet with difficulty, a robust and half-handsome young man turned stupid by his weariness. Alkali coated his scorched face and he could scarcely move his lips and he saw the neatness of his suspended dress uniform and the orderly row of books on the packing case through a red and cloudy haze. He was thinking of the yellow-headed girl when his eyes fell on the diary. Suddenly he said, with a thick tongue, 'My God!' and reached for the diary on the packing case. He threw it into a corner, and sat down on the edge of the cot, and rolled out full length. He was asleep before he had drawn another full breath.